A Shadowed Summer

By

Julie Burville

Visit us online at www.authorsonline.co.uk

An Authors OnLine Book

Cover design by Jamie Day from original artwork by © Julie Burville

The Cornish locations that inspired this novel have been disguised with other names, however the incidents and characters portrayed are creations of the author's imagination. Any resemblance to actual persons, living or dead, is coincidental.

ISBN 978 07552 0480 9

Authors OnLine Ltd
19 The Cinques
Gamlingay, Sandy
Bedfordshire SG19 3NU
England

This book is also available in e-book format, details of which are available at
www.authorsonline.co.uk

This novel is dedicated to my grandparents Bertie Edward Joslin and Edith Margaret Joslin née Chitty without whom I would lack my Cornish connection.

JULIE BURVILLE

Julie was born in Cornwall but has lived most of her adult life in Kent. After a brief but varied Civil Service career in Whitehall and The City, marriage, two children and a degree as a mature student she became a teacher. Her poems have been published in magazines and anthologies and she has read her own scripts on local radio.

Her first venture into novel writing was Invaders of Privacy published in 1998.

She co-authored, with husband Peter, The White Cliffs of Dover – Images of Cliff and Shore (non-fiction) published 2001, 2nd edition 2003.

A Shadowed Summer

FOREWORD

Their roots tapped the same Celtic granite yet in class-divided, post-war Britain, Lorna and Jerome were continents apart. Theirs was an unlikely friendship that changed both their lives irrevocably.

Chapter 1

1961 ... blast from the past

In Port Blissey's social calendar funerals were enjoyed almost as much as weddings and on balmy days a burial attracted a considerable following irrespective of the deceased's popularity or their status in life. However the day of Nelly Nancarrow's final rites dawned anything but fair.

As rain beat a brisk tattoo on the windowpane David reached across the breakfast table to cover Lorna's hand with his own.

'Why not give it a miss, love? It's a lousy day for standing around in a graveyard and it's not as if Nelly's family will expect to see you there.'

Though appreciating that her husband wanted to spare her the ordeal of yet another burial as much as a likely soaking Lorna was not to be deterred.

'I have to go. Poor Nelly dragged her arthritic bones to the churchyard for all our family bereavements and I feel obliged to return the compliment.'

She tempered her stubbornness by squeezing his hand affectionately.

They had been married long enough for David to know that his wife had a mind of her own. Not one to pursue a lost cause, he accepted her decision without further debate.

* * *

The downpour meant that villagers less determined than Lorna stayed away and her fellow mourners numbered no more than a handful of Nancarrow relatives and a stranger she could not place. Such a pathetic turnout made her glad that she had braved the weather.

As the funeral service progressed she became lost in private remembrance of more personal bereavements. The family death toll over the previous eighteen months had kept the surviving members in a permanent state of mourning. First to be taken was her father who had slipped painlessly away in his sleep after long years of ill health: a mortality considered by the village, though not by his family, to be a merciful release. Next to go had been her grandfather, the vital old seafarer who had livened her childhood with salty tales of naval patriotism and derring-do. More recently, and most tragic, had been the drowning of Perryn her youngest brother. Perryn of the sweet nature, gap-toothed grin and baby-face who had never taken a razor to his chin and was still a month off the fifteenth birthday that he would never celebrate.

A shuffling of feet on tile alerted Lorna that the coffin was being borne out of the church. Abandoning the pew, she hurried down the aisle to catch up with the other mourners. Once outside the burial party hastily raised their umbrellas.

The eight-hundred-year-old gargoyles, bored with merely pulling faces, spat down on them.

'Bloody church drainage system is spouting water down the collar of my Sunday suit,' complained the deceased's brother.

'Hush, Bert,' protested his spouse, 'remember where you are. We don't want the parson to hear you blaspheming in his churchyard.'

Lorna angled her brolly to make a buffer against the unrelenting elements and followed the other foolhardy souls across the sodden burial ground. One beleaguered umbrella bellowed outwards then, with a clap of ribs, snapped inside out. The surviving umbrellas were collapsed voluntarily, the already bedraggled mourners resigning themselves to endure the driving downpour unprotected.

As they stood at the graveside the southwest wind hurled itself at them with redoubled force. The diminutive minister rocked visibly at the buffeting, his holy office providing no immunity from the assault. Bravely he raised his voice so that it might be heard above the banshee storm that howled as loud in the churchyard yew tree as it did out on the storm-tossed sea.

With the weather obliterating everything beyond the immediate few square yards of turf occupied by the burial party, Lorna's glance fell upon the cluster of nearby headstones. Several were etched with her maiden name of Penrose. She had been married to David Grainger for seven years yet local custom dictated that she was still referred to by her birth name. This continuity was no disrespect to David but rather an acknowledgement that she belonged. The generations of Penrose graves were evidence enough of village lineage whereas her husband's family were Johnnys-come-lately for no Grainger bones rotted in Blissey's hallowed ground.

Her earliest Penrose ancestors were commemorated on memorials of engraved slate, those more recent were carved from granite. The most poignant of the granite head-stones bore the legend:

Perryn John Penrose
1945 - 1960
Taken by the sea
"He bringeth them into the haven where they would be."

Her youngest brother, like his grandfather, had been born with sea-salt flowing in his veins. When the fishing-fleet was in port Perryn loitered on the quays pestering the trawler-masters until they agreed to take him to sea. On one of these irregular voyages a freak wave had washed him overboard. Not until the news came that his broken, bloated body was found cast up on a foreign shore did his family give up hope of seeing him alive again. Shipped home in a cold cargo-hold, Perryn was eventually laid to rest in the sanctified ground of Blissey's churchyard.

Of all her brothers Perryn had been Lorna's favourite for she had cared for him with an unstinting attention that her fraught and hard-pressed mother of six was never able to provide. The memory of her youngest brother's infant freshness turned the damp and decay of the graveyard momentarily fragrant.

Nelly's coffin was lowered into its muddy berth and under the water's onslaught the grave's steep-dug sides began to crumble. Lorna's resolve was similarly eroded, her anguish welling with the rising floodwater. She gazed into the mouth of the gaping grave where muddy rivulets seemed to be enacting the words of a hymn that they had just been singing in the church.

"Time like an ever rolling stream bears all its sons away..."

Lorna's grief was not for Nelly Nancarrow but for her Penrose men-folk: an infirm father, raconteur grandfather and for her sweet brother Perryn.

To distract herself from the pain of remembering she tried to concentrate on the minister's chant of committal: '... the soul of this our sister departed, and we commit her body to the ground, earth to earth, ashes to ashes...'

The gender contained in this rubric helped to banish her male ghosts and return her to a present that Nelly had left forever.

As the minister intoned, 'in the certain hope of the Resurrection,' Lorna gave an involuntary shudder. A saying from her mother's well-worn collection of adages echoed in her head: "*A goose walked over my grave*". Breathing deeply, she looked up.

Through the slanting, slate rain and across the void of the open grave her eyes met those of the mourner opposite. The stranger looked disconcertingly familiar yet still she could not place him.

Embarrassed to be the focus of his interest she lowered her lashes, yet each time her glance penetrated the weather she found the stranger's eyes locked firmly upon her own. His expression was too grim to be interpreted as flirtatious or even friendly.

Made uneasy, she struggled to make sense of such unwarranted attention. Snatches of village gossip concerning Leonard, Nelly's errant son, came flooding back. His whereabouts had been a mystery until an enterprising uncle had tracked him down. Lorna guessed that the stranger with the doleful eyes must be the wandering son returned in time for the funeral though come too late to make his peace with his mother. Satisfying though this identification was, it did not explain the intensity of his scrutiny. Indignant at his impertinence she confronted the disturbing stare with a challenge of her own.

As their looks fused her brain flooded with an unexpected recognition. What she saw in the stranger's eyes illuminated the mystery of a lost summer, a mystery that had dogged her life for the past thirteen years. Abruptly she turned and fled the graveside, slipping on the sodden turf, swerving to avoid the broken teeth that were tombstones.

The more elderly mourners tutted their disapproval in the belief that she was fleeing discomforts that the rest of them were stoically enduring.

'Typical of the young,' Bert complained.

'They just don't have the stamina of us old folk,' his wife responded.

In the lee of the church porch Lorna stopped running. Blood drained from her face, bile exploded from the pit of her stomach and her breath came fast and shallow. Fighting the faintness that threatened to overwhelm her, she stumbled into the sanctuary beyond.

Enclosed in the musty dark of a pew, nightmare pictures came to her in vignette flashes: an indistinct form lurking in the undergrowth, animal eyes peering from the greenness of the bracken, the monstrous Jack-in-the-box that rose up to seize her.

Then the havoc of the violence. The tearing pain.

In the quiet calm of the little church the shock gradually receded. Like a diligent archaeologist she began to gather up the broken shards of the missing part of her childhood. As the pieces came together images from that lost summer gradually emerged.

What she had subconsciously erased was given back when those dejected eyes met hers across the gape of the open grave and the gulf of thirteen years. It was summer, just after her twelfth birthday, a time of happiness and new pleasures. Yet the summer's euphoria had been shattered by an explosion of violence so traumatic that she had buried the recollection of it deep inside some secret fogou of the mind.

* * *

Though the graveside rites were long over and the gravediggers had already reversed their work Lorna remained in the pine pew. Her usually animated face was uncharacteristically grey and rigid. With fingers slotted together in an attitude of prayer she made a perfect match for the marble effigy of Squire Trethewan's wife, a lady made immortal in the seventeenth-century funereal monument that dominated the north aisle.

A sudden and unexpected appearance of the sun transformed the church's dim interior. Raising her face from the embroidered hassock Lorna saw that the pew stall was tinted with vibrant colours. Turning her palms upwards she closed her fingers in a vain attempt to capture the comforting rainbow.

The stained-glass window responsible for this gaudy display was a Great War memorial commemorating the loss of two of Lanhedra's most illustrious sons. Lanhedra House dominated the village from a hillside two miles distant. It was the family seat of the Trethewans who, for generations, had served as squires of Blissey parish.

Looking up at the window, Lorna read the inscription as she had done so many times before. Enlisted as lieutenants in the same artillery regiment the young brothers had been killed in the same action. Her eyes traced the familiar heraldic devices of the Trethewan coat of arms. The bottom of the glass was decorated with the unlikely juxtaposition of a cannon on its sombre gun-carriage and a blond angel, golden gowned and playing on a psaltery. The inappropriate inclusion of a bellow-cheeked cherub in what was essentially a war memorial was a conundrum often pondered by Blissey's parishioners. Consensus opinion was that the cherubim signified both the Trethewans' love of music and their heavenly aspirations.

Even as a small child the glass-maker's heavenly musician had mesmerised Lorna. Now, as her eyes were drawn to him again, a strange metamorphosis took place. Its plump cherubic cheeks became elongated and haggard, the peachy skin paled and the infant chin sprouted a wispy beard. The transformation went a stage further. She imagined herself gazing up at the sensitive face of a young man whose beard, hair and lashes were so fair as to be almost white. Slim fingers on elegant hands brushed back straying locks that fell untidily across his forehead. He looked gently from pale grey eyes and his face broke into the radiance of a smile that was beautiful.

Lorna's lips silently shaped a single syllable of awed recognition, 'Rome!'

But where did Rome, her long lost companion, fit into what had happened? In the depths of that long ago winter she had gone in search of him but had found no trace. The cottage was storm-ravaged and empty. The Haven and its surroundings offered up no evidence of his occupation. Having not so much as a surname to give him, she had long since ceased to believe in him as flesh and blood. Reason told her that he must have been no more than a figment of an overactive imagination, merely a pleasant myth created to fill the void that had darkened that distant summer. Now, with much of that suppressed memory restored, she was certain of his existence.

Both burdened and animated by her newly gained understanding, Lorna abandoned the sanctuary of the church. Passing through the bone-yard with its sodden mound of raw earth she was aware of acquiring more than Leonard Nancarrow's knowledge. Those puzzling missing weeks of childhood had been returned to her: it had taken a burial to uncover the secret.

Chapter 2

Family Penrose

Lorna Margaret, born in Port Blissey Cornwall on the 13th of June 1937, was the third child and first daughter of James and Margaret Penrose. Jim and Margaret, like many of their village neighbours, boasted a fishing pedigree for the waves that battered at Blissey's front door offered a rich sea-harvest.

The village of Lorna's birth was remarkable mainly for the smell of pilchard that wafted from its canning factory and the assortment of non-conformist ministers who ranted in its many chapels. The pilchard odour was more pungent than the preaching for it invaded the Port's twisting, cobbled streets to permeate both homes and places of worship. Outsiders, pretending superiority, claimed to detect the same pong on the clothes of Blissey's residents.

Jim Penrose was a member of the four-man crew on the lugger *Mary Rose*. They fished for cod, dog, skate, ray, ling, pilchard or any other species that could be enclosed by net or tempted by their baited long-lines. Unfortunately for his family, Jim's income from night fishing was more uncertain than his daytime drinking habits. To curb her husband's profligacy Margaret Penrose made it her business to watch eagle-eyed for the fleet's return.

Though slow to nag her wayward husband, she often complained to her mother. 'If I don't get down to the quay before the catch is landed my Jim will be spending his share in the pub and I'll never see a penny of it.'

This prediction was more than part true. Unless intercepted both Jim and his earnings would disappear into The Anchor from which neither would emerge intact.

The young family lived with Margaret's widowed mother, Olive Polmount, in a rented cottage that clung limpet-like to the cliff-side to overlook the harbour. Despite the serious overcrowding, Margaret found herself pregnant again before her husband left for war service.

Fishing was a reserved occupation and, had he chosen, Jim could have stayed in home waters hunting a cold-blooded and more profitable catch. Instead he enlisted. Joining the navy was an act of desperation rather than of courage. The strain of meeting the demands of his growing issue had taken its toll by making him feel increasingly inadequate. When war washed over the village sweeping many of its young men into active service, Jim joined them. The conflict provided him with the excuse he needed to escape his domestic responsibilities.

'It's every Englishman's duty to join up,' he argued.

Margaret questioned her husband's newfound patriotism. 'There's other loyalties you should be thinking about. What about me and our nippers?'

But nothing she said could dissuade him from swapping his oilskins for the bell-bottoms of the senior service.

Jim Penrose's war was somewhat shorter than the Royal Navy's. His destroyer was torpedoed while on convoy protection duties in the North Atlantic. Penrose was one of just a handful of lucky survivors plucked from a burning ocean. His lungs scorched and health gone he never put to sea again, not even as an inshore fisherman.

Jim's family was obliged to survive on the small war-disability pension granted by the Admiralty. This Margaret supplemented by cleaning house for a retired schoolmaster, shopping for two elderly neighbours and taking in laundry. These paid-duties left little time to attend to her own family. When his damaged lungs allowed, her war-pensioned husband gave credence to his new landlubber status by working an allotment. The quantities of potatoes, swedes and greens that he grew were Jim's major contribution to the feeding of his hungry brood.

Margaret's mother, never having been as hard-pressed as her daughter, would often contemplate, 'With all them mouths to feed and backs to clothe I hardly know how my dear girl do make ends meet.'

Being disabled and in indifferent health did not prevent Jim from adding to the numbers of his dependants. Before armistice was declared a further son had to be accommodated in Granny Polmount's small cottage. When the new council houses were built at Treblissey to quarter the returning war heroes, Jim's was one of the first families to be re-housed. Leaving a grateful Mrs Polmount to a less crowded and more peaceful old age, the younger generations moved to the exposed hilltop overlooking the village. There they luxuriated in the spaciousness of a sparsely furnished three-up, two-down, with an upstairs bathroom, outside lavatory, coal-store and generous garden.

In 1948, Margaret gave birth to a second daughter, Gill. Lorna, for so long outnumbered in a family comprising numerous brothers, offered up a prayer of earnest supplication. 'Gentle Jesus, please make my sister grow up fast. Mum and me need some help about the house.'

This was a reasonable enough plea for in the Penrose household domestic chores were undertaken exclusively by females.

'Don't ask the boys to do women's work,' their father postulated, 'or you'll turn them into sissies.'

Illogically his overworked wife subscribed to this chauvinist philosophy.

Grandfer Penrose, whose working life had been spent afloat on the world's oceans as a mercantile deep-seaman, also resided in Port Blissey. Having acquired pensioner and widower status in the same year, both he and his wicked-tongued parrot, Horatio, took permanent lodgings at Polbliss House where they entrusted their welfare to Blissey's most illustrious landlady, Dolly Rosevear.

Dolly, a cheerful soul, renowned for the excellence of her pasties, scones and saffron cakes, kept a comfortable, if not spotless, house on the winding hill leading to Treblissey.

'Two Roses together, it be only right they share the same bed,' quipped the tittering village gossips.

James Penrose senior was Dolly's only permanent lodger though, in defiance of wartime rationing, she entertained numerous visitors by serving cream teas in her front parlour. Her customers, seduced by the lightness of her scones, fruitiness of her homemade jam and generosity of her clotted cream later came back as paying guests, extending their stays to a week or more. In 1950 Dolly raised a sign on her storm porch which elevated “Polbliss House” to “Polbliss Guest House”.

In latter years Dolly boasted of this enterprise to the growing numbers who posted ‘Bed and Breakfast’ signs in their windows. ‘Now don't you go forgetting, it was me who first promoted the holiday trade and put Blissey on the tourist map.’

Far from being disturbed by the influx of ‘emmets’, a derogatory term used by Blissey natives to refer to holidaymakers, James, her permanent lodger, enjoyed the variety of company that summer brought to his landlady’s home.

From infancy Lorna was fascinated by her Grandfather's avian soul mate. When her own vocabulary was scarcely more developed than the parrot's she toddled unaccompanied up the hill from Granny Polmount's cottage to Dolly's grander home. Entertained by his granddaughter's quaint ways, James encouraged these visits.

'Feed ’Orry, Grandfer?' the little girl would suggest and together they would ply the greedy Horatio with sunflower-seeds harvested from the ripened flower heads in Dolly's garden. The co-ordination required to offer up a single seed to the beady-eyed tyrant made the child bite her lip in concentration and despite the irascible bird's habit of nipping her baby fingers, she persisted in feeding it.

'Kiss Lorna better,' she would command, displaying an injured digit for her grandfather's attention.

Taking his granddaughter on his lap, James wiped away her tears, then flicked at the evil bird's offending quick beak with an even faster wagging finger.

'You old devil, Horatio,' he scolded. 'I'll give you what for.'

The reprobate parrot responded to this treatment by screeching, 'Bug, bugger off, bug, bugger off!'

James' explanation to Lorna of this particular recitation was, 'That's just Horatio's way of saying he's sorry. He don't mean no harm.'

This mollifying ritual was completed with a tickling that was guaranteed to turn Lorna's tears into squeals of delight and pleadings for, 'More tickles, Grandfer.'

In attempting an earnest apology for some childish naughtiness at home, Lorna surprised her parents by impersonating the identical imperatives of the raucous parrot.

Hearing his infant swear made Jim chuckle with undisguised amusement.

'Our little maid don't need no schooling. She can pick up everything she needs to know from that wicked old bird of Dad's.'

Margaret pretended indignation. 'Don't you go encouraging her. I've trouble enough getting the boys to mind their language.'

As she grew from infant into little girl Lorna tired of the tetchy parrot but she never wearied of old James' company.

'Teach me to count in Chinese again, Grandfer,' she would beg and soon would be reciting some invented gibberish that the old man taught her.

There were French lessons too. 'San Fairy Anne, Polly Voo, Alley Veet,' and 'Comby Hen.' she would mimic, her small lips contorting into the same exaggerated shapes made by her grandfather's.

Best of all she loved his stories. Grandfer, an ardent celebrant of England's supremacy on the world's oceans, delighted in recounting the illustrious deeds of English heroes with the stirring names of Drake, Raleigh and Lord Nelson. His tales abounded with victorious Trafalgars, defeated Armadas, racing Tea Clippers and brave little Brigantines. The telling was always vivid with swashbuckling, bloody battles, buried treasure and Barbary Pirates.

Grandfer's patriotic stories made Lorna's young heart pound. When still too young to go to school she was able to recite several verses of "Drake's Drum". Like the poem's eponymous hero, she too dreamed "arl the time o' Plymouth Hoe". On one memorable day Grandfer took her on a train to see this famous stretch of green. This treat was her first excursion across the Tamar into 'foreign parts', a designation given to Devon and the rest of England by a majority of the Cornish population. As their train rattled over the bridge built by the exotically named Isambard Kingdom Brunel, Grandfer told her of the great iron ships built by that same engineer.

Lorna believed her grandfather's sea stories to be first-hand recollections and that the deeds and heroes he described were contemporary with his own sea faring. This misunderstanding caused embarrassment at school. Reintroduced to Francis Drake in a history lesson she raised her hand and in infant-school sing-song proudly announced, 'Please Miss, Sir Francis sailed with my Grandfer.'

She had been quite non-plussed when her teacher snapped, 'Put your hand down, Lorna, and don't be silly. Only naughty girls tell lies.'

* * *

In 1948, Lorna amazed her family by passing the scholarship entrance examination to the Girl's County School situated eight miles distant in Budruth.

'I be as proud as punch of my little maid,' both father and grandfather declared to the village. Her mother had mixed feelings about her daughter's success for her first-born sons, having displayed no such academic acumen, were obliged to complete their education at the village school.

Margaret could not disguise the injustice she felt on behalf of her boys. 'It don't seem fair that Lorna should get this opportunity for advancement when our Jimmy and Tommy don't.' She expanded on the injustice by adding, 'After all, it's the boys who have to grow up and be the providers.'

This certainly wasn't the case in their own family and her pronouncement made her husband squirm uncomfortably in his easy chair.

A more practical reason for Margaret's lack of enthusiasm over Lorna's County School place was the expense of the obligatory uniform. To raise the money she would have to cash out the insurance policy paid for by scrimping and saving from her hard-earned wages. On those rare occasions when she was alone, Margaret liked to take the important-looking document from its brown envelope, absorb the legal language and indulge in dreams of the treats she would be able to afford when it matured. The policy was her only bit of financial security for the future and its loss was deeply felt. The insurance man, who fortnightly knocked on doors to collect his clients' premiums, did his utmost to persuade Margaret to start another policy. But the dream had evaporated and she did not have the heart to begin again.

Lorna looked upon her scholarship in much the same way as her father had regarded his war service: a County School education was a heaven-sent opportunity to escape the demands of home. Disappointingly, this expectation proved a mirage.

With six children to raise and her other outside responsibilities, Margaret Penrose needed every scrap of help she could get about the home yet she persisted in excusing the boys from what in the male-dominated household was regarded as women's work.

'I don't need boys under my feet. Lorna should be the one helping with the housework. She needs to learn how things are done or how else is she to manage when she gets a home of her own?'

In Lorna's reckoning she already possessed a more than adequate knowledge of how a house should be run but such logic was wasted on her mother who could never be convinced that further practice was unnecessary.

The County School, rather than providing the hoped for relief, made Lorna's life more difficult. The leisurely nine o'clock start at the village school was exchanged for a rush to catch the bus that left for Budruth some eighty minutes earlier. The long bus journey also meant that it was early evening before she arrived home. Homework, a rarity at the village primary school, became a nightly commitment.

With scant regard for these new demands on Lorna's time, her mother expected help around the home as usual.

'Don't you go slipping away upstairs until you've cleared away those tea things, my love,' was but one of the nightly injunctions that kept Lorna from her studies. Later it would be, 'Get your nose out of that book, Lorna. It's time to get the little ones ready for bed.'

When Lorna did find time to open her schoolbooks it was difficult to concentrate for there was no quiet corner in their bursting-at-the-seams home. Inevitably, she began to fall behind, particularly in new subjects like Science, Latin and French. The discovery that Grandfer's highly valued tuition in modern languages was too eccentric to be of help came as a bitter disappointment. At the village school Lorna had been used to coming top in most subjects but the competition at the County School was of a different calibre. She was ashamed to be out-performed by so many of her new classmates.

Another irritation was her smart grey and maroon uniform with its badge and beret. More used to being clothed in jumble sale bargains or neighbours' hand-me-downs, she had been so proud of her stylish new outfit. Never had she imagined that her finery would make her the target that it did. Blissey children, even those previously numbered among her friends, became her tormentors.

'Think you're too good for us now, Miss Know-all, Miss Know-all!' they chanted, snatching her beret and tossing it to one another just out of her jumping reach.

Suffering oppression enough from her two elder brothers, this unwarranted unkindness incensed her. To escape the taunting she sought the companionship of the fictional characters found in her books. Grown into a compulsive reader, she craved the printed word in much the same way that her sugar-rationed peers craved their sweets.

To find the quiet needed for reading, Lorna often slipped away to her Grandfer's lodging where the good-natured Dolly Rosevear made her welcome. The drawback of this location was that Margaret Penrose knew where her daughter could be found. Often, she would send one of the boys to hammer on the doorknocker. If the response wasn't immediate they would holler through the letterbox, 'Lorna, you got to come home quick. Mother wants you.'

To avoid the risk of a summons from home, Lorna began taking her books out on the cliff paths or down to the beach. In winter, she read as she perambulated, awkwardly turning pages with gloved fingers and frequently finishing a chapter in the fading natural light.

This behaviour merely confirmed the opinion of those less gifted village children who pestered her.

'Show-off, book-worm,' they taunted. 'Look at her, that County School have addled Lorna's brain.'

At times, when the pressures of home and school grew too much, Lorna was inclined to believe that they were right.

Chapter 3

Spring 1949

At Number Seven Treblissey Crescent Margaret Penrose waged a never-ending war against the invasion of dirt. Her sons, having other priorities, actively collaborated with their mother's enemy by infiltrating her home with muck on their boots and grime on their clothes and person. Margaret, who considered cleanliness next to Godliness, frequently threatened to throw her grubby boys into the washtub along with their dirty linen.

While the chief perpetrators of household dirt played on regardless, their mother press-ganged their sister into active service. Armed with mop and broom, cleaning duties became the order of Lorna's days. Being born a girl and to be forced into domestic servitude were twin injustices that rankled.

The prospect of spending another morning in a kitchen pungent with the odours of stale cabbage and soaking nappies filled Lorna with dismay. It was too glorious a day to be faced with the tedium of household chores and so unfair that she should be cooped up indoors when her brothers were free to do as they pleased. A beckoning sun made her more rebellious than usual and as soon as her mother's back was turned she made a bid for freedom. As a slight to her carefree brothers she took with her the brass telescope, a present to the boys from their Grandfer Penrose.

Once free of the house, she kept running until she arrived at the granite wall above Blissey beach. This centuries-old barrier both guarded the unwary from a two-hundred-foot perpendicular drop and made an excellent viewing-point over the bay. Resting the expanded telescope on the lichen-covered stone she squinted through the eyepiece and scanned the horizon for the billowing sails and Frenchie flags that would signal Boney's invasion. Grandfer always made his Franco-phobic version of the Napoleonic threat sound menacingly immediate. Despite her reputation as a bookworm and scholar Lorna had not outgrown childish games and she liked to pretend that the security of the nation depended upon her vigilance.

When the invading fleet failed to appear she turned her attention to the waters below. It was too early in the season for mackerel to be running and the only craft visible in the bay was a crabbing tosher. Yet the details of the boat and the froth of its bow wave evaded her unpractised focussing and all that Lorna saw through her sweeping eyeglass was an expanse of empty sea. Not until the crabber heaved-to alongside the buoy that marked a trot of pots was she able to home in on her intended target. The fourteen-foot boat looked close enough to touch and the blue guernsied figure of Jack Mitchell was instantly recognisable. She watched with interest as, hand over hand, Jack pulled the inkwell-shaped pots into his boat. Some contained gangling-legged spider crabs others the blue-black elegance of lobsters.

In a fancy script, on the tosher's side, was painted the craft's name, *Sea Nymph Sue*.

The name made Lorna giggle. Formerly, the boat had been known simply as *Sea Nymph*. Jack had added the *Sue* while courting the girl who had recently become his wife. The joke was that Susan had always been an ample body but now, in the late months of pregnancy, she was enormous. Jack's inappropriate coupling of names resulted in his frequent taunting by Lorna's big cousin Bernard Polmount and the other fishermen. She had overheard some of their good-natured teasing.

'While you're getting the new babe baptised, Jack, you can always ask the minister to re-christen your boat Sea Monster Sue.'

Not to be outdone, the other fishermen came up with their own suggestions.

'How about Titanic Sue?'

'Or Leviathan Sue?'

'Which name d'you favour, Jack, me 'andsome?' they taunted.

Though amused by their teasing, Lorna was somewhat disappointed that the good-natured Jack made no defence of his insulted wife.

The throbbing of the tosher's inboard motor reminded Lorna that she had lingered too long at the wall. It was not the first time that she had gone absent without leave and she knew from experience that continued liberty was not guaranteed until she was out of range of older brothers who were only too eager to spoil her fun. Folding the telescope and slipping it nautical fashion under her arm she continued on her way

A squeaking kissing gate gave direct access to the undulating cliff path. At the bottom of the first descent were steps that led down to Blissey beach. There was no prospect of a cooling paddle for the whole stretch of strand was visible from the wall above and so offered no immunity from her brothers' detection. With a defiant toss of her head, she continued towards the headland and the freedom of the open fields beyond.

The pastures were steep, their uncomfortable gradient terraced by narrow parallel paths trodden by generations of grazing cattle. Lorna ran a zigzag gauntlet between the flanks of the brown dairy herd and the newly-emerged horse flies that buzzed in chorus over every steaming cowpat. Coarse grass stems speared her socks through the cut-open toes of her scuffed shoes and hindered her progress. The surgical modification to her footwear was not an aid to ventilation but an expedient practised by an insolvent but enterprising mother in an attempt to accommodate growing feet in shoes already outgrown.

Reaching the stream Lorna was presented with another choice. Passage to the far bank could be made either by way of a wooden bridge or a row of rarely used stepping-stones. Lorna chose to ignore the bridge and take the uneven stones for a more adventurous crossing. With arms and telescope spread for balance, she imitated Blondin whose spectacular Niagara feat was illustrated in her much-thumbed "Bumper Encyclopaedia of Knowledge". Her passable imitation of a tightrope walker parted swarms of midges that were performing a bobbing dance above the gurgling water. One insect cloud remained with her, circling her head in a dark halo. Her triumphant gaining of the other side was greeted by the applause of invisible spectators, an accolade she acknowledged with an exaggerated bow before flapping her arms to disperse her nigglesome midge companions.

Beyond the stream a steeply ascending path wound its way between bushes of gorse in full and brilliant bloom. As she climbed to the crown of the hill the golden gorse gave way to pasture. Sticky and uncomfortable from the unseasonable heat and exertion, she paused to peel off both cardigan and socks and then sat to recover her breath.

Before her the whole bay and its embracing coastline was spread out like a picture postcard. Directly below was the deserted stretch of Blissey beach and, at its centre, a cascade of white water where the stream that she had forded spat itself out of the cliff. Beyond the beach the waves glistened with a million diamonds and from somewhere in the cornflower-blue above a skylark sang.

The view, like the weather, was perfection, but at the back of Lorna's mind was a nagging worry. In two more days her freedom was to be seriously curtailed, not by her brothers' summons but by the demands of a new school-term that heralded the fright of the dreaded summer exams. It was a sobering thought.

She picked at a scab adorning her knee and fantasised about absconding more permanently. Her camp at the nearby Pencarrick Point would make the perfect hide-away. There she would be safe from detection, could live off berries, roots and seagulls' eggs and never go to school again.

From where she sat daydreaming she could see the roofs of the council houses perched on the exposed hill above the hidden village of Port Blissey. By now she was certain to have been missed and she fancied that she could hear her mother calling. 'Where are you, Lorna? I want you to peel these potatoes,' or 'Come here and amuse your baby sister,' or, 'Keep an eye on our John and Perry: they'll be sure to get into some mischief or other if they're not watched.' More than likely she would be expected to perform all three of these duties at the same time. This thought and the realisation that silhouetted on the hill's brim there was still a chance of being spotted by her treacherous sharp-eyed brothers was enough to spur her to her feet.

Stuffing socks into a pocket and tying her cardigan by its sleeves about her waist, she set off again. The land dropped away steeply beyond the boundary of the next hedgerow and primitive steps formed by widely-spaced slate slabs projecting from the earth bank gave access to the adjoining field where she would be safe from detection. These steps negotiated, Lorna breathed more easily.

Her destination was the promontory known as Pencarrick where a jungle of gorse and blackthorn separated the arable land from both the cliff and the sea view. Beyond the vegetation of this stunted wood was her hideout. Though she regarded the Pencarrick camp with a proprietary pride it did not really belong to her. Dirty Dingle was the true owner of the magic and secluded spot. Dingle's coastal paths followed fox and rabbit ways that were less accessible than those used by Lorna and she guessed that it was he who had beaten the secret track that gave access to the wide grassy ledge.

Dingle was a tall, black-bearded man whose shabby dark clothes and greasy trilby hat added to his sinister appearance. Most of Port Blissey's mothers used the threat of the vagrant to correct the wayward natures of their disobedient offspring. 'I'll get that Dirty Dingle to come and take you away if you don't mend your troublesome ways,' was a frequently used intimidation.

Like all village children, Lorna was wary of the unsavoury vagrant and retained a healthy respect for him. That she might find him out on the promontory should have made her fearful of going there but the irresistible enchantment of the place overcame all feelings of caution. There was also comfort in knowing that in the hours she had spent at the hide-away never once had its rightful occupier disturbed her.

Though Lorna had never seen Dirty Dingle at Pencarrick, she was often aware of his presence elsewhere on the cliffs. Frequently on her rambles she noticed a furtive stirring of the cliff vegetation when the wind was still. A closer examination sometimes revealed the line of his trilby-hat poking above the blackthorn.

One winter's afternoon, perched with a book on the steps leading down to Blissey beach, her innocent curiosity was attracted by the antics of a courting couple enthusiastically unwrapping themselves on the bleak sands below. A rustle in the cliff scrub distracted her and she spotted Dirty Dingle apparently engrossed in spying on the lovers. Anxious to maintain a safe distance from his person, she had slunk away before she was noticed.

In the damp of the Cornish winter the old tramp abandoned the cliffs to frequent the village. There he found his accommodation on the harbour-side, either by making his bed beneath a boat's tarpaulin or under an upturned punt on the launching slipway. But Lorna was aware that on fine nights he slept out under the stars and she guessed that Pencarrick served as his bedroom. In sharing his special eyrie she did no harm and hoped that the old man did not resent her using it.

This was her first visit of the year and already fresh growths of bramble and nettle were choking the entrance to the camp and doing their best to prevent her from reaching her goal. Tucking the telescope into the elastic of her knickers, she jumped up to catch the branch of a wild crab-apple tree. When her grip was firm enough to take her weight she swung out over the scrub and dropped lightly onto the concealed and overgrown track beneath.

The path through the undergrowth twisted and turned and she did what she could to protect her vulnerable arms and legs from the clawing thorns and whipping stingers. Frequently she had to stop to unhook clothing or skin from the grabbing hooks that barred her way. The raking brambles beaded her arm and legs in blood and pulled stitches in the home-knitted cardigan tied about her waist yet such trivial damage to person and property was but a small price to pay for the pleasure to come.

The battle with nature over, Lorna emerged onto a springy carpet of sun-lit turf dotted with a profusion of sea pinks and white campion. To her imaginative eye the grassy sward was a magic Persian carpet flying above the finger of granite that dabbled in the blue of the bay. Throwing herself down on the spongy grass she examined the beaded punctures on her bare legs and spat on them, repeating the treatment more generously on the already itching blisters raised by nettles. She administered to the bloody tattoo on her arm by sucking it.

Spittle was her mother's recommended remedy for everything from a sting to a laceration if seawater wasn't readily available. 'Better than all those expensive antiseptics the chemist sells,' was Margaret's frequent assurance to her accident-prone children.

Expedition wounds treated, Lorna lay on her tummy to spy through the telescope. Scanning the bay she traced the coast past the massive headland of Penblissey to the red and white stack of Blissey's lighthouse that stood on the outer arm of the Port's harbour. Sweeping in the other direction she picked out the magnified teeth of the Carrick rocks and, although it was too far off to be heard, she could see clearly the rocking bell buoy that warned mariners of the presence of the hazardous reef. Proud of her newly acquired competence with the spyglass she attempted to follow the flight of a great black-backed gull as it rode the cliff thermals.

The sun climbed and the day grew hotter. Sticky with heat, Lorna peeled off her dress. She draped it over a gorse bush to avoid adding grass stains to its creases. Neatly folding her cardigan, she made a pillow for her head. The comforting warmth combined with an early awakening by restless siblings who shared her bed made her doubly drowsy. It was not long before the brass telescope dropped from her hand and rolled along the turf.

* * *

Dirty Dingle was at home on his cliff haunts. He approached the headland not by Lorna's route but by traversing the cliff itself, wending his way at a height where the undergrowth was thick enough to conceal his passage. The gulls were nesting and he was partial to their raw eggs.

Far below him he saw a pram dinghy with its two occupants pulling towards the pebbly beach that edged the Pencarrick cliffs at low tide. He growled under his breath as he watched the two lads beach the small craft. The stocky youth with wild curls who was issuing the orders was that no-good Bill Padley, the skinny one with the mousy hair was Nancarrow's son. For the past fortnight these two youngsters had been raiding all his best nesting sites. He'd heard talk in the village that the lads were selling the gulls-eggs in Budruth's Saturday market and felt aggrieved. He regarded their enterprise as a commercial exploitation of what was rightly his, though in reality the cliffs and their riches were free to all so there was nothing he could do to protect his interests. Not wanting to be seen by the boys, he abandoned his quest for eggs and headed inland in the direction of the rabbit warren to check his snares.

* * *

The youths pulled the dinghy up the beach and parted company so that each might search a different area of cliff face. It was a strange partnership. Bill, founder of the egging enterprise, was sure-footed as a mountain goat and loved the exhilaration of cliff climbing. Len disliked heights, it was the prospect of making some extra money that drove him to climb. Being risk averse he opted to search the lesser gradient closest to the promontory. Bill, a more competent climber, tackled the steeper cliff to the west.

Len climbed gingerly, his moss-lined canvas bag slung from his neck. Almost immediately he was rewarded by a clutch of herring-gull eggs. They lay in an impression made in the sparse grass of a narrow ledge. Encouraged he looked about him. Above he could see several birds that looked to be laying or incubating, but caution convinced him that these higher perches were too precarious for him to reach. Seeking what he hoped would be easier quarry, he picked a more comfortable route across the cliff face to another nest-site. Here the adult birds bombarded him; their raucous cries, evil eyes and blood spotted bills were the stuff of nightmares.

'Bloody birds!' he muttered, as their beating wings forced him onto a hazardous course that he had not intended.

Lacking the courage to face another attack from these aggressors he climbed higher. Arriving at an overhang his nerve failed him and his commercial interest in eggs evaporated. He wanted only to regain the safety of sea level. With his shirt sticking to his back he surveyed the cliff-face but could see no obvious route down.

At last he found a ledge wide enough to rest on. As his pulse returned to normal, he looked about making a further reconnaissance for his descent. To his right, some ten yards away, a much wider green sward projected from the cliff. Lying supine upon it was the body of a near-naked girl. Len uttered a blasphemous expletive. The sweat of fear began to trickle salt into his bolting eyes. Just as his mouth opened to call for Bill's help, the corpse moved. Only then did he notice the frock hung over the gorse and the woollen garment folded beneath the child's head.

Len's racing heart quietened as the girl, her eyes firmly closed, rolled to face him. She wasn't dead, nor even hurt, but merely sleeping. He saw that her left hand was pressed comfortingly between her legs. Silly little bitch, he could have her knickers off and his own hand on her fanny before she even knew he was there. That would be something to tell Bill about. His imagination excited him; it also blinded him to the fact that the ten yards separating him from those knickers were ten yards of sheer cliff without a single foot or handhold.

Remote on his ledge he continued to watch the girl and began to wonder how she had got there. His first assumption was that, like him, she had climbed from the beach below. But he realised that this was impossible as the only access to the beach was by boat and theirs was the only craft in sight. Only then did it dawn on him that there had to be an easier route from the cliff-top path.

After a cautious and circuitous descent he arrived back at the beach grateful that his bones remained intact and that his head had not been broken in a spectacular fall. His business partner was waiting for him on the pebbly shore, impatiently skimming flat stones across the smooth water.

'How d'you get on?' Padley drawled.

Len opened the drawstring neck of his canvas bag to reveal his eggs. Padley looked unimpressed.

'It's not a bad haul,' Len defended. 'Most of the nest sites on my side were out of reach.'

'Bet I could have reached them.'

Padley's boast annoyed Len. He didn't appreciate the intentional slight on his climbing ability.

Although he had prepared several versions of his encounter with the maid on the ledge, all colourfully embellished to titillate his companion, he decided to keep them to himself. However, throughout the long row back to Port Blissey, and for a long time afterwards, Leonard's mind remained preoccupied with the unexpected sighting of the girl asleep in nothing but her knickers.

Chapter 4

Family Trethewan

War was the watershed in Jerome's young life. Every memory of his pre-war existence was harmonious: his mother was beautiful, his father strong, both parents were loving and their home comfortable and tranquil. There were no rivals for his mother's attention. Although seven-years-old Jerome was baby enough to satisfy Sarah's maternal instincts so she felt no inclination to provide him with a sibling. Cocooned in material comfort and parental devotion, the security of his early years seemed absolute yet changing world politics was about to create a very different state of affairs.

A cloud of contention came to overshadow the sense of well-being that had previously defined family life. The unfamiliar dissension of raised voices and his mother's frequent tears created a bewildering and disquieting atmosphere that fed Jerome's insecurity. For the first time in his young life he felt afraid and vulnerable.

At first the war made little difference to the daily pattern for their routine went on much the same as before. On weekday mornings his mother delivered him to his day school in South Kensington and when lessons ended she could be depended upon to be there to meet him. Their mews home lacked a garden so, on fine days, mother and son would walk either to the park or, as Jerome preferred, take the other direction down to the embankment. After these walks he would try to recapture in pencil and wax crayons the brightly coloured Thames' houseboats or the cheerful flowerbeds and shady trees of Kensington Gardens. While he played the artist his mother Sarah played the piano. When he tired of drawing, she read him stories from his favourite books. As his competence as a reader grew their roles reversed and it was Sarah who listened, attentive and admiring, while Jerome read to her.

When his mother was occupied with household affairs, Jerome retreated to the privacy of his bedroom to play with imaginary comrades. These games of make-believe were instantly abandoned when the grandfather clock struck six for this was the signal for his father's homecoming. With nose pressed to the windowpane, he kept impatient watch over the mews below for sight of the familiar city bowler, striped suit and swinging briefcase. If the wait proved longer than expected, he amused himself by drawing ships and planes in the mist that his breath made on the glass. As soon as his parent came into view he hurried downstairs to throw the door wide in welcome. His father responded by discarding the briefcase and scooping his son into his arms. From this elevated position Jerome babbled his account of the day's events directly into John Trethewan's ear.

One evening, sitting as usual in his window-seat, Jerome spied an interloper entering the cobbled mews. The stranger was dressed in the blue uniform of an RAF officer and he came directly to the Trethewan's front door. Intrigued Jerome ran to the top of the stairs only to be halted in his tracks by a terrible lamentation that filled every corner of the small house. It was an unending wail that raised the hair on the back of his neck. The inhuman howling was like nothing he had heard before yet the sound issued from his own familiar front hall.

Curiosity overcoming fear, he peeped through the banisters. What he saw was inexplicable. The inhuman cries came not from some wild beast but from a woman whose features, though distorted, were instantly recognisable. The agonised sounds were being made by his own mother. As she cried, she beat her fists against the breast of the airman's blue tunic. With a further shock of recognition he saw that the man being struck was his father.

When the wailing subsided it was replaced by a disturbing tirade that continued throughout the evening. For the first time in his life Jerome was ignored as his father tried to soothe his distraught wife. The soothing changed to reasoning but Jerome could not follow the arguments employed. What he did understand was that his father's discomfort was as great as his own.

The dispute continued past his bedtime and late into the night. Kept awake by his mother’s raised voice, he heard the street-door slam. Even though peace was restored to the Mews, he could not sleep. When Sarah came to his bedroom he saw that her eyes were red and swollen from weeping. She sat on his bed and stroked his hair.

'Your father doesn't deserve us, Jerome. He's a bad man who has done a very wicked thing.'

He rarely contradicted his mother but a torn loyalty made him defiant in his father's defence.

‘Daddy is a good man, Mummy, and you mustn’t be cross with him.’

His distraught mother would no more listen to her son's reasoning than she had his father's. Like Lady Macduff, she interpreted her husband's love of country as proof of his disloyalty to herself. But unlike Macduff's lady, Sarah's heart held no forgiveness. Pressing her son to her breast and talking more to herself than to the child, she revealed the enormity of their breadwinner's offence.

'Your father has always been rash and now he's being selfish too. He could have taken a desk-job in Intelligence but that wasn't glamorous enough for him. He wants to play the war hero rather than stay at home to take care of us. It's obvious where his priorities lie. We don't matter to him any more.'

A desk-job in Intelligence was a concept beyond Jerome's understanding but his mother's rantings gave no opportunity to ask for an explanation.

'He's a bad father and an even worse husband. He's betrayed us both.'

Jerome, hating to see his mother so upset, tried to understand her complaint.

'What does betrayed mean, Mummy?'

'It means your father is a traitor.'

And Jerome, like a true son of Macduff, asked, 'Are all airmen traitors?'

* * *

Sarah's hysterical sense of betrayal was seeded in an abandonment from her past. Her parents, in a zeal of Christian fervour, abandoned their five-year-old daughter in England and travelled to South America to devote themselves to the continent's pagan aborigines.

Sarah was left in the care of a wealthy, childless widow, a distant relative on her mother's side. Although Agnes, her guardian, loved her dearly and spoiled her ward in every conceivable way she was a poor substitute for the child's natural parents.

Photographs that arrived from the other side of the equator added to Sarah's overwhelming sense of inadequacy. One showed Sarah's father teaching a row of squatting native Indians, in another her mother was nursing a sick infant. Clearly these dusky-skinned competitors were more important to her absent parents than her pale self. Next day Agnes discovered her ward transmuting her white skin with the stain of a brown boot polish.

The sense of rejection was made complete when Sarah was orphaned at the tender age of nine. Her parents contracted a tropical fever and died far from medical aid in the middle of a Brazilian rain forest. The small annuity they left was barely sufficient to feed and clothe their daughter but the kind-hearted Agnes, already charged with the moral and practical responsibility of bringing up the orphan, accepted the financial liability too.

At eighteen, with an expensive schooling behind her, Sarah and her faithful aunt went on holiday to the French Riviera. It was there that she was introduced to John Trethewan. John was travelling to seek distraction. He needed to forget the painful terminal months of his mother's fight against cancer. As her only beneficiary he now enjoyed the addition of a private income. This fortune though insufficient to make him independent of paid employment at least ensured that he could indulge in some of life's luxuries. Sarah, he swiftly decided, was in quite another category: she was definitely one of life's necessities. He was bewitched by her innocence and found her pale skin, blue eyes and blonde frailty irresistible. Instead of continuing to Nice with his companions as planned, he remained in Hyères to court her.

John was adoring and Sarah considered him to be handsome and gallant. Being twelve years her senior he was the father-cum-husband of her desires. Three months later, despite some muted opposition from her aunt, they married in haste and set up home in the London mews house that had belonged to his mother. Jealously possessive of her husband and her marriage, Sarah was unmindful of how much she owed her aunt. There was no vacancy in her new exciting life for her former guardian.

Shamefully neglected and deeply hurt by Sarah's culpable negligence, the embittered Agnes cooled towards her former angel. This was the state of their relationship when, crossing Victoria Street on her way to the Army and Navy Stores, Agnes tripped. Her head struck the kerbstone and the resulting haemorrhage proved fatal.

Unfortunately for Sarah, Agnes had that very day changed her will in favour of a ne'er-do-well nephew. Her erstwhile favourite was bequeathed only some hideously fashioned and not very valuable jewellery. This was Sarah's second betrayal.

* * *

Like most men of his age John Trethewan had enjoyed a carnal past. Prior to encountering Sarah he had enjoyed a two-year liaison with Mrs Julia Smithson. In the absence of a husband, who was serving his country in one of the colonies, this good lady did her bit to service his fellow countrymen at home. John was well aware that he was but one of a number of young men whom the Major's wife generously entertained. Eager to devote himself to Sarah's pale beauty, John ended the former adulterous relationship without so much as a pinch of regret.

Though initially content to worship Sarah's virginity, after marriage to his child- bride John found it a dry and disappointing shrine. After several weeks of their union his young wife continued to lie unresponsive beneath him. When making love to Sarah he began conjuring Julia: her arching back, the way her smooth long legs gripped his buttocks, how she fed his searching lips with her swollen nipples. His discontent made him feel nostalgic for the shared secrets of the older woman's moist welcome.

No outsider suspected Sarah's frigidity. In public she clung possessively to her husband's arm and in more intimate company was openly demonstrative, fondly pecking his cheek or whispering all sorts of nonsense into his ear. John's friends and business associates told him what a lucky fellow he was to have such a charming and desirable young wife.

Yet, in their more private moments Sarah was far less spontaneous in her demonstrations of affection. Though permitting her husband's cuddling and fondling, she discouraged anything beyond this gentle foreplay. That she wished there was some less painful way of satisfying her darling than through the awkwardness and humiliation of the sexual act was made quite obvious.

John was an honourable man. Wanting to stay true to his marriage vows he convinced himself that he had outgrown his lust and must settle down to enjoy the routine of a marital love that was so much warmer in the vertical than in the horizontal, so exciting in the overture yet so muted in the main performance.

* * *

John's determination to fly for his country, which necessarily obliged him to fly from Sarah, was in her view betrayal number three. She beat her small fists upon his uniformed breast and screamed abuse into his anguished face. Her own pretty features were distorted with the vehemence of rage. It was Sarah's first and only truly passionate display towards her husband.

'If you really loved me, you wouldn't have enlisted. Not after I begged you not to,' she accused, raining blows on the resented uniform.

John's argument that he had joined-up in order to protect his family from the threat of invasion only drove her to sting him with a different complaint.

'Haven't I given you everything you ever asked for? You know I never liked you inside me. It hurts and gives me no pleasure, yet I never deny you. Even when I was pregnant I permitted your beastliness. And now you do this to me. How dare you, John Trethewan? I hate you, I hate you!'

John, who had been frequently denied, could not believe his sweet wife capable of such lies and vitriol. Full of self-pity, he left his harridan hoping that Major Smithson might again be serving overseas and that the obliging Julia might be found at home.

* * *

Deserted for a second time, Sarah withdrew, tortoise-like, into her shell. Her every close relationship had ended in a painful rejection and she did not intend to let herself be hurt again. She sat for long hours, running vague fingers over the piano keys and paying only limited attention to her son.

Jerome tried to console his mother hoping that he might restore her to a happier state but Sarah's insularity made him feel unequal to the task. As the weeks went by he became accustomed to his mother's swollen eyes and cheerless company and thought of his father less often.

The telegram, when it came, regretted that Pilot Officer John Trethewan had been lost in action. His Lancaster had been shot down by an enemy fighter over the North Sea. It was his first tactical bombing mission. The news did not draw Sarah's tears. Instead of crying, she sat for hours her face rigid, her body cold and unmoving. It frightened Jerome to see his mother turned to stone like the evil witch in one of his fairy stories.

With the return of her sensibilities came a renewed anger and, once again, Jerome was terrified of the wild creature that his mother had become. It was not until weeks later, when Sarah was preoccupied with preparations for their evacuation to the country, that the significance of the Admiralty telegram overwhelmed him. With the shutting-up of the home he loved, his sense of loss and isolation was complete.

* * *

The remaining war years were spent at Lanhedra, the run-down Cornish estate of Jerome's dead father's two spinster aunts. The young widow barely knew her husband's relatives and would not have chosen to go to Cornwall had she been offered some other refuge. But Sarah was a friendless orphan and too inexperienced to know how to go about renting a house. Had she been on her own she would have stayed in London for she did not fear the Blitz, being quite fatalistic about it. However, the closure of Jerome's school and the fact that other children were being moved out of the reach of German bombs awakened her sense of responsibility to her offspring. She made the decision to abandon London for the duration of the war and was presented with no option other than to accept the sanctuary offered at Lanhedra.

Lanhedra proved to be an uneasy household. The two resident spinsters, in consequence of being deprived of their brothers and cheated of husbands by the Great War, might have been expected to show sympathy and understanding towards the young war widow and her fatherless child. This was far from being the case. Though they dutifully provided their blood relative and his mother with a home, the Trethewan sisters showed no compassion. At best Edith and Maud were indifferent towards Sarah. At worst they seemed to relish that another generation was to suffer the deprivations that had been visited upon them.

The spinsters frequently reminded Sarah that the income inherited from her husband was really Trethewan money and as such it belonged to Lanhedra. They even expressed their dissatisfaction with Jerome. The pale skin and fair hair inherited from his mother bore no resemblance to the dark and ruddy complexioned Trethewans.

Even his Christian name was cause for contention.

'What possessed you to give the boy such an inappropriate, papist name?' they asked their nephew's widow. 'First born sons of the Trethewans have always been baptised either Henry or John.'

They were right in assuming that the name had been Sarah's choosing. John, intent on pleasing his wife rather than his distant family, had given way to her fancy.

Sarah for her part made no effort other than to be coldly civil towards the two older women. When the last of the Lanhedra servants, a young housemaid called Lily, left to join the Wrens, Sarah made it clear that although she was prepared to fend for her son and herself she had no intention of playing skivvy to her aunts by marriage.

Lily had been a capable, hard working girl, and without her domestic attentions the house slipped into slovenly neglect. Despite her loyal endeavours to satisfy demanding employers, the good-natured girl had managed to find time for Jerome. He took to following her around the house, chatting to her as she worked. After Lily left it was he who missed her the most.

One thing that the three women did agree upon was that the rough and tumble of the village school was an unsuitable establishment to educate the heir to the Trethewan estate. Port Blissey's church organist, a sharp nosed and sharp tongued woman who was burdened with the care of an invalid parent, came once a week to give Jerome music and maths lessons. Otherwise his education was left to his mother. In reality, Sarah became more and more introspective, shutting herself away with her grievances. Rather than teaching her son she would select books from the Lanhedra library and leave him to explore them on his own.

The books smelled musty, many had mould growing on their covers and all had pages poxed with a brown rash. The only volumes to be lavishly illustrated were a set of ancient encyclopaedias and it was with these that Jerome spent much of his study time. He was an avid reader and from the hours spent with these tomes he managed to acquire a diverse, if somewhat out-dated, education.

Although current events were of interest to him, he was unable to follow the course of the war as closely as he would have liked. In the isolation of Lanhedra House, effectively cut off from the rest of the world, there were no companions of his own age with whom he could discuss the hostilities. The only wireless set was guarded jealously by the great aunts in their den, a room to which neither Jerome nor his mother were invited. When the occasional daily paper was brought into the house Jerome read it avidly. In 1943 he saw newspaper photographs of the fall of Stalingrad. The vivid depiction of death and desolation made him sad. Though barely eleven years old he was aware of Sarah's emotional scars and the crumbling ruins of that Russian city reminded him that his mother had been similarly ravaged by the war.

Lanhedra was a large rambling house and the sisters fought but lost a spirited battle to prevent the army from commandeering the dilapidated east wing. The three women and Jerome lived on in the more structurally sound central portion of the old house, their isolation penetrated.

Relishing the diversion that the army's occupation offered, Jerome disobeyed his mother by seeking the company of the soldiers. Though he delighted in their colourful language, particularly the non-military aspect, he had the good sense to conceal this newly acquired vocabulary from his Trethewan women folk.

A few of the infantrymen, understanding something of the boy’s lonely existence, took pity on him. But no sooner did Jerome find a companion when his new soldier friend was drafted elsewhere. He began to wonder if the pain of losing a comrade wasn't worse than being cooped-up exclusively with his three bickering relatives.

Though stationed at Lanhedra for just four months, Major Robert Fuller was the only officer ever to be invited into the Trethewan private quarters. The spinsters tolerated the Major because his generous gifts of black-market goods benefited the otherwise impoverished household.

During the short period of his residence Fuller instructed Jerome to call him "Uncle Bob". Despite these companionable overtures the boy distrusted the Major. He wanted to like him, made the effort to like him, but found it impossible for he noticed the way that the Major's jocular smile never quite reached his steely eyes.

It wasn't that he felt any resentment of the officer's fawning attentions towards his mother, just the opposite, for once again he heard his mother's laughter. Yet her laugh had a different ring than before. It saddened Jerome that it sounded both harsher and less musical than in his memory.

Chapter 5

Summer 1949 and earlier.

Paddington station was bustling with travellers, many taking their first excursion since the war. A long wait at the ticket office meant that Jerome Trethewan was the last passenger to board the Cornwall-bound express. A porter bundled him and his belongings onto the train and slammed the door shut just as the couplings clattered in response to the pull of the engine. Burdened with guitar and other luggage Jerome made an awkward passage along the carriage. Finding all the compartments full, he resigned himself to standing in the corridor. The train gathered speed, blurring the bomb-damaged and smoke-blackened buildings that lined the track. Jerome felt a growing sense of elation to be escaping the ruins and pollution of London.

At Reading, a few passengers were disgorged. After stuffing his bulging haversack into the baggage rack he claimed a vacated seat and sat stiff and self-conscious with his precious guitar case clenched safely between his knees.

A middle-aged couple seated opposite studied him with a prim distaste. He caught their disapproving whispers.

'These bohemian types with their long hair,' the woman sniffed, 'what do they think they look like?'

Her companion nodded. 'They need sorting out, if you ask me. A stint in the forces under the tender care of my old drill sergeant would do them a power of good.'

Jerome flinched. The criticism of his collar-length hair was all too reminiscent of the frequent gibes directed at him by his military stepfather.

Noticing Jerome's pallor and general nervousness, a moustachioed fellow in a corner seat inquired in avuncular fashion, 'You all right son, you look all in?'

Jerome made eye contact with his amiable sympathiser but limited his response to a nodded affirmative. The ample moustache looked very RAF and he was already in too high an emotional state to enter into conversation with someone who was a reminder of his dead father.

His female critic monitored this minimal response. 'Manners!' she snorted.

After this initial stirring of interest his fellow travellers paid him scant attention. He preferred it that way: anonymity was what he desired above all else for no one must suspect his secret.

His body rocked to the train's motion and his eyes, heavy with lack of sleep, closed.

The hypnotic rhythm of wheels over track should have lulled him but instead they taunted with a monotonous chant: *You're running away, you're running away, you're running away.* Crossing the points the tone changed but the accusation remained the same. *You're running away, running away, running, running, running away.* So distinct was the reproach that Jerome was convinced that others in the compartment must hear it too.

Though his lips did not move he challenged the tormenting refrain. 'All right, so I'm on the run. Now tell me something I don't know. Tell me what I'm supposed to be running *to.'*

He could give several cogent reasons for running away but had no precise idea where his flight was taking him. His connections with Cornwall had made that county a natural choice but his ticket to Penzance had been bought not because he knew the town but because it was located at the end of the Great Western Railway Line. The irony of Penzance being, quite literally, a last resort seemed most fitting. Though still worrying about his ultimate destination, he managed to doze off.

At Exeter, the jolting of the carriage awakened him. With an exhalation of steam the train shuddered to a halt. Opposite Jerome's compartment, a platform hoarding displayed an advertisement. Beneath the colourful illustration of a rocky cove was the slogan *"Cornwall by monthly return ticket. Any Time, Any Train, Anywhere by Great Western Railways'*. The cove in the painting was not identified but looking at it Jerome was struck with the solution to his conundrum. The obvious rightness and sheer brilliance of the idea almost made him exclaim aloud.

This initial optimism was soon overlaid with doubts. An all too reasonable fear played in the emptiness of his stomach. That single visit had been so long ago when he had been no more than a child; what if his memory was playing him false? He vacillated between uncertainty and conviction. Surely so distinct a memory had to be real. Then a new anxiety gripped him: even if the recollection proved accurate, after so many years, would the refuge still exist? And if it existed would it still be unoccupied?

The engine halted at the foot of a gradient to gather its steamy breath for the uphill struggle ahead. Because of the uncertainty awaiting him at journey's end Jerome welcomed the pause. He found himself wishing that the delay would be unending. What was the adage, "*Better to journey hopefully than to arrive*"? He contemplated the rest of his life in suspension on the Great Western Railway Line. In the confinement of this carriage he could remain a stranger without history amidst others of the same ilk. He plagiarised to coin his own motto: "better to travel with uncertainty than to arrive to disappointment". For a while, at least, he wanted nothing more than the security of the smut-blackened upholstery of his present surroundings.

* * *

Before armistice was declared, Jerome and his mother left the Cornish great-aunts to their selfish seclusion and moved back to London. Their old home in Clement Mews SW10 had escaped the blitz and suffered from no more than the ravages of neglect.

Closed-up for the duration of the war, it smelt of must and decay much like the rambling old manor in Cornwall. The mould that grew on walls and furnishings was reminiscent of the fungi that flourished on the fallen trees in the Lanhedra woods.

Plaster ceilings displayed maps of damp; a cartography of black continents set in off-white oceans. Dust lay like a shroud over everything. Jerome hardly recognised it as the sunny home of his early boyhood.

Returned to civilisation, Sarah emerged from her depression and, for the first time in years, addressed her son's educational needs. She enrolled him at a newly opened day school in the borough.

Having been imprisoned so long with only adults for company, the school and especially its pupils proved a novelty. At first Jerome felt uncomfortable in the society of his peers for he had forgotten the social skills of boyhood games and chatter. The classroom was quite another matter. Having been starved of formal education, he welcomed the structured existence that school discipline imposed and took a rare enjoyment in his lessons.

Despite the missed years of tuition, he found no difficulty in keeping pace with his fellow pupils. Thanks to the dusty reference books in Lanhedra's library he was the possessor of an impressive diversity of general knowledge. This erudition earned him the admiring nickname of "Cyclo", a diminutive derived from Encyclopaedia. Settled into the new London routine, Jerome again began to believe in the possibility of happiness.

Sarah, emerging from a winter of discontent that had lasted almost five years, began to blossom like her son. With her new-found energy she refurbished the house, restoring it to its previous good order. It was not just the bustle of London, undiminished by the bombing, or even freedom from the oppression of the Trethewan sisters that invigorated her. There was a more intimate reason for the personality change, one that she hid from Jerome.

Major Robert Fuller was one of the lucky ones: he had seen action in North Africa, and later in Europe at Monte Cassino, but had returned unscathed. The next time Jerome saw “Uncle” Bob he had been transformed into an unwanted and resented stepfather. The Major was equally lacking in enthusiasm about his acquisition of a stepson. From the start he was adamant that the boy must go to boarding school. This created an early source of friction in the marriage for Sarah was reluctant to be separated from her son.

Jerome's life had lacked a male authority figure for so long that he found the Major's military discipline overbearing. Discovering Dickens, he instantly recognised the character of Mr Murdstone in his own stepfather. The difference in his situation from that of Copperfield’s was that he lacked the comfort of a Peggotty, Ham or Emily. The chill that had crept insidiously over the mews' house during the war years returned, a chill that seemed intent on settling on his life for ever.

In the pretence of doing his prep he sought refuge in the basement, though in reality his sojourn there was a ploy to avoid his stepfather. In the warmth of the kitchen he chatted with the latest in a long line of daily helps for these worthy ladies seemed to give notice almost as soon as they arrived. The current charlady was a bird-like, perky cockney called Mrs Handley for whom Jerome had a particular liking. He feared that she would stay no longer than the rest for already she was complaining about the Major's interference in the domestic arrangements.

'He thinks he's still in the bleeding army,' she fumed, as she brandished the smoothing iron and attacked with a frightening zest Robert's dress-shirt spread prostrate on the cross-legged ironing board. 'Throwing his weight about, issuing orders, telling me how he wants things done. I didn't go through the blitz just to have some tin-pot general come jack-booting it into my kitchen to order me about. Don't know how your poor Ma puts up with him, honest I don't.'

Jerome didn't know either, but it would have been disloyal to say so.

Despite his reticence to take sides against the Major, Jerome was uncomfortably aware that his stepfather's initial attentiveness towards his mother had changed into a frequently expressed irritability. As for his mother, the tenderness she had first shown towards her new husband was no longer apparent.

Robert had not sought employment since his military discharge and was seemingly content to live off his wife's income. His time in Civvie Street was spent either carousing at his officers' club or moping around the house. When at home, he exploited every opportunity to nag his newly acquired family or to bully the latest daily-help. Jerome much preferred it when his stepfather was out, but his mother, though unable to live in harmony with her second husband, became even more agitated without him.

From snatches of over-heard argument, he understood that his mother was jealous. Frequently, she accused her husband of having been with other women.

'Don't lie to me, Robert,' was a common complaint. 'I can see in your eyes what you've been up to. I've even smelt her on you. God you disgust me.'

At other times, wallowing in self-pity, Sarah would plead with him, 'Who is she, Robert? Is she pretty? Do you buy her nice things with my money? How can you, can't you see how ill this is making me?'

Jerome found these conversations deeply embarrassing; they added to his reasons for seeking refuge in the kitchen.

Mrs Handley had finished the ironing, and was preparing to leave.

'I better be getting back to the North End Road. My ol' man will be wanting his supper and I'll miss the bus if I don't look sharp.'

'I'll put the clean laundry away in the airing cupboard for you Mrs H.'

Jerome liked to be helpful for he was eager to compensate for his stepfather's rudeness.

'Bless you, ducks,' she accepted. 'You'd better do it neat and proper though or General High and Mighty will put you on a charge.'

They both giggled. The bonhomie made him regret that she had to go. Her friendship made him feel that he had an ally and since his mother's renewed indifference towards him he desperately needed to count someone on his side.

Robert's garments made up most of the neatly pressed and folded laundry. Jerome disliked the intimacy of touching his tormentor's clothes; even when newly laundered they were offensive to him. In contrast his mother's things seemed dear, fragile and vulnerable, just like herself.

Taking up a silk undergarment he buried his nose in the material enjoying the softness of texture and the cleanliness of its freshly laundered smell.

He believed himself to be quite alone until the Major's unexpected and scornful blast startled him.

'Dear God, what are you doing boy? Sarah, come here woman. Come and see what this precious boy of yours is up to.'

His mother's pale face appeared behind the Major's crimson one. Jerome was still holding the fragment of silk.

'Will you look at the little pervert. Almost fourteen years old and I catch him drooling over his mother's knickers. He needs the discipline of a good boarding school before it's too damn late.'

* * *

Jerome hated his minor public school quite as much as a younger Robert Fuller had loved his. His disposition was ill-equipped for the rough competition of team games and the Major had deliberately chosen a school where triumph in the sporting arena was held in greater esteem than academic achievement. Jerome was quite unsuited to such an ethos and his keenness in the classroom could in no way compensate for ineptitude on the sports field.

The institutional discomforts of boarding school distorted his recollections of domestic life at Clement Mews. He remembered with nostalgia the pre-war idyll of his mother's companionship. Such memories made him homesick and he yearned for the familiarity of his own room and possessions. Towards the end of his first term he found himself ticking off the interminable days until the holiday. When the time came to travel home he felt deliriously happy.

His first evening at the mews was intimidating. The rosy tints of his recollections left him mentally unprepared for the Major's taunts and bullying. Even more shocking was the unexpected change he found in his mother. There was an unfamiliar, haunted expression in her pale face. Frequent recourse to the whisky bottle whetted the bully's aggression and at every opportunity he scorned and snapped, his sensual lip curling with contempt. The well-honed humiliations and mental cruelties previously reserved for his stepson were now extended to his wife. Jerome saw how these assaults sapped Sarah's confidence and destroyed her self-esteem. She was no longer capable of fighting back. He also noted the little nagging cough that troubled her, but there had been nothing then to connect it with the bloody racking of tuberculosis.

With his friend and ally Mrs Handley long gone, Jerome took refuge in his bedroom to avoid the domestic turbulence. One such night, lying propped on an elbow reading, he heard the now familiar anger of his stepfather's raised voice rising from a room on the floor below. This was followed by unfamiliar and more disturbing sounds: grunts and laboured breathing accompanied by a softer whimpering and the percussion of something being thumped up the stairs a single riser at a time. With his heart drumming against his rib cage Jerome opened his bedroom door.

With bolting eyes he saw the Major holding his mother in a neck-lock while she clung stubbornly to the banisters. He heard again the grunt as Fuller, straining from his exertions, dragged the choking woman up another stair. The boy stood rooted to the spot watching the unequal battle of strength and will. The Major, with the advantage of both muscle and health, dragged his captive up the final riser and onto the landing.

At this precise moment Jerome sprang onto his adversary's back and sank his teeth into an ear lobe. With a howl of rage Fuller released his grip on the mother to direct his violence at the son. An elbow smashed back into Jerome's ribs. Winded, he slipped from his opponent's shoulders. A fist exploded into his collarbone, knocking him backwards. As he fell his head collided with the doorjamb. Stupefied he sat like an expressionless rag-doll, his back supported by the wall he had fallen against. He barely responded as an out-of-focus Mr. Murdstone bent over him breathing alcoholic fumes into his face.

'You young puppy, bite do you? I'll thrash you senseless for that.'

His eyes cold with hatred he hauled Jerome to his feet by the shirtfront. A ripped-off button skittered across the landing. The fist was raised again and the boy flinched away from the certain punishment yet the threatened blow did not fall for his mother was hanging onto their assailant's arm. When her desperate pleading failed, she bit him herself.

Roaring like a wounded bull, the Major released the boy and re-directed his aggression to his former target. Jerome heard, rather than saw, his mother's gown ripped from neckline to waist. Fuller had her pinned against the wall and from his worm's eye view Jerome saw the hated thick fingers with their curling sprouts of coarse black hairs scrabbling at the material of his mother's skirt. The fabric was pushed aside to expose stocking tops, suspenders and clenched-tight, white thighs. To the still stunned Jerome, it felt as if he must be part of someone else's nightmare.

Fuller was struggling single-handedly to release his belt buckle as his mother begged, 'Not in front of Jerome, Robert. Please, not in front of the boy. Let's go to the bedroom and I'll do anything you like, but not here, please.'

Her appeal went unanswered and Sarah screamed instead at her son.

'Go to your room, Jerome. I won't permit you to watch. Do as you're told. Go. Now.'

At the rising crescendo of this command, a sobbing Jerome crawled on all fours into his bedroom. Once inside he shut the door by falling against it. Stuffing his fists into his ears he attempted to deaden the animal sounds emanating from the other side. As Robert ejaculated, Jerome vomited over his carpet.

* * *

Four years on, sitting with his back to the engine on the rocking, Cornwall-bound steam-train, Jerome was as whey-faced as the thirteen-year-old boy who had sat on the shaking foundations of his young life, his back to a marital rape, staring into the fetor of his own puke.

Chapter 6

1961: reflections

Still reeling from her graveyard encounter with Nelly's son, Lorna was thankful to be returning to an empty house. David had promised to meet Rachel from school and take her to his office at the workshop where he could keep an eye on her. On their way home father and daughter would make the diversion to Treblissey to collect little Perry who was being cared for by his grandmother. Lorna hoped that these arrangements would give her time to compose herself.

She hung her still-damp gabardine coat in the downstairs cloakroom. It was the same raincoat that she had worn for the recent Penrose funerals and its ominous black folds looked strangely alien against the colourful warmth of her modern home. Unsettled by the knowledge gained from the graveside encounter, she retreated to the sanctuary of their marital bedroom. The room was comfortingly familiar and so much at odds with the shocking brutality that played on her mind. Throwing herself onto the bed, she claimed and hugged David's pillow. Never had she felt more protective towards him.

Catching sight of her windswept and damp hair in the mirror she rose, smoothed the creases made in the bed's floral-patterned eiderdown and reached for her hairbrush. Her cabinet-maker father-in-law had expertly crafted the dressing table at which she sat. Apart from the house itself, it was the material possession that gave her most pleasure. Tracing the pattern of its walnut grain with a forefinger she reflected on how greatly her circumstances had changed since childhood.

Looking into the bevel-edged glass she examined the large eyes and full lips that looked back at her. Usually, she could examine her mirror image with some satisfaction but this afternoon her appearance was disturbing. The woman she saw in the glass looked ravaged by self-doubt: the confidence that marriage and motherhood had given her was missing.

It was not difficult to imagine herself as she had been then - a child of few expectations who acknowledged her own plainness. Even her mother, who might have been expected to show partiality towards her elder daughter, had been liable to exclaim, 'You must have been standing near the end of the line when God dished out beauty, Lorna, my lovely.' Taken in its entirety this statement was not without irony, but Margaret Penrose was as unaware of this as she was insensitive to the hurt that such an unfavourable appraisal caused.

If dissatisfied with her daughter's appearance, Margaret had done little to improve it. Lorna's hair had been allowed to grow unkempt, the weight of her tresses making it straight and lifeless. Then her hair had hung in an unflattering emphasis of her thin face; now, styled and cut to a fashionable length, it framed and complemented her regular features. Brushing vigorously, she addressed the storm damage. Restored to its usual order her hair waved attractively and shone where the light caught it. She wished that the inner damage she felt could be repaired as easily.

Her dark eyes and lashes had always been her most striking features. In early photographs they appeared as shadowy pools that emphasised the waif-like quality of her drawn face. Now they burned with a shame that verged on anger as she attempted to come to terms with the revelation of a childhood trauma that her mind's innermost workings had kept hidden until today's graveyard encounter.

The mystery of that twelfth-birthday summer had always teased and puzzled her, containing as it did so many forgotten and unexplained things. Now, with her self-protective amnesia erased all was changed. With her new-found ability to trawl back through the whole of that summer's lost weeks, she began to re-examine and place into context those details that had always been known to her.

She remembered vividly her return to consciousness. Waking she expected to see Gill's familiar cot alongside the bed, to feel John's accustomed pulling of her hair or Perryn's gentler attempts to tickle her awake. Instead, her eyes opened to the peace and solitude of a white cell. Her arms were pinned, not by the crush of sharing a bed, but by unruffled bedclothes that held her as though in a straightjacket.

For a frightening moment she thought she must be dead, a belief that seemed to be confirmed when her cry of distress summoned up a white apparition. This spirit proved to be no angel for it spoke with a familiar local accent and introduced itself as Nurse Coombs. She was welcomed back to the land of the living, a country that revealed itself to be Budruth Hospital. With no recollection of being admitted she asked how she came to be there but the question went unanswered. A thermometer forced under her tongue prevented further enquiry.

Her parents came to visit wearing their best clothes. Her father's tears confused her, as had the unsympathetic reprimand dealt him by her mother.

'Don't you go being so daft, Jim, or you'll upset our little maid.'

Though she begged for an explanation, neither parent would give her a cogent reason for her presence in the hospital.

'No need to go worrying your head about that. What you have to do is concentrate on getting better, my 'andsome,' her father recommended.

She must have followed his advice quite efficiently for, though weak and unsteady on her feet, a few days and medical consultations later she was allowed home.

Exposed to the outside world, she was amazed to see the last remnants of brown leaves on the otherwise bare branches. It was November. Though the intervening weeks since early September were lost to her, she was able to recall the long summer holiday with something approaching clarity. In particular she remembered how she had spent a part of every day with her new friend, Rome.

Her parents did not even suspect Rome's existence. Fearing that in some inexplicable way he might be connected with her stay in hospital and wanting to protect him, she resolved to keep him a closely guarded secret.

Other recollections were more vague and confused. With a natural curiosity she interrogated her parents about her memory loss but her innocent enquiry caused them such obvious discomfort that she was never bold enough to ask again.

When, eventually, she was allowed out onto Blissey's streets, people seemed to be avoiding her. Yet despite their reluctance to meet her eye she had the uncomfortable feeling that the whole village was looking at her. This was not the only change: no longer did she have to suffer the bullying and taunts of her peers and even her elder brothers treated her more gently than usual. Such altered behaviour made her harbour the suspicion that every inhabitant of Port Blissey, bar herself, knew why she had been in hospital. Didn't her father regularly claim, 'You've only to scratch your arse in this village and every soul knows about it.'

Whatever intelligence the villagers may have possessed no one volunteered to share it and to question outsiders when her own relatives, including Grandfer, were reluctant to tell would have been tantamount to disloyalty. In retrospect she understood that the real reason for her reticence was childish pride for to ask would have meant admitting her own ignorance.

There was something frightening about a secret that belonged to her but was known only to others. Yet, because of her parents' embarrassment and the avoidance of the subject by everyone else, it seemed prudent to pry no further. Instead she attempted to account for the missing weeks in her own way. It was obvious that she had been very ill indeed and the only logical explanation was that she had caught and been cured of some rare disease too terrible to mention.

As a child she had come upon Gilbert Ford writhing on the ground in Chapel Street. Joyce Clemo's mother had put her fingers into his mouth. Her own mother had explained that this was done to stop him swallowing his tongue. For weeks afterwards Lorna had been haunted by what she had seen. Remembering that incident, she thought it possible that she had suffered a fit similar to Gilbert's and began to worry that her own tongue might disappear down her throat to choke her. She wanted to seek confirmation of this possible explanation for her hospitalisation from her parents but part of her said it was best not to know. She hoped that ignorance might be the charm that would offer protection against such a fit from happening again.

Even when she was fully recovered and positively bursting with good health her family continued to treat her like an invalid. It was particularly noticeable that her mother was more considerate towards her than of old.

'Why don't you take yourself upstairs and read your library book. I can manage down here,' she would prompt.

Occasionally Lorna was excused in an even more remarkable manner. 'Don't you go bothering with that, Lorna. One of the boys can help me.'

Her father imposed new rules, forbidding her to go out unless she was with one of her older brothers. This restriction made her wretched, especially as Jimmy and Tom resented playing nursemaid to a younger sister when they wanted to be off kicking a football or risking life and limb by dilly racing down Penbliss Hill.

Grandfer, with no such distractions, was more than happy to keep an eye on Lorna. The bait he used to tempt her to his lodgings was old copies of *John Bull* and *Picture Post* hoarded at the back of Dolly Rosevear's kitchen dresser. When their pages were thoroughly read, Lorna clipped the more interesting pictures and created collages in the scrapbook that Grandfer had bought for her. Though considering herself far too grown-up to sit on his lap, she still loved listening to his yarns. Old James continued to oblige, filling her head with his own version of English maritime history presented, as before, in a confusing chronological cocktail.

As a toddler Lorna had been a frequent visitor to Penbliss House and it continued to be her refuge. She took delight in the high-ceilinged rooms, the bulky upholstered chairs with their antimacassars, the patterned carpets that were soft to walk on and the glass-fronted cabinet that displayed Dolly's porcelain knickknacks. The luxury of her Grandfer's lodging was a far cry from the utility of her parents' linoleum-floored, sparsely furnished, modern council house.

In the past, Dolly had always made Lorna welcome but now the warm-hearted soul positively pampered her.

'I'm going to fatten you up my 'andsome,' she would declare as she spooned yellow gobbets of clotted cream onto her young visitor's jam scone. This was the first real spoiling that Lorna encountered before David came courting.

She became accustomed and almost contented with the routine of days divided between mornings spent helping at home and afternoons of leisure with Aunt Dolly and Grandfer Penrose. Several weeks were idled away in this manner. The days began to lengthen, winter was passing, yet her return to school went unmentioned. This inexplicable lapse of responsibility on her parents' part Lorna put down to good fortune.

Not until a younger brother began to complain about this educational discrimination did she feel any guilt over the missed lessons.

'Why do I have to go to school when our Lorna don't? It baint fair.'

Lorna found herself in agreement with the disgruntled John. She was beginning to miss the purpose and structure to life that school had given and decided that the question of her future should not be put off any longer.

'When am I going back to school, Dad?' she asked tentatively.

Her father looked ill at ease and exchanged a furtive glance with her mother across the breakfast-table. Her rowdy siblings became quiet as if they had an equal interest in their parent's reply.

'You got to build up some more strength first, Lorna maid,' her father replied.

She never returned to the Girls' County School in Budruth. In early Spring, she was enrolled with the mixed seniors at the village Board School where education, though unexamined and uncertified, was deemed complete on a pupil's fifteenth birthday.

On her first day back at school she noticed the nudges exchanged between some of the older girls as they looked in her direction. Such clandestine attention made her uncomfortable. During afternoon break, Georgie Polmount, a cousin to the Penrose brood on her mother's side of the family, leant over the wall separating the girls' and boys' playgrounds and shouted something rude. Though not fully understanding the words, Lorna knew they were intended for her.

One of the other girls must have told on her cousin for, when the enforced segregation of playtime was over and the children trouped back into their shared classrooms, their fiery little headmaster thundered into their lesson. Seizing poor Georgie he led him away by the ear.

The infrequent appearance of Mr Wilks signified one thing only: a miscreant pupil was in for a caning. The unfortunate George returned red-faced, tear-stained and with both hands pressed to his posterior. Their female class teacher had shown more mercy than the headmaster.

'It might be for the best, George, if you stand rather than sit at your desk for the remainder of the afternoon.'

Lorna tried to remember Georgie's taunt. Across the distance of time his actual words refused to come back, but it didn't matter, she could guess at the gist of them. She thought of Leonard Nancarrow and shivered.

* * *

After the awakening in Budruth hospital, Rome's wonderful companionship had been one of her first recollections. It was not until months later when her parents finally relaxed their curfew that she went to Kilcarrick in search of him. But Rome had gone, as had all trace of his occupation. It was as if he had never been. Such a total disappearance worried her for it endowed him with a ghostly quality.

Certainly his music continued to haunt her, filling every quiet moment by playing and replaying in her head. But with the passage of time the tunes faded and that was when she first began to doubt the singer's existence. She had known only his Christian name and even that seemed unlikely. No one else she knew was named after the saintly scholar who had removed a thorn from a lion's paw.

Eventually she came to believe that her exotic friend had been no more than a figment of a fevered imagination, the same fever that had landed her in hospital. For no reason that she could explain, the cherubic minstrel in the church memorial window always made her think of Rome, but other than in church she put him out of her mind. It was an exclusion that was made complete when, some years later, David came to replace him in her affections.

Now Rome's existence was no longer in doubt. The vision that appeared to her as she sat in the church pew had been as vivid as the original: a sensitive face framed by fair shoulder-length hair, the bony body and lanky legs giving the impression that he was even taller than his measured height of six feet.

Staring into her mirror, she conjured up the gentle youth again. Her bespoke manifestation was so accurate that he might have been standing before her. Looking up into the pale eyes, she repeated the inquiry made all those years earlier.

'Do you ever get dizzy up there in the clouds, Rome?'

His imagined laughter rang rich and warm as of old.

She remembered how his long, artistic fingers teased vibrant notes from the strings of his guitar. Forgotten lyrics and tunes floated back to her across the years and she was able to reconstruct the rich timbre of his singing as he belted out his beloved folksongs and blues. As the notes died, the soothing tones of his cultured speaking voice arranged itself inside her head, making a surprising contrast with the rough energy of his folk singing.

It seemed incredible that after so many years of ignorance she could now unravel the many misunderstandings of her childhood. Yet the knowledge made her feel guilty for it seemed almost a betrayal of all those years of careful protection. After such a time-lapse how could she admit that what had been unconsciously suppressed was now remembered? She knew that she could make no such admission and her reasons were two-fold. Her husband, a relative newcomer to the village, knew nothing of the secret in her past, of that she was certain. Secondly, to seek retribution now would serve no purpose other than to dredge-up a past better forgotten. The retrieval of memory must be hers alone and something to be guarded from others. To preserve her secret she needed to compose herself before David returned home with the children for he was a man not easily fooled. Yet it was impossible to divert her thoughts to the mundane and domestic. Her busy mind kept returning to the events of that shadowed summer and it was a revisiting that played havoc with her emotions.

Chapter 7

Lorna and David

Demotion to the village school had its compensations for in a less competitive environment Lorna became a shining star and rarely regretted the loss of her County School place. Relieved of the double burden of travel and homework she found more time for books and, having freedom of choice, her reading greatly exceeded the limited literary canon studied by the young ladies at the syllabus-structured Grammar School.

The scholars of Port Blissey School received a sound but basic education that included neither the sciences nor the novelty of studying dead and exotic languages. Its pupils left their alma mater at the tender age of fifteen without taking any form of school-leaving examination. Lorna, like her peers, graduated with no more than a last report plus the Headmaster's handshake and his best wishes for the future.

Erudition gained from self-education counted for little in the cut and thrust of the working world so when Lorna secured employment at the village Post Office her appointment was considered to be quite a coup, not only by her family but also by the rest of the village.

'Did 'e hear? Harry Endeoc have taken on the Penrose maid to work at the Post Office counter.'

'Fancy that. And her with no educational certificates neither.'

'Ah, but she've always been a sharp little maid.'

Lorna, possessing a native quickness combined with an acumen for figures, soon absorbed the bureaucratic routines of the job. Her efficiency so impressed Post-Master Endeoc that he felt justified in extending his lunch-break drink at The Anchor into an afternoon snooze. This left his competent young assistant to reopen at two o'clock and to service his customers unaided for the rest of the working day.

David Grainger became a regular customer at the Post Office. Lorna found his daily purchase of a single postage stamp puzzling. Trying to be helpful she asked if he might prefer to buy his stamps by the book, a suggestion that induced a red tidal wave to sweep over the islands of his freckles. This unexpected response prompted a similar darkening of Lorna's own cheeks.

His embarrassment surprised her. Though only three years her senior he possessed a quiet maturity that, compared to the behaviour of her harum-scarum brothers, made him seem very grown-up indeed.

She favoured David's freckled, open face and startlingly blue eyes, respected his quiet manner and admired the educated accent that was so different from the speech of the other young men of her acquaintance. That his rationed buying of stamps might be a deliberate ploy to see and speak to her filled Lorna with wonder and the more she thought about this possibility the more it became a cherished hope. But after their mutual awkwardness David stayed away from the Post Office and by the end of the week she was convinced that she had frightened him away for good.

David Grainger was not a local boy. His parents had moved from the Coventry area some years after the war, both having lost members of their family in the destructive air raids. Unable to shake off the horrors of the bombing and carnage, Marion Grainger insisted on making a clean break by moving to another part of the country. With fond memories of a pre-war holiday spent west of the Tamar, Cornwall had been Marion's first choice.

Her husband, Arnold, was a skilled craftsman and despite the shortage of materials in post-war Britain he saw their move as an opportunity to start up his own carpentry business. Blissey natives usually treated with suspicion those unfortunates who were born beyond Cornwall's borders but Arnold Grainger's amiability ensured that he was soon accepted as a "proper decent chap" and his joinery and cabinet-making venture prospered. David inherited his father's love of wood and was enthusiastic about entering the family firm. His schooling over, he became his father's apprentice.

Marion Grainger found it harder to win acceptance from Blissey's chapel-oriented community. Several factors told against her; chief of these was that she was High-Church rather than Low or non-conformist. The locals spotted other oddities in her nature: in a village sporting fewer than a dozen private vehicles she was that rarity - a woman driver. Her preference to pay her bills by cheque rather than with cash was a practice that local shopkeepers and tradesmen found bemusing. She wore rather more make-up than was considered respectable for a married woman and sent her son as a weekly boarder to a private school 'down West', an expensive educational option previously enjoyed exclusively by the son of Port Blissey's fish buyer made affluent by his monopoly of the trade.

These and other lady-like habits and attitudes meant that the more narrow-minded residents of Port Blissey regarded Mrs Grainger as something of a stuck-up foreigner long after her husband and son were accepted as being ‘Awright’.

* * *

It was Friday and the Post Office closed as usual at 6 o'clock. Although the nights were drawing in and it was already dusk, Lorna took the unlit cliff path that was her usual and preferred route home. Hurrying up the narrow cobbled steep that rose directly from the quayside she was startled by a figure that materialised from the shadows. Already out of breath from her exertion on the slope she let out an involuntary gasp.

The hand that grasped her arm was firm, yet the voice that accompanied it faltered.

'It ... it's only me, David. I'm really sorry if I frightened you. I should have realised that it wasn’t a good idea to appear out of the dark like that.'

‘It was a surprise more than a fright.’ She was trying to present an outward composure that would disguise her inner turmoil for David retained his protective hold on her arm.

'The least I can do after giving you such a shock is to see you safely home.'

She readily agreed to him playing the gentleman and felt pleased that her choice of route made it perfectly reasonable for them to link arms in mutual support as they navigated the dark and hazardous cliff-path.

As they drew near to her home, Lorna found herself visualising the Graingers’ neat detached villa with its gravel drive and well-tended lawns and flowerbeds. Not wanting her escort to see the gate hanging from its hinges, the ubiquitous line of washing or the dilly and drift-wood-strewn garden that invaded the rows of winter cabbage at Number 7, Treblissey Crescent, she made him turn back before reaching the stark council houses.

Next day was early closing and, as secretly hoped, she found David waiting for her at the spot of his previous ambush. This time he was bolder and asked her to go out with him. It was the declaration of interest that Lorna had been waiting for. In accepting his invitation she made no attempt to disguise her enthusiasm.

For their date, David took her to Budruth’s picture palace and borrowed his family’s saloon car to drive them there. Their means of transport struck her as being more exciting than the movie for Lorna could count on one hand the number of times that she had ridden in a private motor vehicle. This was not the only factor that made it difficult for her to concentrate on the silver screen.

When the film's lovers engaged in a prolonged and searching kiss, Lorna could not help wondering what it would feel like to be kissed by David. It was something of a disappointment when he failed to take advantage of their back-row seats. Avoiding greater intimacy he seemed content to squeeze her hand.

On the return journey to Blissey Lorna luxuriated in the comfort of the Standard's leather seats and blessed the convenience of private transport.

'It's such a treat not having to rush off for the bus before the end of the film.'

'Why would you do that?'

David's question made her realise what different lives they led. Obviously he had never been inconvenienced by the dictates of the Western National Bus Company's timetable.

Feeling slightly embarrassed she explained the predicament faced by out-of- town and public-transport-reliant moviegoers.

'Coming from Blissey it's usually a choice between missing the end of the film or missing the last bus home. The only solution is to arrive in time to catch the ending at the afternoon showing of the same programme.'

'What a swizz. Seeing the denouement first must ruin the plot.'

She loved his clever way of expressing things.

'It does, but it's better than being faced with an eight-mile hike in the dark.'

David took a hand off the steering wheel to give her knee a sympathetic pat.

'That's one problem solved now that you have me as your chauffeur.'

This assurance rather than David's goodnight peck on the cheek was what Lorna chose to remember. She regarded his statement as a disguised declaration that he considered them to be going steady.

A week later they repeated the cinema trip. This time the main film was a war story with minimal romance yet David seemed keener to exploit the privacy of their seat in the dark by slipping an arm around her. Lorna reciprocated by squeezing his free hand.

Taking this for the encouragement intended, David held her closer throughout the subsequent on-screen carnage, only slackening his hold when the lights came up. Once their intimacy was illuminated they both moved shyly apart.

David chose to drive home by the old road, a hilly route little used since the new wider highway had been opened up via Trecarrick. At the lay-by half way up the hill, he pulled over.

Nervously Lorna teased him. ‘Have we broken down?’

There was a definite hiatus while he searched for an explanation.

‘I wondered what those lights might be out on the water.’

Leaning across to wind down the steamy passenger window, he drew her attention to a distant glimmer out in the bay. Their bodies touched as they peered into the darkness.

‘It must be the fishing fleet. My elder brothers are out there tonight.’

‘Not the best of weather to be bobbing about on a boat.’

Lorna gave an involuntary shiver and David placed a protective arm about her.

‘You need keeping warm,' he mumbled.

She snuggled closer, inhaling the tweedy smell of his jacket as she had done in the cinema. Not wanting him to think her too forward, she began to chatter nervously.

'Do you know why this place is called Carters Leap?'

‘No, though at a guess I’d suggest that Carter was pining with unrequited love so ended it all by jumping off the cliff over there.’

Lorna laughed. ‘Wrong, Carter is an occupation not a disappointed lover.’

‘What a shame, I was sure that it had to be something romantic. Blame it on the mood I’m in.'

His lips played gently on her cheek and she felt the intimate pressure of his hand on her breast. Inexperience made her chatter on.

‘In a way it is romantic. My Grandfer tells how back in the days of horse transport one poor creature dropped down dead from exhaustion because of the steepness of the hill so the carriers took to leaping from their carts to lighten the load.'

‘I see, hence Carters’ Leap.’

Lorna was surprised that David was still listening for his actions suggested that his mind was on other things.

Her nervous twittering continued. ‘According to Grandfer even paying horse-bus passengers were made to dismount. Then it was shanks’ pony all the way to the top before they were allowed back on again.'

David surprised her by jumping from the car and hauling her out. 'Then we ought to continue the tradition.'

With no intention of walking her up the hill, he opened the car’s rear door and ushered her into the back seat.

Glad that he had overcome his shyness and heady with the pleasure of his kisses, Lorna made only a half-hearted attempt to restrain his wandering hands.

Later they completed their journey to Blissey in silence. With passion awoken rather than gratified both were impatient for the next instalment.

* * *

Margaret Penrose was delighted by David Grainger's attentions towards her daughter. So far, the local boys had steered shy of her and Margaret preferred to believe that it was Lorna's bookish ways that discouraged them rather than attribute their lack of interest to anything more sinister. Since puberty Lorna had lost much of her plainness. She might never be a great beauty but she was, as her father liked to boast, 'developing into a pretty maid with a tidy figure,' and young David seemed besotted. What's more he had prospects, him being in business with his father and all. Yes, Margaret decided, David Grainger would be a good catch for any Port Blissey girl.

Marion Grainger felt very differently. She said very little to her son, but complained bitterly to her husband.

'Why did we spend all that money on his schooling if he's going to end up with a girl like that?'

'You're not being fair, Marion, she's a good girl. Harry at the Post Office can't speak too highly of her.'

'But her family, Arnold. All those children! Jim Penrose has never held down a proper job and those boys of his are wild. The eldest visits Elsie Steadman's cottage when her husband's away. You know that woman's reputation and she's old enough to be his mother.'

'You surely don't hold the girl responsible for what her family gets up to? Come on love, it's not like you to make that sort of judgement.'

Arnold was youthful enough in outlook to understand why his son was attracted.

The little Penrose girl lit-up that dreary Post Office with her smile.

* * *

Early in their courtship David spoke of taking Lorna home to introduce her to his parents. It was a prospect that made her nervous in the extreme and she wasn't in the least sorry that the proposed visit was a long time in the planning. She accepted without bitterness that Marion Grainger might well expect her fine upstanding son to do better than Lorna Penrose from the council estate.

Marion's opposition persisted even after their marriage. Though when

Rachel was born she softened somewhat and with the birth of Perry Arnold, whose auburn locks were such a striking reminder of her own son as a baby, she capitulated completely.

She even went so far as to invite Margaret Penrose to take afternoon tea with her and further surprised Arnold by expressing both sympathy and admiration for Lorna's mother.

'I like her, she's good company and completely uncomplaining about the hard life she's had bringing up that family with only half a husband to help her. Through it all she's kept her sense of humour. It makes one grateful for one's own lot.'

As a demonstration of this gratitude, she plonked a kiss on Arnold's balding pate.

* * *

Until her marriage Lorna's childhood haven, the pebble-dashed Penbliss Guest House, continued to be a place of refuge. As of old, whenever the distractions of her overcrowded home on the Treblissey estate proved too much she escaped to her Grandfer's lodgings. No small part of the appeal of Dolly Rosevear's home was its secluded garden. This retreat perched high upon a natural, inland cliff and was reached by climbing rough-hewn steps at the back of the house. It was Dolly's proud claim that these steps had been laboriously pick-axed from the slate and granite by an ancestor.

As long as the days were mild, Dolly's garden offered a place of peace for Lorna to indulge her obsession with reading. Her favourite seat was a homemade bench concealed behind a shrubbery of hydrangea, fuchsia and veronica. On rainy days she retreated into the shelter of the large shed standing at the top of the terraced garden. This was equipped with deck chairs and was grandly referred to by Dolly as her summerhouse. Though not as splendid as this title suggested, it provided a welcome refuge from the damp of the Cornish climate.

Her grandfather was a frequent companion in Dolly's garden. Though tolerant of her lodger's impertinent parrot and tall stories, Dolly wasn't fond of the fumes of his pungent tobacco. James was an obliging houseguest and to keep both his landlady and her living rooms sweet he willingly retreated to the garden for his smoke. Unlike Dolly, Lorna enjoyed the comfort of the shag's aromatic burning. They kept contented company: James Penrose indulging his nicotine addiction, his granddaughter her reading habit.

It was in Dolly's garden that Lorna accidentally overheard something that should have been the catalyst to jog her memory as to the events of those missing weeks of five summers earlier. It was during the time of David's unofficial courtship and she supposed that being happy and in love she had not wanted any unpleasantness to intervene for she had simply refused to link the evidence to herself.

During her lunch-hour, when the Post Office was closed, Lorna regularly called in at Dolly's house to see her Grandfather. She often found him smoking his Digger Shag on the bench in the high garden. On that particular day, they had not sat long together before he excused himself.

'This sun's a mite too warm for me at this time of the day. I think I'll just go inside for a bit and catch the end of the Home Service news.'

Lorna, enjoying the sunshine, was not the least bit eager to return early to her dark Post Office counter.

'You go ahead, Grandfer,' she encouraged. 'I'll stay for a few minutes more.'

His parting shot was unexpected.

'By the way, should I be putting aside my pennies to buy a wedding present for you and this fine young Grainger fellow?' he teased.

'What nonsense you talk, Grandfer,' she protested.

'Nonsense is it?'

Lorna's scarlet face gave her away and the old man chuckled. 'As I thought, my 'andsome, I'm not so wide of the mark.'

The positioning of Dolly Rosevear's garden bench, high above the twisting and climbing street and quite hidden from that thoroughfare, was not an accidental feature.

This particular route out of the village had been carved, many generations before, through the sheer inland cliff. The rock sides channelled the street's sounds with an acoustic amplification into the garden perched above. Conversations of the travellers up and down the hill could be heard quite distinctly. Lorna supposed that this was how Grandfer had heard gossip about her and David for as yet their courtship was supposed to be a guarded secret.

While considering this likelihood, she was struck by the coincidence of hearing David's mother's name spoken in the street below. Two gossips, whose voices she recognised, stopped to catch their breath before struggling-on up the hill with their loaded shopping baskets.

'They do say Mrs Grainger is none too pleased about it.'

'Well, she wouldn't go much on it, would she? That Marion Grainger's always been lah-di-dah. She thinks herself too good for the likes of us.'

'Does she know, d'you think?'

‘Hard to tell. Though if she does she must be out of her mind with the worry. I know I wouldn't be too keen if it were my son. You know what they said after it happened?'

'I heard a lot of things. What in particular?'

'May's sister, you know the one who was orderly up at the cottage hospital, said they had to do so much stitching inside that no man would be able to do it to her again.'

There was a giggle from the other woman. 'Well, I must say that might be a blessing, 'twould make married life a bit more tolerable.'

'But do her young man know?' continued the other, ignoring her companion's opinions on conjugal relationships.

'If he don't he's in for a big disappointment on his wedding night, that's for certain sure.'

'Disgusting it was. I heard it from her mother that the child was covered in his semen, poor little thing.'

'Tragic too. Some said she was so damaged that she’s never likely to have children of her own.'

The two voices faded as the women continued on their way. For a moment Lorna sat stunned yet she had not allowed herself to brood on or attempt any sort of interpretation of the ugly words that she had overheard. She had simply refused to link them to herself and thought instead of David's strong fingers inside her and of her overwhelming desire to be joined with him. Only the fear of pregnancy, instilled by thoughts of her mother's numerous brood, held her back from abetting the consummation of their urgency.

Now, with the events of those missing childhood weeks returned to her, Lorna wondered at her ability to shut out such vital evidence. Some subconscious fear must have warned her that to illuminate her ignorance might spoil everything so she had blotted out the overheard conversation just as previously she had repressed all memory of being attacked.

* * *

Hearing familiar voices and the sound of the back door opening, Lorna roused herself from her reverie. The looking-glass showed a peaky face so she pinched some colour into her bloodless cheeks.

'We’re home darling.' came her husband's cheerful call. 'Little Perry is full of all the good things your mum's been plying him but our Rachel says she's starving and wants her tea. If we don’t feed her soon she’ll fade away and won't be our little pumpkin any more.'

Hearing Rachel's delighted squeals Lorna guessed that her daughter was being tickled. She heard her son demanding similar attention. When the laughter stopped, she heard both children begging, 'Do it again, Daddy. Do it again.'

Thank God the gossip had been false. She had proved herself healthy and fertile. Rachel had been born ten months after their honeymoon, with Perry's planned birth coming three years later. Her glance was drawn to the bed where they shared so many marital pleasures. She was sorry for the village scolds who failed to enjoy their husbands' bodies as she did her man's.

'Just coming my loves,' she called, a fraction too brightly.

David studied her anxiously as she entered the warmth of the Rayburn heated kitchen.

'How was the funeral? It was foul weather.'

She turned away to embrace her son and daughter before responding.

'It always seems to rain for funerals but I'm glad I went.'

'You look all in, love. Can I make you a cup of tea?'

David seemed to be studying her pale face and to prevent further examination she released the children and offered him the fullness of her lips.

With a tightening of heart she realised that if she did not tell him immediately about the awful thing she remembered then it must be hidden forever. Seeing her husband's concerned face, she knew that she could never visit upon him this newly resurrected hurt that belonged to a time before she had known him. What previously had unwittingly been buried must now be consciously suppressed.

By evening she still looked peaky and David ordered her to bed. Solicitous as ever, he brought her up a hot cocoa. She waved the proffered nightcap aside and pulled him down beside her.

'Make love to me, David.'

It was a delicious surprise to find his wife so vigorously recovered and David responded enthusiastically to the piquancy and energy of Lorna's passion.

Chapter 8

Summer 1949: Kilcarrick Haven

Jerome disembarked at a railway station two stops short of the destination printed on his ticket. Noticing this anomaly the ticket collector viewed both his person and luggage with suspicion.

'This isn't Penzance, young man. You've got off too early.'

Jerome mumbled something about a change of plan and hurried through the barrier. His pale face, rucksack and guitar-case made him a distinctive figure likely to be remembered. Yet he was not concerned about covering his tracks for his reluctant guardian was unlikely to come looking for him. In his imagination he could hear the Major growl, 'Good riddance to bad rubbish.'

The bus-timetable posted outside the railway station showed an infrequent service so he decided to cover the distance on foot. There was no need to ask for directions: the first miles of his journey followed the familiar country road that eventually led to his wartime home at Lanhedra.

There were few vehicles on the road but, as a light drizzle began to fall, a lorry slowed to offer him a lift. Jerome waived the driver on. Though not concerned about pursuit by the Major, he was about to commit trespass and so was keen to keep his ultimate destination secret.

For the final stage of the journey he abandoned the metalled road and took to the muddy coastal path. As he tramped the worry that had tormented him on the train journey returned. It was emotional uncertainty rather than physical exertion that made his breathing become laboured. What would he do if the place was not as he remembered? Worse still, what if the memory proved false and the picture in his head was just the figment of a childhood dream? The thought that something so vivid might have no existence in physical reality induced a panic that he could not suppress.

Breaching the headland he forced himself to look down. The dark clouds that had dogged his hike suddenly parted and shadows raced across the inlet below. His heart lifted at the sight of glittering wet slate. Drawing nearer to the cliff-edge he saw cob walls lit by the same shaft of sunlight. Some of the elation of this moment stayed with him, even after he reached his goal and discovered how much the intervening years had taken their toll on the cottage.

* * *

During the war, when he and his mother lived at Lanhedra, Edith, the younger and more active of his father's eccentric aunts had taken him to Kilcarrick. Occasionally, more to annoy his mother than out of any fondness for her young relative, Edith enlisted him to accompany her on tours of inspection of what was left of the run-down Lanhedra estate. She would steal him away from his books or collect him from the yard where he spent monotonous hours kicking his heels. Once, soon after dawn, she had invaded the high-ceilinged bedroom that he shared with his mother and physically dragged him from the four-poster bed.

'Come on young shaver,' she never used his disapproved-of name, 'slip those apron strings or you'll become as lethargic as your blessed mother. Best foot forward now, you're coming with me.'

His mother, ignoring the jibes, feigned sleep and Jerome went as he was bid not daring to complain about his lack of breakfast.

Edith was a big-boned, muscular woman with bobbed hair and slacks. At their first meeting, Jerome had mistaken her for a man. This had been in those blissful days before the war, when he had gone to Lanhedra with his father. He had been an infant of three or four at the time, but he felt that Edith had never forgiven him for this offence. Several years later, as an evacuee at Lanhedra, he overheard one of the recently billeted young soldiers make the same mistake by addressing Edith as 'Sir'. He expected fireworks from Edith but, to his surprise, rather than correcting the error, she had deepened her voice in reply.

On one of his aunt's impromptu tours of inspection they had beaten their way to the overgrown walled garden on the southern side of the house. Edith brandished an elaborate machete, one of a number of exotic implements including a dozen kukri knives that were relics of colonial adventures taken by past generations of Trethewans. More usually these weapons were displayed for decorative purposes on the walls of the grand staircase of Lanhedra House, but Edith disliked seeing them collecting dust and was apt to requisition the blades for more practical use.

She thrust the machete at Jerome for his inspection. 'No good keeping tools that are unfit for purpose. Try the edge on this one, young-un.'

Obediently he ran his thumb along the blade. The razor edge cut deeply into his flesh. At the sight of the welling blood he expected sympathy, but already Edith was striding off and calling back over her shoulder, 'Come on, slow-coach, try and keep up.'

He suppressed his tears and after sucking the wound wrapped it with his handkerchief. Catching up with Edith he hid the evidence of his carelessness in his pocket.

He had not much liked the walled garden, for under the tangle of choking weeds there seemed to be acres of shattered glass. Edith told him that these shards had once been cloches that covered the melon beds. That night he dreamed of rows of melons lying tortuously on earthy beds and imprisoned in glass tombs. Each melon wore a face like Edith's, their tendrils replicas of her long limbs. Some thrashed out at him, hacking at his vulnerable skin with jagged shards of splintered glass.

The same machete accompanied them on another venture when Edith took him deep into the woods that skirted the boundary of the estate. He had been careful to keep out of her way as she swung the hooked blade in a vigorous attack upon the encroaching undergrowth. From time to time she let out uncharacteristic whoops of delight. Oblivious of brambles and nettles, she seized him by the collar and forced him to gaze on some tropical rarity that she had partially freed from the grasp of its indigenous cousins. He learnt how these botanical exotics were specimens brought back to England as seeds or seedlings by their globetrotting ancestors.

Pressing his face dangerously close to the leaves of a particularly noxious smelling specimen, Edith took pleasure in warning, 'If a single drop of this plant's poisonous sap goes in your eye you'll be blinded for life because there's no known antidote.'

In her own way Aunt Edith had been as big a bully as the Major.

Even more terrifying was the day when she hacked away some clinging ivy and other creepers to reveal an ancient-looking stone structure. She'd barely time to tell him that these three-century-old walls were bee-boles when they heard a tremendous vibration of sound. Furious at being so rudely disturbed after decades of peace, a vast squadron of wild bees swarmed from the uncovered nooks. With no thought other than for her own safety his intrepid leader fled, followed by a trailing formation of the buzzing swarm. No thanks to his guide, Jerome reached the house unscathed. Edith didn't appear again until breakfast next day when both her face and the backs of her hands were measled with red and swollen eruptions. She made no reference to her ordeal and the ferocity of her look silenced Jerome and the others from making either comment or enquiry.

They had not made a single excursion together that Jerome could remember with untainted pleasure, though the jaunt to Kilcarrick Haven had definitely been their most companionable. Petrol rationing meant that the fuel-guzzling Bentley was relegated to the barn and Edith proposed that they should walk the whole distance – a suggestion that his mother tried to veto.

'The Haven is too far for Jerome. You forget that he's been brought up in the city and isn't used to cross-country route marches.'

'Nonsense,' Edith snorted, 'the walk will do him a power of good. In the last war boys not much older than this young whipper-snapper were proud not only to march, but to fight and die for their country.'

'Taking Jerome on a country marathon is unlikely to do anything for the present war effort,' Sarah commented with some sarcasm.

But as usual Edith had got her way.

They walked by road as far as Trecarrick Cross and were just about to take to the fields when the sky was filled with the throbbing sound of approaching aircraft. Looking up, Jerome saw the lumbering shape of a low-flying bomber and, in the distance, a smaller fighter in pursuit. Fascinated he stopped to watch but Edith caught him fiercely by the arm and dragged him unceremoniously and painfully towards the hedge.

It was from the bottom of a ditch, with Edith's bulk sprawled on top of him, that he heard the first explosion. A second followed and then a third, more distant. They did not speak until the sound of the engines had died away.

'Was it a German plane?' he asked.

'Much good you'd be in the service of your king and country when you can't even recognise the enemy,' Edith pronounced dismissively, though her usual strident tone was modulated by a distinct tremble.

'But why did they want to kill us?' He had taken the bombing very personally.

'I doubt if the pilot saw us. He was far too concerned with the Hurricane on his tail and trying to improve his chance of escape. He dropped the bombs to lighten his payload.'

After this life-threatening experience Jerome expected them to turn back and said as much. His suggestion of retreat was met with scorn from his great-aunt who was busily picking pieces of vegetation from her clothing.

'Not frightened by a little bit of high explosive are you? You don't take after your father, he was quite fearless at your age.'

They discovered the first bomb crater several hundred yards away in the middle of a field but saw no sign of any other damage. The next day Edith reported how a cow had been killed at the valley farm and that the third bomb had fallen harmlessly on a deserted beach. The fate of the German bomber was not known.

After the bomb scare, the unlikely companions pressed on, crossing the fields diagonally. Climbing over a final gate, they dropped down to the Haven by following the meandering course of a stream as it gurgled on the final yards of its seaward journey. As they first glimpsed the cottage that signified journey's end the ground beneath their feet became boggy. Forced to divert around the edge of the reeds, they climbed again until they arrived at the very edge of the cliff. Here a precipitous path zigzagged down across the rock face into the Haven.

Kilcarrick charmed Jerome for it possessed everything that a boy with imagination could desire. At the back of the inlet a little cottage grew from the bank of beach. Its slate roof sprouted not only a chimney but also a garden of strange flowering mosses and lichens. A limpid stream flowed swiftly past, falling to form a pool on the beach before spreading itself into invisibility under the darkened sand. In the cliff face a cool cave yawned an invitation to explore.

The receding tide uncovered barnacled rocks that were camouflaged brown and green with wrack. In hollows the sea had left behind numerous pools that were populated with anemones, crabs, colourful snails, small prawns and tiny brown fish with large heads and tapering bodies. Jerome was further entertained by the discovery of a whelk shell with a resident hermit crab fiercely brandishing its armoury.

His delight over his discoveries and the unqualified approval he gave the place seemed to please his great-aunt. She boasted how the Trethewans had once owned every acre of land from Lanhedra down to the high-water mark at Kilcarrick. Just as Jerome was starting to revel in the idea of having such an illustrious family, Edith began to bemoan the political misfortunes, reckless ancestors and imprudent marriages that had combined to reduce the estate to its present impoverishment. The wartime property comprised only the house at Lanhedra, its surrounding fifteen acres of woodland and the Kilcarrick outpost with its cottage, boathouse and immediate foreshore.

'Who lives in the cottage, Edith?' he asked jealously.

'In father's time it was rented to a fisherman, but the place is so remote that no one has lived here for years. The only reliable access is by sea and that can be tricky when there's a blow on the water. The direct approach down the valley is impassable unless the mire dries and it takes a rare and long drought to bring that about. Of course, there's the zigzag we used, plus those rough-hewn steps in the cliff over on the Blissey side of the cove, but both routes are impassable at high water and sometimes at other states of the tide if there's a stiff south-easterly blowing.'

Jerome liked to hear Edith talk of Lanhedra's past. He was proud to stand at the end of a long line of Trethewans, stretching back into history. It made him feel privileged, but also slightly awed by an unfamiliar sense of responsibility. Keen to please Edith, he wanted to say that when he was a man he would restore the estate to its former glory but was shy of making so rash a promise. Instead he contented himself to thinking about the wonders of Kilcarrick.

The isolated cottage seemed to offer protection from the war that was going on in the rest of the world. He decided that it was the most magical of places.

'When I'm a man, I'd like to live here,' he announced.

His enthusiasm moved Edith to be pleasant.

'The estate might come to you one day. Though the way we're going it's likely that Kilcarrick Haven will be the only bit of the Trethewan inheritance left.'

But she spoilt this limited generosity by adding, 'Though it will hardly make an appropriate residence for the fine city gentleman that your mother wants to make of you.'

* * *

Approaching the stone boathouse, Jerome saw that it was no longer the bastion it had been on that first visit with Edith. Its walls, once offering protection from the worst of the south-easterlies that drove unbroken into the inlet, were breached in several places. The cottage itself also showed signs of decay for the elements had been eating away at the cob. The windows, once shuttered though not glazed, mostly presented blank black eyes whilst the surviving shutters were hanging at odd angles. The front door was smashed and stood resting against, rather than hanging from, its frame. The roof, that on first viewing had looked sound, was holed. Yet Jerome entered reverently.

The floor inside was of uneven flagstones. The cob walls rose up to the roof timbers where daylight streamed in through a jagged hole. There was evidence of damp where the weather entered unimpeded. Built into the right-hand wall was a massive chimney that, apart from the slate roof, was the building's only stone structure above floor level. In the hearth were the charcoal remnants of a last fire.

Jerome remembered how his aunt had sent him out to the shore to gather driftwood for fuel. The high-water-mark was strewn with timber from smashed fish boxes and he had returned laden. Edith propped the thin planks against the hearth and stamped on them with her walking boots to break them into more manageable pieces. Having created an uncertain flame with her cigarette lighter, she fanned it with her breath until the fire was coaxed into more vigorous life.

The cottage had been securely shuttered then, the only light entering from the open door, but when the wood caught and blazed it painted the room orange with its dancing light. Edith had smoked a cheroot, sitting before the hearth with her long legs crossed. Encouraged by the warmth, he had sat close beside her. They'd stayed like that for a long time, not sharing their thoughts but silently looking into the flames.

Jerome had forgotten that the cottage was partitioned into two rooms: to the left of the unporched front door a break in the wall opened into a smaller chamber. This was divided from the roof timbers and slates by a partial attic, reached by wooden ladder. Both rungs and upper floor were quite rotten but Jerome saw with relief that here at least the roof above was sound and the walls tolerably dry.

Satisfied with his inspection, he parked his guitar, slipped his arms out of his haversack and lowered himself to the flags. Sitting with his back resting against the wall, he looked around him. That this unfurnished cell was to be his new home was a stark prospect, yet it pleased him. He was excited by the challenge.

There was a momentary panic when he saw the trail of wet footprints on the flagstones for he wanted no Man Friday to share his self-imposed exile. Realising that his own boots had made the prints, he scorned his nervousness and marked his territory by stamping further identical damp impressions on the flags.

His sodden boots were a souvenir of a making tide that had been washing over the rocky shelf that led from the zigzag to the foreshore. The part-submerged shelf was to become a familiar route but on this occasion he had negotiated it gingerly, his feet inching their way along the water-covered rock.

Anxious to lay proper claim to his kingdom, he unpacked his belongings. On the windowsill he arranged an aluminium saucepan, enamelled plate and pint mug, in the latter he stood knife, fork and spoon. In a corner he built a small pyramid with the tins of food he had stolen from his own larder. He assembled the Primus stove and unwrapped the bottle of paraffin from its protective layers of newspaper.

His room boasted the only window-glass in the house: some previous occupant had replaced the door to the rear with one that was quarter-glazed. Although cracked, these panes were otherwise intact and wiping at them with the side of his hand Jerome peered out onto the tangle that had once been a garden. He drew back the rusted bolt intending to explore, but the swollen door would not budge, not even when he put his shoulder to it. Fearful of breaking the already tender glass, he shot the bolt again, and left as he had entered by squeezing past the leaning front door.

Outside, he scanned the detritus-strewn beach. The collaboration of unruly wave and relentless tide had driven both flotsam and jetsam into the inlet and a few minutes of scavenging gave him good reason to be grateful for these deposits. A wooden crate and empty oil drum became his table and chair. A scarred lifebuoy with part of its circumference missing improvised as a pillow. His greatest prize was a stoppered but empty magnum bottle. Washed and filled from the stream it made a storage vessel for his drinking water. Lodged high inside the cave he found a useful square of stiff tarpaulin that made an effective damp course to separate his sleeping bag from the evasive moisture that permeated both the flagstones and cob walls of his new home. Looking around his furnished cell, he congratulated himself on a job well done.

The self-satisfaction did not last. Without shutters and a working front door the cottage offered no security for either him or his possessions. There were necessary sorties to be made into the outside world when he would be unable to take his belongings with him. His chief concern was for his guitar, chosen for him by the young music master whom he idolised and paid for with a last gift of money received from his mother.

The only hiding place that the cottage offered was in the roof-space above his sleeping quarters. Climbing onto the oil drum, he fed the guitar through a hole in the rotten timbers of the attic. Satisfied that its shapely case could not be detected from below he breathed with relief. To deter anyone foolhardy enough to climb the loft ladder he removed what remained of its rotten rungs. With these measures in place he began to relax.

Despite the discomfort and strangeness Jerome felt safe in the cottage. That night he was able to sleep more peacefully than he had done at any time over the previous weeks.

Chapter 9

Lorna and Jerome

Either rain or the threat of it prevented Jerome from exploring far beyond Kilcarrick. On the fifth day, with food supplies dwindling, he braved the weather to embark on a first shopping expedition.

Fearing that the appearance of a stranger would create too much curiosity in the village community of Port Blissey and in the nearby hamlet passed en-route from the station, he opted to shop further afield in the market town of Budruth.

His desire for anonymity stemmed from his unofficial tenancy of the cottage rather than from any threat of pursuit from London. For all he knew Kilcarrick might have been sold-off to pay his aunts' debts. Even if the cottage remained part of the family estate his Trethewan blood gave him no legal right to be there. His mother's rash second marriage had put an end to his prospect of becoming Lanhedra's eventual beneficiary. The Trethewan sisters had been furious that their nephew's inheritance had fallen into the hands of an outsider and they had written Sarah a curt note informing her that they wanted no further intercourse with either their nephew's widow or his son.

Jerome's shopping sortie took him on a jolting, thirty-minute journey by Western National bus from Trecarrick Cross. Budruth was a sprawling town with terraces of grey granite houses but, being market day, the bustling streets and persistent lowing from the cattle-market enriched and enlivened the solemn architecture.

The mouth-watering sights in a grocery store brought home to him one serious oversight in his planning. Though he had escaped his stepfather's clutches, the Major remained keeper of his ration book. Without food coupons to exchange, such staples as cheese and bacon were denied him.

In the shadow of the ancient Parish church was a covered market. There Jerome bought fresh fruit and vegetables, a broom-head, galvanised bucket and a short-shafted camping spade needed for digging a latrine. He noticed how some customers haggled over the price of their purchases but not wanting to draw attention to himself he paid in full. The smell of fresh baking wafted on the air and there was talk in the market about the end of bread rationing. Jerome hoped this rumour would prove true for his youthful appetite lusted after the yeasty pleasure of a crusty loaf.

On his return the heavens opened again and, just minutes after getting off the bus, he was soaked to the skin. The trees above the Trecarrick Valley were stunted by the prevailing southwesterly winds and offered little shelter so he had no choice but to press on through the downpour.

Dripping into the cottage with his purchases he found the main room once again pooled with rainwater that had driven in through both the doorway and hole in the roof. Fortunately a sloping floor kept his sleeping-cell free of the flooding. These satisfactory drainage arrangements proved a considerable comfort when, in the night, he was woken by the thump of the high tide breaking against the boathouse and the sound of the sea sloshing in at the open cottage door. Thankfully this salty invasion progressed no further.

* * *

Prolonged wet weather placed the Penrose siblings under house arrest and all were restless in their incarceration. Lorna was weary of her brothers' squabbling exuberance and her baby sister's fretful crying. To make matters worse, her confinement had been turned into a sentence of hard labour thanks to her mother's incurable obsession with keeping her elder daughter busy.

'Take your nose out of them books, Lorna, and come and help me. The devil finds work for idle hands,' was an all too familiar summons.

The slow passage of time added to Lorna's gloom.

With the reappearance of blue skies her thoughts turned to the prospect of six weeks holiday from school and to the glorious freedom of beaching and bathing that it promised. The welcome sunshine also worked their magic on Margaret and in a rare show of consideration she dispensed with her daughter's services. To exploit her liberty to the full Lorna scrabbled through a chest-of-drawers in search of a bathing costume. Having found her last-year's, now a size-too-small, swimsuit and liberated a threadbare towel from the over-loaded garden washing-line she made a skipping beeline for the cliffs.

It was a longer than usual trek to her favourite beach at Kilcarrick Haven for recent rains had created a quagmire underfoot and made the path treacherous. The squelchy journey was no deterrent for although Kilcarrick's pebbles were harder on the feet than the sweeping sands of

Blissey, Lorna much preferred swimming there. The sudden shelving of the inlet meant that one moment the water would be only knee-high and the next her toes could not find the bottom. The gently sloping sands of Blissey were for little kids, not for her.

Conditions that Lorna viewed as advantages deterred other people from using the Haven as a bathing place and the certainty of finding seclusion there added to its attraction. The inlet with its ruin, stream and wilderness of garden was the stage on which she acted out solitary games of imagination, games that were always greatly influenced by her current reading matter. Dolls' houses were for babies, Lorna preferred to play on a bigger scale.

* * *

Waking, Jerome was dazzled by the light slanting across his sleeping cell. It was his first sight of the sun since the day of his arrival and he greeted it with gratitude for he needed to dry the clothes made sodden from the previous day's drenching. Freeing himself from his sleeping bag, he pulled on some dry trousers and hurried outside. Feeling the warmth on his face and body, he stretched like a contented cat.

After draping his wet clothing, damp sleeping bag and scavenged groundsheet across the low sea wall by the boathouse he lay down beside his belongings and, for the first time in days, began to feel warm. As he soaked-up the sun's rays, small lizards crept out from crevasses in the wall to practise the same archaic ritual. Affinity with the little reptiles gave him a novel sense of unity with the natural world, a feeling that generated an inner warmth.

The boathouse obscured his view of the cliff approach from Port Blissey and the sudden appearance of a slight figure just twenty yards off gave him something of a shock. The intruder was a young girl who walked slowly but purposefully across the beach, her dark head bent in a close examination of the pebbles and coarse sand.

Jerome cursed the array of belongings draped over the sea that were unintentionally flagging his presence. His every instinct urged him to hide but moving was sure to result in detection so he flattened his body to the top of the wall and watched.

The girl stopped to plonk her bottom on the pebbly strand. Leaning forward she raked the beach with her fingers, pausing every now and then to recover some small object that was quite invisible to Jerome. She deposited these finds onto a square of handkerchief spread out beside her. Absorbed in her quest she was oblivious to his presence.

* * *

It never ceased to amaze Lorna that the sea could be such an efficient sorter. The shore was a bit like the rag and bone man's junkyard, though presented in a much more orderly fashion. At the high tide mark was a regular line of flotsam tangled in seaweed. Lower down the beach the rocks had captured a jumble of scrap metal. By the foot of the Blissey steps empty scallop and giant whelk shells were heaped in abundance. On smoother stretches small pieces of sea-polished glass glinted like emeralds whilst the gravel patch she was searching hid a treasure-trove of cows-horns and shilly-billys, miniature shells that were to be found nowhere else on the beach. Shifting her weight onto her other buttock and leaning the opposite way, she began to sift again, this time left-handed.

Not until she paused in her search did she sense that she was being watched. In the expectation of seeing Dirty Dingle she cast a furtive glance over her shoulder.

* * *

Seeing the pale face set with large dark eyes turned towards him, Jerome sat up.

'Hello, what are you up to?' It took effort to sound casual.

Gathering up her finds the child sprang to her feet. Wiping a gritty hand on the skirt of her frock, she studied him with soulful eyes.

'I'm not doing any harm, mister. I'm only collecting shells.'

"Mister"! Obviously she saw him as a man, someone with authority. He had forgotten the days of soft growth on his cheeks and chin. Also her words inferred that it was she, not he, who was the interloper.

'No, I can see that, I wasn't accusing you of doing anything wrong.'

The little girl was taking rather too much interest in his steaming personal effects draped along the wall. To divert her attention he jumped down onto the beach and hid his agitation with a reassuring smile

She cocked her head on one side and frowned before asking, 'No one has lived here for as long as I can remember. Does the cottage belong to you?'

To claim ownership of Kilcarrick seemed to be the most natural thing in the world and with an expansive sweep of his arm he found himself echoing Great-Aunt Edith's words. 'Yes it does; both the cottage and all the foreshore as far as the high water mark.'

They had been walking hesitantly towards each other but at this declaration of ownership she stopped. Checking the beach, she indicated the tide-line of weed and debris higher up the shore and grinned cheekily.

‘So I'm not trespassing then, am I?'

He conceded her point with a nod of his head.

The child's grin grew wider and she ambled to his side.

'If anyone is the trespasser it has to be you!’ she exclaimed, surprising him with her confidence.

The line “Forgive us our trespasses” from the Lord’s Prayer echoed grimly in his head though what he said was, ‘What do you mean?'

‘The top of the beach may belong to you but this bit where we’re standing is owned by Father Neptune and the Cornish.'

Raised in a socialist household Lorna was used to her unemployed father's tirades against the oppression of honest workers like himself by the capitalist landed classes.

“If it weren't for old Neptune, they'd make us pay for the right to put to sea.” was one of Jim Penrose’s conclusive proofs against the injustices imposed by the gentry.

Catching the girl's mood Jerome relaxed.

'Oh, Poseidon's an old friend of mine. I allowed him to come in through my front door last night and in exchange he told me I was welcome to use his bed whenever he wasn't actually sleeping in it.'

She puzzled over the unfamiliar name. 'Poseidon? Who’s he?'

'It’s just another name for Neptune.'

'A sort of nickname do you mean?'

He felt suddenly old and wise. 'No, not a nickname, just the opposite. Old Nick is the devil but Poseidon is a god, the sea-god of the Ancient Greeks.'

Gravely she studied the foreign look of his tall fairness, a stature and appearance in marked contrast to the familiar sturdiness of her swarthy brothers.

'Are you a Greek?' she asked.

Suddenly the tension of the past weeks and months evaporated, he threw back his head and laughed. ‘I’m as English as you are.’

His laughter was musical and infectious.

'I’m Lorna,' she volunteered, deciding that she liked this interesting stranger who seemed to know so much.

‘And I'm Jerome. Pleased to meet you, Lorna.'

He offered a formal handshake and felt the grains of coarse sand transfer from her small fingers to his hand.

‘Lorna is an unusual name. Is it Cornish?'

He believed that this was the sort of question a grown-up might ask for he was trying to act out the adult role attributed to him.

‘I don’t know about my name but my family is proper Cornish, born and bred,' she told him proudly.

He responded by claiming his own Celtic blood-ties.

She studied him, frowning. ‘Jerome doesn’t sound very Cornish.' She tested the two syllables of his name again. 'Jer-ome. Sounds much too hoity-toity for Cornwall.'

'Hoity-toity?'

'You know, all la-di-dah, sort of posh.'

Her quaint expressions made him laugh again.

Lorna, looking up with an open glowing face, offered her friendship. 'You’re nice, I think I’ll call you Jerry.'

His smile died. 'No, not Jerry!' he blurted.

Confused by his change of mood, she apologised. 'I didn't mean to be rude. It’s just that Jerry sounds nice.'

Immediately he regretted his churlish response. The name did sound nice the way she pronounced it, with a rolling emphasis of the double *R*.

It needed only a half-lie to explain his aversion. ‘Jerry makes me sound like a German. That’s why I don't like it.'

When he’d first arrived at his boarding school, a bully had taunted him over his name. 'Jerry!' his tormentor had sneered, 'Jerrys are Nazis. We've got a stinking Nazi here fellows. What shall we do with him?'

Jerome knew the hurt felt at Lorna’s utterance of that diminutive had little to do with the war or school. It was the recollection of his step-cousin's usage that made it so painful. These last few days he had successfully driven Freddy from his mind and he resented being reminded of someone whom he would rather forget.

'What can I call you then?' the girl persisted.

Before he could reply she answered her own question. 'I know, how about Romeo?'

He was taken aback for he had never linked the second syllable of his name with Shakespeare's tragic hero.

‘If you like,' he said. 'What do you know about Romeo?'

‘Romeo is a Montague and one of Shakespeare's star-cross'd lovers. That’s a quotation. We read lots of Shakespeare at school.'

Her indignant expression was what his old ally, the cockney Mrs Handley, would have called ‘an old-fashioned look’. It made Jerome smile.

He indicated her clasped handkerchief. ‘What have you been collecting?’

She showed him by carefully unwrapping her collection of tiny shells.

'They're to make a bangle for my baby sister,' she explained.

He examined the almost closed lips of a little decorated cowrie shell that she called a shilly-billy and asked, 'How will you do that?'

Her expression suggested shock at this admission of ignorance but she answered civilly enough.

'You pierce each shell with a needle and thread them together with button twine.'

When he enthused over the idea of a chain of delicate shells, the little girl made a shy offer.

'I could make a shell necklace for you if you like.'

Such generosity from a stranger touched him. 'What about your sister's bracelet?'

'Oh, there are plenty more shells. I can make Gill a bangle any old time.'

It seemed to Jerome that, having gone native, nothing could be more appropriate than to adorn himself with the shells that were the emblems of his seashore home.

They sat together cross-legged on the pebbles and sifted the beach for more cows-horns and shilly-billys. As they searched Jerome remembered the direction from which she came and questioned his companion.

'Do you live in Port Blissey?'

'I live on the Treblissey estate,' she replied. 'Do you know where that is?'

'I've never heard of it. Is your father a tenant farmer?'

His question seemed to puzzle Lorna, but then her thin face broke into a delighted grin.

'Treblissey isn't a landed estate like the one up at Lanhedra. It's the council estate at the top of Polbliss Hill.'

The misunderstanding embarrassed Jerome. His upbringing had protected him from the world of ordinary working people. He tried to compensate for his ignorance by showing an interest.

'So what does your father do for a living?'

Lorna became solemn. 'Father's not able to do much. He used to be a fisherman before he joined the navy. But his ship was torpedoed in the war and he was in the water for a long time before he was rescued. There was a lot of burning oil, it damaged his lungs and insides.'

'Poor fellow,' Jerome sympathised. 'Won't he recover?'

She shook her head. 'He loves his pint of brown ale better than anything else, but after a visit to the pub he suffers with his stomach something awful. Mother says he used to drink like a fish and she used to hate it but now she's sorry and wishes that he could have his bit of enjoyment without the discomfort after.'

It was a sobering story. Jerome told how he had lost his own father in the war. The shared confidences drew them together.

The deprivation of war was not the only thing they had in common. Like himself, Lorna enjoyed losing herself in an alternative reality found in books. He was amazed at the sophistication of her reading. She knew Dickens and Austen, claimed to have read "The Pilgrim's Progress" all the way through, was familiar with Robert Louis Stevenson, Louisa M. Alcott, Charles Kingsley, Captain Marryatt, R.D. Blackmore and Sir Arthur Quiller Couch. When he confessed his ignorance of the latter, she began a detailed account of the plot of her favourite Cornish adventure, "The Splendid Spur".

'Your school must be first rate,' he acknowledged.

She dismissed this suggestion. 'Oh, English lessons are mostly about grammar with some poetry and plays. I mostly read novels in home time. The lending library comes to the Methodist hall once a fortnight and I have lots of books of my own. Grandfer buys them for me every Christmas and birthday and the rest are prizes I've won for attendance at Sunday School.'

Throughout their conversation, Jerome was careful to sit facing his visitor. He did not want her to see his naked back. Its decoration of red welts and yellow bruises was sure to frighten and repel her.

While they had been exploring each other's tastes in literature, the tide turned and was already lapping at the westerly steps that gave access to the coastal path leading to Port Blissey.

Noticing the sea's advance, Lorna groaned. 'We've been so busy nattering that I forgot to keep an eye on the tide.'

She looked regretfully at the towel containing her bathing costume abandoned further along the beach. 'No swim for me today, I must be off.'

She sprang to her feet but he grasped her wrist to prevent her from running away.

'Wait,' he pleaded.

'I can't, I'll be cut off by the tide.'

'You won't tell anyone that I'm staying at Kilcarrick, will you?' Desperate to win her co-operation he improvised. 'I'm a musician and I've come down here for the peace and quiet to work on some scores. I'd rather not be pestered by visitors. '

She bit her lip in disappointment. 'So how will I be able to give you your shell necklace? And you said you'd like to borrow "The Splendid Spur".'

It was obvious that his plea for privacy had been interpreted as a personal rejection.

'When I said ‘visitors’ I wasn't including you. You must come back tomorrow for your swim. But please don't bring any friends with you.'

Her plain, thin face broke into a cheery smile that made her almost beautiful.

‘That suits me, I don't like crowds either. But if I don’t go now I'll have to swim to the steps. As it is I’ll have to paddle.'

Chivalrously, Jerome rolled his trousers to the knee and made a courtly bow. ' You mustn't get your frock wet. May Romeo be permitted to transport madam to dry land?’

She collected up her towel and trustingly held out an arm so that he could carry her. She clung to his neck, a mere featherweight, her long dark lashes fluttering against his cheek.

He waded calf-deep to deposit her onto the cliff's granite-cut steps.

She beamed her thanks. ' Safe and dry. See you tomorrow then, Rome.'

He accepted the contraction of his name as an avowal of her friendship.

Lorna’s company made him realise how lonely he had been. As he waved her on her way he was already looking forward to a further visit from the super little girl.

* * *

All the way home Lorna thought about Rome. As he’d carried her to the steps his soft whiskers had brushed her cheek and tickled. It had been a nice feeling. Thinking about him made her go all funny inside.

Chapter 10

Friends

Jerome, at seventeen, was fast approaching manhood whilst Lorna was barely a month past her twelfth-birthday yet despite this disparity the friendship struck on that July day blossomed. Lorna brought more than frequent companionship to Kilcarrick: she supplied her new friend with books from her personal library and the out-of-date magazines that she liberated from Penbliss House. In return Jerome entertained with his guitar and gave Lorna an undivided attention that she never enjoyed at home. What began as a natural compatibility and shy regard was soon transformed into a liberality of affection on both sides.

Jerome was already a competent pianist when John Blake, his boarding school's newly appointed music master, introduced him to the guitar. The youthful music tutor's eclectic tuition went beyond the classical for Blake's real enthusiasm was for the traditional Folk and Rhythm and Blues of twentieth-century America. Before long Jerome was infected with an identical passion.

By popular demand, master and pupil entertained an appreciative audience of senior school pupils. These informal soirees never quite elevated Jerome into the first division of the school's popularity league but it did turn him from a misfit into someone respected and sought after by his peers.

Lorna's musical knowledge was more limited. In Port Blissey music meant just three things: the popular tunes played on the BBC's Light Programme, the sacred choirs of church and chapel and the instrumental repertoires of the peripatetic silver bands who hailed from Budruth and its nearby clay-mining villages. Blissey's adult population, well versed in the Lutheran hymnbook, honoured the names of Isaac Watts and the Wesley brothers. The bandsmen too favoured hymn tunes, though their extended repertoire was livened by military marches and renderings of the traditional Floral Dance. During the Port's annual feast celebrations the smartly uniformed musicians played and puffed their way through the narrow garlanded streets to lead the more nimble villagers in a skipping and Bacchanalian dance.

The more exotic sounds of Leadbelly, Guthrie, Josh White and Muddy Waters had not reached Lorna’s corner of Cornwall and so Rome's renditions of the earthy American rhythms were a revelation. Watching the speed of his fretting and the way the fingers of his right hand plucked melodies from the vibrating strings she was dizzy with admiration. It was difficult to decide which she liked best: the grating timbre of his singing voice or the vitality of his playing. So instant was her conversion to his alien music that it supplanted even her former passion for books.

Though musically untutored, Lorna was quick to pick up a tune and memorise a lyric. Practising a Southern States version of English and travelling on Rome's passport she entered a new world vibrant with sound. Soon their spirited duets were transforming the Cornish Haven into an outpost of Dixie. Kilcarrick sprouted “Ol' Cotton Fields” colonised by “Boll Weevil” while a waltzing “Irene” rode the “Midnight Special” as it shone its “ever lovin’ light” on a granite “Rock Island Line”.

Paying for music lessons were way beyond the means of the indigent Penrose family but her association with Jerome fired Lorna with the ambition to become a musician. Without being asked he taught her some basic chords and simple fingering. Pressing on the metal strings left an imprint that made her fingers sore but despite the pain that accompanied the learning process she persevered and soon acquired calluses like her tutor’s. Proud of the hard pads on her fingertips, she almost made the mistake of showing off her left hand to her brothers. Just in time, she remembered that her association with Rome was supposed to be a secret.

Lorna made contributions of her own to their musical repertoire by introducing the popular songs heard on the wireless at home. The Haven was soon rejoicing in the harmonious optimism of “Powder Your Face With Sunshine” and “I'm Looking Over A Four Leaf Clover”. In more raucous mood, the duo made the cliffs ring with the maniacal laughter of “Woody Woodpecker”.

Jerome, though flattered by Lorna's rapturous appreciation of his music, worried that her adulation was becoming dangerously addictive. When she was with him he felt happy and alive but in her absence his loneliness was akin to a physical ache. Even the solitary nature of much of his childhood was proving to be inadequate preparation for the isolation of Kilcarrick. He worried about his growing dependence on his girl companion and regarded his misery as weakness.

* * *

It was a fine evening and Lorna wanted their music-making to go on forever. It took the lengthening shadows to remind Jerome of his responsibility.

'It's late,' he said putting aside his guitar. 'You should be on your way home. We can't risk your parents coming to look for you.'

'Just one more song and I'll be off,' Lorna bargained.

One song extended to a second yet still Lorna refused to budge. Resorting to more physical measures Jerome began to drag her towards the Blissey steps. Lorna resisted by digging in her heels and it took an anguished appeal before she agreed to head homeward with good grace. Usually he walked partway with her but tonight he remained on the beach preoccupied with his over-reliance on their friendship and the uncertainties that clouded his future.

As the setting sun dipped behind the hill a bird struck up a trilling song from the cover of a copse in the valley. The bubbling solo provided a welcome relief from his solitary reveries. It was unusual to hear such liquid notes coming out of the twilight and he wondered if the songster could be a nightingale. The cascade of notes continued and certainty overcame disbelief: no other songbird would warble so richly in the almost owl-dark.

Feeling both humbled and honoured, he tried to recall Keats' Ode but could get no further than the first lines:

"My heart aches, and a drowsy numbness pains
My sense, as though of hemlock I had drunk."

Though unsure of how the poem continued he remembered the gist of its content. As a brother in suffering, he felt an affinity with the poet, yet the sense of oblivion expressed by the consumptive genius was very different from his own exhilaration on hearing the nightingale's song.

Sitting on the boathouse wall, he took up his guitar again and composed a paean of his own to Keats' darkling. It was an emotional counterpoint to the bird's rich crescendo of repeated musical sequences. Communion with the nightingale roused him from his self-pity and brought about an unaccustomed sense of fulfilment.

That night, lulled by the gentle plash of wave over pebbles, sleep came swiftly and untroubled.

* * *

Meeting her blond musician transformed the humdrum of Lorna's life. If she thought of the past at all it was in terms of 'before Rome', and the 'before' bit had been boring. She was living for the present and for a flesh and blood hero whose friendship was precious and who made every hour they spent together varied and exhilarating.

Organising a daily visit to Kilcarrick was far from plain sailing. Although adept at juggling her domestic duties to coincide with a falling tide, gaining parental permission to spend so much time away from home called for much crafty ingenuity. To gain her freedom she played on her mother's good nature and gullibility. Her ruse involved lying and, like all the best lies, her fabrication was rooted in truth.

A sickly girl called Eileen Stone was in the same year as Lorna at the County School. Eileen lived in a solitary mansion several miles along the Budruth Road yet, apart from travelling on the same school bus, the girls had little in common. Eileen's father was a solicitor in the county town, a professional status that qualified his daughter as a member of the town set despite her rural residence. Town girls thought themselves rather superior to the daughters of fishermen and china clay labourers who travelled to school from the outlying villages. Though the two girls exchanged few words it was Eileen who became Lorna's alibi.

She cunningly chose a moment when she and her mother were harmoniously sharing the chore of bedmaking.

'Poor Eileen,' she sighed as she changed a pillowcase, 'she's never been strong and it's so awful for her being ill in the holidays. She hasn't any brothers or sisters and nobody her age lives nearby. She's fed-up and bored being on her own all the time and as we're best friends at school her mother's asked me to go and play with her. Can I go and keep her company? She really needs me.'

Margaret Penrose was impressed. She may have succumbed to her husband's proselytising by voting Labour but she was proud to think that her daughter was associating with such grand people. She often admired the Stones' mansion from the top deck of the bus going into Budruth. It was well known that the family employed that post-war rarity, a live-in help. As further proof of their affluence they had a man in full-time to do the garden. Margaret had seen the Stones' gardener trimming the beech hedge that screened the big house from the road. She'd also noticed the polished brass plate outside the father's offices announcing, *Pascoe, Stone and Pascoe.*

'Poor little maid, what a shame,' Margaret sympathised. 'Of course you must keep her company. But mind you watch your Ps and Qs. We've always brought you up proper so you know how to behave in polite company, so don't you go letting us down.'

To prolong the deceit, Lorna made frequent reports on Eileen's medical progress coupled with imaginative descriptions of Mrs Stone's wardrobe and the house interior. She provided just enough colour and detail to satisfy her mother's curiosity and snobbish failings. She didn't tell Rome of her deception for she suspected that he wouldn't approve.

Jerome, anxious to preserve his anonymity, asked, 'Don't your parents worry and ask where you've been when you're away from home for so long?'

'Oh, they don't mind, they think I'm with friends.' She was becoming a most convincing liar.

Though Lorna was able to manipulate her birth mother, Mother Nature was far less obliging and put all sorts of obstacles in the way of her careful planning. The short neap tides were the biggest problem as they rationed the time that she was able to spend with Rome. On neaps the sea barely withdrew from the steps to Kilcarrick before the waters came rushing back in again.

As much put out as she was, Jerome complained, 'Anyone would think moon and tide were conspiring against us.'

Lorna was too spirited to let even elemental forces outwit them. 'I've been thinking. Why don't I come and go via Trecarrick and the zigzag? That route is passable when the Blissey steps are under water.'

This suggestion cheered Jerome until he visualised the extended journey that she was contemplating.

'It's a long way by road from Blissey to Trecarrick and to reach the zigzag you have to circumnavigate the marsh. It will add miles to your journey.'

'Not miles, barely more than one in each direction. It will be worth it for the extra time that I'll be able to spend here with you.'

Jerome was flattered by her loyalty but the lengthy walk was not his only concern.

'The zigzag is treacherous when waves are breaking. You're just a kid, you mustn't take risks.'

Previously he had treated her as an equal and now he was calling her a kid.

'I'm not a baby,' she protested. 'Besides, I'm not likely to do anything silly. In these parts respect for the sea comes with mother's milk.'

This piece of wisdom was borrowed from her father.

Hearing the catch in her voice Jerome decided that the best apology he could make was to accept her sacrifice.

'I'm honoured that you're prepared to make such a long trek but you must promise never to use the zigzag when there's an onshore wind.'

Lorna promised that she wouldn't.

Later when Jerome waded through the incoming waters to deposit her safe and dry on the zigzag, she refused to relinquish her hold until he had given her a whiskery kiss on the cheek.

* * *

Noticing her elder daughter's new found animation Lorna's mother remarked to her husband, 'Having that Eileen Stone for a friend has made such a difference to our Lorna. Just you look at the colour in her cheeks. And she's that much more cheerful than when her head was forever buried in them book of hers.'

Jim, never missing an opportunity to spout his working class allegiance, grumbled, 'We don't want our maid getting ideas above her station.'

Yet, in reality, he was as delighted as his wife to see his little girl happy.

* * *

Despite warning of its hazards, the zigzag was Jerome's usual route in and out of the inlet and on all but the longer tides it became Lorna's for at least one leg of her journey. He felt a cad when he thought of the little girl hiking those extra miles. His chief hope was that the prolonged dry spell would lower the water level in the marsh and open up the more direct route from Trecarrick Cross. Daily he inspected the stream-fed mire at the back of the cottage but it remained as boggy as ever. On one such survey he had a sudden rush of inspiration. The last big tide had brought a quantity of timber into the Haven and stranded it there. It was exactly the material he needed to conquer the fen.

A slipping tide meant that even the zigzag would not be negotiable until mid-afternoon. Condemned to spend most of the day alone, Jerome decided to test the practicality of his idea to bridge the bog. After tying a length of shore-scavenged rope around one of the larger pieces of timber he dragged the weighty bulk past the cottage and into the reeds beyond. By trial and error he developed a technique for up-ending the timber and influencing the direction of its subsequent fall. Mud splattered in all directions as the bulky timber hit the mire and the disturbance gave off an acrid smell of rotting vegetation.

With the first timber in position, he manhandled a second along its length then repeated the procedure several times more. Some of the woods settled deeper into the marshy ground than others, yet all of their upper surfaces remained clear of the swamp. Laid end to end, the timbers created an uneven, narrow causeway from the shingle mound on which the cottage stood to the comparative solidity of the rising pasture on the Trecarrick side.

Unused to such hard labour his musician's hands became blistered and previously unsuspected muscles painfully announced their existence. Some of the splinters that pierced his flesh were too deep to be extracted with broken fingernails. As remedy for his several ills he took his fully clothed, mud-splattered and sweaty body to face the full force of the cleansing waves.

With salty ablution over, there was time only for a rapid towel-drying of his head and a wringing of shirttails before setting off for Trecarrick. He needed to intercept his visitor before she made the now unnecessary diversion around the mire. Crossing his engineering feat he felt proud of his ingenuity and his spirits soared. He had bridged the bog and the Major for all his military training could have done no better.

As he climbed the sunny fields leading to Trecarrick, the straight growth on some pollarded sycamores caught his eye. Using his Bowie knife, he cut two saplings to use as balancing aids to cross the uneven causeway.

His wet clothes steamed and dried on his body and the patterning of salt residue that whitened on his dark trousers reminded him of the abstract Celtic scrolling on Trecarrick's ancient stone cross.

Trecarrick Cross stood on a triangle of grass made by the junction of two lanes. The cross had been planted in the dirt for a thousand years but had been excavated when the new road was cut and grandly mounted on a modern granite plinth. Wary of walking further in the direction of Port Blissey, Jerome seated himself on the plinth to wait. It was one thing to be Lorna’s escort on the privacy of the coastal path, but quite another for them to be seen walking together on the open road. Lorna had faithfully guarded Kilcarrick’s secret and he wanted to keep it that way.

The ancient Christian monument was in the traditional Celtic style: a tapering upright swelling into an elaborately carved roundel of headstone. Tracing the complexity of the granite-carved knots and scrolls, he wondered if the original masons who had worked and raised the cross had been some ancient line of devout, stone-working Trethewans.

* * *

Recognising the distant figure lounging at the base of the cross, Lorna broke into a run.

'Rome,' she panted, 'you're the last person I expected to see. What are you doing here?'

'I thought I'd make a pilgrimage and pay dutiful homage to your famous Cornish Cross.'

'What a funny thing to say!'

'It's Geoffrey Chaucer, not me. He wrote something like that in his prologue.'

'Aren't you're a bit muddled? Chaucer's pilgrims went to Canterbury, not Cornwall.'

'There's no time for a literary discussion,' his impatience was difficult to contain. 'Let's hurry, I've a surprise for you. Here, take your magic wand.'

Perplexed, she accepted the shorter of two cut staves.

'What are these for?'

'Wait and see,' he teased and, with no further explanation, claimed her free hand and broke into a high-spirited run.

'You'll land us both in a cow pat if you're not careful,' she scolded, as he dragged her at break-neck speed across the field.

His response was to whoop like the carefree boy he had never been.

They continued their headlong descent down the steep and tussocky pasture. Where the land began to flatten and the course of the little stream became lost amongst withy and rushes, Lorna tugged at his arm.

'Where are you taking us? We'll be sucked in the bog if we go any further in this direction.'

'Not anymore we won't. Just hang on to that magic staff, my lady, and trust me.'

Pushing through the osiers, he led her to the end of his day's labour.

'Dah daah!' he trumpeted. 'Surprise.'

If Lorna had been an ancient Briton gazing for the first time on the wonder of the Fosse Way she could not have been more amazed than she was at the miracle of the wooden causeway.

'How did you build it so quickly?'

'I waved my magic wand of course.'

'It must be magic. It's my best surprise ever.'

The marsh safely negotiated, Lorna skipped with excitement as the full significance of the short cut struck home.

'It's brilliant. In future I'll be able to stay at Kilcarrick for as long as I want whatever the state of the tide.'

Jerome doubted that this modest shortening of her journey gave quite such a degree of freedom but he didn't spoil her pleasure by expressing the thought aloud.

Lorna thanked him with a generous hug and a smacking kiss on his whiskered cheek. Such obvious delight was reward enough for his recent hard labour.

Initially they christened the causeway 'Wake's Way' after Hereward, but came to refer to their passage across it as 'walking the plank'. Jerome, borrowing from Peter Pan, pretended that the marsh was inhabited by a crocodile whose digestive system was challenged by a swallowed clock.

'Don't forget to keep your eyes peeled for the croc when you walk the plank,' he warned.

Lorna responded with a convincing, 'Tick-tock, tick-tock, tick-tock.'

Kilcarrick Haven had become their Never-Never Land where Jerome as well as Lorna indulged in make-believe.

Chapter 11

Hunter-Gatherers

Inland, beyond Kilcarrick's newly built causeway, the course of the little stream widened into shallow pools. The seclusion of the pools made them ideal for fresh-water ablutions but Jerome abandoned their use as a bathing place when he realised that the floating plants were watercress. With a limited larder and never enough food to satisfy his youthful appetite the addition of a fresh green vegetable was an unexpected treat.

Lorna arrived to find him munching on a bunch of freshly gathered cress.

'What's that funny stuff you're eating, Rome?'

'Watercress and it comes from our very own stream. Here, try some, it's delicious.'

Raised in a predominantly male household where any salad crop was regarded as rabbit food, his enthusiasm for such insignificant-looking leaves surprised her.

She spat out her first sampling.

'Ugh! How can you eat such bitter stuff?'

'I would say that cress is tasty rather than bitter and it's also very nutritious.'

He tried to prove his point by nibbling rabbit-like at the green stems and making appreciative noises as he chewed.

Anxious to show solidarity, Lorna persevered and began to develop a taste for its crisp iron tang. Helping him to harvest it, she thought it shameful that such a freely available treat was unknown on the table at home.

Lorna reserved her opposition to drudgery exclusively for the Penrose household. In her second home at Kilcarrick she was a most willing pair of hands. Helpmate in Rome's every enterprise, she tackled even the most onerous of tasks with enthusiasm. Secretly she nurtured the fantasy that they were homemaking. By adopting the wifely role she accepted responsibility for his wellbeing so when she found him scouring the low-tide rocks for winkles she issued a dire warning.

'What are you doing? Don't you know it's the wrong time of the year for winkles? They're not safe to eat unless there's an *R* in the month.'

Jerome disparaged this particular piece of local folk wisdom. 'That sounds like an old wives' tale to me. How can it be dangerous to eat them in August yet safe to do so in September?'

As she was unable to provide a satisfactory explanation for this anomaly he chose to ignore the warning.

Not even their tantalising cooking smell could tempt Lorna to try the winkles and she anxiously watched Rome for signs of poisoning. When it was obvious that the out-of-season snails caused no damage her attitude changed and winkles became a regular feature on their shared menu. Spearing the snail whorls from their shells with darning needles borrowed from Margaret Penrose's workbox, each playfully dangled the curled delicacies for the other to eat.

With the Haven's supply of larger winkles dwindling they turned their attention to the more abundant mussels. When exposed by the falling tide the larger rocks were camouflaged by an armour of these blue-black bivalves. Had the gatherers been greedier they could have harvested them by the bucketful.

Jerome was fascinated to discover how the gregarious mussels clung to their precarious perches.

'I've often wondered where the expression "to hang on by a whisker" came from and now I know. It's exactly what *moules* do. How amazing to think that they can withstand the might of the sea by hanging on to the rocks by just their beards.'

Unfamiliar with the French term, Lorna corrected him. '*Mool*? That's a silly name, they're mussels.'

He enlightened her. '*Moules* is what they're called in Brittany.'

Lorna was impressed. Her own experience of travel was limited to rare visits to the cathedral city of Truro and a single trip to Plymouth and its Hoe.

'Have you really been to France, Rome?'

'A long time ago, before the war.'

He was aware that he had seen and experienced so much more than his younger friend. But his past was dangerous ground and to escape further interrogation he made a hazardous leap to the inhospitable and barnacle-encrusted granite of the next rock.

Later, when feasting on the bivalves, he was amused to hear Lorna using her newly acquired French culinary vocabulary.

'We wouldn't dare eat these *moules* if they came from Port Blissey.'

Jerome scooped an ovoid of meat from its casing with an empty half-shell and sucked it into his mouth.

'Why ever not? They're more scrumptious than oysters.'

Lorna's experience of oysters came from literature where they were associated with the decadence of the rich man's table. Though delighted with Rome's favourable comparison it didn't stop her from elaborating on her story.

'People who eat shellfish from around Blissey harbour get the squirts something chronic. Mum says it's because of the drain outfall.'

'Thankfully Kilcarrick Haven is drain free so there's no need to worry about these.'

'That wouldn't convince my Grandfer. He says mussels are scavengers and that to eat them is as risky as supping on sewage.'

Not at all put off by her grandfather's scaremongering, they finished their mussel meal with relish.

Another source of protein was provided by the tiny prawns that hid in the bladder wrack of the low-tide rock pools. These were easy to catch and quick to cook but being so small were much too tedious to shell. The two shrimpers crunched the pink carapaces whole, discarding only the long-feelered heads.

The only ornament in Jerome's Spartan cottage was a washed-up crab-pot retrieved from the beach. It would have continued to sit like a redundant skeleton in the outer room had it not been for Lorna's ingenuity.

'We should put this old pot back into service. There's bound to be crabs living in the Haven.'

Jerome was dubious. He often saw a potting boat operating out in the deep waters of the bay and crabbing looked a skilful business.

'A pot this size won't fit into the rock pools and we'd need a boat to drop it further out at sea.'

'No we won't. My brothers set their pots by wading out from Harbour beach at low water and do the same to recover them on the next low tide.'

'And do they ever catch anything?'

'They wouldn't waste their time if they didn't.' She turned thumb and index finger into snapping pincers to threaten Rome's aquiline nose. 'Some of the crabs they catch have gigantic claws.'

Jerome kicked at the pot's torn netting with his toe.

'What about the holes? Anything crawling in would just as easily crawl out again.'

‘If my brothers can repair an abandoned pot then so can we. Come on, pass over a length of that beachcombed rope and I’ll show you how.’

Under Lorna’s instruction they unravelled the rope into its separate strands and then set about closing the biggest of the holes with a series of improvised knots.

Not wanting to be outdone, Jerome proved himself just as adept as Lorna at tying knots. As the work progressed he studied the round entrance built into the pot's wicker structure.

‘A crab has the whole sea bottom to explore, why should it want to climb in here?’

Such ignorance shocked Lorna. 'You are an old dafty! We have to bait the pot. They won’t bother to go in unless we give them something to dine on. '

Her name-calling was affectionate and he didn’t object. 'Then you'd better show old dafty how we go about baiting it.'

Usually Rome was the teacher and she was his pupil, the chance to reverse their roles gave Lorna a sense of equality that she relished. As a mere girl she was used to being scorned by older, more practical brothers who were adept at most tasks other than those disparagingly dubbed “woman's work”.

Following Lorna's instructions, Rome whittled with his knife to make two double-pointed wooden skewers. This done, they prized a dozen fat limpets from the rocks to use as bait. Both were squeamish about gouging the live limpets from their cone-like shells and then skewering the raw meat, but it had to be done. The loaded skewers were threaded through a piece of old netting that Lorna suspended inside the crab pot.

At the next low water Jerome waded into the sea to jam their repaired, baited and stone-weighted pot amongst the rocks. A square of beachcombed cork, attached by a length of rope, served as their marker buoy. The added delight for Jerome was the fact that everything necessary for their crabbing enterprise had been scavenged on his own doorstep.

'Aren’t we lucky that old Poseidon sends us so many useful presents,' he enthused.

Lorna gave an old-fashioned sigh, 'What would we do without him?'

Influenced by Rome, she had discarded the familiar Sunday School image of God the Father being a stern old man with white, flowing hair and beard. Her substitution was far more benevolent. She imagined him as a genial green man with scaly skin, seaweed hair and pearls for eyes. Like Britannia on a penny, he carried a trident, sat on a rock and gloriously ruled the waves.

Their pot's first catch of an undersized crab did little to satisfy hunger yet was celebrated with a victory caper and noisy ululation that owed much to a Hollywood version of the Sioux war-dance. Jerome, proud of his increasing self-sufficiency, enjoyed playing the noble savage. When cooked they declared the crab's watery meat to be sweeter and more delicious than anything previously tasted. There was extra satisfaction in knowing that the sea was the provider not only of their meal but also of their means of catching it.

Rome dubbed her with the grand title of 'fishing consultant' and Lorna justified the accolade by raiding her brothers' tackle boxes to improve their fishing armoury. She used the stolen items to fashion a long line weighted with leads and hung with a dozen dangerous-looking hooks. Following her brothers' example, though not sharing their enthusiasm for the task, they apologetically baited the hooks with live prawns. At low tide they strung the line across a gully between their mussel rocks. Returning after twelve hours Jerome was disappointed to find that the hooks had caught nothing but a tangle of seaweed.

Their luck as fishermen went unchanged until one morning, following a stormy night, Jerome found a jumble of net and kelp cast up on the beach. Trapped in the net's mesh walls were several still-live mackerel and a gasping codling.

Lorna arrived at Kilcarick to find Rome sitting on the beach painstakingly trying to extricate the still thrashing fish. Patiently, she showed him how to separate the walls of the tangled trammel net to release its catch.

They baked Poseidon's latest offering in the hot ashes of a driftwood bonfire, the oily odour of cooking mackerel making their nostrils tremble and mouths water. The codling fell apart in the ashes so that nothing could be salvaged but the mackerel were held intact by their crisp-cooked skins. Using their fingers, they tore at the blackened scales to feast on the flesh inside.

The salvaged fishing net was made serviceable again in much the same way as they had repaired the crab-pot. The advantage of a trammel net was that it did not depend upon the whim of fish appetites and so needed no baiting. Unlike their improvised line of hooks it caught anything and everything of edible size that came cruising through.

Regular catches of mackerel, pouting and tiny plaice were sometimes supplemented by a magnificent sea bass. Attracted by an easy meal of captive fish, crabs and even the occasional lobster enmeshed themselves in the tarred net-walls. With such productive results, they both relished the anticipation of pulling in the net to see what torpedo and shelled shapes it might contain. Poseidon's gift of the trammel net meant that their success as fishermen was transformed. The sea became their larder making frugal meals and hunger pangs a thing of the past.

Jerome regarded the sea's riches as a benevolent miracle. Even Lorna, brought up on a salty harvest, was impressed with their success. In a haze of heady incense that was the fish-smoke rising from their cooking fires, they turned overtly pagan. The noble savages gave thanks to Poseidon, uplifting their voices in a jointly composed idolatrous hymnal sung to the accompaniment of a classical guitar.

* * *

Their summer idyll at Kilcarrick did not go unobserved. Nicholas Dingle often followed Lorna as far as the cliff top above the Haven. Port Blissey had its share of young rakes and willing wenches and Nick was an opportunistic voyeur of out-of-door acts of fornication. He relished a glimpse of female flesh: the roundness of a naked bosom or the creaminess of an exposed thigh and the repertoire of moans that punctuated human desire made a change from the plaintive cries of sea birds. Some of the wenches he watched, pretending innocence, put up a struggle that only served to add to his vicarious pleasure. His own breath would quicken in time with the panting urgency of the courting couples whom he spied upon.

Nick's carnal knowledge came exclusively from watching the couplings of others yet such voyeurism was a bitter pleasure. At the climax of his excitement he was always reminded of the tragedy of his lost love and, sobbing, he would beg, 'Flora, my lovely Flora. Come back to me.'

It was not the prospect of witnessing such goings-on that made Nick follow Lorna. The Penrose maid was no more than a child and if the young foreigner was tempted into fornication Nick had no intention of standing by and permitting her violation.

Spying on the youngsters' innocuous activities from a cover of blackthorn, he soon realised that this fair stranger was no rascal out to do the girl harm. Yet he continued to watch them for their blameless sport and camaraderie reminded him of his own youth at Lanhedra, before the troubled times when the darkness descended.

Chapter 12

Nicholas

Nicholas Dingle was born in a tied cottage on the Lanhedra Estate. Its four rooms were lit by oil lamps and its water supply was drawn from a communal well that supplied five other families. The occupants of the adjoining cottages shared a single privy located at the rear of a back garden. The dwelling, though humble, was cosy enough as every room had a hearth and fuel came free from Lanhedra's own woods. His father, Joseph, gloried in the title of head cowman; his mother, Winnifred, was a kitchen maid, a title that she regarded as demeaning despite its accuracy for her job was to assist in the kitchens of the big house.

As a boy Nick enjoyed the run of the estate's acreage. From an early age he roamed every corner of the land, fished every stream and climbed every tree that presented a worthwhile challenge. Lanhedra abounded with his secret dens and paths and the estate's fields, hedgerows and outbuildings were as familiar to him as the cliff haunts of Blissey were to become in later years.

It was taken for granted that he would follow his father and earn his living with the livestock on the farm but this was not to be. Colonel Trethewan had decided to sell-off part of the herd and so, at the age of twelve with his schooling over, Nicholas learnt that there was no call for an additional stockman. The only employment available from the squire was in Lanhedra's kitchen garden. This offer of work tempered the father's disappointed but did nothing to appease Nicholas for animals were the passion of his young life.

All God's creatures seemed to bond with him quite naturally. Whenever he crossed the stable yard the farm's shire horses and the colonel's hunters whinnied greetings to him from their stalls. Broody hens allowed him to remove their warm eggs without making so much as a cluck of protest. Stray dogs fawned after him with wagging tails. His father's unreliable ferrets frequently furred his pockets yet never once used their razor-sharp teeth to nip him. In response to another youth's dare, Nick vaulted a field gate to confront the Colonel's prize bull. Despite the beast's fearsome reputation the reception it gave him was docile verging on the friendly.

Wild animals regarded him with a similar trust. A hand-reared, orphaned fox-cub continued to visit long after he had returned it to the wild. Badgers ignored his presence at their sett and even tolerated his company on their lumbering, moonlit ramblings. Fluent in all things avian Nick was able to identify every bird on the estate just from hearing its call or glimpsing the eggs in its nest. Abandoned nestlings that he had raised returned to be fed long after they were fledged and released. His favourite orphan was the robin that tamely perched on his shoulder and piped for crumbs and worms as he worked in the kitchen garden.

Yet with the practicality of a true countryman his love of animals was far from sentimental. He was an expert poacher, illegally bagging the estate's rabbits with the assistance of his father's ferrets and strategically placed nets. When fresh-water fishing he was more concerned with the catch than the sport. A net served him better than hook and line and he would have suffered no dilemma about using dynamite had it been available. Though admiring the bright plumage of cock pheasants, no keener beater was ever employed by the Lanhedra shoot. When the sights of his employers' shotguns targeted the predators of his beloved songbirds, he took a macabre pleasure in nailing the corpses of vermin crows, magpies and buzzards to a gamekeeper's gallows. The height of his youthful ambition was to be the owner of a sporting gun.

* * *

For five years Nicholas laboured in the kitchen garden, cultivating boredom along with the fruit and vegetables and taking little pleasure in tending the inanimates that grew there. He regarded the exotics, particularly the pampered melons and the wall-trained black grapes, as an unnatural waste of good soil. His preference was for indigenous crops that fared much better given only minimal attention. The sheltering high walls of the two-acre garden trapped and depressed him, its half-acre of glass teased his aching head with an endlessly reflecting light. He remembered with longing his boyhood freedom in the fields and woods beyond the confines of his employment.

He was seventeen years old when war was declared in 1914. Swept away on the tide of jingoism he lied about his age and was one of the first to enlist. His ambition to possess a firearm was satisfied, though the one he was issued came with the sinister and unwished-for addition of a bayonet.

From his trench in the Flanders' mud, Nick's enthusiasm for guns soon waned. By the winter of 1916, he seemed to have been fighting over the same few yards of shell-sterilised mud for years and would gladly have exchanged it for the clinging soil and fruity abundance of Lanhedra's walled garden.

On first arriving at the front, he shared with other recruits the romantic ideal of serving his country. He saw glory in the prospect of being wounded for then he would surely be sent home a hero. As witness to the terrible maiming that war inflicted he changed his mind and began to fear grievous wounding more than an early death. There was a time when he mourned the comrades who fell victim to bullets and shells but after two-and-a-half years of fighting staying alive was no longer the enviable option. To go on cheating death meant having to endure the mud, the cold, the rain, the lice, the rats, the silent gas and the thundering of the big guns for ever and ever, with no prospect of the Amen. Survival became a greater enemy than the Hun and daily he prayed, 'Make mine a clean death, Lord.'

The day came when a comrade younger than himself disobeyed the order to go over the top. Instead of patriotically offering up his frail flesh to the barbed wire and enemy machine guns the youth cringed and cried in the mud below the parapet. To encourage others to do their duty, the powers that be made him an example. They executed the lad by firing squad.

The big guns kept up their barrage day and night, testing Nick's endurance to the limit. Exhausted in mind and body he became the next foot soldier unable to answer the call to face that man-made hell. His comrades found him in a foetal position, rooted in the mud and moaning incoherently. They looked for his wounds but found none. His sergeant tried barking orders and then threatened but Nicholas did not respond. One officer wanted to make an example of him but his captain saved him from execution by citing his record as an exemplary soldier.

Dingle had fought bravely at the front for almost three years and had twice been wounded and decorated. Now he was good for nothing so they sent him home.

* * *

Home was no longer the head cowman's cottage at Lanhedra. Whilst Nicholas was on the battlefield surviving the unremitting barrage of death against all the odds, his father, peacefully occupied on the home front, was struck in the head by the hoof of a tetchy milker. The Trethewans' head cowman died twelve hours later without regaining consciousness. The tied cottage was needed for the new employee and his family so widow Dingle moved into a rented two-room terrace in nearby Port Blissey.

Nicholas did not know his mother and his mother did not recognise the shell-shocked wreck returned to her by the British army. Mrs Dingle moved her bed downstairs and Nicholas re-lived his war in the tiny bedroom above a cobbled alley off Chapel Street.

For three months even the softest of sounds set his nerves on edge. Every gentle thud that penetrated his bedroom's thick walls delivered the insidious gas that sent him scrabbling for his mask. He shrank from the Very flares fired by a full moon. But worst of all were the explosions that reverberated inside his head, thundering every bit as loud as the big guns across the channel. As the imaginary shells rained down, he took cover in his trench of blankets.

One April day, his mother returned from shopping to find the street-door wide open and Nicholas missing. Lying in the muddle of his bedding, waiting for the push and the signal to go over the top, he heard a sea bird's plaintive cry. Opening his eyes, he focused beyond the windowpane and saw the beckoning blueness of a spring sky. As if for the first time, he heard the nesting herring gulls crying from the rooftop and smelt salt air instead of corpses and cordite. Responding to the call of the regenerating world outside, he dressed with purpose, found the boots not worn since his homecoming and walked out of the cottage.

He kept travelling, sometimes marching on the tarmac road, sometimes striding along a footpath or stumbling across rough fields. His was a walk of driving purpose but with no destination. He needed to get away as far as possible from the little bedroom where a war raged, shrapnel flew and the guns kept booming.

Though death held Europe in its grip, Nicholas walked through a world awakening. The snows of blackthorn blossom made his eyes ache. The gentler and more benevolent faces of violet, primrose and celandine watched his passage from every hedgerow. Above him, lapwings cavorted in an aerial insanity and rookeries were alive with raucous construction. On branch and viridian budding bush the smaller birds bobbed and flitted in displays of courtship. Nicholas passed on through all this fecund abundance as though attached to the skeins of migrating waterfowl that flew overhead.

Reaching the foot of granite tors that thrust skywards from the bleakness of the moor he collapsed exhausted. Dusk settled and in that strange in-between light his numbed brain began to trace beehive patterns in the random stone that he first assumed to be a natural part of the granite outcrop. Rocks became masonry, masonry became walls and walls took on the architecture of an ancient village, a settlement inhabited by its Celtic builders when Roman rule ordered much of the rest of Britain.

As night fell, Nicholas dragged his sinewy body through the standing ruins into a courtyard formed by a number of dry-stone, roofless cells. Choosing one at random he entered and found in its wall the opening to an underground chamber. Gratefully accepting the shelter it offered, he crawled on hands and knees to tunnel into its deepest recess.

Time held no meaning in this refuge for Nicholas drifted in and out of consciousness. In his stupor he seemed to hear a language spoken in strange poetic tongues. He sensed the bustle of activity of a community going about its daily business and fancied he heard the crowing of a cockerel, the winnowing of grain, the ring of metal being struck, a bladder-bellows rhythmically wheezing and the squealing of a pig as it was bled. In his hunger, he conjured the smell of cooking fires.

* * *

A party of churchwomen conducted by a local historian entered the courtyard of the prehistoric settlement just as Nicholas had done a week before.

'And here ladies, in the wall facing us, you can see the entrance to a slab-roofed subterranean tunnel, known locally as a fogou.'

The lecture was one the historian had given a dozen times before. 'Similar iron-age *souterrains* are found in Brittany and Ireland and, though not uncommon in the Celtic world, they are something of a mystery to archaeologists. It was once thought that such cavities were built as places of refuge in times of attack but, typically, this passage offers no other exit, so possibly their purpose was ritualistic rather than defensive.'

'The fogou looks dry inside. Could it have been used for storage?' asked one inquiring soul.

'Possibly. Being built for ritual would not have precluded them from being put to more practical use.'

'It would make a good larder for storing root vegetables and apples,' an ample woman suggested.

Others in the party liked this suggestion. Domestic activity was easier to understand than pagan ritual.

'Originally,' their guide continued, 'it would have been possible to walk into the fogou standing upright but because of the accumulation of material on the floor the only way to explore today is to crawl. I know because I've tried.'

Some of the women tittered sympathetically but one middle-aged adventurer, her grey head already lowered to the fogou's entrance, asked, 'May I go in and look?'

'If you wish, though I wouldn't recommend it. You risk soiling your clothes.'

Intrigued by the secret of the fogou's origin and undeterred by the warning, the sprightly woman was game to explore.

They had come without torches and the inside of the tunnel was as dark as pitch. When the explorer met an obstruction in the blackness she felt for it with an exploratory hand. Those waiting outside were chilled by a scream that would revisit their sleeping and waking for a long time to come.

A doctor and the local constabulary were summoned. They pulled Nicholas out of the fogou and were surprised to discover a pulse. Picking off the snails and earthworms, they committed him to the county asylum for the insane.

* * *

Roaming the cliffs above Kilcarrick, Nicholas Dingle often spied on the young interloper. He saw that when the youth believed himself to be alone and unobserved a darkness descended upon him. At such times Dingle recognised that he and the blond stranger shared a kinship of tortured souls and he came to identify the youth with his black self.

Dingle's personal torture had begun with the Marne, had intensified at the Aisne and had been unending ever since. The recognition that the youth carried a similar burden reminded Nick of his own destructive history. Recollection and imagination merged.

In his branded mind he was back in the fogou. A young girl came to take his hand and lead him out of his darkness. They made music and danced together in the sunlit courtyard, their voices in harmony. When night fell, he knew he must return to his hide-away in the wall. He begged the girl to lie with him there. At first she teased, laughing and fleeing his arms. But then she returned to his embrace and permitted him to lift the glory of her flaxen hair so that he could unfasten the heavy, bronze brooch that pinned her coarse-woven tunic at the shoulder.

In recalling the face of his Celtic lover, the features that Nicholas conjured were those of his dear lost Flora. Yet the gaunt young man who unfastened the bronze brooch with its scrolled motif and led the naked woman into the fogou was not his stooped, black self but the tall, fair foreigner who had set up home at Kilcarrick.

Chapter 13

A Door Closes

Jerome referred to their beachcombing as 'strand-louping'. Lorna loved this poetic description for it turned their scavenging into something wild and romantic. To give the term credence they threw back their heads and howled a wolf-like duet whenever they discovered some new treasure cast up by the tide.

Lorna's personal scavenging extended beyond the boundaries of Kilcarrick's stony strand. On her way to the Haven she often liberated earthy potatoes, misshapen turnips or dew-glistening cabbages from Farmer Jenkins' unguarded fields. If the farmer happened to be on scarecrow duty she looked elsewhere. At Trecarrick, Mrs Jenkins' wayward hens often laid beyond the protected roosts of the poultry house. If Lorna failed to find an unauthorised nest along the farmhouse boundary she searched wilder hedgerows for more dainty nourishment in the form of wild strawberries.

She rarely arrived at Kilcarrick empty handed and, always appreciative of her contributions to his larder, Rome would ask, 'What yummy delight have you found for us today?'

She felt most pride when she could present him with a clutch of brown eggs.

* * *

Neither Lorna nor the benevolent sea could provide Jerome with all his needs. Being so long undisturbed at Kilcarrick he grew less concerned with anonymity and rather than trek to Budruth to shop for candles and Primus fuel he decided to risk a confrontation with the natives in the nearby hamlet.

He approached the hamlet's general store with some caution and on opening the door was dismayed to find it busy with customers. A jangling bell above the entrance announced his arrival and six expectant faces turned to look at him. Knowing that flight would only arouse deeper suspicion, he conquered the urge to beat a hasty retreat and approached the counter.

With a nod to the assembled gathering he mumbled, ‘Good morning.’

The local cronies took a moment to study his bohemian appearance but then greeted him with salutations that sounded friendly rather than hostile.

Relieved, he fielded the shopkeeper’s enquiry of, 'Where be you staying then, me 'andsome?' with a prepared response.

'I'm camping down at the beach.'

This reply was sufficiently vague to suggest the nearer cove of Little Budruth rather than the more inaccessible Kilcarrick Haven. To satisfy deeper curiosity he expanded by inventing an appropriate role for himself.

'I'm a geology student on university vacation. I’m here to collect rock specimens and study coastal erosion.'

The locals nodded knowingly as one of their number commented, ‘Ah, we be well-versed in the strange interests of you foreigners from across the Tamar.’

The store’s proprietor teased him about his claimed occupation. 'Now don't you go taking away too many bits of our cliffs, me dear, or you'll be letting the sea in and then where will us be?'

His regular customers guffawed at this great wit.

Evidently the shop was used as a social gathering point for further banter followed. His purchases made, Jerome left with their best wishes ringing in his ears and a haversack weighted not only with the essentials that he had come for but with local garden produce that was both reasonably priced and off ration.

His easy acceptance by the residents of the hamlet filled him with fresh confidence and the following day he set out for Trecarrick Farm to buy fresh milk. The direct route took him through an unfamiliar meadow where a bowl-shaped depression in the ground caught his attention. Though overgrown with vegetation, he recognised it as the bomb crater made all those years before. Remembering how his aunt had protected him as they sheltered in a ditch made him feel nostalgic for those past times. Edith had been a prickly customer but in his heart he had believed that she was fond of him. Reminding himself that he was no longer a little boy he brushed sentiment aside and strode out for the farm.

The click of the latch on the farm gate set the dogs barking and, as he stepped across the farmyard, two collies raced towards him. He froze, liking their bared teeth even less than their ferocious barking.

‘Jess, Tess, that’s enough.’ The command came from a woman with a face round and rosy as an apple who appeared in the farmhouse doorway.

The dogs immediately turned tail and began to fawn around the woman’s legs.

‘Can I help you, my dear?’ she asked, wiping her hands on a striped apron.

Her familiar form of address gave him courage.

‘I was hoping that you might sell me some milk.’

She gave a broad smile. ‘Then you’ve come to the right place. Follow me, my dear, the dairy’s just round the corner.’

She led him around the side of the slate-hung farmhouse to a whitewashed single storey building at the back. They were followed by the two collies who were now wagging their tails.

‘Haven’t seen you around here before. Just arrived have you?’

Confident that his broken fingernails, rough hands, unkempt beard and haversack made him look the part, he again offered the mineralogical explanation for his presence.

'One rock looks much the same as any other to me, my lovely, but I dare say there's more to 'em than meets the eye,' philosophised Mrs Jenkins as she ladled the creamy, warm from the cow milk from a churn into his container.

‘A party of you, is there?’

‘No, just me. I’m doing research for my thesis.’

‘That can’t be much fun. It don't seem right for a young man like you to be fending all on his ownsome,' she sympathised.

With motherly concern she filled a paper-bag with samples of her wholesome home baking and refused to accept his offer of payment.

'Don't be daft, my dear. It's a poor old world if a woman can't make a gift of a saffron bun now and again.'

Her personal interest in her young customer meant that Mrs Jenkins was more inquisitive than the storekeeper at the hamlet. Under her interrogation, Jerome let slip that he was staying at Kilcarrick. The good woman's next question made his heart pound.

'Has Miss Trethewan given her consent for you to camp at the Haven?'

With only the briefest hesitation and a flush that he hoped his weathered face would camouflage, he gave the assurance she sought. ‘Yes, I have permission from Lanhedra House.'

This reply satisfied his inquisitor. More usefully, it provided the opening he needed to seek news of his estranged relatives.

'Do you know the people at Lanhedra well?'

Not wanting to raise the suspicions of his informant, he made this sound a casual question though in reality he was anxious for news about the occupants of his wartime home.

Mrs Jenkins was only too ready to gossip.

'Yes, we know the Trethewans though not in any social way of course. They're fine folk who've always been above the likes of working farmers like us but my husband's family has had dealings with them for generations. The Jenkins used to be their tenants until father-in-law bought the farm off them just after the First World War.'

'I'd heard that a great deal of the estate had been sold,' Jerome prompted.

'That's true enough. A grand place it used to be in the old Colonel's day. But they've been plagued with bad luck ever since his first wife died of the influenza.' Mrs Jenkins fell to reminiscing. 'Beautiful lady she was by all accounts. Left him with two young sons to bring-up. The Colonel married again and his second wife blessed him with two daughters. But the outcome of that was even sadder. Only a young woman his second missus was when she died giving birth to Miss Edith. The Colonel took her loss dreadful bad.'

It was strange for Jerome to be hearing details of his family history from a stranger. He'd been unaware that his great-aunts and his grandfather were the progeny of different mothers.

His informant continued to gossip. 'But the calamity that finished the old chap off was losing both his sons in the Great War. He never recovered from the shock of that. Henry, the elder boy, left a widow and child; a fine looking young fellow called John. Sad to say history went and repeated itself. Master John was an airman in the recent war but he went the same way as his soldier father, killed in the service of his country. Master John left a son too. I saw the little chap when he came down here from London with his mother. They stayed up at the big house during the war, but I never heard tell of what's become of him.'

Jerome, now far from a "little chap", felt safe from detection, but it was disturbing to hear his father's death mentioned so casually by a stranger.

He managed to mutter a conventional response. 'What a tragic story.'

'Yes, the Trethewans have had more than their share of tragedy I can tell you. Lanhedra's just a shadow of what it once was. They started selling off the agricultural land in the old Colonel's time; couldn't get the labour after the first war, you see. Since then Miss Maud has sold a lot more just to survive. If the talk in Port Blissey is to be believed then the blessed woman is nigh on destitute.'

Why only Maud? Jerome wondered. Aloud he asked, 'Miss Maud?'

'Maud Trethewan was the elder of the two sisters. She never mixed much with folks round about, though they do say that she was a lively little thing until the Great War took her sweetheart. Having her young man killed like that came as a terrible blow, especially as she'd just lost her half-brothers in the same sad way. 'Twas no wonder really that she never got over it. Became a recluse she did, just locked herself away in that old house and pined for her dead dears.'

Jerome recalled his great-aunt's reclusive nature but it was hard to reconcile the sharp-tongued, angular Maud of memory with the pining sweetheart of Mrs Jenkins' description.

'And her sister?' he prompted.

'Miss Edith was a different kettle of fish from Maud. She was always out and about. Behaved and dressed like a man she did, even into her late middle age. There was a scandal about a young housemaid who lived in up there. She claimed she was obliged to leave because Miss E's attentions weren't natural, but others said the girl was sacked because she was caught stealing. Well, it's all water under the bridge now. But true or not she didn't deserve what happened to her.'

'The girl?'

'No, Miss Edith. It was a terrible accident. She took to going out shooting pigeons and rabbits for the pot with an old twelve bore that had belonged to her father, the Colonel. Some say the sisters owed that much money to the butcher in Blissey he wouldn't deliver up to Lanhedra any more. She was out hunting when the blessed gun went and exploded in her face.'

Mrs Jenkins paused as if visualising the horrific injuries attending such an accident.

'They searched for three days before they found the body. Wild animals had gnawed at her poor corpse and her face was quite blasted away. Those that found her said they wouldn't have known it was a human being let alone a woman they'd known all their lives. My husband says it just proves that females should have no truck with firearms.'

Jerome knew that some comment was called for but found it difficult to speak. 'So Miss Maud is on her own now?'

'Yes, she's the last of the Trethewans.'

Jerome felt the urge to remind his informant that John Trethewan's son was still very much alive but bit his tongue.

Oblivious to his agitation, Mrs Jenkins continued. 'Miss Maud is crippled with arthritis and can't look after herself. A widow-woman called

May Clements lives in and does for her. You must have met May when you called at the big house.'

Jerome, who had been nowhere near Lanhedra, recovered quickly. 'Yes, of course.'

'May's all the staff there is now. And to think that in the old days they had a cook, housekeeper, maids, kitchen boy, bailiff, gamekeeper, gardeners and I don't know what else. Regular community there was up at Lanhedra. Sad to think that everything had to be sold off just to keep the roof over her head. Lives in that great house but poor as a church mouse is Maud Trethewan. Won't take any charity though. My husband tried to help her once but she didn't want to know. Rude she was to him. My Ted says she's too proud for her own good.'

This sounded more like the Maud Jerome remembered.

Paying for his milk and thanking her for her gift, he took a polite farewell. One of the Jenkins' collies nosed at his trouser legs and the other sniffed at his heels as he crossed the yard. Both dogs sat at the gate and whined as they watched his departure.

Jerome was much shaken by Edith's obituary. Thinking about what he had learnt he was barely aware of descending the steep fields down to Kilcarrick. His great-aunt's death affected him deeply for he kept remembering their companionable vigil before the blazing driftwood fire in the cottage's hearth. The thought that he would never again share such intimacy with someone of his own flesh and blood grieved him greatly.

Of Maud he had no such fond memory. During their wartime tenancy at Lanhedra his mother had warned him to stay out of her way. The elder sister let it be known that she did not want to be troubled with children. After his mother's ill-advised remarriage, it had been Maud who had written to sever the family connection.

Though he had never before allowed himself to acknowledge it, he understood that his real reason for coming to Cornwall was that his great-aunts lived here. Subconsciously he had known that when his money ran out or winter arrived, whichever came sooner, he would be able to present himself at Lanhedra, claim his Trethewan birthright and throw himself upon Edith's mercy. With this door closed his future loomed as scary as it was empty.

At Kilcarrick he found Lorna waiting.

'Where have you been?' she scolded. 'I've been worried about you.'

Hiding his misery, he opened his haversack to show her the contents.

'I've been up to the farm for milk. Mrs Jenkins was really decent, look what she gave me.'

He extracted a bun from its bag and held it towards Lorna's nose.

'Saffron, yummy, it's my favourite.'

While they were demolishing the buns, Lorna gave him her news. 'I won't be able to see you tomorrow. It's Mum's birthday and Dad says she's earned a rest and that I have to help at home instead of going gallivanting to see my friend.'

Her words startled him. 'You've told your father about me?'

'Of course not. Everyone at home thinks I'm visiting a girl called Eileen Stone.'

'Who's she?' Jerome knew nothing of Lorna's ongoing deception.

Lorna giggled. 'Eileen's never heard of you either. She's my imaginary friend who's my alibi and your stand-in.'

'Imaginary? You mean she's not real?'

'Oh, Eileen's real enough. It's just our friendship that's imagined.'

'How do you get away with telling such tall tales?'

'I'm a very good actress when I want to be. I often played leading role in the Blissey School plays.'

'I wish I'd seen you on stage. I bet you were a great actress.'

Lorna rewarded his flattery by declaiming a few remembered lines from her last public performance.

Her antics took his mind off Edith's horrific death. Though grateful for the diversion it made him wonder how he would get through the next day alone. He felt an irrational jealousy of Lorna's family for depriving him of her company.

Chapter 14

Watchers

With no prospect of a visit from Lorna, the next day stretched empty and cheerless. Jerome tried to busy himself with chores but by mid-afternoon his restlessness became unbearable. Lanhedra was much on his mind. Previously he had deliberately avoided the place but now some impulse drove him to return to the Trethewan family seat.

Preferring to avoid the roads he travelled across country and approached the house through the woods to the west. Brambles snatched at his clothing and louring branches barred his way. In places the undergrowth grew so dense that he had to force a way through by hacking at the vegetation with his staff. Beating down the yard-high nettles was a reminder of his exploration of Lanhedra's woods with his machete-swinging aunt.

Thinking about Edith conjured up the horror of the gnawed corpse described to him by Mrs Jenkins. The tangle of trees took on new and threatening shapes and sudden, unexplained noises startled him. With drumming heart he beat a hurried path towards the window of sunlight in the distance.

At last the jungle thinned and he reached the edge of the tree line. Before him was a meadow that once had been the expanse of lawn gracing the west front of Lanhedra. The appearance of the big house itself was shocking for the property looked more rundown than he remembered. The east wing, the wartime billet for soldiers, was now a ruin with its roof fallen-in.

He approached cautiously using the cover offered by overgrown shrubs. Close-to the precise nature of the house's decay became apparent: buddleias in purple bloom grew out of the roof, gutters hung askew, lead downpipes had broken away from their wall-mountings and damp patched the walls.

Though the window glass appeared to be intact, paint curled on every window frame. A few curtained windows were the only indication that the house was still inhabited. He identified the first-floor bedroom that he had shared with his mother and bravely swallowed the lump that came to his throat.

On the kitchen side of the house a drooping washing-line was punctuated by a row of redundant pegs. The place looked so deserted that the opening of the scullery door came as a shock. Jerome took cover behind a bushy rhododendron and watched as an elderly woman, whom he presumed to be May Clements the housekeeper, draped the line with a patched sheet and a few ragged towels. He waited until the woman went back inside the house before continuing his secretive circumnavigation.

At the South front, the location of his aunts' jealously guarded drawing room, he paused. Seeing no movement from within he dared to cross the open area of the carriage sweep. There was no danger of crunching gravel giving him away for the drive was effectively soundproofed by a proliferation of weeds and mosses. Peeping in at the window he saw that the drawing room was unoccupied. Further reconnoitre showed him similar drab rooms but of Aunt Maud there was no sign.

He recalled his childhood dream that one day he might restore the Trethewan fortunes. With his face pressed to the cold mullion stone of his former home he felt a sense of deep-rooted guilt. More recently he had cherished the hope that he might be acknowledged as his father's son and reclaim his birthright. That prospect had disappeared forever because Edith Trethewan had died horribly and the only surviving member of his family was an embittered old woman who had refused to acknowledge him even when he had been an innocent child.

Careless of detection, he spun on his heel and made off down the carriageway to the main entrance of the estate. Lacking the courage to face a second encounter with Edith's ghost in Lanhedra Wood he took the metalled road to Trecarrick Cross. All the way home he fretted about his past and present circumstances. Once long ago he had been happy, but it was a dim remembrance. The security of a loving family was gone never to return. More recently he had suffered the bitterest sorrow because of the indifference of the step-cousin he had loved. The repercussions of that relationship were likely to shape the whole of his future existence, a future that was now too painful to contemplate.

In the past weeks, there had been times when he had been able to forget the particular misery associated with his step-cousin. Times when he had known the joy of caring for another human being and having those feelings reciprocated. Lorna's coming had altered his life: she brought to

Kilcarrick something that resembled the dimly remembered pleasures of pre-war life in Clement Mews.

Jerome supposed himself destined to be wretched but it never occurred to him to blame the world for dealing him such a poor hand. He imagined that his inability to be as happy as Lorna was due to some inadequacy within his own character. If he had been blessed with her sunny nature then perhaps life might have turned out differently.

Thinking of Lorna made him wonder about her resilience. From what he gleaned about her home life he believed it to be wretched. She lived in an overcrowded house with few comforts and certainly no luxuries. The head of the household was too sick to provide adequately for his large family. Yet when Lorna spoke of home and family it was always in terms of affection and her lack of material possessions caused her no resentment. She was seemingly indifferent to her low station in life and bore her impoverished lot with fortitude. In contrast he, who had been born so privileged, was frequently miserable. Lorna had taught him so much already, perhaps he could learn from her the most valuable thing of all, the secret of contentment.

Dusk was falling as he approached his refuge at Kilcarrick. Far out in the bay the lights of the fishing fleet twinkled like low stars. Too restless to sleep and needing a distraction from his thoughts he stumbled into the blackness of the cottage to retrieve his guitar from its attic hiding place. Sitting on the boathouse wall, he began to play but his music making failed to provide the distraction he sought.

He remembered a similar evening when a nightingale had serenaded him from a copse in the valley. The exhilaration of those moments had given him a new spirit of optimism about the future but now there was no birdsong to raise his spirits, nor had there been for weeks. It was nearing the end of August and even the warblers who nested in the sedge by the stream had fallen silent. Lorna was the only songbird who could comfort him and she was elsewhere celebrating her mother's birthday.

* * *

Awakening next morning Jerome's depression lifted somewhat. To pass the time until the afternoon when Lorna was due he attacked his domestic chores with gusto. By midday the soaring temperature, scorching beach stones and itching irritation of his salted and sanded body drove him to find relief in the fresh water of the stream.

He walked upstream to where a line of stunted willows screened him from both sea and cliff. In this privacy he stripped to his skin and waded mid-stream where the clear water flowed playfully past his knees. Usually the water's stunning cold took his breath away but the extreme heat of the day made the chill pleasurably welcome.

The gurgling of running water and his own splashing masked the approaching thunder of hooves. His first awareness of the stampeding bullocks came from the vibrations that travelled through the ground to his immersed buttocks. The whole herd was bearing down on him. Terrified and half-blinded by a lather of soap he tried to escape but an underwater root trapped his foot. Falling headlong, his knee struck a stone protruding from the stream's uneven bed. As his head emerged from beneath the water, the bellowing wild-eyed beasts plunged in after him. The intensity of the pain in his knee was temporarily crippling and, unable to rise, all he could do was try to protect his grey-cells from the lethal hooves. Cushioning his head with arms and hands, he awaited his fate.

He smelt the bullocks' pungent farmyard odour and felt the heat of their foetid breath. Expecting to be trampled to death, or at the very least severely maimed, he tensed for the inevitable contact of cloven hoof with his all too vulnerable flesh. Yet the only assault on his senses was a deep lowing at his ear. Peeking from under the shield of his arm he saw a slobbering muzzle just inches from his own. The whole herd had stopped short. The previously rampaging beasts ignored him as they jostled for position and greedily thrust their black and white snouts into the stream to drink.

After the initial relief he felt foolish, especially as his clothes were out of reach, suspended from a sallow willow branch directly overhanging the drinking cattle. Though the bullocks had demonstrated no evil intent, he was insufficiently daring to run their gauntlet. Nor was he shameless enough to retreat back to the cottage naked. Once out of the shelter of the willows he would be in full view of any walkers on the cliff and he did not want to be arrested for indecency.

Not until the water's chill had deadened his senses did he find the courage to penetrate the invaders' lowing ranks to recover his trousers. Nude, shivering and extremely insecure, he pushed his way between the steaming flanks of the vigorous young animals. To his great surprise and even greater relief he found that the cattle were completely indifferent towards him.

Later, on lookout for Lorna, he spied her running crab-like down the precipitous gradient that led to the wooden causeway. Every few yards she made skipping side-steps and he guessed that she was avoiding the ubiquitous cowpats. He understood both her haste and her apprehension for the frisky bullocks grazing the field were taking rather too much interest in her progress.

Ashamed of his earlier timidity, he had not intended to tell Lorna of his own experience with the cattle but when he saw how anxiously she avoided the unreliable beasts he changed his mind. In recounting the tale of the stampede he hoped to reassure and amuse her.

'You could say it was an encounter too close for comfort,' he admitted, 'and one that's completely erased all boyhood ambition to become a lasso-swirling cowboy.'

Lorna's eyes widened with concern. 'You shouldn't joke. A single kick from a cattle hoof can kill a person.'

Brave after the event, he shrugged off her concern. 'There was no real danger. All the bullocks were after was a cool drink and a paddle, they weren't in the least interested in molesting me.'

'You make the bullocks sound like a bathing party but they aren't to be trusted. Show me your knee,' she bossed. 'Does it still hurt?'

He rolled a trouser leg to display the emerging bruise for her inspection. 'It looks worse than it feels.'

Lorna grimaced. 'I'm glad to hear it but you may not be so lucky next time. You must promise me that you'll never again bathe where the cattle come to drink.'

Needing the privacy that the willows offered for bathing, this was a promise that he could not give.

'But you brave that field of horned beasties every time you come via Trecarrick. If you really believe that the bullocks are so dangerous then you're truly courageous.'

His admiration was not pretended.

Lorna preened at the praise but continued to argue for his caution. 'I've no option but to come that way when the steps are under water. It's different for you; you can choose where you wash.'

He gave her a grateful cuddle.

'What's that for?' she flirted.

'For all the sacrifices you make on my account. You're a heroine.'

Glowing with pleasure she snuggled closer.

* * *

Because the tides were uncooperative, Lorna continued to run the gauntlet of the boisterous bullocks. It was later in the week, when the sea was glassy calm, that she changed her routine. Rather than wait for the tide to go out, she swam into the Haven from the still submerged steps. On such a scorching day her dripping shorts and top were a minor inconvenience: she knew from experience that the sun would soon dry her clothes to a starch-like stiffness. Loving the smell and feel of sea salt on her body she failed to understand Rome's aversion to the same condition.

Her premature arrival meant that she found both beach and cottage deserted. Remembering that Rome had been planning to go up the valley to gather some early ripening blackberries, she headed in that direction. Stepping lightly along Wake's Way, she heard his distinctive tenor coming from upstream. He was singing a song that she had recently taught him.

'In a shady nook, by a babbling brook...'

She was about to announce her presence by calling his name when she glimpsed him through the rushes. He was standing calf-deep in mid-stream with legs apart, wearing only her shell necklace. His blond nakedness shocked her.

She knew that the honourable thing would be to creep away while she was still undetected, yet she stayed. Crouching in the reeds she stared unblinking as he soaped his lanky golden limbs and the red swollenness of his private parts. In a home crowded with brothers, she was quite familiar with the appearance of boys' bodies, but it was many years since she had shared a bath with Jimmy or Tommy and her younger brothers' willies looked nothing like Rome's.

He bent to the stream and cupping his hands scooped up water and threw it to the air. The arcing cataract refracted the sun's rays to produce a rainbow aura that outlined his naked body. Rome stood before her looking for all the world like a shining, singing angel.

Her heart thumped in her ribs. She thought him beautiful, though was somewhat disturbed that he should be blemished by the enormity hanging from the golden bush between the thighs.

Not until he turned and trod carefully towards the bank to recover his clothes did she dare creep away. Unlike Rome, Lorna did not tell of her own mid-stream, heart-stopping encounter.

Chapter 15

The Glass Falls

When with Lorna Jerome was able to forget about his fears for the future. Their hours together were filled with the routines of subsistence living and thanks to the enthusiasm of his helpmate even the most humdrum of tasks was turned into fun.

Not least of their daily labours was the collection of wood. Every stick of timber that washed into the Haven was needed as fuel for their cooking fires. If they spotted any driftwood embarked on a more wayward and deep-water course they swam out together to pilot it ashore. Inland, they scoured the willow-copse and hedgerows for fallen or dead branches. All these scavenged resources they carried into the shelter of the cottage and stacked into untidy piles

Lorna decided that their woodpiles looked like the up-side-down nests of giant birds and looking at their ramshackle architecture Jerome had to agree.

'They'd have to be pterodactyls to make nests as large as these but where would they lay their eggs?'

She considered his question. 'Underneath of course. They must be upside-down birds, that's why they build upside-down nests.'

Amused he played along. 'Such unique birds deserve to have a song written about them.'

Clapping her hands, she begged him to compose one.

The nonsense song, which he admitted owed more than a little to Lewis Carroll, included the refrain:

"Take my word, how absurd
is the Tumtum nest
that sits on the Jubjub bird."

Lorna trilled these lines every time they added new fuel to their woodpile nests.

Although their scavenging and fishing activities claimed much of their time the focal point of their hours together were their beach banquets.

Jerome constructed a permanent beach hearth for their cooking fires by erecting two dolmen-like rocks on which he balanced their skewered-fish.

Once the blue-salt flames of the driftwood died back into a mass of glowing embers the fish cooked swiftly, the crisping scales emitting a tantalising, oily aroma. As an accompaniment they baked potatoes in the dying embers, not retrieving them until the skins were crusted black. Impatient for something more filling than fish they sank their teeth into the burnt jackets trying to ignore the discomfort of scorched and blackened fingers and lips.

Jerome received a more dramatic injury when trying to rescue a fallen skewer from the embers. Loving the excuse to mother him, Lorna nursed his blistered fingers. He played down his burns yet her concern touched some raw nerve. His need for maternal attention made him uncomfortable and wanting to hide his emotional state from his companion, he chatted inanely.

'I was right to christen you my Wendy. Barrie must have had someone like you in mind when he wrote his play.'

'If I'm Wendy,' Lorna romanced, 'then you're Peter Pan and you can teach me to fly. Wouldn't it be wonderful to be able to wing my way in a straight line from Treblissey to Kilcarrick and never have to worry about the state of the tides?'

Bird-like, she flapped her arms and at every flap jumped a few inches off the ground. 'Teach me to fly, Peter Pan. Ple-e-ease,' she begged.

Although the literary allusion was originally his, Jerome rejected his casting.

'I'm not Pan. I'm just one of the Lost Boys.'

Sensitive to his altered mood, Lorna changed the subject.

* * *

As August gave way to September Lorna grew pensive and glum. Sad to see her changed, Jerome remarked, 'You're being very quiet; a penny for your thoughts.'

She turned towards him with dark soulful eyes. 'What will happen to us when I have to go back to school?'

Though all too aware that their summer idyll had to end, until today, both had avoided facing the reality of separation.

To counter her misery Jerome could conjure only limited comfort. 'We'll still have time at weekends when we can be together.'

Her eyes told him that two visits in seven days were not nearly enough.

What neither had bargained for was that nature would become a turncoat and conspire to separate them even sooner. The very next day the long summer drought broke with a vengeance. The deluge turned the gurgle of the little stream into a full-throated chorus and then into a torrent that overflowed its banks so that Wake's Way was swallowed into the mire's sticky maw. Once again access to Kilcarrick became dependent on time, tide and capricious wind. To make matters worse, the tides had reached a particularly uncooperative point in their cycle.

With low water occurring before dawn, Lorna knew that her mother, though gullible, would never believe that she was going to see Eileen Stone at such an unearthly hour. Confined to home, she impatiently counted the minutes while waiting for the sea to turn and go out again.

When the time came to set out from Treblissey the sky was so darkly overcast that day was turned into premature night. Although the rain was holding off, the already sodden paths to Kilcarrick had become treacherous and Lorna was forced to take diversions around the worst of the mud.

In her hurry to get to the cottage she slipped from the slimy step of a high stile. For several moments she lay where she had fallen. Recovering from the shock she picked herself up and tentatively put weight onto a twisted ankle. Determined that nothing would keep her from Rome, she ignored the discomfort and went stoically on her way. It was not so much the pain in her ankle but frustration at her slow and limping progress that unlocked the tears. On reaching the crest of the cliff that gave a view into the Haven she saw the welcoming sight of smoke billowing from the cottage chimney.

* * *

Jerome sat by the hearth on a liberated fish-box. It was so late in the day that he had given up all hope of his visitor arriving. Her unexpected, if bedraggled, appearance in the cottage doorway was a delightful surprise. The joy of his welcome turned to concern when he saw the state of her clothing.

'What happened to you?'

She limped towards him and, taking his seat on the fish box, recounted the indignity of the accident at the stile.

Kneeling, Jerome carefully removed her mud-caked shoe and sock.

'Your ankle looks puffy and needs bathing. You're to sit here quietly while I fetch some water from the stream.'

The galvanised bucket he used to carry the water became an improvised footbath.

Plunging her foot into the penetrating cold of the stream water Lorna pretended ingratitude.

‘Call this a cure? It feels more like torture.’

Having doctored the sprain and bandaged her ankle with a strip of rag, he turned his attention to her soiled clothes.

'From the state of you I’d say you've been wallowing in a pigsty rather than falling off a stile. Are you sure that you didn't have your accident at *Swine Lake*?'

Word games like these were their stock-in-trade and soon revived her spirits.

She pulled a face. 'It was definitely not *Swine Lake* and you're a *pig* for suggesting that it was.'

'If you're going to call me names, I'll have to ask you to *trotter* long home, my *Pork* Blissey girl.'

'You're just trying to *hog* all the best jokes,' she countered after the briefest of pauses for thought.

‘*S'ow* d' you make that out? I’m just trying to *cure* you and save your *bacon*.'

'This is getting *boar*ing.'

Jerome's generosity of spirit ensured that Lorna always had the last word in these verbal competitions, but not until he’d made her work for her victory.

'OK, I concede. As usual you’re the punning champion. Now let's get you out of that mudpack and wash your clothes. If I drape them around the fire they’ll soon dry. Your mother would have a fit if you go home looking as if you’ve been mud wrestling.'

As she stripped to pants and vest he offered the loan of what he called his ‘Sunday-best shirt’.

Lorna contorted herself to examine her posterior. Her knickers were as muddy as her outer garments. ‘I’m much too mucky to wear your clean shirt.’

‘A bit of honest mud won’t ruin it. Besides, you can’t stay in those soiled knickers.’

Overcome with shyness, she blushed and accepted his shirt.

‘Promise you won't look until I’m decent?'

He covered his eyes and turned away while Lorna hurriedly undressed and slipped into the overlarge borrowed garment.

When he looked again, she had lifted the shirttails and was dabbing away at the mud on her bottom with a damp handkerchief.

'It might be easier if I did that,' he offered.

Lorna blushed. 'You promised you wouldn't look.'

Immune to her embarrassment, he claimed the handkerchief, rinsed it in the bucket and began to flannel away the mud.

Obediently, though self-consciously, she held the shirt out of the way.

With the mud removed he fetched a towel from his sleeping cell and dried her bottom.

'There, all done and pristine as a new baby.'

Before she could drop the shirttail he planted a smacking kiss on the cheek of her left buttock. She didn't protest. The feel of his mouth and soft beard against her flesh was strangely exciting. She felt a tingling sensation where his lips had touched and wished he would do it again but Jerome picked up the bucket and went outside to collect fresh water to rinse the mud from her clothes.

Ablutions over, they sat at the fireside next to her steaming garments. It was the first time that Lorna had been in the cottage when the fire was lit and she luxuriated in its warmth. Sleepily she listened as Jerome played the guitar. Every so often he put the instrument aside to add some wood to the hearth or to rearrange her drying clothes.

The light thrown by the flames made shadows on the uneven cob walls and Lorna's half-closed eyes were drawn to the flickering patterns. Rome's shadow, as he bent over the guitar, was giant and distorted. Lorna's wild imagination transformed the shadow's shape into a beast that loomed over them both.

Jerome saw her shiver. 'What's the matter? Have you caught a cold?'

'No, it's just a goose walking over my grave.'

The expression filled him with foreboding and to lighten the atmosphere he plucked a jollier melody from the strings.

'Let's sing, shall we?' he invited.

His pleasant tenor took on the dialect of the folk song's earliest interpreters, a rendering suitably matched by Lorna's natural country accent.

Suddenly the joyful harmony of their voices was interrupted and mocked by an intimidating sabre-rattle coming from directly overhead. The aggressive noise grew to an alarming big-gun rumble that was followed by a shell-splintering crash from outside. A sudden squall was launching a vindictive assault on the roof, tearing off loose slates and smashing them onto the stone flags at the rear of the cottage. Lorna gripped Rome's arm in fright as a stronger gust took several slates together. The whole cottage seemed to be creaking and shifting as though it had uprooted from the beach and put to sea.

Jumping to his feet, Jerome dragged her away from the enlarging hole above.

'It's too dangerous to stay here. A slate could just as easily fall in on our heads as pitch down the roof outside.'

He pulled her towards the open doorway where they viewed the carnage beyond. The transformation of the inlet was absolute. Day was turned to dusk. The previously grey, choppy waters had become a white cauldron as the full force of a south-easterly blew through the narrows of the two rocky spurs that offered protection against winds coming from any other direction. Spray lashed the cliffs and both steps and zigzag had disappeared behind a curtain of water.

Rome shouted to be heard above the wind. 'We've got to get you back home.'

Wildly he gathered up her airing clothes.

'Quickly, get dressed.'

The command had to be repeated for his words were sucked away by the wind.

Leaving her dressing in the relative safety of his sleeping cell, he fought his way through the door. Leaning into the force of the wind, he battled across the beach but had not gone far before water swirled about his boots. The suck of water confused him. By rights the sea should have been yards away, making a gentle progress up the beach but the wind, with no respect for tide-tables, had whipped the ocean into a frenzied compliance. Giant waves were already breaking high on the foreshore. He saw with a groan that they were too late. It would be suicidal to try to reach the zigzag, let alone the Blissey steps. Kilcarrick was completely cut-off.

Chapter 16

Raft of the Medusa

Returned to the comparative safety of his sleeping cell Jerome gathered Lorna into his arms. The embrace was as much to comfort himself as his companion.

As his stomach churned with worry the cottage groaned in unison and he voiced the question that screamed in his head.

'Oh God, what do we do now?'

'Will the storm take the whole roof off?'

Lorna's anxiety was reasonable yet it was not the state of the roof that was uppermost in his mind.

'I don't think that's likely. The cottage has been here for centuries and must have survived countless storms as bad as this.'

This reassurance raised her spirits and she offered some comfort of her own. 'At least there isn't a spring tide to flood us out. So as long as we stay put we should be just fine.'

'Just fine?' He was suddenly brusque, pushing her away so that he could look deep into her eyes. 'Have you forgotten about your parents? They'll be frantic with worry when you don't go home tonight.'

'There's no need to be angry, Rome. Mum and Dad won't worry their heads about me.'

She reached out to him, but he turned away, busying himself by lighting a new candle from the nearly extinguished one. Both flames guttered in the eddies swirling through the cottage. He screened the new wick with his hand and when the flame grew strong held it towards her sun-freckled face so that he could see her better.

'You don't seem to realise the seriousness of our situation. Believe me, we're in deep trouble.'

'Why should we be? My parents won't even think of coming to look for me so there isn't a problem.'

She demonstrated her lack of concern by relaxing back onto his sleeping bag.

Disbelief made him snap. 'Are you crazy? Their twelve year old daughter goes missing in the middle of a hurricane and you think they won't be worried?'

That she had cheated her parents caused Lorna little concern, but she had deceived Rome and couldn't bear the agony she was causing him. Tentatively she reached up to take his hand.

'Honestly, they won't report me missing or make a fuss because they'll think I'm staying with Eileen Stone.'

She spoke quietly and because of the chaos outside he didn't catch all of her words.

'They'll think what?'

'That I'm spending the night at Eileen Stone's house.'

'I don't understand. Why would they think that?'

He knew that Lorna lied to explain her long absences from home but as she had never admitted the extent of her deception he was unaware of the elaborate fiction devised to satisfy her mother.

Over the weeks of its telling, the story of her compassionate attendance on the invalid Eileen had developed with such conviction that there were times when Lorna believed in the manufactured alibi herself. Like the time when she discovered the tentacled egg case of a dogfish washed up on the beach. Rome had prised open the rubbery purse and inside was a sad little embryo with huge eyes and a turned-down mouth. Filled with compassion for the tiny stillborn shark, Lorna insisted that they gave it a Christian burial. The tentacled sack with soulful occupant was interred in the overgrown garden at the rear of the cottage. They marked the grave with a miniature rugged cross made by lashing two sticks together. Rome recited all that he could remember of the burial rites intoned at his mother's funeral and Lorna adorned the loose soil of the small mound by planting the woody stems of some sweet scented privet blossoms cut from a nearby bush.

The respectful ceremony over she had exclaimed, 'I bet Eileen's never seen an unborn dogfish. I'll tell her all about it when next I see her.'

Only after the words were uttered did she remember that she and the snooty daughter of the Budruth solicitor had hardly exchanged two words in the whole year that they had attended the same school and travelled on the same school bus.

Absorbed with these thoughts Lorna failed to respond to Jerome's question so he repeated it.

'Why would your parents think that you're staying at your friend's house?'

‘Because...,’ she bit her lip and lowered her eyes to avoid his interrogating stare, ‘that’s where I told them I would be.’

Her confession confused him. He ran long fingers through his pale hair, raking his scalp as if trying to stimulate his brain cells into following her explanation.

‘That’s crazy. How could you make up an excuse in advance when you had no idea that you’d be stranded here?'

She sank deeper onto his sleeping bag. 'I didn’t know for sure but I guessed that getting home tonight might be a problem.'

'What are you, Lorna? Some sort of Celtic witch who can predict the weather?'

She pouted. 'Do I look like a witch? I’m observant that’s all. I saw the coastguard hoisting the storm-warning cone and with the wind in this direction I guessed that Kilcarrick was in for a battering. I told Mum that I've been invited to stay at Eileen's if ever the weather came on bad. If I don’t manage to get home tonight she’s sure to think that’s where I'll be.’

Older and wiser, he believed her confidence to be misplaced.

‘We’ve been fools to think that we could go on deceiving your parents indefinitely. When you fail to turn up tonight the first thing your parents will do is telephone Eileen's people to check that you’re safe.'

She sat up in the sleeping bag, clasping her knees and drawing them towards her.

'No they won't. Mum and Dad never use a telephone. We don’t know anybody who owns one.'

It puzzled her that Rome should have so little idea of the life-style of the ‘working classes’, the label favoured by her out-of-work Dad when speaking of the Penrose family and their village neighbours.

As she looked up at him, her dark tearful eyes reminded Jerome of the little shark embryo that they had buried in the cottage garden.

'Don't cry,' he begged. ‘It will only make matters worse.'

Rome's severity, the destructive violence of the storm and the throbbing of her ankle suddenly became too much.

‘How could it be worse,' she sobbed. 'Because of my ricked ankle I thought you’d be happy to let me stay tonight. I’ve not once slept in your lovely bed even though making it was my idea.’

The echo of an old fear gripped Jerome.

'But you can’t spend the night here. You don't know what people are like. They wouldn't understand.'

What was not in denial was Lorna’s claim about his bed. It had been her idea and she had, quite literally, helped him make it. Sleeping on the unforgiving flagstones had been back aching. To cushion the hardness of the floor they had brought armfuls of pungent smelling seaweed into the cottage, an idea that proved a mistake for with the weed came a myriad of little flies, each one seemingly intent on flying into their mouths and other orifices. Lorna had wanted to replace the seaweed with dry sand but the daily irritation of the sticking grains was already as much as his sensitive skin could take and he had no intention of sleeping in the stuff.

Lorna found the eventual solution to his sleeping problem in the withy moor at the back of the cottage. The osiers that grew there were not a natural feature but had been planted generations before to supply the cottage's fishermen occupants with the materials needed to fashion their lobster pots. Her idea was to weave the withy into a mattress. Jerome had been dismissive, pointing out that such a project required the combined skills of creel maker, basket weaver and thatcher. His argument did nothing to dampen Lorna's enthusiasm for the task and, as in most other things, he let her have her way.

Using his Bowie knife they harvested bundles of flexible withy. Half of the wands were kept intact for the warp and others they cut in half to create the weft lengths. The manipulation of such sharp materials left their overworked hands sore and scarred. For added comfort they padded the wicker frame with more pliable rushes and, finally, with swathes of dried grasses. Their masterpiece took several days and much ingenuity to make. When complete it took up half the floor-space in Rome's sleeping cell.

Although no goose-feathered bed, the new sleeping arrangement gave him his first night of uninterrupted sleep in weeks and he had reported its success to Lorna.

'I've christened your splendid mattress my 'dream raft' because of how efficiently it floats me off to dreamland.'

Lorna, very taken with the concept of a dream raft, told him wistfully, 'I wish we could float away on it together.'

Squatting beside his now sobbing comrade he deeply regretted being so damned enthusiastic about his homemade bed. He should have seen the danger in making the mattress sound so tempting.

'Lorna,' he soothed, 'please don't think that I'm ungrateful. Kilcarrick would be a joyless place without you and it's not that I don't want you here.' It was the closest he'd come to admitting how intolerable his life would be without her. 'It's not me but others who would think it inappropriate. You staying here overnight poses a terrible risk for us both.'

She uncurled from her attitude of misery and threw her arms about his lean body. Her sudden weight overbalanced them both, knocking the candle from his hand and extinguishing it. He made no attempt to rise but stretched alongside her, holding her tenderly to his chest and stroking her dark hair, invisible in the sudden blackness. In very few moments he felt the hypnotic rise and fall of her effortless and regular breathing.

Unlike his companion, Jerome could not sleep. The image of the suddenly extinguished candle stayed with him for it seemed an unhappy omen. He lay with the little girl in his arms, listening to tempest outside and the creaking accompaniment of the disturbed cottage.

Gradually, the elements relented and the sounds of destruction ceased, but the subsiding of the storm did nothing to calm his inner turmoil. He knew this latest cataclysm boded ill for the fabric of his shelter but he did not get up to assess the extent of the damage. How much or little of the roof had been spared would be all too evident in the morning. His immediate concern was not for smashed slate but with the sleeping girl and the likely repercussions for them both of her spending a night at the cottage.

The warmth of Lorna's presence was both the cause of his agitation and a comfort. Lovingly he buried his lips into the dark hair of her sleeping form. At this intimate contact all his suppressed longings surfaced. With will-power weakened, he allowed himself to imagine that it was not Lorna but his step-cousin lying in his arms. The physical stirrings this pretence generated gave no satisfaction but shamed and tormented him with an equal agony of guilt and regret.

Jerome's regret was not that his step-cousin was lost to him but that his life would have been so much simpler had they never met. The situation that he now found himself in would never have occurred had it not been for the Major's nephew.

Chapter 17

1948: Frederick

Sleep was impossible for once he started thinking about his step-cousin the events of the past fifteen months began to roll like a film in Jerome's head.

* * *

It was almost the end of term when Mr Stafford, his housemaster, imparted the contents of a letter received from Major Fuller.

'Your stepfather writes to say that your mother is unwell and he is taking her abroad to convalesce. He regrets the inconvenience of such short notice but wishes you to remain at the school throughout the holiday.'

The Major failed to provide a forwarding address and Jerome's hope that he might receive a more communicative letter from his mother went unfulfilled. It was miserable to be abandoned at the almost deserted school throughout the tedious summer weeks and he felt the hurt of his parent's neglect most keenly.

To keep himself occupied he rambled the Lincolnshire countryside with his sketchpad and pencils. The landscape of flat acres provided little of inspiring subject matter so he drew precise botanical studies of trees, crops and flowering plants. These artistic excursions filled his days. Later, after frugal suppers in the near-deserted refectory, he retreated to the solitude of the dormitory where he either read or took up his guitar to serenade the five unoccupied beds.

The Autumn term was well underway when his housemaster summoned him to a further private audience. Old Stuffy Stafford was a decent sort of bloke who did his best to break the news gently. It was left to Stafford's wife to offer emotional support and prepare the orphan for the ordeal of his mother's funeral.

Jerome harboured no suspicion that his mother's complaint might be terminal. The few letters received from his parent had given no indication of the seriousness of her illness and because of the Major's open aversion to his ‘wife's brat’ he had not been allowed home to discover the truth for himself. Whether his stepfather had lacked the common humanity to prepare him for the worst or had deliberately kept him in ignorance hoping to cause maximum grief later he could not decide.

In front of the well-meaning Staffords he managed to maintain the Englishman's stiff upper lip. When alone he convulsed into a grief that was overwhelming. He mourned not only the loss of his mother but also the waste of a war that had stolen his father's life.

His nights became riddled with uncomfortable dreams always involving his parents. Though he could see them clearly they were always out of reach on the opposite side of some fast flowing river or unbridgeable chasm. Once they looked at him from the back window of a car that was fast accelerating away. Never had his loneliness been more absolute.

The arrangements for his travel and attendance at the funeral were dictated by the Major with the caveat that his orders were to be followed to the letter. It was a timetable that gave Jerome barely an hour at Clement Mews before the cortege left for the church. This wasn’t the deprivation that he expected for without his mother the Mews no longer felt like home.

Neither mourner offered condolences to the other. Closeted in the car that carried them to the cemetery Jerome felt too empty to talk and his stepfather, whose initial greeting had been, 'I hope you're not going to embarrass me by sniffling,' gave him no encouragement to do so.

After the interment the car delivered him directly to the railway station to catch the next train that would return him to school. The Major did not condescend to speak until they were drawing up outside St. Pancras Station.

'Your mother's will names me as the sole beneficiary of her estate or rather of what will be left of it after her considerable medical fees have been settled. She also appoints me as your legal guardian. Don't imagine that I'm overjoyed to be saddled with the expense and inconvenience of another man's son. And as for that school of yours, the fees are way beyond my modest means so you'd better get used to the idea of saying goodbye to it.’

It was a cruel and sneering disclosure. Obviously the widower felt no qualms about his inherited wealth being derived entirely from the fortune of John Trethewan, his dependant's father. Jerome refused to give the legatee further satisfaction by responding.

From snatches of conversation overheard soon after his mother's remarriage Jerome learnt that Fuller had brought previously undisclosed debts to the union. He presumed that these debts were to make prior demands on the Trethewan inheritance at the expense of his education.

Worry about the uncertainty of his future diverted him from grieving too long over his mother's death. When newly widowed Sarah had withdrawn into herself, shutting him out. The pain he had suffered then had been intense. Almost as overwhelming was her neglect when she had taken up with Fuller. Now that she was lost forever he pretended to take comfort in the fact that she could never hurt him again.

Back at boarding school, he threw himself into his studies as a distraction from his personal situation. His single diversion from academic work was his music. Only in the quiet of the dormitory at night when the other fellows were asleep was there time to consider the true wretchedness of his orphaned state. Yet he denied himself the luxury of sentimentality and self-pity for he was afraid that such indulgences would result in tears. To be discovered blubbering would have destroyed every ounce of credence that his guitar playing had earned him.

The autumn term advanced yet despite the Major's threat Jerome's schooling continued without change or interruption. He supposed that either Fuller had been unable to find a boarding school charging lower fees or, not wanting to be bothered with the guardianship of his dead wife's child, was choosing to ignore his dependant's very existence.

Christmas was fast approaching and the school buzzed with an excited anticipation. On the assumption that being out of sight also meant being out of mind, Jerome was reconciled to spending another holiday incarcerated at school. Not that he was the only pupil who viewed the looming festival with sadness. On the shorter vacations there were always a few boarders unable to join parents who earned their livelihood in the remoter parts of the British Empire. Seeing their glum faces Jerome consoled himself with the thought that abandonment caused him less hurt than it did his fellows for anything was preferable to spending Christmas in the company of the Major.

The summons for him to report to Clement Mews came as an unwelcome surprise. His stepfather's terse note made it abundantly clear that this festive hospitality was not extended as a gesture of goodwill: Jerome's services were required to keep an eye on the Major's young relative whose parents had been unexpectedly called overseas.

Jerome expected the nephew to be an infant but Fred turned out to be barely eighteen months younger than himself. The boy's striking resemblance to Robert Fuller was disconcerting. The younger version had an identical stockiness of body with the same black hair, ruddiness of cheek and dark lashes curtaining brown eyes. Thankfully, there were differences in personality and the nephew's winsome grin persuaded Jerome to regard him favourably. More than this, the boy expressed an open dislike of his uncle. Having foreseen no such ally at home, Jerome was so filled with gratitude that, in return, he was happy to indulge his unexpected confederate's every whim.

Clement Mews, though shabbier, looked much as Jerome remembered it. He was surprised to find his mother's piano still gracing the drawing room. It was a valuable instrument and knowing that the Galloping Major was not in the least musical he had expected the piano to have been auctioned off to meet the man's debts.

He was about to seat himself on the piano stool when Fred barged him aside.

'Me first,' the boy demanded and then made Jerome flinch by murdering the keys with a particularly disjointed version of "Chopsticks".

Growing bored with his recital, Fred vacated the music stool to his step-cousin.

Having rummaged through the sheet music, Jerome selected a medley of Gilbert and Sullivan songs because they were the jolliest he could find. To perform melodies that were such keen reminders of his mother was an emotional masochism but his eagerness to please the boy was reason enough to play them.

The notes carried to the Major who strode into the drawing room and slammed down the piano lid, narrowly missing Jerome's retreating fingers.

'I've had enough of that damned tinkling to last me a life-time,' he barked. 'It's driving me mad.'

Jerome wondered what this outburst signified. Was their guardian merely in one of his awkward moods or were tunes so closely associated with his dead wife a too-painful reminder? Whatever the reason, it was the excuse Jerome needed to abandon the piano and its emotive associations. He could recall no other occasion when Fuller had given him cause to be grateful.

Fred produced a pack of cards and they played a couple of hands of whist but the boy soon grew bored with the game and demanded other amusements. Eager to please, Jerome offered to entertain him with his guitar.

Not being witness to Jerome's arrival, Fred was unaware of the guitar's existence.

'Why didn't you say that you've got such a top instrument? A guitar is much better than a boring old piano.'

Fred's enthusiasm was gratifying and although Jerome did not think of a piano as a lesser instrument he resonated with the boy's remark. In their present circumstances the guitar's major advantage over the piano was that it could be enjoyed in the privacy of their bedrooms well away from their moody and aggressive guardian.

Had Clement Mews combusted into a blazing inferno Jerome would have risked incineration to save his guitar. There were both sentimental and rational reasons for his deep attachment to the instrument. Not least of these was the sensual pleasure derived from holding the guitar's perfectly shaped form close to his body. The physicality of that contact had become a substitute for the human intimacies denied him for so many years.

To say that his first term at boarding school had been difficult was an understatement; it had been sheer hell. The school's emphasis on physical fitness and sporting excellence was a regime quite alien to his nature. His inability to conform to the ways of his peers had resulted in him being bullied mercilessly.

The victimisation had continued until he came under the wing of Mr Blake, the new and personable young music master. Blake was quick to recognise his pupil's virtuosity with the guitar and Jerome would never forget the glow of pleasure when his tutor patted him on the shoulder and praised him with the words, 'You're a natural, Trethewan. I'm fortunate to find a pupil with such talent.'

Informal tuition in folk and jazz supplemented the contractual classical lessons and before long the chaps in his dormitory were pestering him to play. Jerome revelled in his mastery over his new instrument for it was a reassuring certainty in a life that in most other respects was outside his control. In time his relationship with the guitar changed: it was no longer something to shelter behind, something that was clasped to the breast like a protective shield. It became a weapon to be used to carve his place in the world, it was his salvation.

His reputation as a minstrel spread throughout the school. Suddenly he was a sought after addition to every entertainment, particularly the illegal ones indulged in surreptitiously after lights-out. As proof of their new regard, his peers affectionately dubbed him "Strings". With the nickname came recognition and an unexpected status that placed him at least on a par with the school's second division athletes. Finding himself suddenly popular made him heady with pleasure. His incompetence on the sports field was excused.

In offering to play for Fred, Jerome hoped to earn the boy's respect just as he had done with the fellows at school. He was not disappointed.

'I didn't expect you to be so good,' Fred remarked, keeping time with his foot. 'You should be on the wireless.'

Such admiration was sweet and savoured, yet when it came to more robustly physical activities Fred was rudely critical about his companion's prowess.

The Major was out and the boys were amusing themselves by hand-patting a Ping-Pong ball across the scrubbed pine table in the basement kitchen.

'Which school teams do you play for, Jerry?'

Jerome bent to retrieve the Ping-Pong ball from the floor. 'None. Ball games and team sports aren't really my bag.'

'You're such a weed. Not at all like me, I'm brilliant at sports and the only chap in middle school to earn a place in the senior rugger team.'

Jerome believed the boy's boast for he possessed the perfect physique for a rugger scrum.

'Let's take my rugger ball to the park and I'll show you how good I am.'

Against his better judgement Jerome pretended enthusiasm for this proposal.

They had barely passed through the park gates when Fred made an unexpected throw. The rugger ball caught Jerome on the side of the head making him momentarily dizzy.

Fred chatted on seemingly oblivious of the discomfort he had caused.

' Don't you think rugger is just the top sport?'

'It's not really my thing, though I wish it were.'

The wish was genuine. He would have given anything to measure up to the ideal of Fred's perfect companion, but, inevitably, his ability with the rugger ball proved a disappointment.

'God, Jerry, you are pathetic,' Fred crowed.

Desperate for approval, he did his best to come up to scratch but every time he ran with the ball Fred's diving tackle floored him.

As he lay winded on the ground his companion imposed a further indignity by sitting on him.

'Get off, there's a good chap,' he pleaded.

'If you want to get up you'll have to wrestle me off,' Fred challenged, pinioning his captive's wrists to the grass.

Unable to match his assailant's strength Jerome gave up the struggle. Such an easy surrender disgusted the younger boy.

'What an old woman you are,' he mocked.

Further excursions to the park revealed similar inequalities. They played soccer with a tennis ball but the shorter, stockier rival succeeded in up-ending his lanky opponent in every tackle.

Tired of being humiliated in the mud, Jerome lay down a challenge. 'How about competing in a race? I can usually manage to run without falling over.'

Though lacking in true competitive spirit he was fairly confident that his longer legs would at least prove a match for Fred's shorter ones.

In a sprint there was little to choose between them. Fred, however, was a poor loser but also shrewd enough to realise that his stamina would be an advantage over a more demanding course. Soon they were racing mini-marathons.

'Just to the fountain at the end of that avenue of trees,' Fred commanded, pointing to a dot in the distance. 'Last one there is a patsy.'

The athletic and far fitter Fred always reached these goals first. With shining eyes and rosy cheeks the victor jeered his fellow competitor home. Awarded the patsy crown, the loser collapsed panting and exhausted.

Proud of his physical superiority, Fred was fond of displaying his well-developed biceps. In doing so he unfailingly commanded, 'Feel them.'

Ever eager to please, Jerome obeyed.

'You've muscles like iron,' was his admiring assessment. 'A regular John Henry.' This was a reference to the "steam-driving man" of his folk songs.

'And who's got fried eggs for muscles, then?' Fred smirked, subjecting Jerome's own arm muscles to a painful squeeze.

* * *

On Christmas morning the only present to appear on the breakfast table was labelled

"To Fred, love Jerry." The recipient eagerly ripped and discarded the brown-paper wrapping that the artistic Jerome had painstakingly hand-decorated with a design of rugger balls and holly.

'Oh, a book.' Fred's disappointment showed.

Hurt, Jerome defended his gift. 'It's a history of rugby football with stories about all the great players of the past.'

Fred flipped through the pages, pausing briefly at some of the illustrations. Clearly the text held no interest for him. With an emphatic closing of the covers he issued a casual, 'Thanks,' then cast aside the carefully chosen gift.

Fred was sufficiently schooled in the social graces to be aware that some exchange of present might be expected. 'I bought you some chocolates, old bean. But you know what a sucker I am for anything sweet. I went and ate the blasted lot.'

Jerome was moved by this imaginary sacrifice of Fred's precious sweet-ration coupons.

'It's the thought that counts,' he responded generously.

The daily help employed by the Major not only cleaned but also cooked their main meal of the day. However, she had demanded time off for the holiday.

' Blasted woman,' her employer complained. 'How am I supposed to feed you two? I imagine you're both expecting a Christmas dinner.'

He made it sound as if this expectation was as unreasonable as his employee's desire to spend Christmas day with her family.

Their not-so-festive meal was eaten in a run-down hotel in the Gloucester Road. It was hardly a joyous occasion for Fuller was in a particularly sullen mood. He studiously ignored his stepson and paid scant attention to his nephew. That the Major's conduct towards his relative was little better than the way he treated his stepson was a comfort to Jerome. He had cultivated a proprietary interest in Freddy and did not want to share him with anyone else, least of all with his old enemy.

To the relief of his charges, the Major was absent from the house for much of the rest of the holiday. Knowing that he was not engaged in paid employment, Jerome voiced an idle curiosity as to what their guardian found to do when away from home all day.

'I reckon the old boy has a floozy tucked up in bed somewhere,' Fred conjectured knowingly.

His uncle's more intimate life was a topic that the nephew had been keen to pursue, but Jerome changed the subject. In his mother's house such suppositions seemed disrespectful.

On the day before the boys were due to return to their respective boarding schools, their guardian announced that he would be spending the night away from home. Catching Freddy's eye, Jerome saw his fellow conspirator give a knowing wink.

Fuller was not one for social niceties and made no pretence of regret at their imminent departures.

'I'll be back tomorrow morning so just make sure you're packed and ready for the off,' he barked. 'I want you on your trains before mid-day.'

He sounded quite jubilant at the prospect of ridding himself of them both at a single stroke.

'Can't wait to be rid of us,' Fred whispered under his breath. 'Well the feeling's mutual.'

This was Jerome's opinion too although he felt ambivalent about the holiday coming to an end. It was a relief to be escaping his stepfather but Freddy had been his constant companion for almost a month. Living under the same roof they had become as close as brothers. The certainty of their imminent separation depressed him.

'Do you think we could keep in touch when we get back to our schools?' he asked on their last night at the mews.

'I've never been one for letter writing.'

This discouraging response caused an uneasy fluttering in the pit of Jerome's stomach.

'At least let me write to you.' He was grasping at straws.

'Please yourself if that's what you want.'

This indifferent permission was given with an equally ungracious shrug.

That night, when Freddy appeared in his doorway, Jerome ducked, expecting a missile. The boy made a habit of wandering into his bedroom. He came under the pretence of borrowing something, but really it was to indulge in a pillow fight or some other rough and tumble. On this occasion his visitor made an unusually civilised entrance.

Sitting on the bed, he asked, 'Shall I come in with you tonight? With the old man's away we can talk without being disturbed.'

In reply, Jerome lifted the bed-covers and wriggled over to make room.

'What's on your mind?'

'Going back to school mostly. You never say much about yours.'

'That's because there's not much to tell. I hated it at first because it's the sort of place that rates sportsmen and you know what a booby I am with a ball. But there are decent masters who compensate and I'm sure there must be worse schools.'

'Being hopeless at sport won't do you any favours.'

This disparaging assessment of his capabilities was too accurate to be resented.

'That's true, especially as the majority of the chaps are morons with big muscles just like you,' Jerome teased.

'Moron am I!'

Pretending indignation Fred jumped astride his bedmate, pinning his arms to his sides. Jerome made no attempt to struggle. He just hoped the pounding of his heart wasn't discernible outside his body. He wasn't at all prepared for Freddy's next question.

'Are there any bum-boys at your school?' Not receiving any response, he persisted. 'You know what I mean, rear-gunners. I bet it goes on, doesn't it?'

'There's talk about some fellows but they're not in my House.'

Still pinning him down, Freddy leant over to place his lips close to Jerome's ear. His voice came strangely hoarse, 'Why don't we try it, Jerry?'

'I don't think that's a good idea, old chap.' Even as he spoke he knew this response was at odds with his emotions.

Fred was too used to getting his own way to tolerate such a lame refusal.

Jerome was overwhelmed as his hand was forced between his darling's thighs.

'I've a hard on,' the boy announced unnecessarily.

And Jerome, lost in the wonder of a sexuality he had only suspected, lovingly fondled the energy of Freddy's manhood.

* * *

On waking, he thought it had been a wet dream, but Freddy was still in his bed. The boy lay on his back with his mouth open, snoring softly. In a rush of tenderness Jerome leant over and brushed his lips across the smooth forehead. He was full of a protective love for the younger boy.

Freddy stirred. He looked confused at seeing Jerome's face so close above his own.

'Get off and don't be so bloody disgusting,' he grumbled, pushing Jerome aside.

Having rolled out of the bed, he groped beneath it for his pyjama bottoms.

'Don't go yet,' Jerome pleaded.

'I need a piss.'

'You'll come back, won't you?'

The wait was in vain for the plea was ignored.

From the bathroom, Freddy went directly to his own room and, to Jerome's chagrin and embarrassment, deliberately kept out of his way until after their guardian's return.

Chapter 18

1949: Jerome and Frederick

Back at boarding school Jerome was uncharacteristically restless. In the classroom he found it difficult to concentrate and in the dormitory the maelstrom of his emotions denied him sleep. Looking at his morning-self in the mirror he barely recognised the dark-ringed eyes and haggard expression that stared out at him from the usual pallor of his face. His schoolwork became scrappy and his housemaster, worried by the sea-change in a star pupil, summoned him to his study.

Jerome sat stiff and awkward in the chair that Stuffy Stafford indicated. The book-lined room with its leather-topped desk and shabby chairs always made him feel anxious for it was here that he had learnt of his mother's death. He was made even more uncomfortable by the analytical way that Stuffy looked at him.

His appraisal completed Stafford gave a nervous cough, an affectation that Jerome recognised as the precursor of bad news.

'What's wrong, Trethewan? Your school certificate results were excellent and your first term's work for your highers was equally promising. In fact, you've always been one of our brightest academic prospects. A few weeks ago we were predicting results that could get you into Cambridge.' Mr Stafford's sad shake of head indicated that the current position was less promising. 'What's happened to you, boy? You mustn't let the loss of your mother destroy your future. She wouldn't have wanted that.'

A rush of crimson tinged Jerome's previously bloodless face. It was not his mother who had been monopolising his thoughts.

'Well?' Stuffy Stafford was awaiting an answer to his question and Jerome felt obliged to give him something.

'I'm not sleeping too well, sir.'

'In that case we'll get the Doc to look you over.' Stafford cleared his throat and began again. 'Though I have the feeling that your problem isn't physical. It's noticeable that you've been a changed man since you went to your stepfather at Christmas. Did something happen at home that you'd like to talk about?'

Talk about what happened! How could he? He had written three times to Freddy, careful, light-hearted, jokey letters. Letters that could cause the recipient no embarrassment. Letters so much at variance with what he really wanted to say. It was a correspondence of correct words arranged into very proper phrases and wooden sentences because emotion-starved epistles were the only ones that could legitimately be penned. After each mailing he eagerly awaited the replies that never came. Impatience turned to misery yet still he dared to hope. Freddy's selfishness was costing him dear.

Again Stuffy Stafford prompted him to talk about his problem. Not wanting to appear discourteous he offered a partial explanation.

'I find Major Fuller a difficult man to get on with, sir.' This much at least was true.

'Your guardian won't be responsible for you forever. You must make your own way in the world and a good education is the key to achieving an early independence. Surely you see that?'

Stuffy continued his well meaning and fatherly advice, but Jerome was only half listening. He was remembering instead how he had tried to kiss Freddy and had been rejected with a "Don't be so bloody disgusting".

The sexual experience with his step-cousin overshadowed everything else. Freddy's words, Freddy's actions and Freddy's neglect tormented him by invading his lessons and destroying his thought processes. These disturbing remembrances plagued him even in the noisy dining hall, though it was at night, in the dormitory, when they were most intrusive. He was utterly bewitched by a winsome grin, dark curls and a bursting physical vitality. Though quite unsuited to a spectre, these characteristics haunted and harrowed him more effectively than any malevolent ghost.

His secret was dangerous for it made him different from his peers. He became wary of other relationships, even becoming more reserved with those whom he had regarded as friends. He felt a growing awkwardness over his intimacy with John Blake, particularly in their sessions of private tuition. In both age and appearance John Blake was little older than the sixth-formers he taught. In questioning his motives for his previous devotion to the young music master, Jerome became increasingly reserved with him.

Stuffy had risen from his chair and Jerome realised with gratitude that the awkward interview was over. Mumbling, 'Thank you, sir,' he made his escape and was part way through the door when Stuffy called him back.

'Oh, Trethewan, I almost forgot. My wife wants to see you. Perhaps you would be good enough to call at our apartment before evening prep.'

It was unusual for a pupil to visit a master's private quarters and Jerome could not imagine why Mrs Stafford should want him to call on her.

The Georgian mansion that housed the classrooms and boys' dormitories had once been part of a large estate. The Staffords lived on-site, in a wing of the old stable block converted to provide family accommodation for the school's senior staff. As he lifted the horseshoe doorknocker, Jerome recalled how Mrs Stafford had tried to comfort him after his mother's death. Since then their only contact had been an exchange of polite salutations whenever their paths happened to cross.

The door opened and Mrs Stafford gave him an effusive welcome. Taking his arm, she led him into a long, low-ceilinged sitting room, enlivened by chintz-covered easy chairs. At one end of the room a cheerful fire burnt in the grate, the other end was graced by a baby-grand with sheet music much in evidence. In the middle of the room, a low table was set for tea for two.

He sat where bid while his hostess poured from the steaming teapot.

'A jam scone?' she offered, passing a plate.

With these civilities over, Celia Stafford bathed him in the warmth of her smile. 'I have a great favour to ask of you, my dear. Did my husband explain?'

Jerome's puzzled expression and shake of the head was answer enough.

'Mr Blake has told me of your reputation as a musician. In fact it is not an exaggeration to say that he often sings your praises. In my own small way I'm a musician too and all three of our children have been blessed with a musical talent.'

She paused in her explanation to take a dainty sip from her cup. 'Our youngest is the most gifted but she was married recently and has flown the nest like her brothers before her.' Mrs Stafford allowed herself a wistful sigh of regret. 'Music making was never meant to be a solitary activity and I particularly miss our duets. Which brings me to my point,' putting down her tea-cup she rested a hand on Jerome's knee, 'would you pay me the very great compliment of joining me at the piano.'

Jerome glanced towards the baby grand, his apprehension turning to pleasure.

'It would be an honour. I've only played on uprights before.'

Sitting at the keys they made an unlikely duo: the middle-aged Celia, elegant in a grey, worsted dress with Chinese collar and Jerome a lanky, untidy schoolboy with his tie askew and legs and arms too long for his trousers and blazer.

Mrs Stafford, who proved herself to be a precise rather than talented pianist, generously acknowledged Jerome to be the superior musician.

'Playing with someone as accomplished as yourself brings a valued cultural dimension back into my life. I do hope that you can be persuaded to come here to play on a regular basis.'

Grateful to be offered a diversion from his preoccupation with Freddy, he was more than happy to comply.

Celia Stafford was a warm-hearted, motherly woman yet initially her well-meaning kindness embarrassed her guest. Such attentiveness reminded him too much of the loss of his own parent and made him miss his mother anew.

Not satisfied with their private music making, Celia organised soirees where they entertained an invited company with duets, both vocal and instrumental. John Blake was an active participant in these musical evenings. With others present, Jerome felt more comfortable in the young tutor's company. He also became more at ease with Celia Stafford and their shared musical interest swiftly developed into a relationship of mutual respect.

With the weekly visits to the Stafford's parlour to look forward to Jerome was able to forget about Freddy for hours at a time. As his obsession with his step-cousin diminished the hurt of rejection also lessened and, once again, he became absorbed in his academic studies.

Stuffy was full of approval. 'Well done, Trethewan. We're all delighted to see you back on course.' These congratulations were punctuated by a double slap on the back.

The Spring Term gave way to the Easter vacation. The Staffords were away visiting their various offspring, and again Jerome was obliged to spend the holiday incarcerated in the sepulchral school in the company of fellow pupils whose family circumstances were little better than his own. In his loneliness he decided to write to Freddy. This letter, like those sent earlier, produced no response. With the return of the Staffords and the start of the new term he disciplined his mind to banish Freddy for good. Several weeks later circumstances intervened to make this banishment wishful thinking.

As the school year was drawing to a close a letter arrived from the

Major. Knowing that his guardian only corresponded to some purpose, Jerome opened the envelope with trepidation. It was the summons of his fantasies but also a summons that he dreaded: Frederick's parents were once again travelling abroad and would be overseas throughout the long vacation. As before, he was ordered back to Clement Mews to play nursemaid.

* * *

Determined to disguise his real feelings, Jerome rehearsed what he would say to Freddy. Yet, no matter how hard he worked at pretending to be detached and casual, the sentences he practised all came out sounding strained and false.

He need not have worried for when they met at Clement Mews Freddy made it easy for him. Throwing the door wide open, the younger boy grinned a welcome.

'Hello Nanny, come to change my nappy?'

He followed the quip by thumping his step-cousin hard on the upper arm.

Forgetting all about his carefully planned script Jerome simply grinned back.

Freddy followed him to his room, making conversation as the newcomer unpacked.

'D'you know any girls, Jerry?'

'Girls? How do you mean?'

Jerome did not much like the new interest that Fred seemed to have acquired since Christmas.

'You know, some crumpet we could take to the pictures.'

Because he numbered no crumpet amongst his acquaintances, Jerome was, as usual, a disappointment.

Jerome's bedroom was unchanged from the way he had left it at Christmas. The neglect was evidence that his stepfather had dispensed with the last in the long line of daily-helps without bothering to appoint another. Dust lay over every surface and the bedding was creased. The sheets had obviously not been changed since he had shared the bed with Freddy. It was a thought that hypnotised him. That night, he lay for hours savouring the stale odour of the bed linen. Part of him was terrified that Freddy might take it into his head to make a second nighttime visit, but another part of him was wretched because his beloved never came.

The first days of the holiday were heavily overcast with a light but drenching drizzle. Jerome was not sorry that the uncooperative weather ruled out sporting contests in the park. Cooped up indoors, they played cards, chess or monopoly but Freddy was in a funny mood and proved difficult to please. He was a bad loser with a tendency to scatter the playing-cards or overturn the boards when luck or skill was against him.

Jerome picked up his guitar to divert Freddy from these fits of pique but, in contrast to the admiration his playing received at Christmas, it now seemed to irritate and soon the boy was complaining of boredom all over again.

The atmosphere was not helped by their guardian who spent much of his time lounging about the house. He interrupted the music making by bawling insults.

'Shut up that pathetic racket, for Christ's sake!'

When they sang, he modified his disapproval to, 'Cut out that bloody caterwauling, damn you.'

'I wish to God he would go out and leave us alone,' Jerome complained.

Blushing, he regretted a turn of phrase that could so easily be misconstrued.

Fred, however, saw no innuendo. 'Must be between floozies.' he suggested.

On the third consecutive day of drizzle, Fred stood moodily at the window watching the weather and complaining.

'My God, this confinement's worse than school. And we're expected to skivvy for ourselves and get our own meals. Prison in term-time and Fuller's black hole for the hols. What a life!'

'It can only get better,' Jerome consoled. 'Anyway what's this about school being a prison? At Christmas you couldn't stop telling me how you're a great sporting hero, always out on the playing field and never at your desk.'

'School's OK if you don't mind the restrictions. Chaps like you who are in uppers get a lot of freedom but my year aren't even allowed off site without supervision. I can't wait to get senior privileges.'

With some relish, Fred embarked on a story that illustrated the reason for his keenness to attain seniority.

'Sixth-formers are allowed to cycle to the village shop during lunch-breaks. What the masters don't know is that not all the fellows go there just to buy tuck and magazines. Some of them are more interested in the extras that are on offer.'

This was said with a leer and nudge to make it obvious that these "extras" were not the usual treats available from a tuck shop.

'The shop owner is an old duffer but his wife is young enough to be his granddaughter and is a real smasher. From what the chaps say her looks and film star curves are wasted behind a shop counter. If she takes a liking to you and you have a few bob to slip her then she can be pretty free with her favours.'

Jerome wanted to point out the contradiction of charging for free favours but, not wanting to upset the raconteur, bit his tongue.

'She takes them into the stockroom to feel her tits but if a chap has real money to offer she'll go a lot further'

The nudge and wink that accompanied this revelation were unnecessary.

Freddy grew more animated as he listed the services available.

Not wanting to hear the sordid details, Jerome vented his cynicism.

'And where's the cuckolded husband while his wife is being so obliging in the back room?'

'Lunchtimes as regular as clockwork he's in the pub boozing so that leaves the coast clear for our chaps. Stewart Clifford, our cricket captain, is one of her regulars. You'll never believe what she did for him.'

With no wish to be told Jerome shifted uncomfortably but, insensitive to his disapproval, Fred continued.

'Elsie, that's her name, backed him up against the boxes, drops on her knees, unbuttons his flies and cool as you like puts his cock in her mouth.' Freddy was positively drooling. ' Can you believe it? She actually sucks him off.'

Seeing the perspiration on Fred's upper lip and the excitement in his shining eyes Jerome supposed that the boy was imagining the scene with himself, rather than the bold captain of cricket, backed up against the said boxes. Finding the conversation distasteful, he asked, 'What's in the boxes? Tins of sardines?'

Fred was deaf to the intended sarcasm. 'Most of my dorm are saving up for seniors' privileges,' he sniggered.

Later that afternoon, with the glass still falling, Jerome put away his guitar. His every suggestion for alternative amusement was met with derision. Exasperated by Fred's uncooperative mood, he gave up trying to entertain his step-cousin and settled into an armchair to read.

Freddy, hating to be ignored, stopped pacing the room, snatched the book from Jerome's lap and hurled it into the fireplace.

Jerome, respectful of literature and indignant about the vandalism, retrieved his novel, blew off the ash and attempted to straighten the bent corners.

‘There was no need for that.'

‘To hell with the book and to hell with this weather. Come on, Jerry, let's go out. I'll go dotty if we spend as much as another five minutes in this dump.'

Jerome’s desire to pacify Freddy was stronger than his annoyance over the damaged book. 'OK. if that's what you want, but it's still raining so we’ll need our mackintoshes. Where do you want to go?'

Fred gave his cunning look, 'Got any money?'

'A bit.'

'How much?'

Jerome told him.

'Not nearly enough, old man. Could you get some more?'

'I've savings in a Post Office account. We could raid that I suppose. But what is it you want to do?'

'How about a spot of excitement in Soho?' Fred wheedled.

'Soho, for God's sake, those women aren't clean. You could pick up anything there. You must be crazy.'

'We don't have to do more than look. Let's go to one of those clubs where the girls show off a bit of bum and tit.'

Jerome couldn't imagine anything more sordid. He tried to sound mature. 'It's dirty old men like the Major who pay to see that sort of thing.'

Disgruntled by the censure Fred turned on him in frustration. 'You’re a real old woman, Jerry, you don't have any spunk. Christ, it would have been more fun staying at school for the vacation.'

Without saying where he was going, he stomped out of the house. An hour or so later he returned, soaked through and still in the same sulky mood. He slammed up to his room without acknowledging Jerome's expressions of concern. When he reappeared, it was apparent that the change of clothing had done nothing to alter his mood.

Fed up with such childishness, Jerome left Fred seated in unaccustomed intimacy with the Major in front of the wireless. They were tuned to a commentary of a heavyweight title fight.

Suddenly it seemed absurd to have suffered so much because of Fred. The winsome smile of memory was absent. He was treated instead to a mouth that was either smirking or sulking. Increasingly Fred reminded him of the Major. It was a small step to believing that he didn't even like him very much. Putting his tormentor out of his mind he climbed into bed with his book. He tried to restore the pages that the ill-tempered boy had damaged by smoothing them between his finger and thumb.

Absorbed in his reading, he was taken completely by surprise when the bedroom door was rudely thrown open. Fred stood in the doorway in an attitude of aggression. He was in his pyjamas. Leaving the door ajar he strode to the bed, dropped his bottoms and, in a voice all too reminiscent of the Major's, commanded, 'Suck me off, Jerry. Suck me off.'

Jerome was paralysed with fear. Fuller was downstairs, separated from them by just a few inches of floorboards and ceiling plaster. His mouth dried-up, he tried to swallow, to speak, but nothing came. Impatiently, Fred yanked back the coverlet and savagely grabbed Jerome's penis.

When the explosion came from the open doorway, Fred leapt from the bed. Jerome was revealed lying on his back, his exposed manhood standing to attention before the Major.

Time seemed to stretch into an eternity before Fuller's face, distorted and purple with rage, was spitting into his stepson's bloodless one.

'You pathetic faggot. I've always known there was something queer about you. I warned your mother what her pandering would do.'

As he spoke he unbuckled his belt and released it from his trousers.

Jerome rolled aside as the buckle-end came swinging down to where his lower torso had been just a fraction before. The second swipe of the leather cut into his buttocks, the next struck his thigh. Then he was fighting with his attacker, trying to grab the strap to ward off further punishment.

Freddy was still in the room standing barely two yards from the bed. His eyes were shining, his mouth was slightly open and his breathing came fast. Jerome recognised the rapt expression. It was the same arousal that he had seen in his stepfather's face when he had raped his mother outside that same room, all those painful aeons ago.

No one could withstand the Major. Jerome stopped fighting and resigned his flesh to the thrashing. He turned towards Freddy and curled into a foetal position. He forced what he hoped would be gagging knuckles into his mouth. He was already martyr to Fred's instincts, now he would be martyr to Fuller's, this was how it had to be.

With each cut, he told himself, 'This is for you Freddy, and this, and this, and this.'

The Major wasted no energy talking, he was intent on causing maximum pain. His breath became laboured from his efforts, but he stopped only when the ache in his arm made the thrashing ineffectual. Then, pushing Fred roughly before him, he left the room without further remark.

Not until he was alone did Jerome permit himself the relief of weeping.

Chapter 19

Runaway

With Lorna snuggled beside him Jerome breathed a heady draught composed of human sleep, vegetable bedding, musty cob-walls and an all-pervading salty tang. Despite the contradiction inherent in these pungent odours, his thoughts remained trapped in the more sophisticated, though less civilised, world not long fled.

* * *

After his encounter with the Major's belt he woke stiff and smarting from his wounds. Every move brought discomfort and each exploratory touch discovered some new tenderness. Swinging his legs over the side of his gory bed he tried to sit but his bruised buttocks made standing the more comfortable option.

Viewing the damage in the wardrobe's full-length mirror he traced the dark welts that scored both his buttocks and back. His abused body reminded him of the map illustrating nineteenth-century railroad mania that was pinned to his classroom wall. Where the lines criss-crossed his skin was broken into blackberry zones that looked like representations of stations. The buckle's deeper scores marked the termini in mulberry crusts of dried blood. Looking over his shoulder at the reflected damage he wondered at his stoicism of the night before.

It was difficult to reconcile the ugly, abused topography revealed by the glass with his previously unblemished flesh. The modification to his appearance stirred an anger tinged with a fierce pride. The pain of the thrashing had been excruciating yet not once had he cried out. His bitten knuckles were evidence of that. To have denied his enemy at least this satisfaction was cause for self-congratulation and he repeated over and over, ‘He could hurt but couldn’t break me.’ The triumph of this mantra-like chant turned defeat into victory.

The murmur of voices and various domestic sounds travelled to him from other parts of the house but no one came near. A new-found stubbornness born of pride gave him the determination to stay in his room. Physically he might be no match for the Major's bull strength but there were other ways of fighting. If he refused to make the first move then Fuller would have to come to him. There was comfort in the pretence that if it came to a battle of wills the contest would not be so unequal.

The front door slammed and a silence settled on the building. Jerome went to the bathroom, drank greedily from the tap and bathed his wounds. The towel proved too abrasive for drying tender flesh so he wrapped his damp body, toga-like, in his soiled bed-sheet. The mirror's reflection of his pale self in the bloody Roman garb transformed him into Caesar about to become a corpse. In a defiant parody of Mark Antony's funeral oration, he shouted his lines for all the mews to hear.

'Look! In this place ran Fuller's dagger through.
See what a rent the envious Major made.
Through this the well-beloved Freddy stabbed,
And as he plucked his cursed steel away,
Mark how the blood of Jerry followed it...'

Choking with self-induced emotion he whispered, 'For Freddy, as you know, was Jerry's angel.'

For most of the long day he lay prone and unmoving on the bed because turning onto his back was too painful an option. Each time he rose to drink from the bathroom tap he re-examined his battle scars in the wardrobe mirror. The Major had abandoned him without even bothering to check on his condition. This indifference as to whether his ward lived or died sparked a renewed anger in Jerome: being ignored was as great an insult as the thrashing.

If his mother could see him now would she blame herself for the consequences of her rash second marriage? Thoughts of his mother led naturally to remembering the more recent kindness of Celia Stafford. How horrified that dignified lady would be to find him in this sorry state. Imagining Mrs Stafford's sympathetic response to the viciousness of his beating weakened his resolve and brought tears to his eyes. Ashamed of indulging in such weakness, he steeled himself to accept the fact that lacking a single ally in the whole of London he would have to face the enemy alone.

In the evening, the sound of a key scraping in the lock and the slamming of the front door warned him that he was no longer the sole occupant of the house and that his excursions to the bathroom must cease. If he were left to starve then he would accept starvation for he was determined not to leave his room. The tyrant must be made to pay whatever the cost.

* * *

On the second morning after the beating Jerome dressed. The friction of clothing on his tender back and sore buttocks made him flinch.

In the afternoon Fuller knocked aggressively at his bedroom door but made no attempt to enter. 'Get yourself down to the drawing-room at the double,' he barked. 'I want to speak to you.'

Jerome ignored the command for he had no intention of showing even the slightest obedience to the man he despised.

On the third day of his self-imposed exile, Jerome turned to the outside world again. Watching the mews from his window he imagined himself as a child awaiting his father's return from business in the city. While he was conjuring his ghosts, the front door slammed shut. Concealed behind the cover of a curtain, he spied the bulky figure of the Major progressing along the cobbled mews. Forming his fingers into the barrel of a gun he took a careful aim at the retreating back.

Momentarily he wished that he possessed a real weapon, but his hatred was not so all consuming that he did not feel ashamed of entertaining such a murderous thought. With the house to himself again he was tempted to end his hunger strike but with a stoicism that was little short of a brainsick obstinacy he confined himself to drinking the metallic-tasting tap water.

Eventually, as he had willed, his adversary came to him. The Major entered without knocking. He brandished a rolled copy of *The Daily Telegraph* that he drummed against his palm as if considering Jerome to be no more than a bothersome fly that he intended to swat. Light-headed with hunger, Jerome giggled inwardly as he pictured himself as a more aggressive insect seeking revenge with its sting.

Fuller addressed him through clenched teeth, conducting his words with emphatic jabs of the Fleet Street clarion.

'You dirty little pervert, you deserve worse than the thrashing I gave you. How am I supposed to tell my sister and brother-in-law that my dead wife's brat has been buggering their kid? Answer me that, will you?'

The spittle generated by these words showered Jerome's face. As distasteful as he found the Major's body fluids he made no attempt to wipe them away.

'I could have you locked up, you pathetic Nancy. Buggery is a crime in this country. But I don't suppose you considered that.'

His glare was a mixture of triumph and contempt and the sneering voice droned on and on.

Jerome focused on the blue-patterned wallpaper that his mother had chosen, tracing its motifs with a concentration so absolute that he became at first immune and then deaf to the unjust allegations.

Fuller's fist crashed onto the occasional table standing near the door, making its flimsy legs rock.

'Dear God, I don't think you're even listening!'

For the first time in the encounter their eyes engaged.

'Didn't you hear what I said? I've made some phone calls and spoken to some brother officers. It's all arranged. By the end of the week you'll have signed your pathetic life away to the regular army. Try any of your faggot practices when your bum's in khaki and the army will have your balls for grape shot.'

The significance of the words burst like a shell in Jerome's head exploding his resolve into tiny fragments. His determination was demoted to the insignificance of the dust motes that floated in the rays of sunlight against a background of blue wallpaper.

'But I'm going to university next year...'

He was unable to control the tremble in his voice.

'Uni-bloody-versity?' Fuller crowed, making Cambridge sound scatological.

'The only university you're destined for, you pathetic poofter, is the university of life. Your education is over. Any learning you acquire from now on will be drilled into you by an army N.C.O.'

Fuller was not so much speaking as jeering.

'His Majesty's Armed Forces will make a soldier out of you if that's humanly possible.' The voice was heavy with sarcasm. 'Though I very much doubt that your namby-pamby hide will survive the rigours of square-bashing.'

His delight at this prospect was as obvious as it was sadistic.

Jerome could not control his rising panic. 'I won't enlist. You can't make me. I'm not cut out for the army.'

'There is an alternative,' the sarcasm was still there, 'perhaps you'd rather I called in the police? They'd be very interested to hear about your sodomy of a minor.'

It was the Major's trump card. His victorious sneer signalled that Jerome had lost not just the battle but the whole campaign. Unjust though the accusation of sodomy was, his innocence could not save him. There was no point in wasting his breath. His mother's widower was out to destroy him. There would be no mercy. He accepted that he was beaten.

Triumphantly the victor rolled his newspaper even tighter, turned on his heel and went whistling down the stairs.

The army! Jerome conjured up the awfulness: the deprivations and coarseness of barrack-life, the physical punishment of square-bashing under bullying drill-sergeants, the stifling restrictions of regimentation and uniformity. Fuller was right, how could he possibly survive a regime so at variance with anything he had ever imagined for his future?

At school it had been compulsory to join the Cadet Corps but even a few of the more sporting chaps didn't approve. All had vivid memories of the war and most had lost some member of their family in the conflict. Admittedly there were many who enjoyed the war games but a significant minority were critical.

Inspired by the ideals of post-war pacifism, Jerome and those he regarded as kindred spirits were in agreement that they would defer their national service until after varsity. As graduates there was a good chance of getting a short-term commission in the Royal Air Force. Sharing something of his own sensitive disposition they could not entertain the prospect of enlisting as a soldier in the ranks. A few even romanticised about disappearing abroad rather than be subjected to the rigours and regimentation of military service. One chap's elder brother had become a coal miner, regarding that reserved occupation and its attendant risks as being preferable to army call-up. Yet here he was, at seventeen years of age, being forced to sign his life away. All element of choice was to be denied him.

There was no plan of escape, he simply reacted: his flight driven by the bleak prospect of incarceration in a future that he knew would be intolerable. He listened for sounds of the Major quitting the house, watched his departure from his window and than mobilised into action. Having retrieved his haversack from the box-room he packed it with tinned and dried foods raided from the larder. To these supplies he added utensils, clothing and toiletries. In the side pockets he stuffed his passport, Post Office savings' book, a bottle filled with tap water and finally a bread and cheese sandwich to fortify him on his journey.

Hunger combined with the exertion of these preparations left him feeling faint. To restore his equilibrium, he fixed himself a meal of toast and scrambled eggs. It was the first food that he had eaten in three days. He ate slowly, aware that this meal was to be the last that he would take in the little house on the cobbled mews.

As he passed through the hall the sight of a football jammed between the curved legs of the coat-stand jolted his memory. For the first time in hours he thought of Fred and wondered where Fuller had sent him.

He was abandoning the home of his childhood and that of his father and grandmother before him, a home that rightly should have been his inheritance. Leaving no note he walked away without so much as a backward glance. Though laden with his guitar-case and heavy haversack that rubbed the abrasions on his back the real burden he carried was the one inside his head.

At the nearby Post Office, he withdrew all his savings. At the corner ironmonger's he made some miscellaneous, though purposeful, purchases. From South Kensington tube station he rode the circle line to Paddington where he transferred to the main-line station. It was not until he was standing in the queue at the ticket-office that he thought of booking through to Penzance. There was some satisfaction in the bitter irony of choosing what was literally a last resort.

The ticket-office clerk advised him that the Cornish Reviera was about to depart. With a swift pocketing of his change and with his one-way ticket gripped between his teeth, he gathered up his belongings and sprinted to catch it.

It gave him a peculiar feeling remembering how he had embarked on that westward-bound train journey without having consciously considered his ultimate destination. It had been years since he had thought about Kilcarrick's rocky cove and the ruined fisherman's cottage. It was seeing the advertisement at St David's Station, Exeter that had jogged his memory. Balancing on the edge of the seat in the swaying carriage, he visualised the Haven as it had been in the war years when his great-aunt, Edith Trethewan, had taken him there. Remembering his childish delight in the charm of the place, he had known that he could go nowhere else.

Chapter 20

Threat and a Promise

Careful not to wake Lorna, Jerome extracted his trapped arm made numb by the weight of her body and flexed his fingers to restore the circulation of blood. When the tingle of pins and needles ceased he lay still to listen to the sounds of the night. The alarming crash of shattering slates and creaking protests of the cottage had ceased. The previous oceanic thundering of the sea's roar was reduced to a more familiar and rhythmical breaking of waves on the beach.

Beside him Lorna stirred in her sleep making small sounds of contentment as she mumbled his name. Her body generated warmth yet his own was cold with fear. How could he have allowed this to happen? He had let a child into his bed and they had been together all night. Once again he experienced the numbing terror that had paralysed him when the Major had burst into his bedroom and discovered him with Freddy.

Not that there was risk of anyone flailing him in his nest of rushes as he had been flailed in that Kensington feather bed. The sea, cause of their predicament, was currently their protector for it would be some hours before the turn of tide permitted anyone to invade Kilcarrick. Yet this temporary reprieve was of little consolation. In all likelihood a search party was already combing the nearby cliffs for their missing child. He and Lorna would not remain safe for long.

What would be done to them when it was discovered that instead of being safely tucked-up in a lawyer's respectable mansion Lorna had slept in a ruined and isolated cottage sharing the mattress of a disreputable runaway? The Penrose parents would discover how comprehensively they had been misled and that the deceit about their under-age daughter's whereabouts had been perpetuated for six long weeks. He knew how this evidence would be interpreted: the platonic nature of their friendship would never be believed.

Out there in the adult world there was little innocence or virtue. All and sundry would assume that he had taken advantage of Lorna's trusting nature and would do their damnedest to soil a companionship that was perfect beyond their perverted conception. After the sanctimonious censorship would come the punishment. He would be locked away for a crime that he was not even tempted to commit. Most unjust of all, in punishing him they would destroy Lorna's sweet innocence.

He cursed his own naiveté. What a fool he'd been to imagine that running away from London would solve his problems. Like a child, he had created a false idyll: one where he was the untouchable sovereign of an imaginary country supposedly immune from the influence wielded by outside evils. His hunger for companionship meant that he had selfishly involved Lorna in the pretence and led her to believe that it was safe to belong to his magical kingdom. How wrong he had been: their invulnerability was no more than a dangerous illusion and his self-created fantasy was in tatters. Even Poseidon whom they had believed benevolent had conspired against them.

Prejudice would label him a violator of children, an accusation that his guardian, Major Fuller, would be only too delighted to corroborate. He knew that there would be no mercy. No one would listen to what he had to say and even if they listened who would believe him? If staying to face the music could serve no purpose then wouldn't it be better to run away? Possibly, yet to flee would be seen as an admission of guilt.

Lorna turned in her sleep and looking at her sweet face he was filled with a different emotion. The selfishness of his actions had turned this innocent little girl into a sacrificial lamb. It would have been infinitely better had she never met him. He wept at his impotence to protect her.

His vacillation over whether he should stay to face retribution or flee to escape it did not last long. In his heart he knew that if abandoned Lorna would have to face the accusations alone. As dawn fingered its way through the shutters to point its own accusatory rays he knew that such a desertion would be unpardonable.

Realising how swiftly time was passing, he rose. The sleeping girl looked so peaceful that it seemed brutish to wake her so he tiptoed into the outer room. With only the briefest survey of the damaged roof he went outside. The sea's energy, so frightening on the previous evening, was reduced to no more than a heavy swell that loped into the inlet to slop against the rocks and fringe the strand with a frill of white lace. He saw with resignation that the tide had relented and that the ledge leading to the zigzag was already uncovered for most of its length. Once again Kilcarrick was connected to the outside world.

The repercussions of Lorna sharing his bed were self-evident: he would be arrested, tried, found guilty and imprisoned. It was an undeserved punishment, one that would destroy him. Yet, despite his fatalistic pessimism, he was determined to do his best to protect her.

Returning to his sleeping cell he shook the sleeping girl.

'Wake up, Lorna, we don't have much time so you'll need to be quick.'

When she didn't respond he shook her more urgently but still she didn't stir. He felt too protective to treat her roughly so became tender, kissing her sleep-swollen eyelids and brushing back her dark hair so that he might whisper in her ear.

'Wake up sleepyhead, it's morning. The storm's blown over and you have to go.'

'How can you be so cruel?' she complained and emphasised her point by snuggling further into the comfort of the sleeping bag.

Hooking his wrists under her armpits, he prised her from the bag in one smooth movement. She yawned, her face flushed from sleep, her bare feet fidgeting on the cold stone flags.

'Sometimes I wonder why I like you so much.'

In contradiction of her harsh words, she threw her arms around his neck in a spontaneous show of affection.

He untangled himself from her embrace but continued to support her weight.

'How does the ankle feel this morning?'

She tested it gingerly.

'Can you walk?' He prayed that she could.

Lorna performed a shuffled pirouette. 'Your water treatment seems to have worked. Thank you, you're a brilliant healer. You should become a doctor.'

Fear keening his every instinct he ignored the adulation and handed over her shoes.

'Can you get these on?'

She worked both feet into the shoes and walked away from him flexing her injured ankle and moving with little sign of discomfort.

His relief was transparent for he had feared that her ankle might be worse. 'You're doing fine, well done.'

'I may not be hobbling like I was last night but I'm not up to doing the Floral Dance.'

He tried to sound lighthearted. 'It's no use playing for sympathy and you can forget about dancing. All that's expected of you this morning is a walk home to Port Blissey.'

Taking her arm, he bustled her out of the cottage.

The bright light made her blink. 'Sunshine! What a difference after last night's tempest.'

Looking towards Blissey and seeing the lower steps still under water she protested.

'Why all the hurry? I can't go anywhere until the tide falls.'

Compared to his own nervous state Lorna's carefree attitude seemed remarkable.

She seemed not in the least apprehensive about returning home after an unsanctioned overnight absence. Still gripping her arm he steered her towards the zigzag.

'We can't wait for the tide. I'm sorry but it has to be the long way home for you today.'

'Why? Mum won't be expecting me back until midday at the earliest.'

'No arguments, you have to go now.'

'You are a bossy-boots,' she complained. 'I shouldn't be made to go on a route march with a sore ankle.'

Wondering at her lack of understanding he tried to reason.

'Lorna, we have no option. You were supposed to be at Eileen's house last night and it has to look as though you're returning from the Budruth direction.'

'Who's going to notice the direction I come from? Why are you being such an old fusspot this morning?'

Her name-calling was an echo of Fred's unflattering terms of address. With nerves already worn ragged he snapped back at her. 'Don't call me names.'

She looked hurt at this show of bad temper yet squeezed his hand and made amends by co-operating.

'What a worrier you are, Rome. But if it makes you happy I'll leave by the zigzag.'

As proof of her compliance she started out across the beach.

Jerome lagged behind, checking the surrounding cliffs for observers. To his relief Lorna negotiated the zigzag path without sign of a limp. He lengthened his stride to catch up with her but paused when they reached the field above.

'I won't come any further for risk of being seen by early travellers on the Budruth road so let's say goodbye here.'

The 'goodbye' sounded so final to his ears yet her bright smile showed that she hadn't noticed.

'OK, you're the boss. I'll be back to see you on tomorrow's tide.'

'No you mustn't. I want you to promise that you'll stay away from

Kilcarrick.' He was unable to keep the panic from his voice.

Her eyes brimmed with tears. 'You can't mean that, Rome.'

'I do.' He tried to make her understand. 'If anyone finds out that you spent the night at the cottage they will make me go away and we won't be allowed to see each other again, not ever.'

Lorna blushed. 'I know what you mean, Rome, but I wouldn't let anyone think anything bad about you.'

'You couldn't stop them. Believe me.'

There was bitterness in his voice.

'But we haven't done anything wrong,' she insisted.

'Of course we haven't, but the truth will make no difference to what people choose to think.'

'Why do grown-ups have to be so nasty?'

Jerome had no answer to that one.

'So when can I come to see you again?'

'Best leave it a week at least.' He could not be so cruel as to say never.

'But I'll be back at school next week.'

She looked and sounded so miserable that he had to offer comfort. 'So come the weekend after. Don't worry, I'll be here and waiting for you. I promise.'

In promising he realised that his quandary over whether to run or stay was irrevocably resolved: there could be no more thoughts of desertion.

Prompted by his gentle push she went on her way but paused every few yards to look back over her shoulder and to throw him an exaggerated pout of misery. He was turning towards the Haven when she called out and came scurrying back to him.

'I'm not sorry about the storm. It meant that I could stay at the cottage and I've wanted to do that for ages.'

She averted her eyes to draw imaginary circles on the grass with the toe of her shoe.

'When I'm older we'll be able to do what we want, won't we?' Not waiting for his reply she continued. 'Then I'll come and stay with you for always.'

His expression must have told her that she was taking too much for granted for she added a qualification.

'That is, if you want me to.'

His hesitation made her lip tremble.

To hide his own weakness he hugged her to his chest. 'Of course I want you to live with me. How could I manage without my Wendy?'

'Will I always be your Wendy? Even when I'm grown-up?'

To spare her feelings he answered in the affirmative. 'Yes, even when we're both grown-up and I've turned from a Lost Boy into a lost man.'

Seeming not to regard this answer as strange she yipped with delight, her previously sad and serious face breaking into a sunny smile.

Standing on tiptoe, she brushed his whiskered chin with her lips. The demonstration of affection was entirely natural, yet for the first time it caused him embarrassment.

'Home,' he commanded, giving her another directional push.

He stood his ground to watch her progress. Every few yards she turned to give an energetic wave.

How could he have even considered leaving her to face chastisement alone? As long as he could convince people of Lorna's essential goodness, of her purity, what they chose to do to him did not matter. The chivalrous action was to stay and accept his punishment. He might never make a modern soldier but he at least shared more than a few qualities with the knights of medieval romance.

Retracing his steps into the Haven he was struck with the irony of that name. He wondered how much longer Kilcarrick would remain a haven to him. One innocent night and everything was changed absolutely.

* * *

Lorna suffered no such burdening thoughts. Rome's promise that she would always be his Wendy made her deliciously light-headed and she tackled her homeward journey in a carefree mood.

Chapter 21

The Staggering Girl

Margaret Penrose was absurdly smug in the belief that her daughter was moving in an elevated circle centred on the lawyer's grand house on the Budruth road.

'Whatever grudges you may hold against people of their class, Jim, you've got to give them some credit for how they've taken to our Lorna. It's done her a world of good. She's smartened herself up no end and I can't recall the last time I needed to nag at her.'

'What difference do it make if our little maid brushes the tangles out of her hair or not?' her husband challenged argumentatively.

'I'm talking about more than appearance. You must have noticed how posh she's taken to speaking.'

Lorna had been doing her utmost to imitate Rome's pronunciation. She had become scrupulous about never dropping her aitches, her rolling *R*s were mere ghosts of their former selves and her flat *A*s became sharper as she mimicked his pronunciation of that vowel. King's English it might be but her modification of accent failed to impress her convinced socialist father.

'Those Stones will be giving our Lorna grandiose ideas that will do her no good at all. They'll spoil her, that's what they'll do. You mark my words.'

'You're talking nonsense, Jim Penrose. Mixing with professional people like them will help her to make something of herself.'

Margaret was more than content for her daughter to further the intimacy with the local bigwigs, even if it meant the personal inconvenience of sacrificing much of her daughter's help around the home. Despite the bosom relationship of their respective daughters, it did not enter Margaret's head to engage the solicitor's wife in conversation. She knew her station and was as unlikely to venture the social leap of making herself known to that good lady as she was to amaze her husband by flying off Treblissey's cliff.

* * *

The new school year began and faithful to her promise Lorna kept her distance from Kilcarrick. After the novelty of recent weeks she found the boring drone of uninspiring teachers thoroughly dispiriting. She had exchanged a tidetable adventure for a timetable regime that turned classroom into a prison. After weeks of wearing only light clothing, the scratching discomfort of grey serge, choking tie and garter-controlled socks felt as constraining as a straitjacket and she disparaged the uniform that once she had been so proud to wear.

The school bell's ringing insistence separated not so much her lessons as her daydreaming because, for much of the time, her mind was elsewhere having flown away to Kilcarrick to be with her soul mate. This inattention did not go unnoticed and she collected two impositions on the first day back. Her new form tutor icily informed her that the speed of receiving these punishments set 'an unenviable school record' and added insult to injury by awarding an additional black mark.

Already burdened with homework Lorna resented these impositions. The first demanded a five-hundred-word essay unimaginatively entitled "Why I must not gaze out of the window during lessons". Her response comprised no more than a list of reasons, part pedestrian, part contrived. The second task, a monotonous two-hundred lines, was in Lorna's view a pointless punishment. As she laboured to reproduce multiples of the sentence "Dreaming should be a function of sleeping, not waking", it occurred to her that had this been the topic for her essay she might have argued quite convincingly against the proposition. But such were the inexplicable ways of her teachers.

* * *

Jerome, subject to no pressures other than the tides and his own anxieties, was still fretting over what he believed to be the inevitable repercussions of Lorna's over-night stay at the cottage. Her confident assurances that the Penrose parents were used to roving children and that her wanderings would cause them neither concern nor raise their suspicions had done nothing to ease his mind. Familiar only with the rigid regimes of boarding school, a neurotic mother and a bullying stepfather he could not conceive of such careless parental supervision.

In his imagination he lived out his arrest, trial and incarceration. For someone of his temperament there seemed little to choose between life in the army and a prison sentence, but at least the former would have been honourable. He was about to disgrace the Trethewan name and the disgrace was compounded because his supposed crime was linked to the very ground where his illustrious forebears had their roots.

* * *

Weekends were often trying for Margaret Penrose and she was not in one of her better Saturday moods. Lorna was observant enough to notice the causal relationship between her father's recreational activities and her mother's disposition. She knew that he had come home late the previous night for she had heard him swearing as he collided with the kitchen table and knocked over a chair. Later, from the adjoining bedroom, she had heard lowered voices, her mother's complaining and her father's supplicatory. A rhythmical squeaking of bedsprings followed. She recognised the pattern and wasn't surprised when, next morning, her father showed signs of an upset stomach and rueful hangover and her mother demonstrated a shortness of temper.

It was her father's Saturday morning custom to relax in the easy chair by the kitchen range to read the sporting pages of his newspaper. Lorna's mother took her revenge by pre-empting Monday's washday. This meant that the comfort of the weekend kitchen was transformed into the bustle and humidity of a Chinese laundry. Inevitably the husband's punishment had repercussions for the daughter for washday was a major event requiring an extra pair of hands.

'Don't you go disappearing off to Eileen's house this morning,' her mother directed. 'I need you here to help me.'

Although this delay meant missing the first tide the conscript obeyed but instead of being rewarded for her efficient stripping of the beds her mother made additional demands.

'Keep an eye on the wash-boiler, there's a good girl. I don't want the tub boiling over and flooding the kitchen again. Then you can give me a hand with wringing the sheets. Somehow I'm not feeling up to doing much mangling this morning.'

This assessment of her condition was said with an accusatory glance towards her suffering husband.

Lorna sat in the soap-scented kitchen making a half-hearted attempt of tackling her homework while waiting for the boiler to complete its steamy bubbling. Mother and daughter then took turns at rinsing the wash in the deep enamelled sink. This process complete, her mother fed the bedsheets into the mangle's rubbery maw while Lorna cranked the stiff handle.

'Don't turn so fast, Lorna,' Margaret warned. 'You put me in fear for my fingers.'

Never had the wringing process been completed so energetically for the tide was going down and Lorna ached with the desire to be on her way to Kilcarrick. Not until the patchwork bedding was pegged and dancing to the wind's choreography did her mother give a grudging leave of absence. Lorna took off at a run, eager to get out of earshot before her resourceful parent thought of another task that needed doing. She had been separated from Rome for far too long.

* * *

After the Spring egg-collecting expedition, when Leonard Nancarrow had spied the sleeping girl in her knickers, he had gone in search of the hidden access to Pencarrick's grassy ledge. The entry was hard to find for it was not where he expected it to be.

At a spot where the main coastal path veered sharply inland, the ground to seaward fell away into a scrub of blackthorn and gorse and a few wind-stunted trees. A wild crab-apple tree pushed out of this vegetation and something about the distortion of its lower bough attracted his attention. Looking closely he saw that the moss that grew abundantly on the rest of the bark had been worn away on this particular limb. Grasping the sturdier part close to the trunk, he pressed himself up for a bird's-eye-view. Beneath him, in the seemingly impenetrable coastal jungle, he spotted a rudimentary path. It was a simple matter to swing out on the bough and lower himself down.

On that first visit to the promontory's ledge he'd made himself comfortable and enjoyed a smoke in the spring sunshine. The Penrose kid's hideaway met with his approval for it offered a grand view out over the sweep of the bay and its spongy grass was a damn sight more relaxing than his broken bedsprings at home.

The idea for a fine prank formed in his mind. When the little maid next visited he would be waiting for her. Waiting and in hiding. He wouldn't hurt her of course, just give her the shock of her life by pretending to push her off the ledge. He liked the idea of visiting upon another his own barely controlled fear of heights.

Len had revisited Pencarrick many times since but had never once encountered Lorna. Initially this was a disappointment but appreciating both the solitude of the grassy ledge and its spectacular view he soon grew fond of the place. Whenever the taunting at home became more than he could bear he slammed out of the house and headed for the Point. It was somewhere to indulge in his favourite fantasy about suddenly coming upon sleeping girls. In his imagination if not in life their knickers were always accessible.

* * *

Leonard was packing his possessions into the battered suitcase lying open on his bed. Tomorrow he was going away. His call-up papers for National Service had come and he was ordered to report to the barracks in far-away Aldershot. From his bedroom window he saw Lorna as she ran across the back field towards the cliffs. On impulse, he abandoned the sorting of his meagre belongings and followed her.

He sauntered along, taking a last look at the bay. The symbolism of the gulls confidently riding the cliff-currents on effortless wings was not lost on him. He was aware that he too was about to fly and was not sorry to be leaving. He wondered without emotion if he would ever return. In day-dreaming about overseas postings and wider experiences, he entertained no thought that his call-up might actually clip his primaries.

For the past three years he had been working over at Boskelly Farm where his employer treated him like the pig-shit he was paid to shovel. His meagre wages gave him a few coins to jingle in his pocket and a limited financial independence that enabled him to indulge in an evening pint at the pub and a game of darts or billiards. Yet even these harmless outings were spoilt by the ranting confrontations that followed when he got home. His chapel-going, teetotaller father never failed to condemn all recreation in a public house as 'the goings-on of Satan'.

His mother gave him an equally hard time, especially on paydays.

'Now that you're earning you can't expect free bread and board. It's only right and proper that you pay your way.'

Paying his way would have been fair enough but the sum that his mother demanded for his keep was the best part of his earnings.

In these rows over money he was always outnumbered for his father took delight in supporting the matriarch's avaricious demands. 'You don't know when you're well off, boy, that's your trouble. If you don't like the deal you're getting here at home, you can always fork-out like ol' James Penrose does and get yourself lodgings with Dolly Rosevear at Penbliss House.'

The nagging did not stop with the sarcastic and impractical suggestion that Leonard earned enough to afford boarding-house rates.

'What do you do with your wages anyway but piss them up against a wall? Your mother can put your money to better use.'

On cue, his mother would rejoin the attack. 'Thoughtless, that's your trouble, my lad. You've no idea what it costs me to satisfy an appetite like yours.'

Further protest was pointless. To stop the barracking he would hand over the majority of his earnings into his mother's grasping hand.

Sick and fed up with the nagging and the narrowness of his life, Len viewed the arrival of his call-up papers as a sweet relief. The timing was right, he couldn't wait to get away.

Following the coastal path, he caught sight of Lorna as she emerged from the gorse to climb the steep field above Blissey beach but then lost her again as she mounted the stile and dropped down into the lower field beyond.

* * *

Freed from scullery duties Lorna covered the undulating miles to Kilcarrick without so much as stopping for breath. She made the ascents by pressing hands to thigh muscles to urge her legs on. Once over the top she flew down the precipitous slopes with arms outstretched for balance. The miles were covered so quickly that she arrived at the cliff-top above Kilcarrick well before the water was clear of the steps.

Being deprived of Rome's company for a whole week had made her wretched yet the prospect of seeing him again produced symptoms equally dramatic. Her stomach was as knotted as her father's though for a very different reason: Jim's discomfort was due to alcohol abuse of an already damaged digestive system, Lorna's colly-wobbles were induced by the nervous excitement of expectation.

Arrived above the Haven she scoured the inlet for a glimpse of Rome but could see no sign of him. From the state of the tide she guessed it would be a full thirty minutes before the sea receded sufficiently to allow even wading access to the beach. Too impatient to sit passively waiting, she turned and walked back the way she had come intending to wile away the minutes by visiting her neglected camp out on the promontory.

* * *

Today, as on his previous visits to Pencarrick, Leonard found the ledge unoccupied. Responding to the call of nature he piddled over the cliff-edge. Long after the citrus arc had ceased he remained standing there, fighting his vertigo and holding his limp member in his hand. Two white swans leading a flight of their full-grown but grey offspring appeared out of Port Blissey's distant harbour. The powerful beat of wings and the sight of those long necks thrusting towards their destination served as another reminder of his own imminent flight. His spirits lifted: the omens were good. Tomorrow he too would be as free as a bird.

Watching the swans pass close to Penblissey Head, he spotted Dirty Dingle. Idly he wondered what the old goat was doing hiding himself in the cliff blackthorn. A glimpse of sunlight on glass gave him the answer. The vagrant's binoculars were not focused on the family of swans but were directed towards the beach below. Though Blissey's sands were hidden from Len's view he guessed what the old bugger was up to and laughed. If not spying on some woman undressing under a towel he would be drooling over the antics of an unsuspecting courting couple. Letting his imagination dwell on such activities, he lay down amongst the sea-pinks to masturbate.

Alerted by a dull thud and a scuffling in the vegetation, Leonard realised that someone else had dropped from the crab-apple tree. Remembering his intended prank, he wondered if the intruder could be Lorna Penrose. Seeking a hiding place, he wriggled backwards into the curtain of bracken. As Lorna came into view he held his breath and tried not to rustle the jagged fronds that concealed him.

* * *

The magnetic attraction at Kilcarrick meant that Lorna had neglected her Pencarrick camp. Her most recent visit had been weeks earlier when she had shown the secret place to Rome. She expected the hidden path to be overgrown and near impassable with a summer's growth of brambles. Instead she found the way well-trodden and obstacle free. The thought that her special place might have become the playground of other children was unbearable and she hoped that the user was Dirty Dingle for she accepted the vagrant's right to be there.

Breaking cover from the undergrowth it was a relief to find her territory unoccupied. She looked first out to sea and then down onto the granite jaws that jutted menacingly from the swirling water. A pair of cormorants postured on the rocks below, hanging their wings out to dry. The cormorants looked so archaic that she could easily believe that they had been performing the self-same ritual since the age when dinosaurs ruled the world.

* * *

It was the girl who moved first. She seemed to sense his presence and turned wide-eyed to peer into the vegetation where he was hiding. He could see that she was trying to decipher his crouching and unfamiliar shape camouflaged by the bracken fronds. Unblinking, she backed away, staggering towards the cliff edge. Forgetful of his original intention, Leonard moved fast, his reactions sharpened by the many close shaves of his egging escapades. Seizing her by an arm he dragged her away from the precipice.

The silly wench, not understanding that he was to trying to save her, began to scream. He closed his hand over her mouth to silence the noise but she bit into his flesh, drawing blood and began to fight back. Anger aroused, he wrestled her to the ground. She continued to scream, her small fists raining blows on his chest. The ferocity of her fight surprised him.

To pin her thrashing arms he dragged her frock up over her head and to stifle her shrieking he pushed the fabric into her mouth. In raising her frock he not only uncovered the frequently dwelt upon knickers but bared the little buds of her developing breasts. His right hand closed about her throat, the left he pressed to her loosening thighs. Possessed by a monstrous lust he could not stop.

Chapter 22

Dark Webs

The chilling cries coming from the Pencarrick direction had a demoralising effect on Nick Dingle's nerves. He rationalised the screaming as just some silly little maids playing childish games on a Saturday afternoon and put them out of his mind. It was later in the day, when out checking his rabbit snares, that he discovered the obvious disturbance to the vegetation that usually hid the entry to Pencarrick's grassy ledge.

Pencarrick was a favoured haunt for Nicholas for when the weather was fair there was no spot more comfortable. The point gave an uninterrupted view of the heavens and on clear nights he liked to stargaze before he went to sleep. There was one star in particular that twinkled a different colour from the rest and its brightness reminded him of Flora's flaxen, shining glory. He liked to imagine that his Flora was up there, watching over him, waiting for him to join her.

Not much that occurred on the cliffs escaped his attention. He knew that others used his eyrie, namely the little Penrose maid and that young villain Nancarrow who earlier in the year had raided his best egging sites. He rarely visited his vantagepoint during the day and as both youngsters seemed as keen as he was to keep the hideaway a secret he was philosophical about them using it. In fact there was some advantage in sharing the place for the lad dropped his butt-ends there. Nick added the salvaged tobacco to the tin carried in the inside breast pocket of his threadbare jacket.

Today, discovering the trampled vegetation, he was annoyed with the interlopers. A herd of stampeding cattle could not have made the previously hidden path more obvious.

* * *

Dingle's herd of cattle had been no more than one pair of legs. Leonard Nancarrow, coming to his senses and realising the enormity of his offence, was thrown into a blind panic. Ignoring the twisting path he beat a direct route of escape through bracken, gorse and bramble. His single objective was to get away from the horror of the defiled, bloody and motionless thing that he had abandoned on Pencarrick's ledge.

* * *

Nick Dingle followed the path of havoc, muttering his irritation. His grumbling was silenced into a stunned disbelief when he broke through onto the ledge and found himself gazing down upon the part-naked body of a bloodied child. Overcome with an uncontrollable shaking, he sank to his knees.

Closing his eyes did nothing to blot out the violence. Before him he saw a procession of mutilated corpses, their injuries horrible. Some lay half-submerged in the filthy water of shell holes, others were part-swallowed by trench mud or hung, like vermin, rotting on the wire.

'Rat meat all,' Nick intoned over them. 'Rat meat all.'

His basic instinct was one of self-preservation. An inner voice told him to run, to forget what he had found. He struggled to his feet, knowing that he could do no good here. To get involved was likely to bring both grief and trouble and he'd suffered more than a bellyful of these difficult companions already. The sun broke from the cloud to light both Nick's ashen face and the child's violated flesh, but could warm and revive neither.

A recollection of the screams he had chosen to ignore earlier in the day returned to torture him. With the evidence before him he could picture all too vividly the ordeal that the child had suffered. Why hadn't he responded to her cries? Hadn't he heard the terror in them? Was he grown so callous, so indifferent that he could turn his back on suffering? Knowing that he might have intervened to save the little maid increased his anguish. He sank to his knees again, this time to beg forgiveness of a maker whom he knew from experience to be indifferent.

'Dear Lord, forgive me, a poor sinner, for my failings.'

His supplication over, he rose, intending to put as much distance as possible between himself and the scene of such obscenity. In taking a final compassionate look at the murdered child he thought he saw a slight trembling of her rib cage. Though telling himself that the movement was mere wishful thinking or perhaps his rheumy eyes playing tricks, he drew closer to the body. The little chest stirred again and this time he knew that he was not mistaken. He knelt, removed his greasy trilby and pressed the greying bristle of his once black whiskers to the bitten and abused torso.

The detection of a fluttering pulse made him weep with relief. He dragged the child's clothing down to cover the haemorrhage between her thighs then wrapped her tenderly in his tattered jacket. In administering to her, he crooned all the while, 'You poor little maid, don't go and leave old Nick. Don't leave old Nick.'

He understood the risk he was taking, just as he had known that night, after the heavy shelling had forced them to fall back. For hours they had listened to Ted, their comrade, calling out from the midst of the carnage. They had waited for dark, then he and the corporal had crawled out of the trench again, out into no-man's-land, to bring their pal back.

When the flares found them they lay in convincing imitations of the grotesques about them. When the concealing darkness returned they crawled on. The corporal said that someone up there must have been watching over them that night, for they had got back to their own lines unharmed and brought Ted in with them.

Not until they cut away his battle tunic did they realise the extent of Ted's abdominal wounds. He lived only minutes more. The corporal had bought it in the next push. Two more to join the procession of comrades that the mud of Flanders claimed for its own. Yet he had survived. Survived to live on with the guilt of having to remember all those dead dears.

Taking the unwanted responsibility into his arms, Nicholas struggled to his feet. Once again he was putting his head above the parapet. Clutching his limp burden, he pushed through the wire of brambles and strode purposefully into the glare of the public searchlight beyond.

* * *

At first the little maid's weight did not seem burdensome and he reached the stile that overlooked the sweep of the bay without so much as a pause. In the middle distance the beacon of Port Blissey's lighthouse beckoned him on. After the initial climb, the path ran downhill for some distance and gravity helped him navigate the tussocky field. Further into the descent there were stiffer hazards to negotiate. Gorse bushes snatched at his trousers and rabbit holes opened beneath his feet as if intent on snaring him. He gave thanks when he reached the bottom without taking a tumble.

Before him the swollen stream gurgled angrily beneath its narrow bridge. Usually, the slimed wooden walkway presented no obstacle to one renowned for his goat-footed sureness but today was different. His arms were locked awkwardly around the child depriving him of his usual means of balance. Mid-stream, his foot slipped on a greasy plank and he almost dropped his human encumbrance. Perspiration broke on his brow as he adjusted his hold to take a firmer grip. It was sweet relief to gain the Blissey bank without further mishap.

Collecting his breath, Nick embarked on the steep ascent to the crown of Penblissey Head. Barely half way up, his muscles started to tremble, his breathing became increasingly laboured and his heart began to pump alarmingly. He told himself that he was used to painful burdens that could not be put down. His body contradicted him by breaking out in sweat yet not even the bayonet that stabbed mercilessly into his side could halt his progress.

'We can do it, I know we can do it. I'll not let you die, little maid,' he promised. 'I'll not let you die.'

This pledge came from the black fogou of his history. It was the self-same promise made to his lovely Flora as she lay in child-bed agony, her flaxen-hair darkened and fastened to her brow by perspiration.

* * *

Flora had been in labour for twenty-four hours. The midwife had been called away to attend a difficult delivery in a neighbouring village and although Nick went all over the parish in search of the doctor, he was unable to find him. Overcome with the sense of his own uselessness, he could only watch the punishment of Flora's racking but ineffectual contractions. Though he pressed the heels of his hands to his ears it did little to deaden her cries.

'I'll not let you die, my little maid,' he promised.

It had been an impotent vow for Flora had left him, departing this life with the baby still breeched inside her. He buried them both, his Flora, to whom he'd never had the chance to be a proper husband, and the poor little mite who had never taken breath and was another man's child.

* * *

Nick reached the summit of Penblissey Head wheezing from his exertions. His chest felt as if it were about to burst and the pounding of his heart was frightening for its thundering seemed to come from somewhere outside himself. Never before had he experienced such a sensation, not even in the hellhole of Flanders. He was close to collapse but knew that if his heart failed him at a spot so remote from habitation, the little maid would surely die. He cursed his frailty and cried his shame aloud. It would be history repeating itself: his comrade at arms Ted, his sweet wife Flora and now the little Penrose maid, no matter how hard he tried, he could not save them.

His knees buckled and, with the girl still held fast to his breast, he slumped against a granite gatepost. He had failed again.

* * *

After declaring Dingle sane, the doctors opened the asylum doors and ushered him out into a world temporarily at peace with itself. With nowhere else to go, Nicholas returned to his mother's cottage in Port Blissey. He came home to an old woman, for his mother was prematurely aged. As for the cottage, it surprised him to see how untouched it was by the war he remembered raging there. Refusing the offer of his mother's bed, he slept on a mattress in the small sitting room. After the discomforts he had known, the snug cottage seemed like gracious living. His mother had cared for him through the time of his troubles, now it was his turn to support her. Earning a living became his first objective.

The run-down Lanhedra estate was but a shadow of its pre-war magnificence and there was no employment for him there. Being too much of a landlubber to be accepted as a fisherman, he went cap in hand to the canning factory asking for work. The manager was sympathetic, but he wanted cheap labour and preferred to employ women. The out-of work Nicholas was at desperation point when the local fish-buyer, still in mourning for a son lost in the Great War, took pity on him. He was offered and accepted a job as fish packer in the harbour-side store.

The work was repetitive and hard, often starting at dawn when the fleet returned to port. The fish had to be gutted, weighed, then preserved in broken ice that first had to be smashed with picks from great frozen blocks. When packed, the fish-boxes were loaded onto open lorries, their destination the Billingsgate Market, two hundred and fifty miles away in London.

Work in the store was hardest in autumn when huss, otherwise known as dogfish were running in the channel. Nick's job was to spear the evil shark-like heads on hooks fixed to the wall then use bare hands and brute strength to skin the obstinate spotted hides from gills to tail. This lucrative catch was mostly destined for the capital city's fish and chip shops where the sweet pink flesh was battered, fried, graced with the name Rock Salmon and served to hungry customers in yesterday's newspapers.

Nicholas hated the dead eyes, the splattering blood and the fishy stink of his work. Cold-blooded creatures were so different from the warmth of fur and feathers that had been the love of his Lanhedra boyhood. Having to spend his hours of paid employment handling the corpses of marine life was a cruel sentence for a lover of living creatures, but he stuck to his task for there was no other work on offer.

His day's labour over, he would hurry home to his mother's cottage. To rid his flesh of the stink of fish he routinely took the zinc bath from the hook in the outhouse, carried it into the kitchen and set it before the open fire. The tub was filled with water from the kettles and pans that his mother set on the hearth to heat in readiness for his return. Before immersing himself, Nick added liberal splashes of Dettol to the water. The pungent twang of the disinfectant disguised the fishy odour but, no matter how thoroughly he scrubbed, he would still find some glistening fish-scales adhering to his skin long after he had bathed. He told his mother that he thought he might be turning into a fish, and in his wilder moments believed this to be true.

He made a friend at the fish-store, or rather William Way made a pal of him. Willy had been too young for the war and envied the older man his fighting experience.

Despite this envy, Willy paid Nick scant respect, even heckling him about his mental problems.

'D'you know, Nick my 'andsome, you be the only bloody one of us what 'ave been in the asylum, yet only you 'ave a certificate saying you be sane.'

Nick tolerated the teasing because lucky Willy was married to Flora. Flora whose mass of flaxen curls so bewitched Nicholas that he could barely control the overwhelming urge to trail his fingers through their ripeness. In his dreams and imagination he was more daring and would press his lips into their soft tumblings.

Willy's wife had the sweetness of nature so often found in simpletons. Though backward in matters scholastic and equally artless in the ways of the wider world, she kept a tidy house for Willy, fed him well, and idolised her swarthy young husband.

After spending an evening in The Anchor and drinking a few more pints than was good for him, Will chose to boast about aspects of his marriage that more properly should have been kept private.

'Show me a man who goes and marries a woman for her brains and you'd be showing me a fool. My Flora may not be button-bright but she's all there in other departments. She's got breasts as soft as air cushions and the sweetest little fanny a man could ask for. What's more she's happy and willing to gratify my every whim.' He gave a self-satisfied wink after this revelation. 'I reckon I've got everything a bloke needs to keep him in clover.'

Nick found such talk offensive but one of their drinking companions was more than happy to elaborate on William's theme.

'Tis all very well for you to gloat, Willy, but you deprived the rest of us of a community service when you went and married your Flora. Every boy in Blissey chased after her.' Flora's advocate chortled into his pint of mild and bitter, 'And some got proper poetic about her.'

Raising his glass in salute, he declaimed his verse loud enough for the whole of the public bar to hear.

'There's no maid in Blissey more eager to kiss ee, than Flo. Thick as two planks, so there's no need to wank, go to Flo.'

It was Nick who hit him.

* * *

A loss of sensation in his left arm reminded Nicholas of the helpless child he was holding. He knew that he should be concentrating on his present duty, not dwelling on past failures. The little maid had been lying out on the point for hours and needed urgent medical attention. He understood only too well the risks of further delay. Loosening his coat from about her, he listened again for a pulse. The faint rhythm of life was sufficient motivation for him to shoulder his burden again and stumble on.

Two fields and a footpath later he reached the tarmac road, but there was no feeling of elation. His journey had taken too long and he feared that the child had died in his arms. Yet, for once, luck seemed to be with him. Almost immediately he had the comfort of hearing the grind of a large motor coming up the hill out of Port Blissey. Blundering into the middle of the road, he lurched into the path of the on-coming vehicle.

Alf Hicks had been delivering coal on the Treblissey council estate. The sudden mid-road appearance of Dirty Dingle, apparently bent on suicide, gave him a shock. He stamped on his brakes late and only just avoided hitting the old man.

'You silly old bugger, what the hell are you up to?' he shouted from his cab.

Alf saw the camouflaged shape, but not until Nicholas wrenched the passenger door open and pushed his burden up onto the bench seat did the jacket flap open. He gaped, bolt eyed, at what the bundle contained.

'My God man, what have you got there?'

Gathering up the child's bloody body, the vagrant's eyes blazed. Forgetful that Blissey men were not accustomed to taking orders from him, he commanded, 'Get this lorry moving, you fool. We've got to get her to the medics.'

Without further question, Alf put the lorry into a lurching gear. He thrashed the ancient engine all the way to the hospital, testing its suspension on every bend of the twisting road.

Not until he drew-up at the hospital's main entrance did the driver allow his eyes to be drawn from the road to the nightmare in Dirty Dingle's arms. The old man was crying, rocking the little body and stroking its dark hair.

'Poor little maid, poor little maid,' he moaned, pressing his bearded lips to the matted hair. 'Don't leave me, Flora, you mustn't leave me.'

Alf, eager to disassociate himself from Dirty Dingle, explained to the medical staff his own limited role in the mercy mission. At the same time he could not resist passing judgement on the older man.

'God knows what made him do it. He must 'ave lost what are left of his wits, poor soul.'

Chapter 23

Victims

Jerome, nerves taut as guitar strings and his nights ragged with dreams, was convinced that under pressure of questioning from her inquisitors Lorna would be forced to admit to their secret confederacy. His unauthorised occupation of the Kilcarrick cottage and Lorna's fabrication of the Eileen Stone alibi would be more than enough evidence to condemn them for no one would believe in the innocent nature of their association.

With no expectation of reprieve he kept a constant cliff-vigil for the posse coming to arrest him. Alert to the possibility that his seekers might arrive by police launch his ears tuned to listen for the throb of a marine engine. As a boy he had thrilled at the sight of the River Police patrolling the Thames but as an outlaw he dreaded a water-borne appearance of blue uniforms.

The magic of Kilcarrick was transformed utterly. The gentlest of waves took on a threatening aspect, the musical gurgle of the little stream became an irritation and the looming cliffs cast shadows that seemed to be closing in on him. Even the metallic mewing of the gulls, once an exhilarating wake-up call, sounded mournful in the extreme. His playground had become his holding pen.

Sleep was elusive. When unconsciousness did arrive he was haunted by dreams of raised truncheons and prison bars, symbols of punishment and incarceration that stayed with him throughout his waking hours. Yet, in all this nervous time of watching, listening and waiting, the expected invasion of arresting officers failed to materialise.

* * *

In awaiting the arrival of the Cornish Constabulary, the staff at Budruth Hospital detained Dingle by locking him in a small consulting room. This enforced confinement was too much a reminder of his years of detention in the asylum and Nicholas hammered on the door and cried to be released. When the exertion of his pleas and hammering failed to deliver him, he cursed his captors with ripe obscenities that he had not aired since his army days.

The turning of a key did not signify freedom. Instead his gaolers' uniforms changed from the pristine whites of the nursing staff to the dark blue serge of officers of the law. He had known that it would turn out like this. Standing amidst the bloody desecration out on Pencarrick Point he had understood the personal risk involved in trying to save the little maid.

The coppers read him his rights, took him outside and bundled him roughly into the back of their Black Maria. With no more fight left in him, he offered no resistance and went unprotesting. At journey's end they dragged him from the police car just as unceremoniously. Weakened from their earlier exertions his legs failed him and he fell. Resigned to the rough treatment, he made no complaint about the grazes to both his knees and wrist.

Inside Budruth's police station two plain-clothes detectives led him to a windowless room sparsely furnished with a table and three chairs. Once seated the detectives fired a barrage of questions infinitely more menacing than the physical aggression of the uniformed plods who had carried out his arrest.

'All I did was try to help her,' he insisted but his protests of innocence were ignored.

'Why make it worse for yourself, Dingle? You're covered in the child's blood. Do you really expect us to believe that you found her in that state?'

Nick examined his shabby trousers and soiled shirt. The only blood he could see were the smears on knees and cuff that came from the grazes suffered in falling from the police car. He supposed that the blood they spoke of must be on the jacket that he had wrapped around the bleeding child. This they had taken away as evidence.

'Tell us what really happened, Dingle.'

'I told the other coppers as much as I know and I've got nothing to add.'

'We'll see about that, my lad.'

Nicholas was nobody's lad, certainly not this fresh-faced strip of a policeman's.

' I found the little maid and tried to save her and that's the truth.' He ventured the question that was tormenting him. 'Is she going to live?'

'Shut up, Dingle. We're asking the questions, not you,' snapped the heavyweight of the two interrogators. He leant threateningly across the table until his face was only inches from Nick's own. 'You say you found her. But why go out to that forsaken spot if you didn't already know the girl was there?'

'I was walking the cliffs like I always do. When I got to Pencarrick I saw where someone or something had beaten a way through the bushes. I went out on the point to find out what they'd been up to.'

The younger detective took up the questioning, his tone becoming sympathetic.

'You went back for her, didn't you? You hadn't meant to harm her, I can see that. You regretted what had happened so you returned to put things right. That's how it was, wasn't it?'

They wanted him to be guilty, that much was obvious.

He made a token protest, though there seemed little point in wasting his breath.

'I told you, I didn't know the little maid was there.'

'Going back for the girl proves that you didn't intend to kill her. It will save us all a lot of time and things will go easier for you if you come clean and admit to what really happened.'

The use of the word '*kill*' convinced Nicholas that the child was dead.

'Poor little maid. I wanted to save her.'

As usual he had been too late and his efforts in vain. Bowing his head, he wept, the unaccustomed tears making tracks in the ingrained dirt of his face.

A fist crashed onto the table. 'You blubbering, perverted bastard. What about your victim? Did she shed tears when you half-throttled her? Did she scream when you forced your filthy cock inside her clean little body?'

The younger man intervened. 'Easy Stan, no need for that. Look Mr Dingle, our forensic boys are going to find your pubic hair and other unsavoury bits of you all over the girl. It would save us a lot of time and you would be doing yourself a favour if you confess. Get it all over and done with now and you'll feel better.'

But Nicholas wasn't saying any more. He played the deaf-mute, refusing to respond to either their cajoling or their threats. Exasperated, they locked him in a cell. It was five hours since he had found Lorna and no one had so much as offered him a cup of tea.

* * *

What the police believed to be an open and shut case was scuppered when the police surgeon made his report to Detective Inspector Hawkins, the officer in charge of the enquiry.

'Sorry to disappoint you inspector, but there's no way the old man committed the assault.'

The news was unwelcome but Hawkins' facial expression didn't change.

'How can you be so sure? The child's in intensive care and you've been unable to examine her.'

'No, but I've spoken to the doctor who admitted her and I've examined Dingle. According to the medical notes the girl has multiple bruising and external wounds on her limbs and torso. The ones on her back are mainly scratches made by the gorse, but fingernails gouged the others. I've done a thorough check of your suspect's hands and there's not a trace of either skin or blood under the nails.'

'Couldn't he have cleaned himself up before he went back to get her?'

'Cleaned himself up! You've seen the state of him: he has the dirt of ages under those fingernails and none of it has been disturbed recently.'

'What about the blood on his jacket?'

'The blood is on the inside and commensurate with him wrapping it around the girl and carrying her across those cliffs for a couple of miles. That's something your forensic team will doubtless confirm when they've completed their examination. Anyway, the hospital has come up with a conclusive piece of evidence that clears your suspect.'

'And what's that?'

'The girl was bitten on her left breast and her attacker left teeth marks so clear that his dentist could make him a new set from the impression.'

Why does that rule out the vagrant?'

'The rapist has a full set of pearls, the old man's jaw is all gaps and stumps.' He gave a sympathetic shake of the head. 'I'm afraid your enquiry has only just begun.'

The inspector groaned, experience should have told him that it was never that easy.

'It's a damn nuisance, finding this out now. We've lost a lot of time.'

His colleague concurred. 'It's too dark to do anything more out on Pencarrick tonight. The real investigation will have to wait until morning.'

'At least the area is taped and we've posted officers out there to ward away the curious. Keep your fingers crossed that the rain holds-off. If it doesn't, then vital evidence is going to be washed away overnight.'

'What shall we do with the old man?' asked his fresh-faced junior colleague.

'I've a feeling there's something he's not telling us so we're not going to release him yet. Buy him in a decent meal and make sure that he's comfortable. We'll question him again in the morning.'

The inspector cursed their previous heavy-handedness; it would be difficult to win the old boy's co-operation now.

* * *

With the isolation of Kilcarrick Haven still undisturbed Jerome began to share something of Lorna's optimism. Their escape from detection seemed little short of miraculous yet, as day followed uneventful day, his fear of persecution receded. Convinced that some benevolent, supernatural force had intervened to protect them, he stood in the waves and offered-up a heathen prayer of thanks to their old friend and provider Poseidon.

As a diversion from his loneliness he made-up flippant puns about their lucky escape. Obviously the *holiness* of the cottage's roof rendered the strong arm of the law *'armless*. Yet such puns fell flat without a companion to match them. In more sombre mood he swore never again to put Lorna at risk for next time their luck might not hold. Common sense told him that the only certain way to keep Lorna safe would be to ensure that there never would be a next time.

The autumnal storm was a reminder that winter was approaching and a further gale could easily dislodge the whole roof and render the cottage uninhabitable. Until now he had been operating in a time of plenty, subsisting largely on the liberality of land and sea but the onset of winter would bring deprivations and hardships so far unknown. Even in the mildness of a climate favoured by the Gulf Stream's Atlantic drift it was hardly feasible that he could over-winter in the damp cottage. It was time to admit that Kilcarrick had never been more than a temporary refuge and that he would have to go away.

All the wealth he possessed had been withdrawn from his Post Office account before leaving London. The withdrawal was no fortune, barely enough to buy his train ticket and keep him in essentials for a few months. His remaining funds had dwindled to just a few pounds and to survive he needed to earn more. There was little prospect of finding work in Cornwall so his best option would be to go abroad. France was the obvious choice. He was competent in the language and had things turned out differently he would have gone on to read French at university. Recalling the promise of that brighter Cambridge future he mourned the life that now could never be. This brief wallowing in self-pity was an indulgence that he could ill afford and forcing himself into a more positive frame of mind he began to make plans.

His remaining funds were probably insufficient to cross the channel as a fare-paying passenger and anyway he did not relish the idea of arriving penniless on foreign soil. His only hope of remaining solvent was to pick up a France-bound cargo boat at Budruth Quay and perhaps work the short passage. Once landed in France he could hitchhike south to Burgundy or Bordeaux where, at this time of year, the vineyards would be looking for casual labour.

With emigration decided upon, he was tempted to walk to Budruth Quay to arrange an early sailing but loyalty to Lorna delayed him. He knew that in leaving home soil there was no guarantee that he would ever return. Lorna would regard his flight as a betrayal and a breaking of the promise made to her on the morning after the storm. He could not desert her without saying goodbye and telling her why and where he was going. Yet it was a wretched thing to be the harbinger of unhappiness to someone who had brought him so much joy.

Tormented by guilt and regret he stalked his domain and brooded. The stunted valley trees had been stripped of their leaves by the storm so that even the landscape seemed to reflect the barrenness he felt in his heart.

* * *

The weekend arrived but Lorna did not. Her failure to appear prolonged Jerome's agony and left him feeling frustrated and anxious. When they had parted he had urged her to stay away from Kilcarrick but now, impatient to be gone, he was desperate to bid her farewell. The tidal rhythms repeated themselves, first by cutting off the Haven from the cliff approaches and then linking it again. He kept an anxious vigil but Lorna failed to appear.

On Sunday impatience made him pre-empt the tide by wading to the Blissey steps. The idea was to intercept Lorna before she reached Kilcarrick. He hoped that by breaking the news of his departure on neutral and less emotive ground he might be softening the blow.

Cresting the steep field that sloped towards Pencarrick Point he was unsettled by the unexpected sight of a group of milling figures. His unorthodox appearance was made even more eccentric by his recent walk through the waves and he had no wish to draw attention to himself. Fearful of detection, he beat a hasty retreat. Fate definitely seemed to be conspiring against him.

* * *

Had Jerome stayed longer, or been less preoccupied, he would have seen that the intruders on the cliffs were not casual walkers. Some were uniformly clad and like the chief constituents of his nightmares they wore distinctive helmets. The police reinforcements had been at Pencarrick since first light and were meticulously searching the whole area. At the scene of the crime they found fragments of child's clothing that told only too vividly what had happened there.

It had drizzled overnight but not enough to erase the prints they were looking for. On the Point itself the only evidence of the attacker was the flattened vegetation but inland, in the bare soil of the public footpath where cattle rather than walkers had worn away the turf, they found several sets of prints. Some, like the bite mark on Lorna's breast, were near perfect impressions.

Apart from the size elevens belonging to their own ranks, there were imprints of three other soles. From the impressions of the girl's size three sandals they were able to reconstruct her one-way passage as far as the cliff above Kilcarrick and then her return, but only as far as Pencarrick point. By checking back to the police station they established which of the other two sets belonged to Dingle. From deeper imprints it was possible to detect when the vagrant had been burdened by the weight of the child.

It was a third set of boot-prints that interested them most. They found many clear impressions leading from Port Blissey, though none beyond Pencarrick. Several incomplete, though distinct, marks indicated that the wearer had been running on the return journey. The imprints were measured at size nine. Unfortunately, the sole pattern matched that of the most common type of boot sold in local shoe shops. It was the identical footwear worn by the majority of the village's male population.

* * *

Jerome explained away Lorna’s continued absence by a simple piece of self-delusion: she had obviously taken to heart his warning about their vulnerability. Meeting the party of weekend walkers on the cliffs, she must have reacted as he had done and retreated. He sought consolation by telling himself that her decision had been the right one for it was safer to stay away.

Less comforting was the realisation that the demands of school would prevent her from visiting the cottage during the coming week. Five interminable days with only his unhappy-self for company was not a pleasing prospect yet he was resigned to postponing his departure. To run out on Lorna without saying goodbye was a worse option and the coward's way.

The emptiness of a further week of waiting made him lethargic. He no longer bothered to set the trammel net or light a fire. He quelled his hunger pangs by eating beans straight from the can and idled away the days staring out at the horizon in the direction of France. Mindlessly he gathered up a handful of sand, allowing the coarse grains to trickle through his fingers. The action reminded him that time was running out. He would wait for one more weekend but then, see Lorna or not, he would have to go.

Chapter 24

The Village

Dolly Rosevear did not like to question her lodger too closely about the condition of his granddaughter for James had returned from his visit to the cottage hospital looking ashen. In response to her gentle enquiry he muttered, 'It's bad, it's bad,' and without uttering another word retreated to the privacy of his room.

If truth were told, James Penrose senior was not over-fond of children. He was of the opinion that life would have been more peaceful, and certainly more prosperous, had he possessed rather fewer descendants. But, of his many grandchildren, Lorna was his favourite and he felt a real affection for the little girl.

As Dolly was hanging her Monday wash in the high garden of Polbliss House she heard excited voices rising from the street below. Two of Jim and Margaret's Treblissey neighbours were avidly discussing what had become the village's only topic of gossip.

'I've always expected that Dirty Dingle to do something like this. He terrifies my children. If they see him coming they do an about-turn and head off in the opposite direction double quick.'

'It's not just the kids he frightens, the sight of that old man is enough to make my blood run cold,' said a younger voice.

'According to Alf Hicks, Dirty Dingle was covered all over in her blood and Alfie should know for it was him who picked them up in his coal lorry and drove them to the hospital.'

'I heard from her own mother that the poor little mite had marks round her throat like a necklace of blue beads where his finger had been.'

'As if having his wicked way with her wasn't enough. Makes me queasy just thinking about it.'

'It does. He must have all but throttled the child. Hanging's too good for the likes of monsters like him.'

'And her internals are damaged something awful, they do say.'

'Dirty devil, doing that to a child. He deserves to have it cut off.'

'I say it's a blessing that Lorna's in a coma, at least she don't know nothing about it.'

The women passed on up the hill and their voices trailed away as Dolly dropped her pegs and hung on to her washing line for support. A corner of the freshly laundered sheet flapped down to trail in the dirt.

* * *

On the Tuesday, seventy-two hours after the attack, Lorna was still in intensive care and Nicholas remained locked in a cell at Budruth police station. He could not bear to be caged like some poor zoo animal denied its natural habitat. His captors' attitudes had softened and he was being treated as an honoured guest but that was of little comfort when what he really wanted was his freedom. Despite the copious cups of tea, victuals and tobacco they plied him, he remained steadfastly silent.

Detective Inspector Hawkins spoke to his men. 'We can't hold the old boy any longer. If he does know something about the attack then he has no intention of telling us. We might as well let him go.'

'He'd better not be released back to Port Blissey,' warned a sergeant who was better briefed on local matters than his inspector. 'Constable Bullock tells me that feeling in the village is running high and if the mob gets its hands on him there could be a lynching.'

The police had deliberately withheld the fact of Dingle's innocence. It suited their purpose that the real rapist should think himself safe and perhaps be put off-guard.

They were carrying out door-to-door checks in the village, seeking witnesses and examining the boots of all males of fourteen years and older. They justified this procedure to their interviewees by explaining that they needed to eliminate the innocent from their investigation.

The house-to-house enquiries had begun on the Treblissey estate, the nearest dwellings to the scene of the crime. The officer who called at the Nancarrow household found that the old Weslyan's boots were two sizes smaller than the ones they were interested in. On being questioned about the other male occupants, the master of the house told the policemen that his only son, Leonard, was away doing his National Service. The visit was recorded and the law, duly satisfied, left the family in peace.

Efforts by the Budruth constabulary to persuade Nicholas that he would be better off being released into the care of a hostel in the next county fell on deaf ears.

'I'm not going to foreign parts. Port Blissey's my home and that's where I belong,' he insisted.

As a safer alternative to Dingle's choice the inspector offered the continued hospitality of a Budruth police cell. Even with the assurance of an open door, Nicholas could not be persuaded.

'I know my rights. You got no cause to be depriving me of my freedom.'

'We're not depriving you of anything, man, we're concerned for your safety.'

Nicholas brushed aside the sergeant's explanation. 'You said yourselves that I'm innocent. Why should an innocent man be needing police protection?'

He had been restrained for too many years of his life. All he wanted was to return to the freedom of his beloved cliffs.

As a last attempt at persuasion, the inspector called for the help of Port Blissey's resident constable. It was hoped that PC Bullock's personal touch would prove more successful in reasoning with the determined old man.

'Now look here, Nick my 'ansome, you'd better listen and listen good,' George Bullock urged. 'Naturally enough there are people in the village who are angry and upset about the little maid and some of them believe you to be responsible whatever the evidence may be to the contrary. You know what can happen when men get the drink inside them. Take my word for it, it wouldn't be safe for you to come home at the present time.'

Nicholas considered his options but there was only one that he favoured.

'I got to get out, George, I can't breathe in here. If you was to tell the Blissey folk that it weren't me that did it they'd believe you and wouldn't have cause to hurt me.'

Though flattered by Dirty Dingle's confidence in him George Bullock was not nearly so certain that his authority as village policeman carried so much weight.

'I don't know about that. The village is looking for someone to blame and I'm not sure that they're much interested in hearing the truth. They're baying for blood and you don't want that blood to be yours, do you? Be sensible man. For you to go back to Blissey just now would be to court trouble. It's too damned risky.'

Nicholas listened to the warning but was still adamant. 'It's a risk I'm prepared to take. I'm going home, George, and there's an end to it.'

'On your head be it then. Until we've got the real culprit under lock and key there's bound to be folks who will doubt your innocence. We won't know who they might be or what they might do, not until it's too late.' He let this message sink in before continuing. ‘If you do come home, you mustn't expect a bodyguard. I can't play bloody nursemaid to you all the time, I've got other work to attend to.'

'I don't need no bodyguard. I've known these people for best part of a lifetime and they know me. In the past they've been good to me.’

What Dingle said was true. When the fish catches were plentiful, there was always someone willing to buy him a pint or to offer him a generous pinch of baccy. When the weather was at its worse and he needed more shelter than could be provided by an upturned boat, folks turned a blind eye to his trespass and permitted him to sleep in their outhouses. Some of the wives were generous too, providing him with treats and tit-bits at Christmas-tide. The very clothes on his back were hand-me-downs from widows who had the goodness of heart to pass on the belongings of their dear departed.

‘They're good folks I tell you,' Nicholas insisted, remembering past generosity.

'Good folks, they may be,' George Bullock cautioned, 'but these are special circumstances in difficult times.'

‘Just as long as you tell them it weren't me that hurt the little maid then I'll come to no harm.'

Nicholas let it be known that this was his last word on the subject and stubbornly refused to listen to further argument.

Bullock reported back to his senior officers. ‘Dingle won’t listen to reason. He’s determined to go back to Blissey and it’s a waste of good breath trying to persuade him otherwise.’

With some sighing and a clicking of tongues the old man’s would-be protectors gave in.

‘Fair enough, if that’s what he wants. But to be on the safe side we’d better set the record straight before we let him go. At least that might dampen the Blissey blood lust.’

The editor of the twice-weekly local rag was given the story to run in his mid-week edition. With Lorna's identity protected, Nicholas Dingle was hailed as the injured child’s deliverer. The newspaper coverage put much colourful emphasis on his age, infirmity and strength of character. Its headline announced:

GREAT-WAR VETERAN
RESCUES ATTACKED GIRL.

The article ran:

> It was the action of this frail and elderly man that undoubtedly saved the injured child’s

> life. His was an heroic journey, made against all physical odds. In seeking urgently needed medical assistance, he carried the stricken girl over precipitous cliff-tops and across swift flowing streams.

The article's emotive prose was sustained to the concluding paragraphs:

> A police spokesman commended Mr Dingle's unselfish actions and praised the outstanding endurance he demonstrated to effect this remarkable rescue. The matron of Budruth hospital, where the child is being treated, expressed her admiration and confirmed that without Mr. Dingle's prompt action the victim of the attack would most certainly have died.
>
> The parents continue their vigil at their daughter's bedside where her condition is said to be stable but causing concern.

The editor decided against printing a photograph of Nicholas to accompany this accolade. His fear was that the vagrant's unorthodox and suspicious appearance would undo any favourable opinion engendered by their carefully chosen words.

Inspector Hawkins contacted the vicar of Blissey parish and the ministers of the village's four chapels. These men of God were asked to assure their respective flocks of Nicholas Dingle's virtue and innocence and to counsel them to act charitably towards the emancipated ex-suspect.

As an extended part of the rehabilitation plan the local bobby was to spread the same intelligence to those inhabitants with more secular interests. Constable Bullock was told to visit every pub in Port Blissey to broadcast the official police view of Nicholas Dingle's innocence and worthy character. In the cause of furthering goodwill the constable was authorised to offer the drinkers free beer to be funded from petty cash at the taxpayers' expense.

* * *

In the spotlight now focused upon it Port Blissey was a buzz of excitement and indignation. When news of the atrocity broke the population had been greatly relieved that it was accompanied by the assurance that the perpetrator was already in police custody. This relief had been followed by a great outpouring of anger against Dirty Dingle.

The grubby eccentric had been a familiar figure on the edge of community life. Hadn't they always tolerated the anti-social behaviour of his solitary ways? Never had they interfered with the reclusive manner in which he chose to live. There were even those amongst them who encouraged the vagrant by making sure that he had shelter and food when times were hard. Even if mothers habitually threatened their wayward offspring with Dirty Dingle's retribution, in their hearts they had believed him harmless. The news of his arrest for the rape and grievous assault of one of their children kindled a hatred that would not be easily extinguished.

On Tuesday evening, in the cause of justice, Constable Bullock visited the Man o' War, The Anchor and finally The King's Head. At each of Blissey's alehouses the policeman proclaimed Dingle's innocence to the patrons with all the conviction that police petty cash could muster.

While the beer flowed in every sense freely, a few of the older imbibers chose to remember Nick's past deeds and spoke out in his defence.

'I never did believe him capable of doing such a thing. I've known the man all his life and violence baint part of his character.'

'Regular hero he was in the Great War. My father used to tell how Dingle were decorated and mentioned in despatches.'

'That be true. He did more than his bit in this last war too.'

The speaker took a deep draught of constabulary ale before illustrating his statement.

'Some of you will remember how the Behennas and Hunkins sailed their luggers over to Dunkirk to evacuate our boys off the beaches. Well, Clifford Polmount, God rest his soul, was all set to do the same but could find no bugger brave enough to go with him in his little tosher.'

One of the present company had been propositioned by the late Cliff Polmount for this very purpose. Taking the criticism personally, he offered a defence, 'Well, us all thought that old boat of his wouldn't stand up to the seas on the long channel run and a tosher was too small to carry many more than a dozen so it weren't worth the risk, were it?'

Nick's advocate ignored the interruption. 'Well, Cliff couldn't very well go alone, so he'd pretty well given up the idea when Nick volunteered. And him a landsman too.'

There was a pause to allow this intelligence to sink in.

'Many a time, Cliff told me the story of how they came under fire and he didn't want to risk no more than one run because he knew about Nick having suffered shell-shock from fighting in the trenches of the Great

War. But after they'd taken off the first boatload and brought them safe into Ramsgate Harbour, Nick wouldn't hear of stopping. Put Cliff to shame he did. There were thousands of poor devils left on them beaches and Nick said that if they could save only one more soul it would make the risk worthwhile. So they went back and made a second crossing.'

His drinking partners were subdued for a moment, quietly picturing what it must have been like for the two-man crew, already exhausted from the long haul up-channel. They were seamen themselves and could well imagine the terror of those dangerous channel-crossings: the tosher, overcrowded with wounded, being strafed by machine guns and vulnerable to bombing and mines.

'Dingle's always been a good man,' slurred another of the drinkers. 'When Willy Way fell, awkward like, off the back of the fish lorry and broke his neck it were Nick who took his young widow in and looked after her.'

'He did a sight more than that. He went and married the girl, even though she were a simpleton and seven months pregnant with Willy's child.'

'He worshipped that girl and that was what did for him. Flora died in childbirth, taking the unborn babe with her.'

'They do say,' another confided, ‘what with Flora already being heavy with child when they wed, she was never a proper wife to him in the bed department.'

This deprivation was a sobering thought that occasioned much sympathy. The general consensus being that conjugal reward was the least Nicholas deserved for the charity he had shown. Widow Dingle’s death was the final straw and after that he went proper downhill.

'He moved back in with his mother and took it awful hard when the old lady died. Didn't go to work at the fish-store no more and got sacked. Didn't take no pride in himself neither, forgot to launder his clothes or to bathe. That's when folks started calling him *Dirty* Dingle.'

Others, familiar with this more recent episode, added to it. 'Without a woman to do for him, he neglected to clean the house as well. When Vern Pollard, his landlord, called to collect the rent Nick wouldn't let him in. Eventually Vern sent in the bailiffs to evict him. Dingle didn't seem to care, he took to living rough. I suppose it could 'ave happened to any one of us if we'd been cursed with his bad fortune.'

'Poor old bugger!'

'Poor old sod.'

Sympathy often went best with beer.

'You call him old and that's how most folk hereabout think of him but you'd be wrong. Nick may look ancient with that trenched face of his but I could give him ten years,' continued their chief informant. 'He were only a boy when he fought in the first lot, so by my reckoning he can't be more than in his mid-fifties.'

'Baint no wonder he do look so worn, 'tis his grim life that have aged him.'

The others murmured their assent. 'That and being out in all weathers.'

It was a tragic tale and, for that evening at least, Nicholas had a loyal supporters' club.

In the more sober world, the majority of the population felt a general lack of confidence in the way the law had handled the business that had darkened their village. Although Dingle had been freed no other arrest had been made. Unrest was growing. In particular the community disliked the way that the continuing enquiries made suspects of all their men-folk. The mantle of saviour did not sit convincingly on the grimed shoulders of an eccentric who had spent years locked away in the asylum. Feeling against him rumbled on. Some merely grumbled, 'There's no smoke without fire, that's what I says.' But there were others whose prejudices had been sharpened by the sex and violence that had occurred out on the granite promontory and who muttered darker things.

Chapter 25

Betrayal

On Friday the news issuing from the cottage hospital was mixed: Lorna was out of intensive care, breathing without assistance but still unconscious. Margaret relayed this progress to her father-in-law whose face was showing the strain of the past week. She hoped Grandfer James would take some comfort from the report, but he was in agreement with his son that a coma was hardly cause for celebration.

Lorna's eldest cousin, Bernard Polmount, was not party to his aunt's news but was celebrating none-the-less. He was on the beer in the Man O' War. His drinking companions were Jack Mitchell, Ambrose Johns and the Trehennah brothers. It was Richard Trehennah's eighteenth birthday and their celebration marked both Dick's anniversary and the licence it gave him to get legitimately drunk with the rest of them.

'Drink up, Sunshine,' his elder brother, Daniel, encouraged. 'There's just time to get in another round before closing time.'

'Make mine a barley wine, Dan,' demanded Bernie. 'I'm going to need some additional fortification if we're going to give this bugger eighteen bumps after the landlord throws us out of here tonight.'

'Don't know about us being thrown out, but from the look of him I'd say young Dick's about to throw up.'

The birthday boy's unhealthy colour gave credence to Jack Mitchell's prediction.

Not appreciating this aspersion on his manhood, Dick put on a show of bravado illuminated by a sickly grin. 'I'll have a barley wine too. Bilge water's got more body than this here bitter.'

'Get a double in for him, Dan,' Ambrose encouraged. 'Your little brother needs some building up if he's taking Tina out tomorrow night. We don't want him disappointing her, do we?'

'That's my baby sister you're talking about, so watch your lip, tiddler,' Bernard commanded.

Emboldened by alcohol, Ambrose sniggered. 'It's all legal Bernie, she's old enough.' To prove his point he waxed lyrical, 'When roses are red they're ready for plucking, when girls are sixteen they're ready for f...'

He hadn't got beyond the initial consonant of his rhyme when a backhander from Bernie obliged him to duck his head.

'With what's happened in my family this last week, I'd have thought you would have more sense than talk like that.' Bernard was on his feet, his anger genuine.

'You didn't give me chance to finish, Bernie. Ready for *flirting* was what I was about to say.'

An angry Bernard was not a pretty sight and the others laughed in an attempt to defuse the situation.

Part appeased, Bernard sat down again.

'You artful bugger, Ambrose Johns. Too bloody clever by half, that's your trouble,' he growled.

With the next round of drinks in their glasses their camaraderie returned.

Long after the landlord had called time and symbolically shrouded his pumps with a bar cloth the birthday party was still carousing in a corner of the public bar. The publican, with rather more concern for his bed than enforcement of the statutory closing hour, threw them out as Bernard had predicted.

Jack Mitchell was the last of his customers to be assisted to the door.

'You should be ashamed of yourself, Jack, boozing with these bachelor boys when you've a wife and baby waiting for you at home. What will that little sea nymph of yours say when you roll in drunk?'

The others laughed at the landlord's banter for Jack's Susan wasn't noticeably smaller even though she had been delivered of the sprog.

'It's not them nights he's out with us but the ones he spends at home that Jack needs to worry about. From the look of his Sue we reckons he's gone and put another bun in the oven already, don't we lads?' teased Dan, careful to attribute the impertinence to them all.

Tired of these jibes, the skipper of *Sea Nymph Sue* was planning to rename his boat when he could think of something appropriately safe to call it.

'Christening the bloody boat *Albatross* would bring me less grief,' he complained.

Bernard offered the more controversial suggestion that he could always rename his ample wife.

Out on the dark street, Bernie announced that he needed a piss. All five wound an uncertain course onto the dark quayside where they unbuttoned their flies and practised some synchronised splashing as they relieved themselves into the harbour's gloomy waters.

Shaking his cock, Ambrose reminded the others that Dick's initiation to manhood was still incomplete and, with characteristic sadism, suggested an additional refinement to the promised eighteen bumps.

'After we've given him his bumps we'll wet birthday boy's head a second time by tossing him overboard.'

Though pretty far gone, Dick retained enough sobriety not to relish this watery prospect. While his drinking pals were still fumbling drunkenly with their fly-buttons, he broke away at a run. In boisterous spirits the others set off in baying and clumsy pursuit. Not wanting to be cornered at the end of the quay where the current ran swiftest, Dick wheeled onto the fish jetty. Amidst the jetty's confusion of nets, pots and fish-boxes he sought a safe hiding place.

His companions, not so drunk that they were unable to hear this manoeuvre, came whooping after him. Crouched in concealment behind a jumble of inkwell lobster pots, Dick grew nervous. His pursuers, though clumsily routing through the stacks of fish boxes, were closing in. He was trying to clear his fuddled brain to decide on his next move when he heard Bernie's triumphant cry.

'Got you, you young bugger. Now you're for it.'

But it wasn't Dick who rose silently from a makeshift bed on the tarred netting.

'What the hell?'

'Who've we got here then?'

It was Bernard who made the identification. 'Christ, it's Dirty Dingle!'

Dick came out of hiding as his boozing pals closed ranks about the old man, their mutual high spirits instantly transformed into a common baying for blood.

* * *

With his eyrie at Pencarrick despoiled, Nicholas had chosen to make his bed on the harbour. He lay in the relative comfort of a tumble of fishing net, lulled to drowsiness by the gentle lapping of water against the jetty. After his recent confinement he was grateful to have stars for his roof.

Disturbed by the bawling of youthful voices he became anxious. Anxiety turned to panic when powerful hands seized his shoulder in a vice-like grip. He could smell the drink on them and sensed as something tangible the blood lust radiating from their impetuous aggression. Looming over the jetty was the pointing forefinger of a derrick. Lit by the beams of the flashing lighthouse it cast an ominous gallows-like shadow. Remembering P.C. Bullock's warning, Nick regretted his bravado about returning to Blissey.

Their handling of the old man was contemptuous. What started as an accusatory and spiteful jabbing of fingers progressed to a cuffing that dislodged his trilby. When he was bareheaded the aggression escalated into more serious violence. Hands clenched into fists so that the ill-tempered prodding converted into punches. One set of knuckles buried themselves in the victim's solar plexus and he doubled in pain.

All the while his attackers relentlessly forced Nicholas backwards towards the jetty's edge. The tide was in and he couldn't swim. Drowning wasn't the way he wanted to go. His nerve gave way and so did his bowels. The smell was overwhelming.

His assailants drew back but then began to laugh. 'The old pervert's gone and shit himself.'

'Then we'd better make sure he takes a bath.'

Powerful hands grasped Nicholas by the collar. He was pushed onto his heels so that his upper body was angled to overhang the jetty's edge.

Nicholas cast a fearful look over his shoulder. The harbour waters that not long before had been lulling him to sleep now slopped black and threatening.

It had been easy to hold his tongue under police interrogation but in the hands of these bullyboys his nerve gave way. He was willing to sing like a canary if it could save his skin.

'I know what you're thinking, lads, but it weren't me.' He groped for inspiration. 'It was that young foreigner. He's the one you want.'

The hand on his collar jerked him upright. Nicholas exhaled in relief. He had found the right words, the key to his salvation.

'What young foreigner?' Bernard demanded.

'Don't listen to him, he's lying through his teeth.' To emphasise his point, Ambrose aimed a punch at the old man's head.

'Hold up!' Bernie snapped, intercepting the blow. He repeated his question. 'What young foreigner would that be, Dingle?'

Nick took advantage of the reprieve by rushing his information. 'A tall fair lad. The one who's been living all summer in the ruined cottage at Kilcarrick Haven.'

'Wait a bit.' It was Jack Mitchell who spoke. 'It could be that Dingle is telling the truth. When I've been potting over Kilcarrick way, I've noticed a stranger on the beach. Quite often there's been a kid with him. Come to think of it, the nipper could well have been your little cousin, Bernie.'

Bernard pulled Nicholas back from the watery abyss. The old man felt little relief for he knew himself to be falling into a chasm far deeper. His cowardice had opened damnation's door.

'You told the police about this stranger, Dingle?'

'No, I mind my business and leave them to do theirs.'

Bernard released his grip and, in a gesture of disgust, dropped the old man onto the stone of the jetty.

'Let's go and get the bugger,' Ambrose enthused.

The motion was passed unanimously.

Spread-eagled on his back, Nicholas watched as his tormentors transformed themselves into knights-errant intent on defending the honour of all Blissey maidens. He crawled away from the righteousness of their Arthurian parliament unnoticed.

* * *

On the bench at the old Napoleonic battery, Nicholas cleaned himself up by discarding his soiled underpants. He was too ashamed to sleep for he had thrown suspicion on a lad whom he believed to be blameless. Never before had he sacrificed another to protect his own worthless skin. Better to have been pitched helpless into the harbour and drowned than done anything so cowardly. Contrition made him groan aloud.

Countless times he'd followed the little maid to Kilcarrick to spy on her antics with the fair young foreigner. Initially, the harmless nature of their fun had been something of a disappointment but then he began to take vicarious enjoyment in their play. Envying their innocence, he’d wished he were a boy again so that he might be admitted to their camaraderie. Now that idyll was over. The little maid was cruelly violated by God knows who and he had knowingly put her gentle and innocent playfellow at risk. Nicholas was filled with self-loathing and a choking remorse at what he had done. He recognised that the boy, like himself, was one of life's victims. How could he have betrayed someone who was so obviously a fellow in the brotherhood of suffering?

In his wretchedness he sought false comfort. Surely once the young foreigner realised the police were snooping around he would have had the sense to move on. But common sense told him that in the isolation of Kilcarrick the lad may not have heard about the terrible thing that had been done to his playmate and even if he’d heard, being innocent, he would have seen no reason for flight.

Nicholas consoled himself by reasoning that the Blissey boys were too far-gone with drink to do anything that night. The youngster would be able to sleep unmolested and, at first light, he would slip over to Kilcarrick to warn the lad off. Satisfied with his rescue plan, Nick fell into an uneasy sleep.

Chapter 26

Paradise Defiled

In a quest for information about possible channel passages Jerome hiked the six miles to Budruth Quay. Having never visited the port before he was disappointed with what he found there. Instead of the expected hive of commercial activity the only craft in the dock was a rusty hulk that looked as if it hadn't been moved for aeons. A white powdering of China Clay dust was evidence of recent industrial loading yet the quays were completely deserted. Having no contingency plan, France and the continent suddenly seemed far away.

As he pondered the prospect of having to seek a passage at one of the larger ports further along the coast an unexpected voice hailed him.

'You there, didn't you see the notice? The harbour is private property and there's no public right of access.'

A bulky figure stood in the doorway of a nearby concrete building. Before Jerome could respond a second man appeared. The two bore down on him, their faces stern.

From the overalls they wore he guessed that they were stevedores.

He was quick to offer an apology. 'I'm sorry about trespassing but I came to inquire about cross-channel sailings.'

The men came to a stop and looked him up and down.

'Travelling are you?' asked the larger of the two as he scratched his stomach.

'I was hoping to get a crossing to France from here.'

He expected short shrift from this enquiry but, after a mumbled consultation, the men relaxed, their officious challenge seemingly forgotten.

'There's nothing doing today but a small cargo vessel is due to dock tomorrow and return to Brittany first tide on Monday. Would that be of any interest to you?'

'A sailing on Monday would be perfect. How do I go about arranging a passage?'

The men exchanged glances and nodded.

'We could likely fix it for you if you were to make it worth our while.'

To make his meaning plain the spokesman stuck out an open palm.

Jerome considered his dwindling funds. 'How much do you want?'

The man grinned. 'You don't look as if you're in the money so let's say just the price of a couple of pints of bitter for two thirsty dockers.'

Jerome tried to conceal his surprise at the modesty of this demand.

'The captain's well known to us and he isn't one for formalities. If you can make yourself useful on board then he'll probably carry you for free. Just turn up in plenty of time for the sailing and be sure to bring your passport.'

Ignorant of the cost of pints of bitter, Jerome handed over a ten-shilling note. The recipients nodded with approval and sealed the deal with knuckle-breaking handshakes.

The prospect of an imminent departure lifted his spirits and, heady with the success of his negotiations, he whistled a jaunty accompaniment to his stride all the way back to Kilcarrick. As for Lorna, he would be able to bid her goodbye for she would not let another weekend slip by without coming to see him.

That night, encased in the comfort of his sleeping bag, he dreamt of hectares of vines ripening under a southern sun. In his dream he played his guitar with fingers that were stained purple from gathering the heavy clusters of luscious fruit.

* * *

While Dirty Dingle was indulging in the self-deceit that the lad at Kilcarrick would be safe until morning, the inebriated Blissey boys were already heading out of the harbour. They rowed as quietly as the creaking rowlocks of Jack's dinghy would allow with four of them pulling a single oar apiece. Dick sat in the bow priming the hurricane lamp that he had collected from the Trehennah's net-loft.

There should have been a waxing moon but the night sky had grown leaden with a covering of low cloud. Darkness suited their mission for they had no wish for their departure to be silhouetted against a silver sea. Even without the moon the intermittent beam of Blissey's lighthouse washed over them and illuminated their midnight egress from the harbour. All were thankful when their craft passed beyond the range of the prying light and into the cover of night.

The tide was with them and all four oarsmen were in prime condition from rowing in gig competitions during the summer's regattas. Pumped with the adrenalin of their purpose they made the fourteen-footer fairly fly across the bay with a rhythmical accompaniment of grunting effort punctuating their progress.

At the mouth of the Kilcarrick inlet they shipped oars, allowing the drift of the tide to take the dinghy into the beach. Gripping the painter, Dick jumped into the surf. Misjudging the distance in the dark, he found himself thigh deep in the sobering chill of the sea.

'Shit!' he expleted, as he tried to find his feet on the sloping shingle.

'Shut your noise, damn you,' Bernard hissed from the boat. 'D'you want to give notice that we're coming for him?'

Recovering his footing, Dick pulled on the painter until the keel grounded. The others jumped from the bow onto dry land.

'Tide's still making,' Jack reminded, 'we'd better drag her up several yards more unless we want to walk home. Heave when I say.'

The pebbles made a noisy clattering as they pulled the boat free of the water. With backs still bent, the landing party froze into statues. They held their breath, ears cocked. Their objective, the silent cottage, loomed as something more solid in the uncertain blackness at the head of the beach.

'Christ, we've made enough noise to waken the dead. Anybody would think I'd brought a crew of bloody landlubbers with me,' Bernard whispered, straightening his back.

They waited, ears straining for any sound of movement coming from the echoing darkness. Apart from the sough of surf on beach and their own heavy breathing, the night was quiet.

'Well have to carry her over the shingle. Ready?'

Gripping the gunnel above the thwarts, they flexed their muscles and lifted in unison. Treading carefully, they carried the heavy, clinker-built boat out of the tide's reach and deposited it onto sand.

They advanced cautiously for in the pitch dark there was no telling where the silent sand would betray them by turning into clattering pebbles. On reaching the low wall that separated the cottage from the shore Dick lit the hurricane lamp. Grown accustomed to darkness, the others were blinded.

'Can't see a bloody thing now,' Bernard hissed. 'Keep that damned light out of my eyes, will you.'

'Give it here,' Ambrose demanded. Taking charge of the lamp, he led the way over the wall and on into the cottage's unguarded interior.

* * *

The furtive shuffling and whisperings that invaded the outer room also invaded Jerome's unconsciousness. His dreams absorbed these noises and converted them into a ritual trampling of the grapes. The oozing of juices between his bare toes was pleasantly sensual and he went on dreaming.

All summer he had been living in splendid isolation with Lorna his only visitor. That their illegitimate night together had apparently gone undetected renewed his belief that the Haven offered a magical immunity from interlopers. It took the splintering of a tripped-over fishbox to free him from the clinging tendrils of his dream vineyard.

Wakefulness revived his previous feelings of insecurity and returned him to the sickness of the real world. He could smell their male presence and on opening his lids he saw the unmistakable glow of an artificial light shining from the outer room. It was an awakening that turned his comfortable dream into a premonition of the grapes of wrath.

From the near darkness he heard a voice, deep and resonant.

'By Christ, he's still here!'

He was still trying to gather his wits when the lantern blinded him. Clawing at his sleeping bag he struggled to get free but callused hands gripped with bruising force to hold him down. A clammy perspiration broke over his body.

The same, deep voice came again. 'Hold the sod still.'

He tried to swallow but terror dried his mouth and disabled his tongue. His first thought was that the invaders were thugs sent by the Major, yet the voice had a distinctly Cornish ring.

He tried to say, 'What do you want with me? I'm doing no harm here,' but couldn't be sure whether he had spoken the words or if they remained locked inside his racing brain.

The Blissey boys had come for action. Without further instruction a steel-capped boot made contact with his fragile frame. More kicks followed.

The bag offered meagre protection from the attack. He tried to curl himself snail-like to protect his most vulnerable parts. He winced as a rib cracked. With an even sharper pain, he heard another go.

'Please, don't hurt me.' There was no doubt that his voice was working now. He was shouting, pleading with them. 'Why are you doing this to me? I've done you no harm.'

The leader of his attackers spoke again. 'Get the bugger out of his sack. Let's see what we're doing.'

At this command, the blows ceased. A hand entangled in his hair and pulled hard enough to scalp him. Yet still Jerome clung to his sleeping bag refusing to be extracted. A memory of prizing winkles from their shells floated before him.

There was a tearing of fabric as the bag ripped. Numerous hands manhandled his naked, vulnerable body.

'For Chri'sake, give us some light. Somebody pin his arms. Are you all bloody useless?'

With his arms restrained, Jerome kicked out at his attackers, panic overcoming his pain.

'Get hold of his legs you damn fools, he be slipperier than a bloody eel.'

There were too many of them, his resistance was soon subdued.

'We'll show him what we does to buggers who sod about with our little maids.'

The threat made, Bernard raised his right leg to carry it out. 'This is for my little cousin, you pervert.'

Deliberately he ground the heel of his boot into Jerome's genitals. An eruption of pain seared the youth's groin, spreading tongues of fire through his body.

Their victim screamed and Dick's head, already throbbing from the drink, could take no more. 'Shut your screeching,' he ordered.

When the dreadful noise would not stop, Dick grabbed the object nearest to hand from its resting-place against the wall. He raised the instrument by its neck and then brought it crashing down from high above his head. The edge of the guitar caught its owner on the side of the face, simultaneously smashing soundbox and cheekbone. At this violation, Jerome joined Lorna in a merciful unconsciousness.

Panting, the four attackers backed off to look at their handiwork. Ambrose, who had led them so boldly into the cottage, played no part in the violence other than to illuminate the action by holding the hurricane lamp high. He was both frightened and excited by what he had witnessed. When the naked man screamed his agony he became sexually aroused. As the others stood looking at their handiwork, he placed the lamp on the floor throwing their shadows giant and monstrous upon the theatre of the cottage wall.

In holding back from their victim it seemed to him that they were making way for his turn. He wasn't aware of picking up the spade and afterwards had no recollection of how it had come to be in his hands. In an execution imitative of Dick's solo performance with the guitar, he raised the tool two-handed above his head. Swinging it in a complete arc, he dashed it down upon the still body. As the spade liaised with its target, he felt the sticky rush between his thighs.

The metal blade cut like a machete. Against the force of the blow not even the bone showed much resistance for the neck was almost severed. There was a reek of blood, so primitive and frightening that it obliterated all other smells and smothered their four other senses.

There followed a moment of utter stillness, when the five living souls in that cell had no more use for breathing than the dead man. It was Dick Trehennah, so newly arrived at boozing manhood, who interrupted the impious pause. He broke ranks to stumble towards the doorway in a retching rejection both of their manly deeds and his night's ale. Dan, his elder brother, sank to his knees and, in an uncharacteristic trembling falsetto, began reciting over and over a prayer heard every Sunday in the Methodist Chapel.

'My God, Ambrose, what have you done?'

In asking this rhetorical question, Jack Mitchell spoke for them all.

Ambrose stood wild-eyed. He could not associate the gruesome carnage before him with any action of his own and was bemused when Bernard gripped him by the shoulders and began shaking him like a terrier with a rat.

'You fool, you bloody young fool, you've gone and done for us all now.'

'Don't say that Bernie, don't ever say that.' Jack Mitchell felt the sweat of panic oozing from his pores. 'How will they know it was us? They won't as long as we get away from here.' His croak was unrecognisable. 'Come on, we got to make ourselves scarce.'

He made to run for the boat, but Bernard's shout halted him.

'Come back, you silly sod. It's no damn good getting into a buggers' muddle. We'll all be hanged for this night's work if we leave it like it is, that's for certain.'

'What are us going to do Bernie, tell us what to do?' Dick whimpered.

'We've have to get rid of the body, you half-wits.'

Jack tried to concentrate his thoughts on Susan and the baby; his duties as a husband, his responsibilities as a father; for their sakes he must pull himself together. He would put his trust in Bernie. Good ol' Bernie always knew what to do for the best.

As if in acknowledgement of this unspoken confidence, Bernard clouted the kneeling Daniel about the ears.

'What good is praying going to do us, you soft 'appeth? Get yourself up.'

When Daniel didn't respond, he hauled him up by the collar.

'Get off your knees man, it's not divine intervention that's going to save us. If we want to avoid the rope we have to sort this thing out for ourselves.'

Bernard drew the spade, Excalibur-like, from the part-severed neck and then forced the body back into the torn and blood-sodden sleeping bag. In obedience to his orders, the others scoured the two rooms, collecting together all items foreign to the cottage.

Bernard fed the broken guitar, haversack and smaller belongings into the already bulging sleeping bag. Last of all he added the murder weapon and, with rope fetched from the boat, began lashing everything together into an ungainly parcel.

'How shall us weight it, Bernie?'

'We'll have to sacrifice Jack's dinghy anchor and chain. We don't want this little lot dragging with the tide and fetching up on Blissey beach, do we?'

Ambrose did little to help. He stood mesmerised, staring into the pool of blood with its fiery sun that was the reflection of their hurricane light.

'What about the blood, Bernie?' Dick asked. There was so much of it.

'One thing at a time.' Bernard was still occupied in securing his bloody parcel.

Jack swallowed bile. 'Christ yes, we have to clean up in here. I saw a bucket in the outer room. Shall I fetch some water to slosh around?'

Bernard looked up from his knots to be confronted by Jack's blood splattered trousers.

'It's not just the floor that needs water. Before any of you gets in the dinghy you better go for a wash in the sea. Up to your necks if necessary. Make damn sure your clothing is clean. It won't do for us to take his blood back to Blissey.'

Bernard was in charge. He was the only one not to panic, the only one with enough wit to think straight and the others were looking to him to save them. Despite the desperate circumstances he was beginning to relish the role of leader. After all, Dan was older than he was and Jack was a married man, but it was to him that they looked to get things done.

Filled with a new-found confidence he began to plan ahead.

'Hold up with that water, Jack. Don't start swabbing yet. This rush bed is saturated with blood and we don't want it damper than it is already. It's got to burn.'

He pulled the woven mattress away from the wall and into the centre of the cell.

'Get rid of the evidence, that's what we have to do. Dick, go get me some of that dry timber that's stored in the other room. Is there any fuel in that Primus stove?'

Jack shook the Primus. ‘It’s full.’

'Go steady with it then, we don't want too big a blaze or the roof timbers might catch. We can't afford to have the whole place going up.'

'Why not? Why don’t we just burn the whole cottage down?' The hooligan in Ambrose was reviving.

'And bring down the law, the Budruth fire brigade and anyone else who's interested? Use your brain you numb-skull, why don't you?'

He appointed Ambrose and Dick to take charge of the blaze with strict orders not to let it get out of hand. Jack went to make ready the boat and free the anchor and chain. Dan was made his fellow bearer for transporting their gruesome burden.

'You won't go off and leave us here?'

Even with the corpse removed, the cottage and its surroundings made Dick's flesh creep. His brother put an arm about his shoulders to reassure him.

'We can't take everyone off this trip but we'll be back as soon as we’ve got rid of the... sack.'

Dick could well understand why his brother could not bring himself to say *body*.

The less sensitive Bernie offered a typical piece of his black humour. 'There's only room for the burial party and that’s one party you'll have to miss, Birthday Boy.'

As Bernard and Daniel carried their ghoulish load down the beach, an owl hooted from higher up the valley. It was more than Dan’s fraught nerves could take. With a whimper, he dropped his end of the burden and even Bernard’s ripest curses could not persuade him to take it up again. It was Jack who helped Bernard load the corpse into the boat.

Letting the other two row them out of the inlet, Jack busied himself by chaining his anchor to the unwanted cargo. Once in deeper water, Bernard gave the order to ship oars. Helped by Jack, he lifted the unspeakable thing over the side. They lowered gently, not from any sense of reverence for their once-human bundle but because their nerves could not cope with the drama of a telltale splash.

'Our Father which art in heaven, hallowed be Thy name, Thy kingdom come, Thy will...' Dan gabbled automatically.

'Shut it, Daniel.'

As though in countermand, the disobedient clouds parted, unveiling a full moon that lit the seascape and silver-plated their guilt.

The fire crew, anxious to get away from the nightmare of Kilcarrick, was already waiting on the beach. Bernard refused to take them off without first checking the cottage.

'There's things still to be done in there,' he snapped. 'We got to wash down the floor and get rid of the bucket and that Primus stove.'

None of the others were bold enough to confront the scene of their violence again. Taking up the hurricane lamp Bernard re-entered the cottage muttering scorn at his companions for the superstitious fools that they were.

The lamp revealed that the withies and rushes had turned to charcoal and ashes on the flagstones. The flames had obligingly blackened both the floor area and walls to obliterate the more telling stains they had made there. Satisfied that the evidence was destroyed, Bernard stamped on the still glowing embers to snuff them out. Not until the fire was safely extinguished did he rejoin the others at the boat.

'The water wasn't needed,' he told them. 'All that's left to do is get rid of the final evidence that someone's been living here.'

He handed the Primus and the bucket into the boat, the latter rattling with a few domestic utensils previously missed.

As soon as they were over deeper water Bernard dumped the incriminating items over the side.

'Just as well we've got the world's biggest scrap-yard at hand to lose the evidence in,' he commented grimly.

Dick took his brother's place at the oars, pleading that he needed something to do.

There was a stink in the boat making all aware that, for a second time that night, someone had shat himself. Only Dan, their elder statesman, knew for sure who that someone was.

The return voyage was against the tide, but this was not the only reason for it being slower. No one spoke until they had moored at the deserted Port Blissey quayside. As they tied up the boat their admiral gave his final command.

'Now you all listen to me, if you breathe a word of this anywhere we're up shit creek without a paddle. If your mothers or wife want to know where you've been for most of this night, let them think you've been lying in the alley drunk or shagging some maid up in Lanhedra woods. You keep your lips buttoned about what happened or we're dead men, understand?' As an afterthought he added, 'But don't forget what that bastard did to my little cousin. He deserved what he got, we just saved the law a job, that's all.'

It was a necessary reminder for they were so aghast at their night's deed that the motive had been forgotten. Thanks to Bernie, by the time they reached their homes, they had almost convinced themselves that they had acted in the service of justice.

It was next morning before some of them discovered the blood on their clothes, on their faces and in their hair. Jack's dinghy also bore witness to their deed, but Blissey's boats were too frequently splattered with fish blood for that to register as being of any significance.

Chapter 27

1961: Confrontation

Once the children had gone to bed Lorna relapsed from artificial cheeriness into unaccustomed silence. She sat by the fireside supposedly reading but David had not seen her turn a page in twenty minutes. Instead her eyes were drawn to the flames in the hearth, her thoughts clearly elsewhere. David hated seeing her so unnaturally tense. She was not usually subject to mood swings and he assumed that her present preoccupation was connected with her afternoon attendance at Nelly Nancarrow's funeral. Laying his own book aside, he took her hand and attempted to rally her spirits.

'Come on, sweetheart, you look all in. Let's go up for an early night.'

'That sounds a good idea but only if the offer includes a kiss and a cuddle.'

David was not fooled by her skittish enthusiasm

'You've not been yourself since the funeral. Won't you tell me what's wrong?'

Lorna, thinking that she was making a good job of dissembling, wasn't prepared for his question. Their marriage had always been based on truth and mutual trust but telling him about the trauma punctuating her unorthodox childhood was something that she could not, must not do. A resurrection of the past would lead to rumour, speculation and scandal that would bruise the respectability of her husband and children.

Determined to keep her new-found knowledge to herself, she confessed only as much as he already suspected.

'You were right and I should have listened. Nelly's funeral was too much of a reminder of burying my little brother.'

This explanation contained more truth than lie and she hoped that David would accept it on face value.

David, with no reason to suspect that her preoccupation was caused by anything more sinister, offered the requested comfort of his arms. Lorna fell into them gratefully only shaking off the embrace to lead him up to the bedroom. She needed his intimacy to rid her of blacker thoughts and her encouragement ensured that their cuddling led to something more fervent.

* * *

After their lovemaking Lorna usually slept soundly but tonight her brain was hyperactive. Village memory, like the Blissey's grapevine, was long and she was sure that the crime against her innocence must still be whispered about in the gossiping corners of the Port. Incredibly even the community's most spiteful gossips had united in silence to spare her their knowledge. Rather than disillusion her protectors she would adopt the safer course and go on pretending a state of blissful ignorance.

Many villagers still referred to her as Lorna Penrose yet the skinny waif brought up in the Treblissey council house had been transformed with a new identity. That unremarkable child had become the confident Mrs David Grainger, mother of two lovely children and owner of a smart new villa on Lanhedra Road. Her present position in the community was a far cry from her childhood when less able peers had picked on her, making her feel an outcast. She had become a respected mother with secrets no darker than those of any other daughter of Blissey.

Her husband turned over in his sleep and she spooned herself gratefully around his back. Marriage to David had brought her status for he was partner in his father's successful business and to be an employer in their essentially working class environment made him one of the elite. According to the village, David Grainger was 'a chip off the old block' and, like Arnold his father, they accepted him as a Blissey man. This was a flattering adoption by locals who were apt to regard anyone originating from 'foreign parts', more accurately designated 'the rest of England', with a deep and lasting suspicion.

Local regard for David was such that he had been voted onto the Parish Council in preference to a long-serving local man. This had proved a wise decision by the electorate for their new councillor was full of energy and fresh ideas and served the community with an unstinting dedication. In support of the husband she loved Lorna also busied herself in local affairs.

'Them young Graingers be the pillars of the community. It's a pity there aren't more of their generation like 'em,' a customer told Harry Endeoc, over the Post Office counter. Overhearing this accolade, Margaret Penrose proudly carried these words back to her daughter and son-in-law.

Lorna's life had changed for the better and she wanted to keep it that way. To revive memories of the horror that lurked in her past would taint her new life. To prevent that from happening she knew she had to conceal the recovered memory - even from David.

* * *

Two mornings later David watched as his wife cut Michaelmas daisies from their garden. He guessed that these blooms were to be votive offerings for Lorna regularly went to the graveyard to place fresh flowers on the more recent of the Penrose graves.

He joined her outside. 'Isn't one churchyard visit enough for this week? You've looked quite washed-out since Nelly's funeral.'

Lorna refused to be diverted. 'I have to go, there's weeding to be done. Perryn's plot has grass growing through the granite chippings and you know how Mum hates to see a neglected untidy grave. In her eyes it's an advertisment to all and sundry that the relatives don't care.'

David accepted that he was beaten for he knew the importance his wife placed on boneyard duties: they were her labour of love.

'Have it your own way. But don't take our delinquent grave robber with you. I'll drop him off at my mother's. You know how she welcomes the chance to have him to herself for a couple of hours.'

The offer was accepted for Perry Arnold their two-year-old son was a handful. There was nothing he liked better than to fill his pockets with stone chippings from the graves. He was particularly fond of the green ones, as Lorna discovered when she investigated an alarming rattle coming from the drum of her twin-tub washing machine.

* * *

Relieved of the hindrance of her acquisitive infant, Lorna busied herself in the deserted churchyard. She was on her knees weeding when footsteps crunched on the gravel path behind her. Absorbed in her task she took no notice until the feet stopped nearby.

There was no need to look up; some sixth sense told her who was standing there. On her knees and feeling vulnerable, she prepared to defend herself. Swivelling to face him she saw that his mournful eyes were reading the dedication on the tombstone.

'I'm sorry about your brother. I didn't know that he'd died. The sea can be a cruel master. Wasn't Perryn the little lad you used to take for walks in the pushchair?'

Lorna's thoughts whirled. She had assumed that Leonard Nancarrow would flee the village as soon as his mother was buried; yet here he was, deliberately seeking her out and making conversation.

She sprang to her feet but was betrayed by trembling knees that made her stagger. Not wanting to touch Nancarrow's outstretched hand she flinched from his offer of assistance.

Taking the hint he withdrew a pace.

It took supreme effort to disguise her weakness. Poised to run, she brandished the hand-fork, menacingly pointing the prongs at his throat.

He gave a sad shake of the head. 'There's no need for the fork. I mean you no harm.'

Her eyes conveyed that it would take more than his weasel words to persuade her to lower the makeshift weapon.

'You obviously know that it was me.'

Though he made no attempt to elaborate she understood him perfectly.

'Yes, I know you were my attacker. Now go away and leave me alone!'

It took effort to make her words sound like a command rather than a plea.

Shaking his head, Nancarrow ignored the injunction. 'If you knew, why have the police never come after me?'

Rather than give him an answer she challenged with a question of her own. 'Is it a coincidence that we happen to be in the cemetery at the same time?'

'It's no coincidence. I've been watching out for you.' His Adam's apple rose and fell as he swallowed. 'I spotted you in the village carrying flowers and guessed you were heading here. I left it for a bit and then followed.'

He stood, head bowed, remembering that earlier time when he had followed her across the cliffs to Pencarrick.

His silence made her bolder 'What do you want from me?' she demanded.

He rephrased his unanswered question, his mournful eyes drilling hers. 'Why haven't you told the police about me?'

'Hasn't it occurred to you that I might prefer to forget what happened rather than have…' she'd almost said *my shame,* 'the episode dragged into the public domain?'

Though her eyes blazed the rest of her still trembled.

He frowned and shook his head in confusion.

'I don't understand. Surely you want to see me punished as I deserve?'

She felt that she owed him nothing, not even an explanation. 'I'm leaving now and don't you dare try to follow me.'

He took a step towards her. ‘Please don’t go yet, there are things I need to tell you.’

She couldn’t imagine what he wanted to say but wondered if listening to him might exorcise some of the demons that had come to plague her.

Adopting a bravado she did not feel she tried to take charge of the situation.

'Have I still cause to be afraid of you?' she challenged.

Nancarrow bowed his head. ‘Believe me, I’ve no intention of causing you further harm. Though it may sound trite, I came to tell you how sorry I am, how sorry I’ve been and that I intend to make amends.’

Because he sounded so pathetic and looked too miserable to pose much of a threat her fear began to subside. Withdrawing the threatening prongs, she pointed her fork in the direction of a bench positioned under a yew tree some distance from the graves of her ancestors.

‘If you must talk then I suggest we sit down.’

‘It made me feel such a monster when you ran from my mother's graveside. I swear to God you’ve no need to be terrified of me.’

His sincerity was so convincing that she began to walk towards the bench that she had indicated. Obediently he followed.

She spoke without looking at him, 'It was shock, not fear that made me run from the grave. I’d remembered nothing of you or what you had done until that moment at the burial.'

It was his turn to flinch. 'You had no memory of what I ... what happened?'

She knew that he had been going to say *what I did*. She was not surprised that he wanted to distance himself from his crime.

Because she did not respond, he asked his question again. ‘But you must have known. How can you *not* have remembered?’

How could she begin to explain to him what she did not fully understand herself? That by some not-understood process of the brain's self-protective and unconscious workings her mind had locked away all knowledge of the assault.

‘I recalled nothing of you or what happened on Pencarrick and no one, not even my family, spoke of it. It was recognising you at the funeral that triggered the memory.’

She did not add that she was still trying to come to terms with her newly gained knowledge.

He shook his head in disbelief. 'What a shock. To find out so suddenly I mean.'

They arrived at the bench. Wanting to show that she was the one in control she sat down and indicated that he should do the same.

He sat with his knees together, careful not to invade her personal space.

'Thank you, I'm really grateful that you're prepared to listen. I don't suppose it will be much comfort, but I want you to know that not a day goes by without me regretting and cursing what happened. I may have fled from Pencarrick but the nightmare of it has haunted me ever since.'

Again his sincerity seemed genuine yet it was strange to think of him remembering down the years, when for her what had occurred out there on the promontory had been no more than a mysterious void lurking in her past.

Her silence obliged him to continue.

'I was so certain that I'd left you for dead. Then I received a letter from my mother telling me you were in a coma. Not that she had any idea that I was responsible, of course.'

'Your mother wrote to you?'

'Yes, I left Blissey for my National Service before you were found. That's why I never came under suspicion.' His head dropped. 'I expected you to regain consciousness and name me. Sad to say I was depraved enough to hope that you would never come round. My only concern was to save my own wretched skin.'

Lorna shivered. 'Why choose me as your victim?'

He started visibly. 'No, believe me, it wasn't like that. I never intended to harm you.' He rocked his upper body and hid his face in his hands. 'It just happened.'

'Unprovoked assault doesn't just happen.' She couldn't bring herself to use the word *rape*.

'Truthfully, I never intended to do more than frighten you but everything got out of hand.'

'Losing control doesn't excuse what you did.'

'No, you misunderstand. I'm not making excuses. What I did was criminal, evil, unforgivable.'

He dropped his hands and she saw how bloodless his face was.

'My mother's letters were full of nothing else. She wrote about how the congregation prayed for you every Sunday. When her letter brought news that you were on the road to recovery I was terrified. I couldn't sleep, I couldn't eat. Every day I expected to be arrested. I went into the army weighing over ten stone and came out two years later weighing barely eight.'

'And you never came back to Blissey until your mother's funeral?'

'Not once. I was too scared to return. It was a relief when my army service was up. It meant I could cover my tracks and disappear completely. I travelled the country, moving from job to job, never staying in one place long enough to settle or for people to get to know me.'

'And your parents? Surely they knew where you were?'

'No. The whole point was to cut myself off from home. That way I thought I could escape the consequences of what I did.'

'But you're here now.'

'It was my mother's dying wish to see me again. Then fate took a hand.'

'Fate?

'There were only half a dozen mourners at the funeral and one of them turned out to be you.'

'How did you recognised me.'

'It was your eyes, they've haunted me ever since. When you looked at me across my mother's grave, they looked exactly the same as they did out on Pencarrick Point. How could I not have known you?'

He gave a strangled sob and began breathing deeply as if to control his emotions.

The silence lengthened and Lorna felt obliged to fill it. 'How did you learn that your mother was dying?'

He gave a wry grimace. 'I grew careless. Eighteen months ago, I joined a car components manufacturer in the Midlands. In the normal way of things I would have moved on by now, but I met a woman. For the first time in years I felt I had roots. It got me thinking about my mother. I sent a note on her birthday and later a Christmas card. I withheld my address but the Birmingham postmarks gave me away. It wasn't difficult for Uncle Ted to track me down. Without evidence of identity it's impossible to get well-paid work so I'd never changed my name.'

She was curious about the woman he mentioned. 'So you're married?'

'Married? How could I marry with this awful thing from my past hanging over me? What happened out there on Pencarrick ruined my life as well as yours.'

She was struck by the ironic justice of the perpetrator suffering more than his victim.

'You didn't ruin my life. I've been very lucky. I'm married to a wonderful man and we have two lovely children.' She thought but did not add, 'I have so much when you seem to have so little.'

'I'm happy for you,' he said generously. 'You deserve some recompense after all the suffering.'

He made her sound like a martyr. It was not a role that she deserved or coveted.

'I wasn't aware of suffering. When I rejoined the land of the living my body was healed and I had no memory of what had happened.'

'Then your loss of memory was a blessing.'

'For us both,' she suggested.

'No, not for me. I'm glad that you were spared the knowledge but it would have been better if I'd faced my punishment. By now I would have served my sentence and been a free man.'

'You are a free man,' she reminded.

'I'm not free in here,' he struck his forehead several times with an index finger, 'and haven't been for all these years. I knew the risk I was taking in coming back to Blissey, but I welcomed it. I need to settle things once and for all. I can't keep running for the rest of my life. It's better that I give myself up.'

His words frightened her. 'You mustn't talk like that.'

'But don't you see? It's the only restitution I can make. The police will be delighted to close the file on a thirteen-year-old crime.'

His cynicism panicked her.

'If you really are here to make amends then try to see things from my point of view,' she urged. 'The last thing I want is to have my name dragged through the law courts. I have two children who are happy and secure. I don't want them to learn what happened to me. To revisit the past means punishing my family and I won't let that happen.'

Leonard sat as though stunned. 'But if I don't confess, what am I to do?'

It was such a pathetic appeal coming from a grown man. She couldn't help comparing him to her husband. David, once a shy youth, had matured into a capable, decisive adult. Leonard was an inadequate and she found herself pitying him.

He was looking to her for advice so she gave it. 'My pain lasted only a few minutes, Leonard. Yours seems to have lasted years. Why let a single mistake made when you were a youth destroy the new life that you've built for yourself?'

'It's already destroyed any chance of happiness I might have.'

'That can't be true. What about the woman you mentioned?'

She would clutch at any straw that might prevent him from handing himself over to the police.

'Helen? She's a divorcee, a couple of years older than me. Her ex-husband was an abusive alcoholic. The last time he beat her so badly that he put her in hospital. The irony is that she's always telling me what a good man I am. You and I know that's not true. I'm a fraud. I've been living a lie. '

'A single act of aggression in your youth doesn't make you a bad man. Helen sounds as if she needs you. Forget the past, go back to the Midlands and marry her.'

'Helen has a ten-year-old daughter from her marriage. I can't get it out of my head that Carol is almost the same age as you were when...'

Lorna clapped her hands over her ears. 'Don't tell me any more, I don't want to hear.'

His lip trembled. 'Christ, I don't mean that Carol's at risk from me, though I suppose you have good reason to think she might be. The child trusts me. I'd thrash any man who tried to touch her. But how can I ask her mother to marry me with this in my past? It would be deceiving them both.'

His protest was too earnest not to be believed and she tried to make amends for her misjudgement.

'Look at me, Leonard. How much of Lorna Penrose do you see in me now?'

He studied her features. 'Very little, apart from your eyes.'

'So you agree that I've changed. I'm not the same person I was then and neither are you. You're not the Len Nancarrow who jumped out of the bracken to almost frighten me to death. We both have to move on. We have to unshackle ourselves from the past.'

A muscle twitched below his eye. 'What did you say?'

'We have to unshackle ourselves...'

'Not that, I mean about me jumping out from the bracken?'

He held his head as though squeezing something from the rat-hole of his memory.

'My God, you're right. That *is* what happened. It's why I grabbed you. I was hiding in the bracken when you spotted me. You reared back like a frightened filly and I thought you were about to go over the cliff. I jumped out to save you.'

He looked stunned, the recollection making his eyes bolt.

'So why hide if you weren't planning to attack me?'

'I told you, it was just a juvenile prank. I wanted to scare you, not do you physical harm.'

She was a girl again, out there on Pencarrick. Over the past days she had enacted the scene many times.

‘I thought you were going to push me off the cliff.’

‘Just the opposite. But when you started screaming I panicked. I was afraid that someone would hear and that I'd get into trouble.' He gave a rueful laugh. 'Back in those days I was never out of trouble. Yet that day I was happier than I'd been for ages because I was going away to start a new life. I didn't want anything to interfere with that. When I pulled your frock over your head, it was only to muffle your cries. I didn’t mean it to go any further.'

The moment was tense as he reconstructed the fugitive memory. 'But you struggled so fiercely that I had to subdue you. Then it all went horribly wrong.'

Lorna tried to absorb what he was telling her.

'All I've ever thought about in the years since was the blood and that you seemed to have stopped breathing. Those are the images that haunt me. I’d forgotten about trying to save you.'

She had to believe him for she knew how selective memory could be. There was relief in knowing that his attack had not been premeditated.

Leonard seemed to think differently. ‘Not that knowing how it started is any comfort. It doesn't alter the fact that I left you for dead.'

'Except that I wasn't dead, but very much alive.'

Much to her embarrassment, he began to weep. Knowing the value of human contact, she tentatively patted his arm. What would the village gossips make of the spectacle they were presenting? Lorna was grateful that the churchyard was little visited on a Thursday afternoon and that their bench was tucked away in a secluded corner.

Leonard found a handkerchief and blew his nose noisily. 'After what I did to you I can’t be allowed to get away scot-free.'

‘Why should I want to see you punished now that I understand how it happened? It’s best that you forget about me and the past. Go home to Helen and Carol. Build a new life. Make them happy.'

'Perhaps if I confessed to Helen she would understand.'

Lorna’s panic returned.

'No, that would be a mistake. Some things are best unsaid. It was our business and we've settled it between ourselves. No one else need know.'

'What about your husband? You must have told him what you’ve remembered.'

She shook her head. ‘I haven’t. And it's love, not deceit, that stopped me from telling him.'

He met her eyes. 'Lorna Penrose, you're a remarkable woman.'

She could not return the compliment for it did not fit this prematurely aged and sad man. It was impossible to believe that Leonard Nancarrow was only three years older than David. His face was haggard, his hair thinning, his shoulders stooped. As a compromise she transferred the compliment.

'I'm sure I'm no more remarkable than your Helen. It sounds as if she's had a tough time.'

'She has.'

'Then you must try to put that right.'

'I'll do my best. And thank you, the last thing I expected was your forgiveness.'

Lorna thought this positive note was the one on which to end. She checked her watch.

'I have to go, I'm due to collect my daughter from school in fifteen minutes.'

They rose in unison from the bench and walked side by side through the churchyard. At the fresh mound of earth that was his mother's grave, Leonard paused.

'Poor mother. There was never much laughter in our house; she wasn't a happy person.'

'Times were hard, especially for the women.'

'Yes, and I didn't make things any easier. I wasn't much of a son.'

'Then you'd better make a better job of being a husband.'

It seemed natural to chivvy him; it was the sort of advice she handed out to her elder brothers.

'Do I really have your permission to bury the past?'

'I insist. It's the only way you can make amends. It's what I want.'

'Then I'll do as you want. I promise.'

He offered his hand. After only the slightest hesitation, she took it.

'Thank you again, Lorna, and goodbye. There's nothing to keep me in Blissey, I'll be leaving this afternoon.'

She made her handclasp firm. It was the first time she had seen him smile and it made him look years younger.

Chapter 28

1961 continued

Lorna felt neither disgust nor hatred towards Leonard Nancarrow, rather she regarded him as a sad individual deserving of pity. The realisation that he had left the village without making any disturbing disclosures came as a relief. The threat to her husband and children was removed and for the first time in days she began to relax.

Despite what she had preached to Leonard about burying the past, she was acutely aware that her married persona could never be totally separated from her Penrose childhood. There were pieces of that long-ago summer that still eluded her and she was far too inquisitive to leave a single shard of that past unexhumed. There were just two other people who could help complete the puzzle. One was the long absent Rome but, without a surname to aid her, finding him would be impossible. The second was both accessible and approachable for that person was her mother.

Lorna and Margaret often met by chance on Blissey's streets but as this was an inappropriate venue for an exchange of confidences their *tête-à-têtes* took place by arrangement in the privacy of their homes. On alternate Tuesdays Lorna climbed Polbliss Hill to lunch in the kitchen at Treblissey, on other Tuesdays her mother made the reverse journey to visit her offspring's comfortable villa on Lanhedra Road.

It was in the kitchen of the Treblissey council house that Lorna swore her mother to secrecy.

'I've something to tell you, Mum. But you must promise not to breathe a word to anyone else.'

Margaret, fondly imagining that her daughter was about to make an early announcement of a third pregnancy, was visibly shocked by the unexpected and unwelcome revelation that followed.

'Oh, my good Lord, I've got to sit down, my lovely.'

In admitting her recollection of the attack, Lorna was careful to provide only an expurgated version and made no mention of what had triggered the memory.

Once over the shock, Margaret became very animated.

'Who was the monster who did it, Lorna? Is he someone we know? The police turned the village up-side-down but they never caught him. For all these years he's escaped punishment and at last he'll get what he deserves.'

Her mother's desire to exact revenge was understandable, but Lorna had no intention of naming her attacker. Leonard Nancarrow had gone away, this time for good and she was glad that at last he could stop running. Misery had dogged the whole of his adult life and she had no desire to add to that by betraying him. Leonard was her secret and keeping that secret was a means to protecting them both.

'That's not going to happen, Mum. I don't know the identity of my attacker. I never saw his face.'

Margaret, with no reason to suspect her daughter of lying, swallowed her disappointment.

'Perhaps that's all to the good, though it doesn't seem right that he should get away unpunished after doing such an evil thing to an innocent child.'

At the thought of this injustice, Margaret snuffled into her handkerchief.

Lorna put a supportive arm about her. 'Please don't fret, Mum. Haven't you always taught us that it's no use crying over spilt milk.'

'I'm sorry, my lovely, it's just that I never expected us to be having this conversation. Your father and I did all we could to keep the truth from you. It was his express wish that you'd never be told and he died believing you would never know. One of the last things he said was what a blessing it was that you'd never remembered.'

'Finding out isn't so bad. In some ways I'm relieved to have those missing weeks explained and it's not as if it happened yesterday. But now the memory has surfaced I want to hear your version for I need to understand exactly what happened.'

'Are you sure, my lovely? Isn't it best to let sleeping dogs lie?'

'It's my life, Mum, don't you think I have the right to know?'

After some deliberation Margaret conceded, 'Well if you're sure. Though I don't want to go upsetting you.'

Lorna drew up a chair to sit next to her mother and encouraged her to continue by holding her hand.

'It was a terrible time. We thought we'd lost you. The physical injuries healed yet you still lay in a coma and it seemed that nothing could rouse you. We'd just about given up hope of ever bringing you back to life but

Grandfer Penrose wouldn't give up. Every day he travelled over to Budruth hospital to sit by your bed. Hours on end, he'd read to you from your favourite books. Your father and me visited when we could, but it was difficult, what with the expense and all. Though it wasn't just lack of money that kept us from visiting daily. After what happened to you we were frightened of leaving the little ones.'

Lorna gave her mother another hug. She could well imagine her parents' fear for the rest of their brood.

'You don't have to apologise, Mum.'

'When you came to, the doctors were worried about your state of mind, but you recovered with all your faculties intact.'

'Not quite, there was the amnesia.'

'Everyone, except perhaps the police, regarded that as a blessing. We were thankful that you didn't remember the awful thing that had been done to you.'

Lorna turned the conversation to what she really wanted to know.

'Who found me?'

She had been romancing that her saviour and rescuer was Rome. She imagined him coming to meet her on the cliffs only to find her unconscious at the secret camp out on the Point. He would have carried her down to the cottage and then run to the Jenkins' farm at Trecarrick to seek help.

Her mother's version turned this fantasy upside-down.

'Pencarrick is such a remote spot that it was a miracle you were found at all. If it hadn't been for Nicholas Dingle, God bless him, you would have died. He carried you in his arms across the cliff-tops to Treblissey hill where he flagged down Alf Hicks in his coal lorry. Alf drove you to Budruth hospital and Mr Dingle went with you. Of course, it wasn't until much later when the police came calling that we found out what happened.'

Lorna's hero was changed from Rome, blond angel and musician extraordinary, into Dirty Dingle, an old and unwashed vagrant. To accept this unflattering transformation took some effort. Like the rest of her generation she had always perceived the tramp as the bogeyman of parental threat, the stuff of childish nightmare. Learning that she owed her life to him was a strange contradiction.

'Dirty Dingle was supposed to gobble-up little children, not save them.'

'That's exactly what the police and most of the village thought. Most unfairly as it happens.'

'The police suspected him of being my attacker?'

'Worse than that, they went and arrested him. It was the medical evidence that proved his innocence. I used to feel real bad about him sleeping rough when we owed him so much. Your father wanted to reward the old chap for saving you. We offered him money, as much as we could afford, but he wouldn't take it. He said that with a house full of kids to feed and clothe we needed it more than he did. Proper upset about you he was, poor chap. Of course, he lives at the old folks' home now and it's good to see him well cared for in his declining years.'

Her mother's reference to 'most of the village' believing Dirty Dingle to be responsible confirmed Lorna's suspicion that knowledge of the rape was common currency in Port Blissey. Everyone, except herself, must have been aware of the attack.

'What I find so unbelievable is that no one in the village has ever told me what happened.'

'That's hardly surprising. We let it be known that you'd lost your memory and we wanted the whole business hushed-up. People respected that wish. Besides, with the villain still on the loose no one liked talking about what happened. The police were still poking around and with the crime unsolved it made suspects of too many of the men-folk. It wasn't just our family that was affected, the affair proper rocked Port Blissey. Your old Grandfer said it caused more of a stir than the great storm of 1891.'

Lorna began to understand their neighbours' motives for keeping quiet. Rather than harbour suspicions of their kith and kin for a crime perpetrated in their own backyard people had chosen to close their minds to it. A sense of denial had prevented the community from talking about the rape and her own selective amnesia had protected her from their knowledge.

'So with my attacker still at large everyone believed that the rapist was still in their midst.'

'That's exactly how it was. Wondering which one of your close neighbours might be an abuser of children is an uncomfortable thing to live with.'

'And my amnesia meant that they could deny the assault had ever happened by ignoring it.'

'That's being too hard on folk. Those close to us were as keen as we were to see him caught but at the same time everyone wanted to spare you the truth. In time your father and I came to accept that it was just as well that the villain wasn't found. Had an arrest been made the case would have gone through the law courts and we could never have sheltered you from that.'

Lorna shivered at the thought of a trial and the unwelcome publicity of newspaper coverage, especially if it had come now, thirteen years after the event. Not just the village but the whole country would learn of the scandal, including David, their children and, of course, her in-laws. Thank God she had been able to persuade Leonard Nancarrow against going to the police to confess.

'What about David's parents? Do they know what happened to me?'

'Not as far as I'm aware. They were still living in Coventry when it happened and later on David insisted we never mentioned it to them.'

Lorna thought she must have misheard. 'David? David knows?'

'Oh Lord, what have I gone and done now? Don't tell me you haven't told your David what you've just told me.'

'I haven't told him because I thought he didn't know and I wanted to spare him the distress. Are you telling me that he's known all along?'

Margaret nodded. 'He found out before he married you. We were obliged to tell him everything.'

Lorna recalled the conversation that she had overheard from Dolly Rosevear's garden all those years ago. 'Did you tell him because you thought I might not be able to bear children?'

'Goodness, no. What put that into your head? The doctors assured us there was no lasting physical damage.'

'So why did he have to be told?'

'It was your brother, our dear lost Perryn, who did it.'

'Perryn was no more than an infant at the time. What had he to do with all this?'

'You must remember how young Perryn idolised David. He would have done anything for him.'

Lorna did remember, but could not imagine what her mother was about to reveal.

'Just after you and David announced your engagement, Perryn was poking around in the Trehenna's net loft. Your cousin Bernard came in off the quay and he and Dan Trehenna started talking about you. They had no idea that the child was up above and overhearing every word they said.'

'What did they say?'

'What he heard didn't make much sense to Perryn, him being only nine years old at the time. But he was smart enough to gather that something terrible had been done to you when you were a little maid. Guessing that he wasn't meant to hear, he slipped away out of a window. As chance would have it the first person he bumped into was your David. Perryn was upset and he blurted out what he'd heard. David came straight up to Treblissey to see your Dad and me. We had no option but to tell him the whole story.'

Lorna was stunned. Nothing in her husband's behaviour had ever suggested the possession of this knowledge.

'Poor David, what a way to find out. How did he react?'

'He took it well. He said that it made no difference to him because he loved you, but that it would be better if his mother didn't get to hear about it. It was David who made Perryn promise never to tell you or to talk to anyone else about what he'd overheard. Then we all made a pact never to speak of it again. And I haven't, not until today.'

Lorna thought she knew her husband so well, yet for years he had been steadfastly harbouring this secret. So urgent was her need to talk to him that she left her toddler with her mother and went directly to the workshop.

The Graingers' cabinet-making business had expanded. Declining pilchard shoals had closed the canning factory and the family firm had moved into new premises built on the old factory site. The expanded business employed nine people and an apprentice. Orders came in from customers from all over the county and beyond.

Entering the workshop, Lorna breathed in the smell of fresh wood-shavings. It was a familiar scent and one that she loved for David carried it home with him. Arnold, her father-in-law, greeted her with a kiss and directed her to the office where she found David immersed in paperwork.

Seeing her without their son, her husband's open features signalled anxiety. 'What's the matter? Where's Perry?'

'Perry's fine, I've left him with Mum.' She squeezed his hand. 'Can you get away, it's important?'

'Sure, I was looking for an excuse to escape these invoices. How long do you need me for?'

'An hour should do it as long as we take the car.'

'I should be able to manage that?' He threw her the ignition keys. 'Where are we going?'

'Wait and see,' she told him, mysteriously.

She drove to Trecarrick Cross then, taking the old Budruth road, pulled into the lay-by at Carter's Leap.

'Do you remember the first time we stopped here?'

David laughed. 'What's this about? Don't tell me you've brought me here in the middle of the afternoon to canoodle.'

'I might have.'

'In broad daylight? You hussy, that's positively indecent. Besides we're an old married couple with a perfectly good conjugal bed at home.'

'I do love you, David.'

He nuzzled her ear with his lips. 'I should hope so, mother of my children.'

'David, there's something I've been keeping from you. Something I've remembered from my childhood.' Their eyes met and she saw that he understood.

She nodded, 'Yes, I've remembered.'

His initial dismay turned into a tender concern.

'Oh, my darling. Your family has always hoped we could spare you that knowledge.'

'It's all right, David. I can cope. But what about you? Mother tells me that you've known since before we were married. Why did you never say?'

'It wasn't my place to tell. It was your parents' decision to remain silent. They wanted to protect you from ever finding out.'

As they held each other, he asked the inevitable question. 'Was your attacker a Blissey man?'

Lying to David was harder than lying to her mother. 'I don't think so. If it had been someone local I would have recognised him.'

It was a white lie, not even that. The youth who had been Leonard Nancarrow was unrecognisable as the tortured adult who bore his name.

'I've known for days that something was troubling you but never imagined it was this. After all these years of not knowing, what was it that jogged your memory?'

She was ready for his question. 'Nothing in particular. It just came to me as I woke one morning and every day since my memory of those lost weeks has become a little clearer.'

'But why didn't you tell me?'

She hugged him. 'You're a fine one to criticise. You've kept quiet about it for years.'

'I kept quiet because it made no difference to my feelings for you. Promise me, Lorna, that you won't let this come between us?'

'There's no fear of that. Now that I've had time to think I'm glad that I've found out and the only difference about knowing is that it makes me love you more.'

For several moments they clung to each other.

David looked at his watch. 'There’s more than an hour before you're due to collect Rachel from school, what say we pop home and finish this canoodle in the marital bed?'

'I suppose that making love in the back of the car is a bit undignified for two such upstanding pillars of the community.'

David repeated his accusation that she was a shameless hussy. Twenty minutes later, in the privacy of their bedroom, she did her best to live up to his description.

Chapter 29

Ghosts

To better understand the events of that shadowed summer Lorna was drawn to the wall that both overlooked Blissey beach and gave an unimpeded view of Pencarrick's granite finger. Although the promontory's grassy ledge was hidden by vegetation Lorna's recently keened memory was vivid enough to carry her there.

She saw again the burning eyes in the bracken and the fiend that rose from its hiding place to terrify her. She felt the sharpness of gorse against her back, re-lived the rough hands tightening round her neck, the excruciating pain of penetration and the terrible conviction that her assailant was intent on tearing her apart. The recollections were as vivid as they were violent and would have been overwhelming but for her recent encounter with her attacker. The sexually driven and violent youth with the wild eyes was transformed into a suffering and prematurely aged penitent.

Her mind's eye permitted her to see beyond Pencarrick. The briefly shared idyll with Rome came scudding around the point like soft clouds driven on a freshening breeze and she was able to recall her childhood companion with a clarity that previously had been missing. She realised that Rome, cut off from normal social intercourse by his hermit existence, was unlikely to have learnt of the terrible thing that had happened to her. She was saddened to think that he had most probably interpreted her imposed absence as a chosen desertion.

Though the shock of revelation had receded Lorna knew that to complete the healing process she should revisit the haunts of that summer, a magical summer that had brought roses to her cheeks and made her heart lighter. So, with her two children left in her mother's care, she went on a pilgrimage to Kilcarrick.

Passing Pencarrick she found dense and flourishing undergrowth where her secret path had once been. She was not sorry to find the point inaccessible. Nature, like the inhabitants of Blissey, seemed intent on closing that chapter of her history.

Arrived at the cliff top above the Haven she saw that a cliff-fall was part-covering the Blissey steps. Undeterred, she scrambled down to the beach, her sliding feet creating miniature avalanches in the shale scree.

The cottage was in a sorry state, its roof fallen-in and its cob walls breached by the sea's battering. Apart from the stone chimney, no part of the walls stood higher than her head. At the rear of the cottage the withy-moor encroached into what had once been the garden and the crumbling cob walls were perforated by the untamed growth of willow.

She picked her way gingerly through the ruin. Enough remained on the inside to distinguish Rome's sleeping cell from the rest. She recalled their hand-blistering labour to weave the ingenious mattress that he had christened his dream-raft. Wondering at her own naiveté, she remembered her innocent desire to share his homemade bed and how this was made possible when a storm-whipped sea conspired to trap her at the Haven overnight.

In those final shared hours Rome had been frantic with worry although she had tried to reassure him that his concern was unwarranted. Her trusting parents had made only the briefest enquiry about her night's absence and entertained no suspicion that she had been anywhere other than safely tucked up in fine bed linen with Eileen Stone. She could clearly recall her mother's delight in believing that her daughter had slept in the solicitor's residence.

'What was your bed like? Was it one of those fancy divans with a sprung mattress?'

At the time Lorna had no idea what a divan looked like but she had replied in the affirmative knowing that this was the answer that would give her mother the greatest satisfaction.

Her present search of the ruin was a disappointment for she could find not a single clue to confirm Rome's occupation of the cottage. Even the fuel for their fires, so carefully stored in the outer room, had long since been washed or carried away. Disheartened, she returned to the beach where the crunch of shingle beneath her feet sounded the same as she remembered and the sea swirled in familiar eddies around the barnacle and mussel encrusted rocks.

The shore was littered with rounded pieces of slate and she began skimming the slim stones across the water. On an exceptionally calm day, Rome, champion of their Ducks and Drakes contests, had set a record of fifteen hops and she had come close by achieving eleven. Today, small waves swallowed her skimmers before any did better than five.

The sound of running water drew her to the top of the beach where the stream gurgled its remembered song. At the spot where Rome collected his fresh water, she dabbled her fingers in the icy flow. Noticing a glittering of green gems in the stream bed, her heart missed a beat. Her 'bottle emeralds' were still there. Over that long-ago summer she had amassed a collection of these sea-polished glass fragments and had scattered them in the stream as a surprise for Rome. Plunging in a hand, she retrieved a single smooth green oval. She wrapped her souvenir in a handkerchief and tucked it carefully in a pocket, glad to have found at least one keepsake connected with her playmate.

Though so little of personal association had survived, the images in her mind were less transitory and from these she reconstructed Kilcarrick as it had been in her childhood. She saw Rome everywhere: he waded into the sea with the lobster pot on his back, built a beach fire between the dolmans, harvested strong wands from the withy moor and played at make-believe on the long-sunken causeway.

Rome was as ubiquitous as the sough of Kilcarrick's surf and it took just a small leap of imagination to hear again the timbre of his singing voice and the harmonies of his music as his long slim fingers coaxed tunes and rhythms from the guitar. She recalled his thousand kindnesses and felt again the intimacy of their closeness as he carried her through the waves, took splinters from her fingers, dried her clothes and shared his warmth. Finally, she resurrected the shining angel who bathed in the stream, her shell necklace strung about his naked throat.

Their companionship had been as harmonious as their music-making - utterly pure and chaste yet at the same time disturbing. Only now, from an adult's perspective could she recognise her adolescent yearnings as the stirrings of an awakening sexuality.

There were less laudable aspects to that summer at Kilcarrick: her petty thieving from both home and Farmer Jenkins' fields and her brazen deceit of her parents in using the elaborate fabrication of a friendship with Eileen, the solicitor's daughter. But nothing, not even her violation, could sully her fond remembrance of that secret, happy time.

Despite the many recovered memories Rome himself remained an enigma. Where had he come from? Why he had chosen to live out a reclusive existence at Kilcarrick? He had told her so little of his history and, as a child concerned only for the present, she had not bothered to ask.

Then she had regarded him as a permanent fixture. Now she understood how impractical it would have been for him to live on at the Haven once winter set in. The cruellest of circumstances had denied them the opportunity to say a proper goodbye.

Where had he gone? Where was he now? There were so many unanswered questions, questions that would haunt her as persistently as the memories recovered from that once lost summer.

Wherever Rome might be, she hoped that he too had fond memories of their youthful camaraderie and that, like her, he had found happiness more permanent than the sweet but transient interlude they had shared.

* * *

Dirty Dingle had become respectable. No longer did the old man haunt the cliffs on secret paths or spy on lovers from his concealment in the blackthorn. It was several years since he had eaten a seagull's egg, made his bed under a tarpaulin or slept like a savage beneath the stars. Gone was the grimed skin, straggly dark beard and threadbare clothing, even the greasy trilby had long ago been incinerated. Mr Nicholas Dingle had become a resident of Blissey House, once the old vicarage, now converted into a council home for the infirm and elderly.

Seeing him out walking, clean-shaven and soberly dressed with his tweed cap worn very straight, the village exclaimed, 'That matron has done miracles with old Dingle, look at him, every bit the country gent!'

Yet not everything had changed: inside his sanitised skin Nicholas felt much the same as ever. Despite his aches and pains, he still coveted the old ways, hankering after his wilder haunts beyond the charted harbour and village. On clement days, when his rheumatism wasn't playing-up, he liked to walk in the direction of Blissey beach.

The climb to Penblissey Head was beyond him now but he was still capable of descending part way to the beach so that he could again feel part of his beloved cliffs.

It was his habit to take the steps as far as the bench that provided a rest station for the climbers returning from the sands below. There he would roll a smoke and wait until he recovered sufficient breath and energy to undertake the ascent back to the top.

Today, stationed as usual on the halfway seat, his attention was drawn to an unusual object being tumbled amongst the seaweed and other detritus along the tide line. Driven by the beach-combing habits of an adult lifetime, and quite forgetting his infirmity and the effort required to climb back up so many steep steps, he continued down to the beach.

* * *

The Kilcarrick exorcism was successful, for now Lorna could lean on the wall above Blissey beach and look across at Pencarrick without feeling any of the agitation of her earlier emotions. Far below her vantagepoint at the wall, she was surprised to see Nicholas Dingle making his way down the cliff steps to the beach.

Since her mother had revealed the debt owed to Dingle, Lorna felt an intimate connection and special warmth towards the old man. Whenever she saw him sitting on the harbour-side or strolling in the village she went out of her way to greet him. Though their paths often crossed they never shared more than a salutation. Twice she had attempted a greater intimacy but her friendly attentions seemed to make him uncomfortable. Respecting his sensitivity she suppressed the desire to engage him in conversation.

Most recently, when out walking with the children, she had met Dingle in a deserted lane. To her surprise he had blocked their way, his attention riveted on dark-eyed Rachel who was helping push Perry's infant carriage.

Uniquely, he had chosen to speak. 'Looks just like her mother,' he declared.

For the first time, his glance met hers.

Knowing that what she wanted to say had to remain forever unspoken, Lorna tried to express her gratitude in the look she shared with him. His nod of acknowledgement and his muttered, 'Be sure to take good care of your little maid,' suggested that he understood what she was trying to convey.

Now, as Lorna watched from her vantagepoint at the wall, Nicholas Dingle dragged his rheumatic bones across the deserted beach below. Stopping at the tide-line he bent and picked something up. Straightening, he examined the object for a long time before pressing it to his breast and continuing his painful walk towards the sea. Though far above, Lorna could see how the old man's footprints made pools as he tramped across the smooth sand still wet from the sea's recent withdrawal.

* * *

Bending to his shiny black boots, already staining white from the sea-salt, Nicholas retrieved the object he had spotted from above. He held it before him, staring into the two empty eye sockets. With a tobacco stained index finger, he traced the shattered cheekbone. From an inner darkness he smelt again the charred remains he had found on that long-ago morning at Kilcarrick's fisherman's cottage. In his trouser pocket he still carried the shell necklace he had found stuffed into a cavity of the cob. It was an amulet that had brought its original owner only bad luck.

He was obliged to acknowledge a truth that he had possessed throughout all the intervening years yet, until this moment, had refused to admit. In a gesture that was both protective and self-comforting, he cradled the cranium to his chest. He was embracing all his lost dears.

'Forgive me my lovelies,' he moaned. 'Forgive me dearest Flora. Ted, my old comrade, I'm sorry.'

He pictured too a nameless, tortured, blond foreigner, his youthful, thin face framed with girlish-length hair.

'I wanted to save you my dears, I wanted to but I couldn't. I was too weak always.'

Lifting his face to the sky, he shouted his agony, 'Answer me this, why are the innocent taken from this world and the wicked left to have their way?'

* * *

Dingle's words did not carry to Lorna, leaning on the wall two-hundred feet above, but she saw the old man straighten his body and, with an unlikely athleticism, swing back his arm to hurl the recently retrieved object out over the sea. As she traced the arc of its circumscribed course the sun lit the sea-bleached bone. Seeing the white streak Lorna shivered. For a moment she thought the shape resembled a human skull.

Protectively she crossed her arms over her swelling abdomen for in her womb she felt the stirrings of a new life. Turning her back on Pencarrick she faced towards Blissey and the future.

Chapter 30

1962

The Trehennah brothers were fishing from their lugger, a vessel named *Fair Annie* after their mother. Earlier the shipping forecast had reported a deep low-pressure system moving in from Biscay. Not relishing the prospect of being caught up in foul weather on the wrong side of the Lizard they shot their nets within sight of the Blissey light. Daniel was in the wheelhouse, Dick and their young deck hand, Roy Clemo, were hauling the nets. In terms of quantity it didn't look bad but the fish were mostly pollack, in commercial terms not a quality catch. Dick, hoping for cod, cursed the low market value of their haul.

As the net came over the side, Roy's eyes alighted upon something foreign caught in the wall of the mesh. While Dick was occupied with shaking the fish into the open hold the boy retrieved the bulbous shape. Recognising the object for what it was he reacted violently and dropped it onto the deck.

'Bloody Hell, Dick. It's a skull!'

The death's head rolled and landed at Dick Trehennah's feet. Stooping, he gathered it up. Even before his hands closed around the bone, his intuition made the connection. He did not need to turn it over and look at the smashed cheekbone for confirmation.

It had been the evening of his eighteenth birthday. With his brain fuddled with celebratory booze he had gone with the others to the cottage at Kilcarrick. Though their violence had been premeditated he had lacked the stomach for it. Their victim's cries set his nerves on edge and he'd picked up the guitar with the intention of putting a stop to the screaming. He'd achieved that all right for what he'd set in motion had led to the horror that, fourteen years on, still had the power to wake him sweating in the early hours.

An excited Roy called up to the wheelhouse. 'Daniel, you'll never believe what we've fished up.'

The beat of the marine engine and the whirr of the winch motor drowned the boy's voice. Daniel Trehennah, who was studying the dark clouds massing on the western horizon, gave no sign of having heard.

'Hush,' Dick warned. 'Don't go telling Dan. You know what his nerves are like.'

The boy, his courage returned, scoffed. 'A grown man baint afraid of skeletons, surely?'

Dick, used to protecting his elder brother, manufactured an explanation.

'It's considered bad luck to bring something like this onboard. Dan's superstitious that way and I'd rather he didn't know about it.'

Certainly Dan was a changed man since the blood-bath of that September night at Kilcarrick. He could be unpredictable at the best of times, but there was no telling what his reaction might be if he saw what his brother was holding.

Roy was not to be silenced so easily.

'But he'll have to know. This could be a murder. It's our duty to report it.'

Dick averted his face while he wrapped the skull in a piece of oilskin.

'Don't be a bloody fool,' he snapped. 'It's the remains of some poor, drowned seafarer, that's all.'

The boy, growing bolder and regretting that he had not hung on to his prize, demanded, 'Give us another look at it,'

Dick moved the oilskin parcel out of reach.

'Show some respect, won't you? This here's part of a man, not some novelty to be played with.'

Roy sulked at this reprimand and they were moored at the Blissey quay before he spoke to his employer again.

'I'll take the skull up to the police station if you like,' he offered. 'After all I saw it first.'

'You'll do no such thing, that's the boat owner's responsibility. And until I've spoken to the law, you'd better keep your mouth shut about it.'

Roy wondered what was making Dick so sour. He was usually the easy going one. It was the elder brother, Daniel, who was the queer fish.

* * *

Dick was wise to wait until they were alone before revealing the unwanted element of their catch to his brother. He made his revelation when they were storing some of their gear in the net-loft.

'We landed more than we bargained for today, Dan. It could spell trouble.'

Daniel, only half listening to his brother, was unconcerned. 'What's the problem? Isn't young Clemo shaping up? I always said there was more lip to him than brain and muscle.'

'It's not Roy, though he could be a complication. Look what dragged up in the net today.'

He unwrapped the worn piece of oilskin to reveal the white bowl of skull that lay at its centre.

Daniel's eyes bolted. 'It's not him. Tell me it's not him.'

'I only wish I could.'

A twitch started below Daniel's right eye. 'Are you mad? What made you bring the thing ashore?'

'I had no choice. Roy saw it first and he's bound to blab. What would it have looked like if I'd thrown it back?'

Daniel wrapped his arms around his body and started rocking. He would have swayed less had he been on the deck of the *Fair Annie* in a force eight.

'It's all going to come out, isn't it? We're done for,' he moaned.

His brother gripped him by the shoulders and shook him. 'Pull yourself together, Dan. What's to connect a trawled-up skull with us? Or for that matter with the stranger at Kilcarrick? It's like Bernard said at the time, we'll be all right as long as we keep our heads and don't tell no one.'

At the naming of their erstwhile saviour Daniel revived somewhat. 'We'd better let Bernard know what we've found. He'll tell us what we ought to do.'

'I intend to. Jack needs to know too.'

'Where shall we meet up?'

'It better not be here in the net-loft, anyone might walk in off the quay and hear what's going on. I'll ask the pair of them to come to your cottage, tonight.'

'Why must it be my place?' To play host to their conspiracy was too central a role as far as Daniel was concerned.

'Because the rest of us have wives and children at home and what we have to discuss isn't exactly a matter for family consumption.'

Immediately Dick regretted his choice of words. Daniel's wife of just twelve months had recently walked out on him. What made matters worse, she was shacked up with Tom Penrose just three doors down in the same street.

* * *

Since the night of their blood lust, these particular Blissey boys had ceased to be drinking buddies. Jack Mitchell had abandoned the pub for a more sober, domestic existence. His wife's second pregnancy had resulted in twins. These births resolved the problem of the renaming of his boat. Removing the dedication to his wife Sue, Jack turned *Sea Nymph* into the plural in honour of his three little girls. Though he talked of being blessed with three daughters, in reality he regretted not having a son. He had been well and truly punished for his involvement in the Kilcarrick madness. The impotency that had been visited upon him made it unlikely that he would ever have a lad of his own to help him with the boat.

Dick also was a changed man. He too had lost enthusiasm for masculine company and alcohol being too busy seducing and then marrying Tina Polmount, Bernard's little sister. Sex became the refuge where he could forget that night's foul deed. He blamed the birth of five children in seven years for turning his hair prematurely grey. Tina, who had borne his five children, retained her youthful looks. Dick envied her unlined face and raven locks but, of course, Tina had no dark secret poisoning her insides.

Of them all, Daniel Trehennah was the most altered for he had suffered a complete personality change. Though become more deeply religious, he had turned too morose to socialise and looked destined to remain a bachelor. It was the talk of the village when he got himself wed to a young woman fifteen years his junior but his moodiness soon cost him his marriage.

Only Bernard Polmount still frequented the Blissey pubs, his florid face and size of stomach bore witness to long hours spent in The Anchor or The King's Head. Even the publicans had ceased to encourage his patronage by warning that he was turning his liver into a beer keg. Ambrose Johns, the fifth member of their Kilcarrick boarding-party, was dead.

* * *

Bernard and Jack responded to the summons as Dick knew they would. They all arrived at Daniel's cottage in Chapel Bank within minutes of each other.

'So what's all this about?' Bernard demanded, as soon as the street door was fastened behind him. 'It better be something important, I don't like wasting good drinking time.'

'Oh, it's important all right.'

Dick placed the oilskin bundle on the velvet cloth that covered his brother's table. After a dramatic pause that had more to do with reverence than showmanship, he solemnly opened the cloth to reveal its contents.

Jack let out an expletive. Daniel began a silent sobbing that was only detectable by the rise and fall of his shoulders. Bernard snatched up the skull, turning it over in his hands to examine it.

'Well I'll be buggered. Where did this fetch up?'

'Out in the bay, it came up with our nets,' Dick told him.

Bernard bounced an eyebrow. 'So no-one else knows about it?'

'As luck would have it the Clemo kid spotted it before I did so I had no option but bring it ashore.'

Daniel's sobbing became audible.

It was Dick whom Bernard turned on. 'For Chri'sake, make your brother shut-up, he do try my patience to the limit. I sometimes think he exchanged his wits for Dirty Dingle's that night.'

Family loyalty spurred Dick to his brother's defence. 'You seem to forget we did more than rough-up Dingle. We killed a man. It's not Dingle's wits Daniel took on board but your guilt. God knows you've never shown an ounce of remorse for what we did.'

Bernard shifted uncomfortably. 'What good would remorse do us? Besides it's all water under the bridge. At the time we believed we were doing right.'

Dick grew bolder. 'Don't deceive yourself, Bernard. We were too drunk to think straight. Do you really believe the lad would have stayed at Kilcarrick if he'd attacked your cousin? We all know what PC Bullock said about the evidence. The boot-prints they found led towards Blissey. The real rapist was hiding out in our own community, not sleeping peacefully at Kilcarrick.'

Jack Mitchell protested, 'Why are you blaming us, Dick? We only went there to teach him a lesson. It was Ambrose who killed him.'

'Bloody convenient to have a dead man to blame isn't it?' Dick snorted, unable to forget that he was personally responsible for things getting out of hand.

'Vengeance is mine, said the Lord,' Daniel intoned, sounding like some fundamentalist preacher. 'Ambrose paid with his life for that night's deed and the Lord God will exact the same retribution from us all.'

Bernard's laugh was grim. 'You fool, Daniel. Ambrose died because he lived for the thrill of taking those bends on the Budruth Road at seventy miles an hour. It was recklessness on his motorbike that that broke his neck, not the Almighty's retribution.'

Dick knew that it was not recklessness but rather a death wish that had killed Ambrose. It was true that he'd always been a risk-taker, but after Kilcarrick he too had changed. Who in his right mind high-dives off Island Rock when the tide's on its way out? Ambrose did that several times and survived. The reason he took the bends on the Budruth Road at excessive speed was because he was looking for a more certain method of breaking his neck. As there was nothing to be gained from voicing this opinion, Dick called the room to order.

'I didn't ask you here to quarrel or apportion blame. We need to present a united front and decide what to do next.'

Bernard re-examined the skull. 'Who's to say this wasn't a sailor killed by a swinging boom or a seaman murdered in a ship brawl? Whatever the explanation the police aren't going to trawl the bottom of the seabed for the rest of his remains. We've had more than a dozen years' practice at keeping our mouths shut so zipping our lips now won't be difficult.'

Jack was comforted by Bernard's confidence. 'Bernie's right, what have we got to worry about? It's not as if the police even suspected that a murder had been committed.'

'Odd thing that,' Dick reflected. 'A lad goes missing yet there was never any enquiry. It was as if the stranger at Kilcarrick never existed.'

'And that's the way we want it to stay.' Bernard's glance travelled to Daniel. 'Are you listening to this, Danny-boy? I don't want to hear any more talk of heavenly retribution. It's ten years since Ambrose smashed himself up on that motorbike. As for the rest of us sinners, well that God of yours must have forgiven us long ago. Understand?'

Daniel was lost in his misery so his brother spoke for him.

'Don't worry, I'll take the skull to the police station and answer their questions. I can't imagine them wanting to speak to Dan. If they should want another witness, I'll give them Roy Clemo. He'll be happy enough to talk and there's no way he can incriminate us.'

Satisfied that Dick could be trusted to handle the police, Bernard and Jack went their separate ways.

Dick stayed on at his brother's cottage. The events of the day had resurrected devils that he needed to exorcise before he could face his wife and family.

'Bernard is right about one thing. It's not death and heavenly retribution we have to fear. Isn't it enough that we're all being punished here and now? One mistake and our lives were altered forever. That wretched night my carefree years were stolen from me. Eighteen years old and I was pushed into a manhood that I wasn't ready for. Every birthday since has been an anniversary of that killing. And I'm not the only one; we've all of us been living in a purgatory of our own making. There's Jack made impotent and you with your nerves so frayed that you can't look any man direct in the eye anymore. Believe me, Ambrose is the lucky one, he's out of it, the rest of us have to go on living with what we've done.'

Daniel considered this assessment. 'What about Bernard? I don't see him doing much suffering.'

'Bernard's not like the rest of us. He's got no conscience. As far as he's concerned someone had to pay for what happened to his little cousin and it didn't much matter who that someone was. But Bernard got it wrong on two counts, firstly our victim was the wrong man and secondly there was no need for revenge. The harm done to his cousin wasn't lasting, Lorna Grainger's living proof of that. It's us who've been permanently damaged.'

Daniel moaned. 'If Bernard don't show remorse he'll fry in Hell fire.'

Dick, a non-believer since his momentous eighteenth birthday, seized on this to comfort his brother. 'You're right. The rest of us are serving our penance by suffering in this life but Bernard Polmount has got his punishment to come.

Daniel considered this proposition without comment. Just when Dick thought that his brother had gone off into one of his trances, he reached out to touch the skull with a forefinger.

'We ought to give him a Christian burial, Dick. That's the least we can do.'

'If that would make you feel better, I'll see what can be arranged,' Dick promised, patting his brother on the back.

* * *

The Christening ceremony over the participants processed down the aisle, their feet treading the several brass and slate memorials that commemorated generations of dead Trethewans. From the church's dim interior, they emerged into the blinding glare of sunlight.

Arnold Grainger played with his light meter and corrected the exposure setting on his camera lens. He was about to record for posterity the latest rite of passage in his family's genealogy. His wife and Margaret Penrose posed for the camera, taking turns to hold their new grandson.

'He's a lovely little chap,' declared an admiring Dolly Rosevear. 'You do have such 'ansome babies, Lorna. Yet it do seem only yesterday that you were just a little maid sitting on your dear Grandfer's lap in my best parlour.'

'We must get a photo of you and the baby, Aunt Dolly.' Lorna turned to address her father-in-law. 'Arnold, could you take one with Dolly holding him, please?'

'Here you are my dear.' Margaret relinquished the baby into her elderly friend's arms, fussing to arrange the christening shawl crocheted eight years earlier for her daughter's first born.

'Marion and me were just saying, Lorna and David have got themselves a full set now, Rachel dark like our Penrose side, young Perry auburn like his Dad and now this little blondie.'

Dolly pulled the shawl away from the baby's face for the photograph. All the while, she clucked to him in the soft brogue of her own particular interrogatory style of baby talk.

'Who be a lovely little man then? Who do look 'ansome in his christening robe? Who be his Auntie Dolly's fair little sweetheart? Who was a good, good boy and didn't cry in church when the parson gave him his lovely new name?'

She paused in her petting to address the baby's mother. 'Jerome is a proper proud name, Lorna. You mustn't let folks spoil it by shortening it to Jerry.'

'No, Aunt Dolly, we wouldn't want that.'

Rachel tugged at her mother's skirt. 'Let me hold baby, Mummy. I haven't had my picture taken with him and I'm his big sister.'

Her grandfather concurred. 'Of course I'll take a photograph with you holding him, sweetheart.'

Rachel glowed with pleasure as she posed for Arnold's camera with her new brother as an accessory.

'Good baby, smile at Granddad. Say cheese.'

The baby obliged by gurgling happily.

'Isn't Rome a darling baby, he does exactly what I tell him to do,' Rachel enthused.

'What did you call him, sweetheart?' asked her father.

Though taken aback, it was Lorna who responded to David's question. 'Rachel called him Rome.'

'Rome? That's an unusual contraction. I wonder how she came to think of that.'

'I've no idea, but even Aunt Dolly can't object to her calling him Rome. It has nice ring to it.'

Reclaiming her son, Lorna kissed the fair hair poking from beneath his satin bonnet and whispered fondly, 'It's time we took you home baby Rome.'

As the Christening party evacuated the churchyard they crossed paths with a more solemn entourage entering through the lychgate.

* * *

Bernard Polmount led the procession. Behind him, acting as escorts to Daniel Trehennah, were Jack Mitchell and Daniel's brother Dick. All four men were soberly dressed in dark suits and ties. Daniel carried an elaborate wooden casket that had been made by Arnold Grainger's most skilled cabinetmaker.

All knew of the purpose of their visit. Margaret Penrose in particular felt proud of the compassion showed by these young Blissey men. When her own son, Perryn, had been lost at sea her worst fear was that he would be washed-up on some foreign shore and not given a proper burial.

She paused to exchange words with her nephew.

'I'd heard you were burying him today. It's a fine thing that you do for the poor unknown soul, Bernard.'

'We saw it as our duty, Margaret,' Bernard grunted, embarrassed. 'Must get on, the parson's waiting for us.'

Hearing Margaret's undeserved commendation, Dick Trehennah's stomach muscles clenched. Inwardly, he cursed Bernard who must have realised that the Grainger's baptism was today. Forewarned, they could have avoided this unwelcome clash. He threw an anxious glance at his brother and saw with relief that Daniel's attention was wholly concentrated on the casket he was carrying and he appeared oblivious of the interchange.

The last time the four of them had come to the church together had been to bury Ambrose Johns. That occasion had almost pushed Daniel over the edge and his collapse at the graveside had almost done for the lot of them. In the presence of other mourners he had ranted on about God not being satisfied until there were four more coffins in the grave. Fortunately, Daniel's reputation for mental instability meant that little notice was taken of his wild words.

Daniel carried the casket past neglected gravestones leaning at curious angles towards a peaceful corner of the churchyard. There, against a wall and overshadowed by a centuries old Yew, stood three simple headstones. Each commemorated an unnamed casualty of a drowning. One bore a date in the previous century, the most recent were both contemporary with the Great War. It was in this spot that a fresh hole had been dug. It had cost the gravedigger only a fraction of his usual effort.

In complete anonymity and remote from the grandeur of the family vault the last of the Trethewan line was committed to sanctified ground.

Only his mourners could put flesh on the bone. Each remembered the youth in his own way. For Bernard it was the delicate frame and long limbs he had dragged from the sleeping bag, for Dick it was the scream, for Jack it was the crunch as spade imbedded in bone, for Daniel it was the spurting of life-blood on the Christ-like, wispy beard.

The clergyman's words interrupted their grim reminiscences. '... in sure and certain hope of the Resurrection to eternal life.'

To which rubric Daniel Trehennah added a loud amen.

END

Lightning Source UK Ltd.
Milton Keynes UK
11 December 2009

147366UK00001BA/7/P

9 780755 204809